THE NIGHT THIEVES 002

AS THICK AS THIEVES

R.E. BOND

This is a work of fiction. Names, characters, places, and incidents either are the product of the authors imagination or are used fictitiously, and any resemblance to actual persons, living or dead, business establishments, events, or locales is entirely coincidental.

The ebook version of As Thick As Thieves is enrolled in Kindle Unlimited and is only legal to read on Amazon.

To the dark romance girlies who dream of being kidnapped from your bedrooms by villains...

So you can be railed by big dicks like the queens that you are.

Spotify Playlist

https://open.spotify.com/playlist/
7aKavXOIU9Gnw6ZNz0dx9K?si=ce62a15c45f4410f

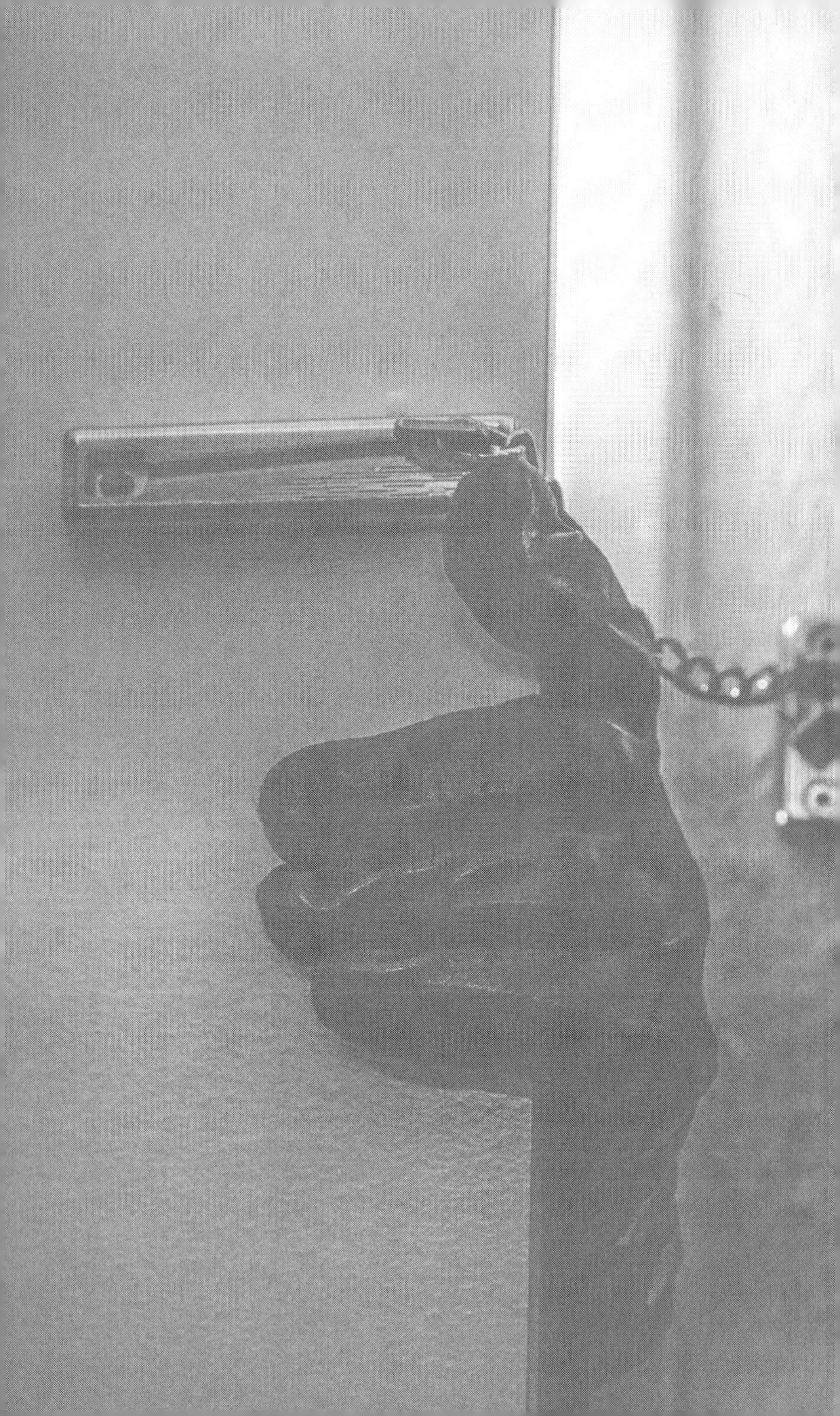

Chapter One

Penn

I'd spent days refusing to eat or drink when Dad first dragged me home. I'd spent most of it in a state of panic from being shut in the dark alone and being beaten, but desperation finally made me cave and he'd now turned it into a game of degradation as he tipped water on the concrete at his feet.

"Hungry?"

Two slices of bread landed in the puddle next and shame washed through me as I grabbed them, hoping to save them from becoming soggy but failing. I fought a gag as I ate the soaked bread, my own stench starting to get to me. Three or four weeks had been like this, but it was the only meal I got. If I was thirsty, I had no choice but to lick the water from the dirty ground.

I wasn't allowed back in my room, I was locked in the basement in the same clothes I'd been dragged home in. Luckily, there was a working toilet but no shower.

I was numb to the pain and fear, going through the motions and praying he either killed me or I died in my damn sleep.

I had no idea what Stone had told the guys, but the fact

that no one had come to save me told me everything I needed to know. I was on my own.

"You stink. Estelle is going to give you a sponge bath," he continued. We'd had a lot of one-sided conversations since I'd been home. "Do you want to get out of here?"

That perked me up.

"You'll let me out?" I croaked, peering up at him. "Back to my room?"

"No, I'll rehome you like the fucking dog that you are," he spat, and I flinched as he towered over me. "I warned you I'd sell you if you wouldn't behave and marry someone willingly. If I sell you to someone in my circle, your threat of spilling secrets won't be a problem. It's not like they'd unchain you from their bed for you to run off and report it."

Dread hit me at the thought of being sold in the skin trade, my bread forgotten as I crawled towards him. "Please, don't—"

He slapped me hard, his voice sharp. "You did this to yourself, Penelope. You let those degenerates inside your pants, so what did you expect? No man wants a wife with a used-up pussy. You'll have to settle for being someone's plaything. It's more than what you deserve."

Tears burned my eyes as he walked away, the lock turning and trapping me in the dimly lit room alone again. I shouldn't have gotten attached to Cruz and Drake, I should've run the moment I had the chance.

The thought made my heart hurt, but knowing they hadn't come to find me told me that I hadn't meant much to them in the first place.

I wasn't alone for long before Estelle walked in with a bucket of soapy water, a gasp leaving her as she saw me for the first time since I'd left. "Oh, Penelope."

My throat was clogged with emotion as she placed the bucket on the ground and sat beside me, pulling me into her arms despite how badly I smelled. I sank into her hold, tears streaming down my cheeks as she comforted me.

"He's selling me."

"I'll never understand that man. You've been through a traumatic experience and he's treating you like it was your fault. You didn't ask to be taken by those awful men. Did they hurt you? Oh my God, did they—"

"I didn't exactly fight them," I sniffed, sitting back to watch her face. "They saved me, Estelle. Well, one was a grumpy asshole and another hated me, but the others were so sweet. I went on my first date, and to Lightning Cove at night to watch the stars. I even learned to use a gun which was cool." Memories flashed through my mind, the sound of crashing waves soothing me with a false sense of security.

"They didn't hurt you though?"

"I went toe-to-toe a lot with Knox and Stone, but Cruz and Drake? They smothered me with sweetness from day one. I guess they were only using me though or they would've kicked the door down to find me by now," I said bitterly, wiping tears from my cheeks. "Drake said he loved me, so why didn't he find me?"

"Oh, honey. I'm so sorry," she said softly, reaching out to tuck my greasy hair behind my ear. "Let's get you cleaned up, and I'll try to find you a protein bar or something. I've been so worried, all we knew was that some men had taken you, but Louis wouldn't elaborate."

"I was fine until I came back," I murmured, letting her help me to my feet.

She stripped me naked and tenderly cleaned me, crying for me as she tried to clean the cuts and bruises that covered my body. Dad had whipped me a handful of times and my skin was split in places, some growing infected.

My back hurt but I hadn't seen the damage, and I knew I had a bad one across my stomach.

I was relieved when I realized Estelle had a small bag of fresh clothes, the sweats and hoodie looking like the softest material on the planet compared to my old worn clothes.

It felt so good when she'd managed to wash my hair in the bucket too. Was it perfect? No, but it was better than it had been.

She brushed my damp hair once I was dry and dressed, her worried eyes finding mine again.

"I have a bad feeling that the small party he's hosting tonight is for people to buy girls, and since he's insisting on me cleaning you up, I think he intends on you being one of them."

"Pray I find a decent new *owner.* I doubt those men exist in his circle, but miracles happen." I swallowed past a lump in my throat, unsure of my future.

"I always pray for you," she promised softly as she collected her things, knowing she couldn't stay longer or Dad would punish me and most likely fire her. "If you ever manage to escape again, try to get a message to me to let me know you're alright. I live in Briar Falls. Seventy-seven Sale Street. Send me a letter or knock on the door if it's safe to do so. I'm usually there each night by six, but you can always go around the back and use the key that's under the pot."

"Thank you, I will," I nodded, loneliness filling me as she left the room. It was ironic how the dark felt comforting now, being the only peace I had. If it was dark, he wasn't down here hurting me.

I tried to nap, it was a little easier now that I felt cleaner, but I never slept for long.

There was a lot of noise upstairs, telling me the party had already started, so I sat in the corner against the wall and waited for what I knew was coming.

Sure enough, Dad thumped down the stairs a few hours later, his voice firm. "Come with me."

"Can't I stay here?" I asked weakly, cringing as he grabbed my hair and pulled me closer to him.

"I gave you that option before and you ran off with a bunch of criminals. Get upstairs. Feel free to throw a tantrum and embarrass me, they like their toys wild."

I wanted to throw up as he escorted me into the brightly lit room, people's conversations dying down as we passed.

"I have a surprise tonight! My daughter's looking for a new home. Sorry she's not dressed up, feel free to test drive her if you want," Dad said cruelly, shoving me and causing me to stumble and land on my hands and knees. Laughter went around the room but I didn't dare look up, humiliation burning through me on top of the pure exhaustion.

"How much? She looks like she fucks good," someone asked, and I closed my eyes as people started bickering over me. I wished the floor would swallow me whole and make it all go away.

"I'll give you a million."

"Make it three," Dad threw back, another man joining in and making people gasp.

"I'll give you five million cash right now."

"She's not worth that," Dad scoffed, but the man seemed way too keen to take me home. Between the lack of nutrition, sleep, and the defeat, I couldn't even find the energy to be angry.

"C'mon, I bet she's got a wild side. She's been broken in, right?" Footsteps approached me, and I flinched as fingers trailed lightly through my hair. It was all a lie, there was nothing gentle about these men.

"My daughter turned out to be quite the whore apparently," Dad replied. "You really want to waste five mill on her? She's a nut job so you'll have to keep her contained or medicated."

"I don't mind paying for experienced pussy, especially if

it's crazy. I don't like timid girls, they bore me," the man replied, continuing to toy with my hair as I stared at his polished shoes. "I have the cash on me."

"No returns," Dad warned as he stepped closer. I closed my eyes as I heard them clasp hands to shake on it, trading my life like it was a used car.

"Wouldn't dream of it. Hey, go get the cash, dude. I'll let you play with her on the way home."

It seemed he had a friend too, and I couldn't help it as tears fell.

"You really want this one?" his friend asked with uncertainty. "What about the blonde we came here for?"

"Hey, Louis. You'll let us take the blonde on a discount, right?"

This conversation was making me physically ill.

They haggled for a few minutes before making a deal, and I refused to look up until a gentle hand squeezed my shoulder and someone squatted in front of me.

"C'mon, babe. Let's get you out of here." I forced my eyes up to find Zavier Lopez in front of me, my mouth opening to speak, but he cut me off quietly. "Fight me a little and play along. You don't know me, got it?" Relief filled me and I almost burst into tears as he pulled me to my feet, motioning to a guy beside him. "Yo, go get the fucking money. I want to get these girls home for some fun."

I had no idea what they were doing here buying girls, but I wasn't going to question it until we had privacy. He was wearing a fancy suit like everyone else, his face hard and void of empathy for the other girls being dragged around the room.

There was no way that he was like my father, I refused to believe it.

His friend ran his gaze over me before nodding, pointing to the blonde girl that was cowering in the corner. "Keep an eye on her too."

Dad kept glancing at me so I forced a disgusted look on my face, sneering at Zavier. “If you think you’re touching me, you have another thing coming.”

“If you think you get a choice, then you're in for a big surprise,” he chuckled, and it was scary how real it seemed. He grabbed my chin, keeping his eyes on mine. “You can’t escape me. You’ll never see your daddy again. That’s a promise.”

His hidden comfort was easy to read and my tears of joy just made me look the part of a scared girl. “Fuck you.”

“Once we’re in the car,” he replied, keeping a hand on my wrist until his friend returned with bags of cash. I had no idea how much business these two did with my father, but considering Dad didn’t feel the need to count the cash, I guessed it was a lot.

“Say goodbye to Daddy,” Zavier growled, and I made sure to pull back and make it look like I was trying to get away from him.

“No! Dad, please!”

“This is what happens to princesses who think they can do as they please,” Dad said bitterly, patting Zavier on the shoulder like they were good buddies. “Enjoy.”

“I will,” he answered smugly, dragging me from the room as his friend grabbed the screaming blonde. We passed Estelle as she held the door open for us, and before I could say anything to try and soothe her worry for me, Zavier leaned closer to her and spoke softly. “She’s fine. We’ll get her out of here.”

Estelle looked surprised as she ran her eyes over me, her face relaxing slightly as I gave her a tiny smile that I hoped the cameras didn’t see. I didn’t want her worrying about me again, so I was grateful Zavier seemed to know who she was.

“Have a good evening, gentlemen.” She held my gaze, not bothering to hide her affection for me. “I love you. I’ll be praying for you.”

"Miracles happen," I choked out. "I love you too."

"We've gotta go," Zavier warned, tugging me out the door and towards a van, his friend struggling with the blonde behind us. It was obvious she had no idea who they were.

We got locked in the back of the van, the vehicle moving from under us as I crawled towards the blonde to comfort her. Zavier and his friend were in the front that was separated from us, so I had to pray I'd read them right and they were saving the girl too.

"Hey, it's okay. They're not bad."

"They bought us!" she screamed, her voice hoarse. "They—"

"I know one of them. They're helping us," I said quickly, taking her hand. "We're okay. I'm Penn."

"Raylene," she answered through tears, but she was still on alert. Panic filled her eyes as the van slowed a moment later. "Why are we stopping already?"

Doors slammed and the back opened to reveal Zavier and his friend.

"You're not really buying girls in your spare time, right?" I asked sharply, and Zavier snorted.

"Good to see you too, Whitlock. You look like shit."

"Asshole," I scowled, but I threw myself at him, hugging him tightly. If he was buying girls, I'd take my chances with him over Dad's basement. "Thank you."

He caught me, taking my face in his hands to carefully inspect me for injury. His thumb stroked across my cheek where Dad had hit me, his jaw clenched. "I can't believe he fucking sold you. We nearly didn't come tonight but we've been looking for Raylene for a while and caught wind of her being there tonight."

"You didn't know I was there?" I asked with confusion, and he shook his head.

"Not as one of the girls for sale. We knew you'd gone

home, Stone said you'd left to stop the Kings from coming after your guys and then attacked him. You shouldn't have done that, we could've helped you."

"Stone said I wanted to go home?" I asked with a frown, and he ran his eyes over me for a second before replying.

"Is that not what happened?"

"Doesn't matter now," I said with a shrug, but inside I was at war with myself. Why had the guys believed that? Stone hated me, so they should've checked to make sure it was true. I was so angry at them for thinking I'd just leave them.

Zavier eyed me knowingly but he didn't mention it. "Let's get you ladies home so you can have a shower and some food. When did you eat last?"

"I got bread daily," I offered, and Raylene nodded.

"Me too."

"We've got soup, so hopefully it won't be too harsh on your stomach. We need to get back in the van, we're heading to the Heights. We have a place set up there that no one knows about."

"What about your girlfriend?" I teased, his eyes narrowing as his friend laughed.

"She's not my fucking girlfriend, you cheeky shit. I'll let you get away with it because I have a feeling that's the first you've smiled in a long time. Get in the van."

"This is the second time I've been kidnapped," I sighed, crossing my arms. "I think I deserve some ice cream."

"I have some at home," his friend replied. "I'm Ander."

"You can't win me over with sugar," I warned, and Zavier scoffed.

"Don't listen to her. Cruz and Drake figured out the way to her heart is with food."

"And good dick," I pointed out, a cocky grin tugging at Ander's mouth.

"I'm your man then, babe."

"Pass. You're not my type," I said and wrinkled my nose, holding out my hand to Zavier. "Can I use your phone?"

"Nope. Pretend you're kidnapped for one more night. I'm not dealing with those dickbags kicking my door down tonight. I'll deliver you to the compound tomorrow," he answered, gently nudging me towards the van. "Please be a good little princess for me, I'm tired."

"I thought you liked your girls wild?" I deadpanned. "And why would you take me to the guys?"

He frowned. "You don't want to?"

"Are they looking for me?" I asked flatly, and I didn't miss the way he cringed. "Exactly. I don't want to see them, Zavier."

"Your call. Do I tell them you're okay?" he asked as he helped me back into the van.

"No. It's not like they're worried anyway," I snorted, getting comfortable as I sat in the corner. "The Night Thieves can go and fuck themselves."

Zavier could tell I was done talking, so he handed me a protein bar and offered one to Raylene who flinched back from him. "We'll get you out of here, okay? No one's going to hurt you. Tomorrow, we'll help you get home to your family, they're worried about you."

"You've spoken to my family?" she choked out, and Zavier gave her a warm smile.

"They've been looking for you ever since you were kidnapped. We've been in touch so they knew we'd found you and were working on getting you out."

"Thank you," she sobbed as she threw herself at him, and I loved how he didn't even hesitate to comfort her. He was a good man.

"C'mon, we need to get moving. One can eat while the other showers, then you can have an early night. Bedroom doors lock too so you can sleep without fear tonight," he promised, pressing the protein bar into her hand, and this time she took it. "You can call your family before bed too if you wish."

Raylene kept blubbering her appreciation, and she cried tears of relief the entire ride to the house. At least one of us had a loving family to go home to.

"Hey, save room for soup," Zavier scolded as I shoveled a spoonful of ice cream into my mouth.

"Leave her alone. Ice cream is dairy, she needs calcium for her weak bones," Ander offered with a grin as he slid a bag over his shoulder and grabbed his keys. "Don't wait up for me, it's a late one."

"She needs *nutrition*," Zavier argued, bringing a bowl over to the table and placing it in front of me, snatching the small tub of ice cream from my hands despite my protests. "Soup first."

"It's just ice cream, not acid," Ander scoffed as he headed towards the door.

"Call me if you need me," Zavier answered dryly, scowling at me as I tried to take the ice cream back. "Hey, do as you're told."

I flipped him off and Ander laughed as he left, but I happily dug into the soup, groaning as I swallowed the hot broth. "This is really good. Did you make it?"

"Yeah. I like soup and it's a cheap way to make a bunch of meals to freeze when I need to," he replied, dropping into the seat beside me. Raylene was showering and going to bed since she'd already eaten, but I was more than happy to hang out with Zavier.

I'd missed having company.

"Do you and Ander save girls often?"

"No offense, but I don't want to talk about it," he grunted, assessing me as I ate. "You're covered in cuts and bruises."

"Yeah, I know. Dad's a piece of shit," I answered, reaching for the bottle of water that he'd already given me. "I'm fine, seriously. I was going a little crazy locked in the basement with nothing but soggy bread and water that I had to lick off the floor, but I'll survive. I'm just glad one of his crazy, rapey friends didn't buy me."

"You need weeks of a nutritious diet, and it couldn't hurt to get a medical check."

"Won't Dad find out?" I couldn't go back in that basement.

"He sold you, Penn. Obviously, I'm not holding a claim over you, I fucking hate that shit, but in the skin trade world, I own you. If I want to take you to get checked out or to the store and events, I'm allowed to. You're free of him, babe," he said gently, and I shoveled more soup into my mouth to try and ease the tightness in my throat.

"Why would you spend that kind of money on me? Where did you get it?"

He leaned back in his seat, glancing at his phone before replying. "You're worth more, but no offense, it's counterfeit cash. Your dad's a dumbass and squirrels it away, so nobody really notices." He slid his phone into his pocket, assessing me for the hundredth time. "Can you tell me if you have any injuries under those clothes?"

The soup in my stomach soured at the thought of him seeing the whip marks, but I knew cleaning them in the shower wasn't going to be enough. Seeing them in the mirror had made me nauseous, and the water had hurt like hell on some of them.

"It's bad," I admitted quietly, pushing the rest of the soup away, my appetite gone. "He whipped me."

"It broke the skin?"

"Some are infected," I said with a wince, meeting his gaze. "I tried cleaning them in the shower but—"

"May I take a look?" he asked, my muscles bunching as I leaned away from him. "If it's infected, you need antibiotics. I'll be gentle, I promise."

"Okay," I forced out, trying to grab the back of the shirt to lift it but the angle pulled at the wounds.

"I've got it," he murmured, standing and slowly lifting the back of my shirt. I leaned forward as humiliation washed through me, flinching as his cool fingers touched my back. "Sorry. Some of these look bad, Penn."

"I know."

He was careful as he inspected them, cursing when his phone rang loudly and scared the shit out of me.

"Sorry, I need to get this." He walked into the other room, and I could hear him cursing up a storm. "I'm busy, okay? Why can't he handle it on his own? I'm not coming home for that. I said I was fucking busy." I got to my feet and wandered towards the room, finding him pacing and raking a hand through his hair. "What part of busy don't you understand?"

"I can leave?" I offered, startling him as he swung his gaze over to me.

"No, stay," he said quietly. "Go finish your food." I went to answer but annoyance filled his face as the person on the phone said something. "None of your fucking business, asshole. Unless he's dying, then I'm not coming to help. Good night." He hung up with a scowl, giving me a look. "Sorry, my friend Logan got into some trouble at the track and expects me to bail him out."

"Is he okay?"

"He's fine, just stuck his damn dick in someone he

shouldn't have and got his ass beat," he replied dryly. "Show me your stomach. I'll have to put some ointment on them, and I'll get you some antibiotic pills tomorrow. If they don't start showing improvement in the next few days, we'll have to take you to the hospital."

"But won't they ask questions?" I didn't want to be grilled for information.

"Not if I call in some help. For now, eat the rest of your soup while I put ointment on these wounds, and then you should get some rest. Keep taking small sips of water, too."

"Thanks for this," I said with a small smile. "I'll be sure to pay you back somehow." Sleeping with him would be a fast payment, but the thought made me feel sick. I liked Zavier, but not like that. "Do you want me to sleep with you or something? I don't have any money."

"Jesus, no. I'm helping you because it's the right thing to do, not because I want you to owe me anything," he said firmly, steering me towards the kitchen. "Don't use yourself like that. I can see you don't want to. Sleep with people because you're attracted to them and want some fun, not because you think they're entitled to it. You're a person, not a pawn."

"What do you want then? I can't—"

"You can take everything I'm offering for free. Stay as long as you like, there's no catch. I just want to make sure you're okay," he said before I could finish my sentence, relief filling me.

"Thank you."

"You're welcome. Now, let's get you ready for bed," he smiled, rummaging in the cupboards for ointment while I finished my food.

Chapter Two

Penn

"Are you sure Dad can't take me again?" I whispered as Zavier steered me towards a booth at the Squashed Melon Cafe, my eyes glancing around nervously.

"I bought you, so I can take you to breakfast," he said casually. "You sure you want unhealthy pancakes? Eggs would be better for you."

"Please. I need tasty, not healthy," I groaned, dropping into a seat and moving over for him to sit beside me. I'd slept like the dead but my body hadn't caught up yet, so I felt terrible this morning. Ander had arrived home really late last night, but he was already gone when I stumbled into the kitchen, apparently taking Raylene to the airport.

"Does Ander sleep?" I asked as Zavier texted someone. "I heard him come home really late."

"He's learned not to sleep much. He runs a lot of businesses, so he's busy all the time."

"Oh? What does he do?"

"Nothing that we can discuss," he said as he lifted his eyes from his phone. "He's on his way here now to join us for breakfast."

Zavier ordered for all three of us, and the food had just arrived when Ander walked in, bags under his eyes from a late night of doing fuck knows what.

"Raylene is on her way home. Her family will be waiting at the airport for her." He sat opposite us, looking me over critically. "You get enough sleep?"

"Did *you*?" I scoffed, studying him right back. "I have a month's worth to catch up on, but I slept all night so it's a start. I'll feel better tomorrow. I did hear you get home though."

"I don't have time for sleep."

"Make time," I argued, his eyes narrowing.

"I liked you more when you were sleepy and scared. Don't mother me or I'll take away the ice cream."

"I might look cute and little, but fuck with my food and I'll turn into a rabid beast," I threatened, his mouth curving into a smirk.

"Cute."

I wanted to punch him in the face for doubting me, but with the lack of food and sleep I'd had recently, chances were high I wouldn't have a lot of fight in me.

I ate so much that I almost threw up, and Zavier gave me so much shit for it that we were all laughing until our stomachs hurt.

Ander wasn't as carefree as Zavier, but that was probably because he was on alert, his eyes constantly scanning our surroundings.

"How did you know Estelle could be trusted when you told her you were helping me?" I asked Zavier as we walked to the car once our food had settled a little.

"I'm good at spotting bad guys, and she was letting out so much worry for you that I'm surprised we didn't drown in it. Cruz mentioned once that there was a woman that worked for your father that meant a lot to you, so I also took a guess since she looked so scared on your behalf," he replied, opening the passenger door for me.

I studied Ander's black Supra as he opened the driver's door, and I raised an eyebrow.

"Is that a race car? Hey, I think I saw you at the track talking to Riley and Luna when Drake took me once." It looked like it went really fast, and I was pretty sure it wasn't road-legal. "Maybe one night you can take me for a spin around the track in it."

"I can do that, but you'd better not throw up on my dash, this car's my baby." He patted the roof before glancing down at his phone, sighing. "I need to go but I'll see you guys later."

"Keep me updated," Zavier replied before Ander got in the car and started the engine, the rumble echoing around the street as it fired to life. "You'll give him a complex if you come in your pants," Zavier teased when he caught me staring, and I punched him lightly in the shoulder.

"I like cars but not that much. What are our plans for the rest of the day?" I asked as I slid into the passenger seat, making him chuckle.

"You don't want to go back to the house and rest?"

"I've been stuck in the basement for a month, I'd like to enjoy the sun for a while," I replied, and he shut the door and moved around to the driver's side, starting the engine.

"How about we go shopping? You need clothes and girly shit."

"I don't have money to—"

"I have money for you. Don't argue, I'm not taking you to Crestford or anything fancy, don't panic," he cut in, reversing out of the parking space and driving towards Ashburn Valley.

"It better be a super cheap store," I scowled, crossing my arms.

"You're giving off major bratty princess vibes right now,"

he grinned, leaning over to open the glovebox and pulling out a phone. "I almost forgot, this is for you."

"You got me a phone?" I asked as I took it, looking it over. It looked flashy like the one Stone had given me, but this one didn't have a parent control on it.

"You need it. Ander isn't always around, and I don't live at the house you're staying at, I'm only there when one of the women are so I can keep them safe. If you're staying long term, I'll have to find somewhere else for you to live or you'll have to stay there alone. I live with Logan, Reid, and Raven, and they're starting to notice my absence more lately. I don't want them to know what I'm involved with. You can call me or anyone you want on there if you need help or if you just want to hang out. You'll make friends the more you hang out at places like the track, or you could even go to school."

"You'll let me?" I asked with disbelief, a sigh leaving him.

"Penn, I didn't actually buy you. I put on a show and those assholes will think you're mine, but I don't cage pretty birds, I teach them to fly. If you want to leave right now, I can take you anywhere you wish."

"I don't have anywhere to go," I mumbled, my face heating. "I don't have family or friends."

"Then you can stay at the house until you want to move on," he smiled, telling me all about the track and filling me in on local gossip until we reached the store in Ashburn Valley.

"I don't need those," I scowled as Zavier shoved armfuls of clothes at the lady at the register. He glared at the small bundle in my arms, acting offended.

"You need more than a few shirts and sweats. I saw you looking at these so I got them."

"You're going to make a sweet husband one day. An annoying one, but sweet," I grumbled, making him chuckle.

"I'll be sure to send my future wife your number to give me a reference then." He slid a credit card towards the lady and winked. "Are you in the market for a husband, gorgeous? Penn can tell you how perfect I am."

The woman turned bright red and giggled, and I couldn't help but roll my eyes.

"He has such a charming personality to make up for the lack of dick in his pants," I deadpanned, and Zavier raised an eyebrow at me.

"C'mon, babe. I know how to use my little pocket rocket. I make women see more stars than an astrology class."

"I bet," I snorted, handing my things over to the woman who was looking even more embarrassed. "Don't listen to him. Size totally matters."

Zavier's fingers gently curved around the nape of my neck, easing me away from the register as he smiled at the woman. "Sorry about her, she doesn't know what she's talking about."

I let him flirt up a storm with her, chuckling as we left, and he cursed about having to carry everything for me.

"You insisted on me buying it with your flashy card, so you can carry it."

"You know, I think I preferred you when you weren't being a princess," he grumbled, but his eyes sparkled with amusement. "And the card's Ander's. Do I look the type to have one of those?"

"Do I look like a Kingslake princess? Appearances are deceiving," I said dryly. "Where to now? Or are you done spending time with me?"

"Is there somewhere you'd like to go?" He shoved the bags

in the car, eyeing me over the roof. "You used to hang out in Stoneleigh, right? I could take you there?"

The gym was somewhere I definitely wanted to go, wanting to catch up with my gym buddy if he was still there, but I needed my strength back before working out and throwing hands.

"Can we watch movies at home? Or are you busy?" I asked as we climbed in, and he shrugged.

"I need to go out in a few hours, but we can hang until then. You'll probably end up napping anyway after all this walking around."

"I am a little tired," I admitted. "I'm probably due for more ointment too."

"Definitely. We'll get you home and comfortable. Will you be okay on your own for a bit tonight?" He looked worried about it, so I nodded. I didn't need babysitting.

"You have good security, and I have a phone, so I'll call if I need you," I answered, fiddling with my phone. There weren't many contacts in there, but it was better than nothing.

"If you get hungry, there's soup in the fridge and random pamphlets on the kitchen counter for places that deliver food. I'll leave some cash with you in case you need it."

"I'll just heat up the soup." I didn't want him spending more money on me. He'd spent enough of Ander's already, and the soup was good.

"Ander's not likely to be home before me, but he has a key. If anyone knocks on the door, don't answer it. No one knows that place is Ander's, so no one should be stopping by. If you think anyone is hanging around, call me," he explained as he drove us home, pointing out things like houses to avoid and the history of a few burned-down places. Most of them were thanks to drug debts, which didn't surprise me.

Once I'd put all my shopping in my room at the house, we

watched a movie until Zavier had to leave. I fell asleep within five minutes of the house being silent.

Cruz

"You racing?" I asked Riley as I leaned against her Corvette at the track. It was still early but the place was crawling with people.

"I told Jett if he beat Beckett I'd race him. We both know that won't happen," she chuckled, peering up at me from under the hood of her hoodie. "You okay? You've been starting to share a personality with Stone lately."

"Sorry, I'm working on it," I grunted, accepting the bottle of vodka she offered me and took a large mouthful.

"Don't worry about a girl who left you behind," she said quietly, nudging my arm. "Besides, it looks like Stone was right and she took off anyway. Maybe she did have a fiance."

The thought gave me fucking hives.

Stone's bullet wound was proof something had gone down between them, but doubt had lingered in my mind. I assumed she'd been locked in her room again, so I'd gone as far as breaking into the damn house to check her bedroom, but she wasn't there.

All her things were gone too, telling me she was either in a facility like Stone suggested, or the fiance was real and she'd gone to live with him. I wanted to believe she'd been taken against her will, but shooting Stone when he was only trying to help her didn't make sense. If Louis had sold her on those dodgy skin trade websites, I would've seen something about it since I made a habit of digging into the dark web to keep an eye out.

Maybe she really had needed medicating and was crazy? I

felt like an asshole for fucking her if that was the case. Was that taking advantage of someone?

"I don't get it," I sighed, handing the vodka back. "It's like she's vanished. She didn't seem mentally unstable, so I'm struggling to believe she's in a facility or something."

"If she'd convinced herself that her father was the devil and you guys were saving her, then she could've come across as quite convincing. She did shoot Stone though, remember? Does she really mean that much to you? You need to let this go before you make *yourself* crazy."

"I would've left with her if she wanted to run," I admitted, scanning the track as two cars took off from the starting line. "I would've taken her anywhere she wanted to go, that's how much I want her."

"You'd leave your boys behind?" she scoffed.

"If it meant having her, then yeah. I'd leave Rawson Grove behind without a second thought," I answered, looking towards the gate as I heard the sound of Reid's black Challenger roll in. Logan and Reid were already here with Raven, so I wasn't surprised when it parked close by and Zavier climbed out.

Apparently, he'd had Reid's car a lot lately.

"Hey," I greeted as he joined us.

"Hey. You seen Logan?" he asked, glancing around the track.

"Yeah, he's got girls cooing over him and his smashed-up face down by the starting line," I grinned. Logan had fucked someone's girlfriend last night and gotten his ass handed to him.

The girl got beat up by her boyfriend's sister too, it was hilarious.

As if on cue, Logan wandered over with Raven scolding him for something, Reid rolling his eyes at the pair of them.

"There you are, you're late," Reid said as he bumped knuckles with Zavier. "Where's your girlfriend?"

"Girlfriend?" I asked with a wide smirk, and Zavier scowled.

"I don't have a girl."

"Who did I hear on the phone last night then?" Reid demanded smugly. "Is she why you're late tonight?"

"Lopez has a girlfriend!" Logan hooted, making me laugh.

"Would you guys shut the fuck up? I don't," Zavier snapped, glancing at me with annoyance. "You prowling for pussy?"

"Uh, no," I chuckled, noticing how tense he was. "What's up with you, man?" I stumbled as he threw a punch at me, making me curse as I touched my burning lip. "What the fuck, Lopez?" He didn't answer me before stalking off across the field, leaving me staring after him.

"Damn, Cruz. What did you do to him?" Riley smirked, but Logan cringed.

"Sorry, bro. I have a feeling that was meant for me. He's hardly been home these past couple days, so I don't know what's going on with him."

Zavier was usually carefree and a bit of a joker, but he was also a murderous weapon when he wanted to be. I had no idea how I'd pissed him off considering I hadn't really seen him in weeks.

"He needs to get laid," Riley stated unhelpfully, pushing off the car. "I'm going to find Beckett. Try not to wreck that pretty face, Cruz."

"Ha ha," I muttered, flipping her off as she walked away, and Logan leaned against the car beside me.

"Have you spoken to him much lately?" he asked, and I shook my head.

"I've been busy. Stone's been sending us on more jobs than normal, so I haven't had a lot of leisure time," I grumbled. "I'm only here tonight because if I didn't get the fuck away from him, I would've kicked his teeth down his throat."

"Trouble in paradise?"

"He's just driving me insane. He's gotten worse since Penn left, barking orders like a drill sergeant while stomping around the compound. He sent Drake on a job with Jai and Will last week, and they're still not back. So Knox is intolerable to be around too," I sighed, checking my phone to find messages from Stone, demanding I get back. I'd been working since four this morning, so he could choke on my dick if he thought I was coming back to do more.

"When's Knox ever tolerable?" Raven asked dryly, joining the conversation. "He's worse than Stone."

"Trust me, you've only seen what they're like in small doses. Living and working with them is very different," I groaned, scowling as my phone started ringing. "See? He's like a clingy fucking girlfriend. I feel like I'm dating a controlling narcissist."

"Break up with him," Raven teased, and I gave her a sly smirk.

"For you? If you insist."

Reid scowled, eyeing me with violence. "Everyone knows you're not dicking anyone, you're still moping about the Kingslake girl."

"So why are you getting so mad?" I threw back, winking at Raven who rolled her eyes, knowing I was just doing it to be a dick. They were way too protective of her if you asked me, the poor girl was never going to get laid.

"Thanks, now they're going to be raging assholes for the rest of the night," she huffed, crossing her arms.

"You're used to it. I don't know how you live with them."

"Me either, it's out of obligation at this point. I can't kick them out of my house and leave them on the streets," she chuckled, but we all knew it was bullshit.

Raven had been best friends with Reid and Logan her entire life apparently, and Zavier had somehow wormed his way into their friendship group too over the years.

"You keep telling yourself that," I snorted, my phone ringing again. I answered and pressed it to my ear, my voice sharp. "What the fuck do you want? I'm done for the day."

"You're done when I say you're done. Knox needs you to —" Stone didn't get to finish.

"You're all good with computers so why the fuck does he need me? If there's no one else, you either need to train people better or fire them," I hissed, walking away from the others to speak more freely. "I thought he was on a job with you and Leah tonight?"

"Leah's vanished and I can't fucking find her, so I need you to get your ass home and help Knox since he took off on his own," he barked, making me frown.

"She's missing? Have you called Jai to see if he's heard from her? They're banging so—"

"Not everyone gets attached to their toys like you. She was in a mood earlier with me, so she's just fucked off to make my life difficult," he bit out, and I couldn't help but laugh.

"Listen to yourself, bro. You're the one making everyone else's lives difficult right now, so don't be surprised when people start avoiding you. Why do you think I'm at the track? Or why Knox has been offering to take so many damn protection detail jobs lately? Everyone's trying to get away from you because you're being a prick."

"Just get home, Cruz. I mean it," he warned, and I almost wished he'd fire me so I could leave. Deep down I knew I'd be devastated, they were my family, but I'd had enough of his bullshit.

"Fuck you, Stone." I hung up before he could explode at me, and I called Knox, wanting to check in with him to make sure it wasn't an emergency. I was mad at Stone, but not Knox.

"What?" Knox gritted out when he answered, and I huffed.

"Hey, I just wanted to check in to see if you actually need me. Stone just called and demanded my presence on your behalf."

"I mean, help would be fucking nice. I'm in Kingslake."

"Stone said you took off alone. Why isn't he with you?" I bit out, jogging towards the car and waving at the others, shaking my head when Reid motioned for them to follow. He gave me a thumbs up and let me leave without question, and I slammed my door and started the engine as I switched the phone to hands-free, catching the tail end of what Knox was saying.

"And then the dickbag tried micromanaging shit, so I told him to fuck off and I left. It's not a huge job, so I'm fine."

I pulled my tablet out from the glovebox and brought up his location, cursing at him.

"Dude, that's a big job. They have loads of security."

"I've shut down most of it and no one's here. I can't even find the dog," he answered, and I was pretty sure I almost reversed over someone on my way out. Loud cursing reached my ears, but I didn't care. I floored it out of there, knowing exactly where I was going.

"You're already in there? Dammit, Knox. Get out and wait for me."

"No, I've got this. Just pull up the security and cover me," he snorted, hanging up on me without another word.

The moment I parked near Knox's car and pulled my gloves and balaclava on, I bailed from the car and made my way towards the dark mansion, hauling myself over the iron gate and jogging towards the window around the back. It was open from where Knox had climbed in, and I lifted myself through it and glanced around.

"Knox?"

He didn't reply so I crept through the house, making my way towards the office. I'd been studying the blueprints of this house for weeks, so I knew it like the back of my hand.

"I told you I was fine," Knox grunted from behind his mask when our paths crossed in the hallway, two paintings in his arms.

"We're a team, dumbass. You wouldn't let Drake go out alone, so how is this any different?" I scolded, taking one of the paintings from him and heading back towards the window.

"Drake's an idiot and would get himself caught," he answered dryly. "So would you."

"Fuck you, asshole."

We made it outside without a problem, closing the window and walking in the shadows silently, my steps faltering as I heard a growl. "Uh, found the dog."

The Doberman snarled, snapping its teeth at us as it emerged from the bushes close by, and Knox didn't hesitate to nudge me. "Move."

Didn't have to tell me twice, getting bitten by dogs sucked.

We tore across the yard, the dog giving chase and closing in on us fast. I scrambled over the gate without destroying the painting, but when Knox grabbed the gate and started lifting himself over it, the dog dove at him, latching onto his leg.

"Fuck!" he snapped, grinding his teeth against the pain. "Take the painting!"

I snatched it from his hand and placed it on the ground,

getting it out of harm's way. Knox was struggling to keep his volume down to avoid alerting the neighbors, but at least he had two hands free now to haul himself up further. We hated running into dogs because they were only doing their job, and we didn't like hurting them. Usually we'd tranquilize them before going in to avoid this.

Knox kicked it with his free foot, the second kick causing the dog to let go so he could pull himself over the gate. He hit the ground hard, a grunt leaving him as he tried to get to his feet as fast as possible, but he'd landed pretty hard on his shoulder. Adrenaline pumped through me as I helped the big bastard up, grabbing the paintings and helping him hobble to his car just as the neighbor's security lights switched on.

They were probably coming to investigate since the dog was barking like mad now.

"Can you drive?" I asked as Knox slid into the driver's seat, giving me a nod.

"I'm fine. Go, someone's called the cops for sure."

"I'll tail you," I said quickly as I headed to my car and jumped in, both of us tearing out of there like our asses were on fire. My tires skidded in the gravel as we left Kingslake and into Pine Valley. It was a smaller town, mainly made up of woodland and cabins. It didn't even have its own grocery store or police station.

Since Stone hadn't called to say we were being followed, we risked it and headed back to the compound in Rawson Grove, parking in the garage and shutting the massive roller door, taking a moment to catch our breaths before climbing from the cars. Knox was limping badly, holding his shoulder as we made our way inside.

Stone was sitting in the kitchen barking orders at some of the other thieves, and I couldn't help but lose my temper. "Who the fuck's on surveillance?"

"You were supposed to be," Stone said without skipping a beat, running his eyes over us. "What happened?"

"I went to help Knox because he was on his own. You were here, so you should've been keeping an eye out."

"It's not my fault you refused to come home and help." I was so close to laying him the fuck out in front of everyone.

"The fuck is wrong with you?" I demanded, seeming to catch his attention because he spun around and glared at me.

"Me? You're the one that's been a pain in the ass ever since that rich bitch left. I knew she'd ruin everything. You should've listened to me."

"Are you dense? The only person destroying this place is you. Look around you, Stone. No one wants to fucking be here!" I exploded, motioning to Knox. "His DNA is now all over the perfectly manicured lawn in Kingslake because the damn dog got him, so don't be surprised if you get stuck dealing with that." I tugged Knox from the room despite his annoyed growl, steering him into the bathroom to stop him from bleeding all over the floor.

He managed to get his shirt over his head, slapping at my hands when I went to unbutton his jeans.

"The fuck, Cruz?"

"Grow up. I'm not going for your dick," I scoffed, going back to the task of removing his jeans. Once he was in nothing but his boxers, I squatted to inspect the bite on his leg. The bleeding had slowed but it still looked nasty.

"So, what's the verdict, Dr. Perv? Will my dick survive?" Knox deadpanned after a moment.

"Get over yourself. I'll need to clean your leg and give you some stitches, but yes, you'll survive. I'll give you a tetanus shot too just to be safe." I stood, carefully moving my hands over his shoulder to test for damage, noticing straight away it was dislocated. "Why didn't you tell me you'd fucked up your shoulder? You shouldn't have driven home."

"We were a little occupied, and the car was automatic so it wasn't that much of a problem," he muttered. "I can deal with my leg myself. Stop fussing."

"You're such a stubborn asshole. I'll do it, then I think we should stop by the Psychos' to see if their medic can look at your shoulder," I replied as I started pulling gauze and everything else I needed out of the cupboard.

"We need our own medic, but I'm fine."

"Shut up and do as you're told. I'll fix your shoulder since you won't go, but don't punch me when it hurts," I scolded, an amused huff leaving him.

"Yes, Doc."

Chapter Three

Penn

"Morning," I said with a raised eyebrow as Zavier stumbled into the kitchen in his boxers. "Rough night?"

"Nope."

"You have one sock on and your dick's poking out of your boxers," I deadpanned, making him curse as he fixed it. "And did you get punched in the face?" His cheek was red and a little swollen, but apart from that he seemed okay.

"I'm fine, I gave Reid attitude last night when he was leaving, so he punched me for being a dick," he muttered, pouring himself a coffee before dropping into the seat opposite me. "Sorry about flashing you."

"It's just a dick, I've seen them before," I chuckled, eating a spoonful of cereal before speaking again. "Why did you give him attitude?"

"In my defense, they were giving me shit, so I'm not completely to blame. Don't worry about it, it's normal for us to fight about dumb shit. He did take his car back though."

"Do you think you could teach me to drive? I've always wanted to," I asked, and he gave me a blank look.

"With what car?"

"Can't we borrow Ander's?"

"You mean the high-performance street racing car? No. You'd kill us in that thing, it's got more power than a fucking jet plane under the hood," he snorted. "Not to mention that car's the most important thing to him in the entire world. No offense, but he's not going to let some random girl drive it."

"Why don't you have a car?"

"I did for a while, but it blew a head gasket, and then someone stole shit off the body, so I scrapped it. It's not so bad now that Logan has a car too, but that was before I started doing all this shit with Lavaro," he sighed, sipping his coffee before changing the subject. "Cruz was at the track last night."

Anger burned through me and I fought to keep it off my face. "Bet he was having fun."

"Not really. I punched him."

"Why?"

"Felt like it," he shrugged, finishing his coffee and fiddling with his phone while I ate the rest of my breakfast. I recognized the sound of Ander's Supra as it pulled into the driveway, but I wasn't expecting him to walk in covered in blood.

"Oh my God, what happened?" I demanded as I flew to my feet, trying to find the damage.

"It's not mine, don't panic," he grunted, my eyes widening.

"Don't panic? Who the fuck does it belong to then?"

"Lopez!" he snapped, confusing me until Zavier grabbed my wrist and gently tugged me back, and Ander stalked off towards the bathroom, slamming the door behind him.

"Why's he mad at me?" I asked with a frown, and Zavier cringed.

"He's not mad at you, but it's better that you keep your nose out of his business." He motioned to my coffee, giving me a smile. "Finish that and get ready to head out for the day."

"Where are we going?"

"Wherever we want," he grinned, and it really started to sink in that I could do whatever I pleased. I wasn't being chained to the house, I was free.

"Can I get my own ID? Oh! A job?"

"Slow down. I organized your ID already but maybe you should wait on the job. You need to build your strength and let your body heal," he scolded, taking my coffee from the table and handing it to me.

"I need to stop at the bar in Ashburn Valley to see Beckett about something. Are you okay with tagging along or do you want to stay hidden a little longer? I can't promise she won't tell Cruz about you being around," he said as he checked his phone again.

"Last time she saw me, she beat me up," I groaned, a laugh leaving him.

"She's over it, you'll be fine."

I quickly got ready for the day, grinning when I checked myself out in the mirror. The black cargo pants were insanely comfortable, and the overly large T-shirt made me feel like I was giving my father the middle finger. He'd never allow me to wear stuff like this.

I left my blonde hair loose around my shoulders, applying some mascara and a little eyeliner before wandering back into the kitchen, earning a wink from Zavier.

"Look at you, street rat."

"They're a little big but I didn't see the point in buying a smaller size, only to need bigger ones in the next few weeks," I shrugged, eyeing the documents on the table. "What's all that?"

"Birth certificate, photo identification, and bank card," he replied, keeping the papers piled together but handing me the plastic cards. "Keep these on you. I know you don't have money right now, but I set up an account for you to use when you're ready. All the information you need is on this piece of paper."

"How did you get all this without me?" I asked suspiciously as I took the cards and turned them in my hand to look at them. I'd never had my own cards before. "And where did you get this photo of me?"

"Mind your own business," he teased. "Just say thank you."

"Thank you," I deadpanned, sliding the cards into my pocket with my phone. "Is Ander coming with us?"

"Nope, he's showering then leaving again."

"So what car are we taking?" I asked slowly, frowning when a car revved outside. "Who's that?"

I didn't realize I'd started biting my nails nervously until he tugged my hand away from my face, his voice gentle. "It's just Reid. I asked him to pick me up alone. Put your shoes on and we'll go."

I found my black high top sneakers and laced them up, following Zavier outside.

"Are you sure Beckett won't beat me up again?" I whisper-yelled as we walked towards the car, and Zavier ruffled my hair.

"If anything, she'll beat me up instead. I can distract her while you run."

"That's not funny," I scowled as he opened the door, and Reid's smug expression dropped as he studied me.

"You've got to be fucking kidding me. You're banging *her*? Jesus Christ, Lopez. Are you insane?" Reid snapped, and I didn't mean to, but I jumped at how angry he sounded.

Zavier scowled, pulling the passenger seat forward and motioning for me to slide into the back. "I'm not sleeping with her, I'm helping her, asshole."

"Do the guys know?"

"The guys who abandoned her? No, and they don't fucking need to. Keep your mouth shut." He turned to me, softening his face when he realized I hadn't climbed into the car. "It's fine, get in. Everyone just thinks I have a secret girlfriend and this dumbass thinks it's you."

"Care to explain why you've been so sketchy then? If it's not a secret that you're spending time with her, then why aren't you telling people?" Reid argued as I finally got into the back so Zavier could fix the seat and climb in.

"You know her father's a piece of shit, so I'm just helping her get on her feet. She doesn't want to see the guys, so drop it. I'm not hiding it, I'm just giving her time to figure out what she wants to do," Zavier answered, glancing back at me. "Right, Penn? You don't owe anybody shit."

"I owe you," I muttered, earning a dirty look.

"You don't owe me anything. You needed help, so I helped you. End of story."

"I'll take you to Harley's bar, but I'm not sticking around for this shit show," Reid stated firmly as he started driving towards Ashburn Valley. "Just remember that Stone and the guys can see literally everything through security cameras, so they probably already know she's with you."

"They don't, or they would've already shown up for a pissing contest," Zavier snorted, ending the conversation.

"What the fuck, Lopez?" Beckett bit out as we walked towards a booth in the back of the bar, her eyes burning into me. She definitely wanted to beat me up again. "What's she doing here?"

"Good to see you too, Donovan," Zavier deadpanned, ushering me into the seat opposite her before sliding in beside me. "Her father sold her, so I'm helping her out."

"You can't just hide her from some rich kingpin on your own!" Beckett hissed quietly. "Do you know how dangerous that is? What if they go through Raven's fucking house looking for Penn? You're going to get people hurt or killed!"

"No one's looking for her because I was the buyer," he explained, continuing before she could lose her mind. "If I didn't do it, some creepy abusive dickbag would've bought her, and she could've ended up anywhere."

"Where did you get that kind of money? The skin trade is insanely priced, and I doubt Louis would let her go for cheap."

"It was counterfeit cash."

"For fuck's sake," Beckett groaned, scrubbing a hand over her face before assessing me again. "You wouldn't have needed saving if you hadn't shot Stone and run off."

I frowned, confusion washing over me as her words sunk in. "What? I didn't shoot him. Stone delivered me to my father with some big speech about me needing help. My father had convinced him that I was mentally unstable and was taking everyone for a ride, so to speak. Stone got shot? He was fine when I saw him last."

Her eyes narrowed skeptically as she glanced at Zavier. "You knew this and didn't tell Cruz or Drake?"

"No, I didn't know," he replied tightly.

"Why did you bring her here? I thought we were talking business," she asked as she changed the subject, checking her phone and replying to a message.

Zavier shrugged. "I wanted to talk about the skin trade, so I thought I'd bring her with me since she might know a few things. Also, she's been locked up since she was taken, so the fresh air and carbs might do her some good."

Beckett's eyes lifted to me once more and she took a long look, her expression softening the tiniest amount. "She could definitely do with the carbs. Get her some pasta or something."

"She needs nutrition. What is it with you girls and your empty carbs? All she wanted when I brought her home was fucking ice cream," he grumbled, and Beckett actually gave him a genuine smile.

"If I'd been locked up for a month, I'd want ice cream too. And some whiskey. You'd better have given her the fucking ice cream, asshole."

"Lavaro did."

"You got her involved with him? Are you stupid?"

Ander seemed nice, but I also understood her concern. After all, he had just stumbled through the door covered in someone else's blood.

"He helped me get her out."

"Are you two attempting some vigilante justice bullshit?" she demanded, her smile fading. "Oh my God, you are, aren't you?"

"I'm the son of the Devil, I think I have it handled," he said dryly.

"Yeah, and look how the Devil fell when we got our hands on him," she said flatly, but he turned to me and changed the subject.

"What do you want to eat?" I didn't even have to think about it.

"Grilled cheese and some pancakes with coffee."

He blinked at me for a moment but Beckett chuckled. "Yeah, you're not getting nutrition into her. Let the girl eat what she wants, at least she's eating."

"Her stomach won't—"

"Just shut up and buy her the shit she wants. She's an adult, she can handle an upset stomach," Beckett snapped, and I jumped as someone spoke from beside us.

"Can you guys not fight in my bar? Who's your friend, Lopez?"

I glanced up to find a middle-aged man looking at us with a dishtowel tossed over his shoulder. He seemed kind, but everyone could put a mask on when they wanted to.

"This is the princess that broke into Mom's house," Beckett said without missing a beat. "You know how Zav likes to pick up strays."

"He's only around because he was *your* stray," the man answered and rolled his eyes, but his face had hardened. "Why's she with you guys now?"

"Because Mr. Lopez over here bought her from her daddy."

"Donovan," Zavier whisper-yelled, earning a half-assed shrug from her.

"What? You just said you bought her."

"Never mind," he grunted, giving me the side-eye. "Tell everyone I'm not holding you against your will."

I rolled my eyes, giving Beckett a small smile. "It's not like I'm trapped in a cage. I mean, he let me eat today."

"Whitlock!" he snapped, and the man grinned.

"I like her. I'm Harley Bates." He reached out to shake my hand, my eyes going wide as I took it.

"You're one of the Psychos?"

"Yep." He didn't elaborate. "What can I get for you guys?" His smile was warm but he had a hard edge to him that screamed danger.

"Grilled cheese, pancakes, and coffee for the princess," Zavier said dryly. "Eggs and bacon with coffee for me, and—" He glanced at Beckett, motioning for her to speak.

"I'll grab pancakes and coffee," she said as she texted on her phone. "Extra syrup." Harley said he'd be back soon and wandered off to organize the food, and Beckett pinned her gaze on me. "So, what do you know about the skin trade?"

"Well, it sucks to be on the product side of things," I deadpanned. "And Zavier sucks at haggling. He paid five mill for me after Dad asked for three."

"Well, aren't you a big spender, Moneybags," Beckett said with a raised eyebrow as she assessed Zavier. "Would you think she was worth that much if the money was real?"

Zavier leaned back in his seat and crossed his arms. "If I had that kind of money, then yes. What was I supposed to do? Leave her there? People were fighting over her, Beck. I wasn't going home without her."

"Why didn't you tell me you were this deep in that shit?" she scolded under her breath, genuine frustration in her eyes. "Those guys trust you or you wouldn't have been invited in the first place. How long has this been going on for?"

I leaned back but shot forward with a wince as pain shot up my back from the wounds, and Zavier grimaced. "I think you should let Jade look at them. If they go septic—"

"Who's Jade?" I asked through clenched teeth, willing the pain to go away.

"Harley's girl. She does a bunch of medical stuff for the crews, she's really good at it."

"I can tell if it's bad or not," Beckett said and got to her feet, pushing me forward and lifting the back of my shirt without waiting for permission. I tensed, but I let out a slow breath to calm myself when she didn't touch me. "Damn, Whitlock. Your dad did this?"

"Yeah. He whipped me a lot," I mumbled as she fixed my shirt. "Zavier's been putting ointment on it."

"You need strong as fuck antibiotics and to bandage it. Jesus, Lopez. Why didn't you bring her by Mom's house to get checked properly?" Beckett growled, and he let out a light laugh.

"Um, I don't know. Maybe because the last time she was there, she was caught breaking into it? She's not exactly welcome. Not to mention, I can't force her to get checked out, and she didn't want to."

"Sure you can. You bought her."

"Donovan," he huffed, but Beckett looked down at me with a scowl. "And you. Why the fuck don't you want it looked at? Zavier's risking his life by getting involved with you, and you're just happy to die on him? The fuck?"

"No, I—"

"I don't like you," Beckett said sharply. "But I don't want you keeling over and dying on Zavier after he put so much effort into keeping you safe. Once we eat, we're going to the Psychos' shed."

"I can't just walk in there!" I threw back as discomfort burned inside of me. "I disrespected your family. I have no right to ask them for help."

"You're not asking," she shrugged and sat back down, grinning as Harley returned with our food. "Argue with me later, I'm starving."

"Penn? What the fuck, Beckett?" Hunter demanded as she practically dragged me into the Psychos' shed an hour later. I knew Skeeter was glaring at me from the other side of the room, but luckily, he stayed away.

Beckett motioned towards me, continuing to drag me through the room with Zavier right behind us. "Is Jade here? I need her medical expertise."

"What happened?" he asked as he followed, studying me. "And why is she with you?"

"Zavier bought her, long story," she replied, and Zavier let out a huff of annoyance.

"Stop telling people that."

Hunter huffed out a breath, opening a door to an office and blocking the doorway.

"I don't even want to know, forget I asked." He turned, his voice softening. "Hey, Hotshot. I gotta steal Red for a minute."

"Get her out," someone snapped, and I took a step back, not that I got far with Beckett's hold on me.

"She needs medical treatment."

"Then she can go to the fucking hospital."

"They will only ask questions, and Lopez bought her, so it's complicated," Hunter replied dryly, a chair scraping as someone walked towards the door. Rory Donovan was intimidating as fuck in real life, her sharp, blue eyes roaming over me slowly. She tilted her head, sliding her gaze to Beckett.

"Give me a reason not to throw her out."

"Lopez put himself in the middle of this shit, so I don't want his efforts wasted if it goes septic and she dies," Beckett shrugged, glaring at Zavier. "We can talk more while your rent-a-girlfriend is being treated." Rory's critical eyes seemed to search my body, and Beckett added, "Her back's messed up."

"From?"

"Whipping. She's been in a basement for a month apparently," Beckett answered, and my muscles locked up as Rory moved closer and grabbed the back of my shirt to yank it up. She was silent for a moment, some of the harshness leaving her tone.

"This was your father?" It took me a moment to realize she was speaking to me.

"Yes," I squeaked out, trying to relax but failing. I never thought I'd meet Rory in person, so I was both fangirling and shitting my pants at the same time.

"Zavier bought you from him?" Disapproval lined her

voice as she put my shirt back in place. "Was it a private sale or open?"

I didn't understand the question, but Zavier took over. "Louis was hosting a sale in his house. I'll explain the details of my presence later, but I was there to buy someone else when he dragged her out. Lavaro and I took both of them home, and the other woman is currently back with her family, while Penn is with me until we can organize something more permanent."

"We'll definitely be discussing this in further detail, considering you've got your foot in the door with the business we're trying to tear down," Rory replied bluntly. "I want her out of here the moment Red's checked her over." She walked off but paused as I called out to her.

"Wait!" She didn't turn around so I continued. "I'm really sorry about breaking into your house. You're like, my idol, I love what you and your family do. You're the only people I know with money who use it for good. I honestly had no idea it was your house, I was just trying to prove to Stone that I could fit into the family he built because I had no one."

No one spoke, and Rory didn't respond before continuing towards the bar where Skeeter was currently glaring at me, and Beckett snorted. "You're something else."

My face heated as everyone stared at me, but a kind woman appeared in the doorway, giving me a smile. Her hair was as red as a fire truck, her voice soft. "Let's take a look at you. Beckett, you two go wait by the bar."

Nerves raced through me as I glanced back at Zavier, and he ruffled my hair with a grin. "You're in good hands, promise."

I didn't get time to thank him before Beckett was scruffing his shirt and dragging him away. "You and I gotta talk, Lopez." He went willingly so I tried not to worry about him, turning my attention back to Jade.

"Follow me," she said sweetly, my eyes catching on someone in the office as she closed the door. I was pretty sure it was Caden, the guy who'd held a gun to my head when I'd broken into their house, and he didn't seem pleased to see me either.

Once in a private room with a locked door, my entire body relaxed, and I let out a shaky breath, making Jade chuckle. "If you think that small lock will keep them out, you're stupid."

"Let me enjoy my false sense of security," I joked lightly, amusement flashing across her face.

"They act tough, but they're a sucker for damaged women, no offense. You're pretty safe in here, especially if Rory allowed you to stay. Sit up here, and I'll check you out so you can get out of here." She patted a low table in the middle of the room before finding some gloves. I hauled myself up, hesitating, before pulling the shirt over my head and keeping it pressed to my chest. "Have you been putting anything on it?"

I flinched as her fingers touched my skin, and she mumbled an apology as she poked and prodded carefully.

"Zavier started applying antibiotic ointment when he brought me home the other night, so he's been keeping it clean, but before that, I didn't touch it. I hadn't even seen it until I left Dad's house. He wouldn't let me shower, so it was kept pretty dirty while I was in the basement," I admitted, keeping my eyes on the ground in front of me. "I don't know where to go next. I can't stay with Zavier forever."

"I'll give you some strong antibiotics. They'll mess with any contraception so be careful," she warned, making me snort.

"I keep my legs shut."

"You're not on anything?" she asked slowly, and I shrugged.

"Cruz was going to put the implant thingy in my arm, but we never got around to doing it. I'm not having sex anyway."

She was quiet for a while as she cleaned and patched my back, not speaking again until she was in front of me, repeating the process with the wounds on my stomach.

"I don't want to scare you or anything, but I think the implant is a good idea. In this world, women are pawns and weaknesses, so even though you're no longer with your father, someone could try to cause you harm. We've seen a lot of girls and women abused and raped by the hands of men who think abuse is power, and many have ended up with unwanted children because of it." She winced when my eyes went wide. "Sorry, that sounded awful. Hopefully, nothing happens, but I like to prepare for the worst. I've had past experiences, and so have some of my close friends. The reality is even though we have these crews behind us to keep us safe, no one is guaranteed to avoid trouble. Nothing says *fuck you* to someone you want to hurt by raping a woman they care about and knocking them up."

"People do that?" I whispered as I stared at her, my stomach twisting in thought. "Use babies as revenge?"

"Yep. I keep myself protected as much as possible. Besides, all it takes is one drunken night of fun and boom, baby," she chuckled. "It can't hurt to be safe."

"Where do I get contraception from? I don't have money or—" I wasn't going to let anyone use me in a sick game like that. Sure, they could cut it out of me if they really wanted to, but it was better than nothing.

Jade opened a cupboard and pulled out a small box, waving it at me. "I can do it right now if you like. We keep them stocked for a lot of the girls who work for us."

"How much? I don't—"

"It's free. Women's healthcare is fucking stupid, so we try to ease the strain of it. If you need other women's products, I can help you. I doubt Zavier thought of those kinds of things," she smiled, not waiting for my reply before pulling tampons and sanitary pads out. "I'll give you my number so if you need more, you can just let me know."

"I appreciate your kindness, but give those to people who need it. I'll figure it out myself," I said, hating the thought of taking things that others might need.

"You need it." She tossed in a box of antibiotics and smiled. "Would you like the implant inserted now?"

I nodded, wanting to throw up when she'd numbed my inner arm and I saw the huge needle she had with the implant.

"Ugh, that's huge."

"That's why we numb the area. I have one and I'm a little bitch, so you'll be fine," she teased. "Would you like me to get Zavier to hold your hand?"

"No, that would be weird," I said with a wrinkled nose. "We're just friends."

"He'd do it, he's a good kid," she replied before stepping closer. "You ready then?"

"Does it hurt?" I asked softly, relief filling me as she shook her head.

"Nope. It'll bruise and be tender for a few days afterwards, but that's it. You'll have to replace it in three years."

"Okay, do it," I murmured as I squeezed my eyes shut and held my arm out.

I felt it, but it wasn't painful, and my entire body relaxed as she stood back with a grin.

"See? All done. I'll put a bandage on it and you'll be good to go. It can take a few weeks to be reliable, so be careful. It gives you time for your antibiotics to be over too."

"Thank you. I'm grateful for your help."

"Any time."

I pulled my shirt back over my head and shuffled off the table, accepting the small paper bag she handed me before she gave me her number and led me out towards the bar where Zavier waited. He seemed deep in conversation with Beckett and the others, but his eyes still ran over me to make sure I was okay. Rory's eyes burned into me but she didn't say anything, and Zavier said his goodbyes before thanking Jade.

He steered me outside and I frowned when Beckett didn't follow. "We didn't bring a car."

"Lavaro's picking you up and taking you home. I have something to do with Beckett," he answered, eyeing the bag. "What else did she give you?"

"Girl stuff. She put that implant thing in my arm too," I explained, pointing at the bandage.

"She's really nice. Sorry, I didn't even think of getting you stuff like that, usually the girls are only with us a day or two before we send them to their families," he cringed. "Shit, did you need them right now? Should we get more ice cream and chocolate? Raven's a fucking demon when she's on hers, so we throw sugary shit at her and keep our distance."

"I'd be a demon too if you threw food at me like a dog," I snorted as Ander's car pulled up, and Zavier smirked.

"That doesn't stop you from liking the idea of belly rubs and being called pretty when you're cramping, though. How's that any different?"

No one had done that for me before, but I imagined it was nice. "It just is." He opened the car door and I climbed in, eyeing Ander. "I hardly recognized you without all the blood."

"You can walk home if you wish," he replied dryly, leaning over me to speak to Zavier. "Do I need to come back for you later?"

"Nah, Beckett can drop me off. I'll see you guys later," he smiled, giving me a wink before walking back into the shed and letting us head home.

Chapter Four

Stone

I SCOWLED as Drake ignored my phone call for the millionth time. He'd been back for a day, but he'd spent the night in Ashburn Valley at Beckett's house with Jett and Maddox. Since he was avoiding me, it meant Knox was now pissed because his boyfriend wasn't home.

Which was apparently my fucking fault.

I needed a fucking cigarette, but since I was the one who made everyone quit months ago, I didn't think it would go over too well if I got caught smoking. I hadn't thought of one even when Penn first arrived and fucked shit up, but now it was all I could think about.

Cruz was working at the computer beside me, but he hadn't said much. I'd been overworking them all, I knew that, but I was trying to keep them occupied.

I scanned the screen when I got a notification that someone had driven through the gate, and I bit out a groan when Beckett's Mustang parked out front. She only showed up to hit people or cause trouble.

Cruz gave me a look when I sighed, closing out of the other footage I'd been going through. "What?"

"Your friend's here," I muttered, his eyes sliding to my screen and making him chuckle.

"Face it, you like her."

"False. She set that asshole on fire here, and I can still smell it," I grumbled. That was the last time I let her store a torture victim here, even if they deserved it.

Someone let Beckett in and she entered the office with a smirk on her face, which instantly put me on edge. "Afternoon, you two. I've had an interesting day."

"Spit it out, Donovan. You know I don't like your cryptic bullshit," I growled, but Cruz was more than happy to play along.

"Maddox finally stuck his dick in Jett? I knew it. They have so much sexual tension between them. I bet that got your rocks off."

She laughed, grabbing a chair and turning it to face us so she could get comfortable.

"I wish, but that'll never happen," she grinned, leaning back and eyeing me. "I just had breakfast with a mutual acquaintance of ours."

"Satan? How's he doing?" I deadpanned, my stomach dropping when she raised an eyebrow and replied.

"A particular runaway princess."

Cruz tried to act unbothered, but his voice filled with interest. "You saw Penn?"

"I've spent most of the morning with her. Won't lie, she looks like shit. Her daddy did a number on her this time."

She knew. I could tell by the way she was staring at me that she knew what I'd done.

"Well, I'm glad she's out and about. I'm surprised she was allowed to spend time with you, though. Louis really wouldn't like you," I said lightly, but Cruz shuffled closer and spoke over the top of me.

"Is she okay? What happened? I thought she was in a facility? Why's her father letting her wander the streets? And how the fuck did you end up having breakfast with her in the first place?"

Beckett slid her gaze from me to him, her face softening a fraction. "She's not doing too good. She wasn't in a facility, he's had her locked in the basement this whole time, and she's skinny as a rake. He only gave her bread and water. Louis sold her a few days ago."

"That can't be right," I mumbled, frowning. "Why would he do that? He was supposed to help her."

"Is that what Louis told you?" she scoffed, crossing her arms. "She's lucky her wounds didn't turn septic and kill her. She's not crazy, Stone. He lied to you. The only thing wrong with her is that she's impressionable and easy to coerce because she doesn't have a proper understanding of social skills. She'd follow the Devil to the pits of hell if he promised to be her friend."

Cruz turned to me, fury in his eyes. "What the fuck did you do to her to make her shoot you then? If she isn't crazy, then she was scared and trying to defend herself."

My heart slammed in my chest, and sick satisfaction filled Beckett's eyes as she watched me struggle to dig my way out of it. "Yeah, Stone. Why'd she shoot you?"

"She wanted to go with him," I said weakly, surprised when Beckett got to her feet and walked towards me, the amusement gone from her face as she looked down at me.

"You mean *you* wanted her to go with him. She never would've left the guys behind without warning. I don't know her well, and I don't particularly like her, but she's so desperate to please people so that she'll belong. You handed her back to her father for your own gain. I'd like to know how you got shot, because from what Penn told me, you were fine when you handed her over."

I didn't dare look at Cruz as the guilt ate me alive. I'd

wanted her gone, but I didn't think it would be that bad for her. I'd be lying to myself if I really believed she was enjoying her time with him, but I figured he'd just lock her back in her room.

"I wanted her gone, and he wanted her to get help. I thought I was doing the right thing. I didn't know—" Beckett's fist slammed into my cheek, surprising me.

"You sold her out! She's done nothing but beg for you to accept her, and you threw her to the wolves, asshole! She's been locked in that basement for a month, being beaten and degraded until she was sold! If you didn't think it was the wrong thing to do, why did you lie? Why did you stage a shooting?" She hit me again, and I let her because I deserved it.

"Where is she?" Cruz asked in a flat voice, refusing to look at me as Beckett stood back. "I need to—"

"No offense, but she wants nothing to do with any of you."

"Where the fuck is she, Beckett?" Cruz barked, getting to his feet. "I need to see her."

"He won't let you near her until she's ready," she answered, motioning to me. "And she didn't shoot this asshole either. She said he was fine when she saw him last."

"Who the fuck has her?!" Cruz shouted, getting in her face. "Tell me!"

"Back off, Lennox. I stopped by to tell you I've seen her, but that girl's traumatized and broken. You can't go playing the white knight card when, right now, you're one of her villains." She turned and glared at me next. "You're lucky I don't drag you back to the shed and pin you with assisting with the skin trade, you dick. I can't believe you were so selfish that you'd blindly believe that shitbag over her."

"I thought she was sick and I was helping," I insisted, my face burning from her fists. "It was just a bonus that it meant she wouldn't be here anymore."

"You're so fucking stupid. You had a loyal girl who meant the world to your best friends, and you fucked it up." She stalked from the room and I stared after her, the room silent as Cruz stared at me. I couldn't look at him, and he snorted when I didn't move.

"Got nothing to say? Did you seriously shoot yourself or something?"

"I didn't know—"

"Save it!" he snapped, turning to face his computer, and I glanced over to find multiple surveillance screens up while he scoured them for Penelope. I knew the moment he found her because the keys stopped clicking and he went still.

It was a recording of Harley's bar in Ashburn Valley, Penn sitting at a table with Beckett and Zavier. He rewound the footage a little, pausing it on the spot where Zavier and Penn arrived together.

"What the fuck?" Cruz whispered under his breath, rewinding more until it was at the start when they arrived in Reid's car. He switched cameras to follow their tracks back to a house in the Heights, his knuckles cracking as he balled his hands into fists when it showed they'd left together.

It seemed she was Zavier's mystery girlfriend that Cruz had been joking about.

"Cruz—" I didn't know what to say, but I had to say something.

He didn't let me though, standing and walking towards the door.

"Fuck you." He left without another word, leaving me sitting alone like an idiot. I went through the footage again and again, the guilt getting worse. She looked so tiny, her clothes hanging off her small frame and her cheekbones more prominent than usual.

The thought of what she'd been through because of me made me feel sick.

Cruz

I tracked Zavier's phone to Raven's house, slamming my car door as I stalked towards the porch. I wanted to tear him to pieces for not telling me she was okay.

I slammed my fist against the door, trying not to take my anger out on Raven as she opened it with a frown. "Hey, what's wrong?"

"Where the fuck is he?" I gritted out, her frown deepening.

"Who?"

Footsteps sounded from behind her, and Logan moved into view, scowling at Raven.

"Why the fuck did you open the door? It sounded like a psychopath pounding on the door. What if you'd been hurt?"

I tried to push inside but Logan's arm shot out to block me as he pulled Raven behind him out of harm's way. "Dude, what the fuck?"

"Where is the piece of shit?" I spat, and he was lucky I didn't punch him in the face for keeping secrets from me too. Had they all known?

Of course they did, Zavier told them everything.

"Who the hell are you looking for, man? Calm down," Logan grunted, motioning for Raven to get back from us. "Don't barge your way into our house demanding shit."

"Did you know?"

"Look, you're making zero sense. I don't know what you're even talking—"

"Penn," I bit out.

"What about Penn?" he frowned, confusion filling his face. I calmed a fraction when I realized he didn't know, lowering my voice.

"Lopez's secret girlfriend is Penn. He had breakfast this morning with her and Beckett."

Logan raked a hand through his hair, blowing out a breath. "Jesus Christ. Maybe they were just eating together?"

"Zavier arrived with her. Reid dropped them off at Harley's," I answered, and Reid materialized beside him and crossed his arms.

"Can you calm down? You've got your wires crossed, bro."

"Tell me where Lopez is or I'm going to turn this house upside down to find him myself," I warned, my blood boiling as the man in question finally joined us. He looked way too calm for a dead man.

"You've got it wrong, Cruz."

I didn't let him say more before throwing a fist at him, the pair of us stumbling back to the ground. Zavier got some good hits in, and I didn't understand why he was so pissed at me. I wasn't the one fucking the girl he loved behind his back.

"Break it up!" Reid barked as he and Logan pulled us apart, Reid's arm hooking around my neck to yank me back. "Enough!"

"He's fucking Penn and didn't have the balls to tell me!" I growled, some of the anger leaving me as Reid snorted.

"No, he's not. He's just helping her."

"But—"

Zavier shoved Logan away and glared at me, looking ready for round two.

"I haven't touched her, dumbass. I can't believe you guys didn't track her down. She waited for you, you know? She was beaten, tortured, starved, and you didn't do shit to save her."

"I did look for her!" I snapped, jerking against Reid's hold on me. "I checked footage and even broke into her fucking house, but she wasn't there! Stone had been shot and made it awfully convincing that she'd wanted to go, so what was I supposed to do? Why didn't you tell me she was okay?"

"She doesn't want you to know anything, and she's not okay. Apart from dropping twenty pounds, her back and stomach are a mess. Louis whipped her to the point of broken skin which turned infected."

I noticed that Raven and Logan were looking at him like he'd grown two heads, and I realized they'd been kept in the dark about the entire thing.

"How did she end up with you? Beckett said she was sold," I asked as Reid finally let me go now that my anger had subsided, and Zavier eyed me silently for a moment before answering.

"She just did, and it's not your business. Stay away from her, I mean it. You and your boys are the last people she wants to see."

"Can't do that," I murmured. "I know she's staying with you in your secret house on the other side of the Heights."

Reid moved around me, giving me a look. "That's one of Lavaro's houses."

"Ander fucking Lavaro got caught up in this?" I hissed, and as much as I liked the guy, he was trouble. "Are you kidding me?"

"He's done more for her than you'll ever know," Zavier said cooly. "Next time you want to talk, call me. If you come into this house like a bull in a china shop again, I'll shoot you."

"Jesus Christ," Raven huffed before walking off, sick of our pissing contest, and I gave Zavier a nod.

"Penn and my guys are off limits to you. They're the only reason I'd kick your door down."

"Then I hope you know you're getting shot," he scowled, following Raven up the hallway.

Reid eyed me, annoyance in his tone. "I think it's best you leave, man."

"Like you wouldn't tear my compound apart for Raven," I threw back before leaving, slamming the door behind me.

Penn

"What the fuck happened to you?" I gasped as Zavier walked through the door later that night, scrambling off the couch when I saw his swollen jaw and nose. He pulled back when I went to touch his face, letting out a sigh.

"Seems Beckett told the guys about our morning. Cruz practically kicked Raven's door down to get to me this afternoon. He was under the impression I was keeping you as a secret girlfriend and lost his shit."

"Cruz did that?" I asked as I tried to touch him again, but he put a hand up between us.

"I'm fine. He knows where you are, so if you don't want to be found, we'll have to move you."

Dread filled me, and I glanced towards the door as if he was going to bust it down any second. "Is he mad at me?"

"No. It seems the truth came out, though, because he's freaking out about needing to see you. Apparently, he broke into your father's house to look for you after you left, but you obviously weren't in your room. He thought you really were in a facility," he answered. "I wouldn't be surprised if he shows up within the next day or two. What's the plan?"

"What about the others? Does Stone know?"

"If Beckett went there and told them, then he's probably got a bruised jaw and ego right now. Do you want to stay here? Now that Cruz knows the truth, he's likely to follow you to the ends of the earth. He's a little in love with you," he chuckled dryly. "Or you can face him and send him packing."

I dropped down on the couch and groaned. "Why would Beckett tell them?"

"It's probably her way of getting payback on you for the whole, *breaking into her parents' house* thing."

"I wish she'd just hit me again," I grumbled, a light chuckle leaving him as he sat beside me.

"If you ever watch her fight in the cage, you'll change your mind fast. That girl's a weapon."

"I can fight, but not that well. Hopefully, once I train more, I'll be better at it," I smiled, turning to face him and crossing my legs.

"As much as I enjoy your enthusiasm, you need to heal first, Penn. Do you want me to find something for you to do? Are you bored?"

"I'm used to doing nothing," I shrugged, his phone pinging with a message. He sighed as he read it, typing a response while speaking to me.

"I stopped by to let you know I'm staying at home tonight. Cruz's visit spilled a lot of secrets that I'd been keeping from Rae and the guys. They're a little pissed with me so I think I owe them a half-assed explanation and some time at home."

"You don't have to explain yourself, I'm fine alone. I'm sorry about Cruz taking his shit to your house, that wasn't fair," I sighed, but he ruffled my hair and gave me a wink.

"I get it, trust me. I should've expected it since Beckett has zero loyalty to you. We can hang out for a while if you want, though?" he offered, but I shook my head.

"It's fine, spend more time with your friends. I can watch a movie and have an early night."

"Call me if you need me. Lavaro's with Riley tonight, so fuck knows what trouble they're getting into. He's likely to have his head under the hood of a car so he won't hear the phone," he said with a wry smile. "It's probably why his girl left him."

"Where's your girlfriend then?" I teased, laughter filling

the room and making the place feel homey. I really enjoyed having company again.

"Smart-ass. I don't have time to let another person in, and it wouldn't be fair on someone to be a second priority."

"If we get to fifty and we're still single, I'll marry you. We can get a dog," I grinned. "Then we can just hang out all the time and won't be lonely."

"You won't be lonely," he said seriously, a soft look on his face. "You make friends easily, and now that you're free to do whatever you want, you'll have a social life in no time. If we're lonely at fifty, though, we'll buy a condo on a beach for sure. Deal?" He was humoring me, but it was nice to pretend I'd never be alone again.

"Deal."

I watched TV alone for an hour once he'd left, then I got hungry and rummaged in the cupboard. Ander had told me that noodles were easy to make, so I put them in a pot and figured out the right knob to turn the stovetop on, then I went back to the TV.

It was fine until I smelled smoke and the fire alarm started screaming through the house.

"Fuck," I cursed as I flew off the couch and into the kitchen, smoke coming from the pot.

I switched the stovetop off and grabbed the pot, tossing it in the sink and turning the water on. It sizzled as the metal cooled, and I huffed as I stared at the burned noodles, not understanding what I'd done wrong.

My phone rang and Ander's name popped up on the screen, his voice sharp as I answered.

"What tripped the alarm?"

"I did. I thought you said noodles were easy! I burned them!" I whined, making him chuckle.

"How the fuck did you burn noodles? Did you cook it for too long and all the water evaporated?"

I frowned, glaring at the pot because it was obviously to blame. “What water? I just put the noodles in the pot.”

“New rule, you don’t cook. Not even toast. You’ll have to open the windows to let the smoke out or the alarm will keep going. Wave a dish towel at it or something,” he sighed. “And order yourself something to eat.”

“Can’t I just wash the noodles?” I asked as I started opening windows, snatching the dish towel to flap at the awful alarm.

“Jesus Christ, no. Throw them in the trash, Whitlock. You can’t wash fucking noodles,” he said with exasperation. “Do I have to come and supervise you?”

“How do I heat up the frozen soup that Zavier made? Maybe I can—”

“You don’t. You hang up the phone to me, then call the pizza place for a delivery. Don’t touch anything else,” he demanded, making me pout.

The alarm stopped but I continued waving the air around, praying it didn’t start again. “But—”

“Since you have everything handled, goodbye,” he huffed before the line went dead, giving me no choice but to order pizza.

I couldn’t decide which one I wanted, so I ordered three, then I sat on the couch to wait.

Chapter Five

Cruz

I PARKED the car down the street and opened my laptop on the passenger seat, taking two seconds to hack into the security system to disengage everything. I'd already been on one job tonight but it had been faster than expected, and Leah had offered to take the sculpture with her and Jai, so I'd detoured.

I hadn't bothered going home to change, preferring to hide in the shadows in my black gear, so I climbed from the car and started walking along the road towards the house. I snuck along the side until I reached the backyard, peering through the windows. It was one o'clock in the morning, so most of the curtains were closed, but they weren't shut properly. With the security off, it was easy for me to sneak in through the backdoor, moving on silent feet through the dark house once I'd locked the door again behind me.

I poked my head into one room, finding it empty. I'd seen the basic layout of the property so I knew which doors were bedrooms, trying them all until finally finding the one I wanted.

The lamp was on, casting a warm glow around the room, my heart calming the moment I laid eyes on Penn. She looked peaceful as she slept, her arms wrapped around a pillow and one of her feet sticking out from under the blanket.

I moved closer, fighting the urge to touch her.

I didn't make a single noise, but her eyes suddenly flew open and she screamed, scrambling back in a panic.

"Penn!" I hissed, cursing when I remembered I still had my mask on, pulling it off so she could see me. "It's Cruz!"

The screaming stopped and her eyes turned to slits, launching her pillow at me with a scowl. "What the fuck, asshole? You scared me to death!"

"Sorry," I winced, raking my gaze over her. She was definitely skinny, but the spark in her eyes was blazing strongly.

"How did you even get in here? The security is insane," she bit out, getting back into bed properly but keeping her distance from me.

"Where do you think Lopez got his system from? I made it, so I can shut it down," I snorted, intending on sitting on the edge of the bed, but she threw her other pillow at me.

"What do you think you're doing? Get the fuck out. I don't want you here, Cruz."

"I know, Lopez told me," I shrugged, raking a hand through my hair to fix it since I'd worn my balaclava for the past few hours. "I had no idea, baby. I broke into your dad's place to see you but your room—"

"Why didn't you come after me that day?" Her voice was so soft I barely heard it. "You believed Stone? After everything he'd done to me?"

"He came back to the compound with a gunshot wound, claiming you shot him and ran. I didn't want to believe him, but it was a little hard not to. I mean, he was shot," I said with a sigh. "Since you told Drake you'd go with your father to stop the Kings shooting at us, we figured—"

"I told Drake I wouldn't leave!" she snapped, tears burning her eyes. "Why didn't you find me? A month in the basement being hurt and degraded, and I got through it because I was waiting for you to save me. Why didn't you save me?" Her voice cracked as she angrily swiped at her cheeks to brush away the tears, and I didn't give a fuck if she was pissed at me, I sat beside her and pulled her against me.

Her scent filled my senses and I breathed her in, clinging to her as she tried to fight me off.

"Don't touch me!"

"Baby, stop," I murmured into her hair, relief moving through me as she sagged in defeat. She started sobbing and I hauled her onto my lap, shuffling my back against the headboard so I could hold her properly.

"You didn't save me," she choked out, burrowing into my chest more and soaking my hoodie with tears.

"I know, I'm so fucking sorry," I whispered, kissing her temple, rubbing a soothing hand up and down her back, but she flinched back sharply. I'd forgotten about the injuries Beckett had told us about. "Show me."

"Show you what?" she asked quietly, refusing to look at me.

I slowly reached out to cup her chin, her eyes finally sliding to mine. "Show me what he did to you."

The hesitation on her face dug into my chest as she contemplated it. I didn't want her hiding from me.

Finally, she sighed and moved to sit in front of me on the bed, turning so that her back was to me, and I carefully lifted the bottom of her shirt to find most of her back bandaged. I gently took the corner in my fingers and pulled it back, pure rage rushing through me as I saw the slashes across her skin.

"It's so ugly," she whispered, and as much as I wanted to tear the bandage off to get a proper look, I put it back in place.

"Nothing about you could ever be ugly, Penn."

Her tear-filled eyes burned into me as doubt lingered below their depths, and I wanted nothing more than to kiss her pain away. The shame reflecting on her face made me want to tear her father apart even more, especially when she looked away as if she couldn't face me.

"No matter what, my feelings for you will never change," I said softly, and I swore she stopped breathing.

"How do you feel about me?"

I crawled around her so that I was directly in front of her, holding her unsure gaze.

"I love you. You're all I want. You want to get out of here and never look back? I'll go with you. I'd follow you to the ends of the earth."

"You can't leave the guys behind," she said weakly, but something settled across her face as hope filled her. "Or your job."

"No? Watch me. I'll walk away from everything for you," I promised, taking her face in my hands. Her lip trembled with overwhelming emotion, and I couldn't hold back any longer as I leaned forward and kissed her.

She didn't even try to fight me off as she accepted the kiss almost desperately, her fingers threading through my hair to keep me close. I wanted to push her back and sink inside her, but I'd only end up hurting her wounds.

"Stop!" she suddenly blurted out as she pushed me back. "I'm still mad at you!"

"How's that working out for you?" I chuckled as I drew her against me again, not wanting any distance between us.

"Do the others know you're here? They're not outside, are they?" she scowled, only relaxing when I shook my head.

"Nah. I'm selfish and wanted to see you alone. I won't keep it a secret from them when I get home, though. My fist has an appointment with Stone's face anyway."

"I don't want you guys fighting."

"I'll skip the fighting and go straight to fucking murder," I snorted. "Is there anything else he did to you that you didn't tell me about?" The flash of worry in her eyes was small, but it was there, anger simmering inside me again. "Penn, what the fuck did he do?"

"It's nothing."

"Why are you protecting him?" I asked with a frown, her eyes dropping to the blanket as she fiddled with her hands on her lap.

"I'm protecting you, not him."

"From what?"

She looked back up at me, and guilt flickered across her pretty face. "Because if I tell you, it's going to tear you all apart, and I don't want to be the reason you fight. I was also worried you'd all get in trouble over it, so I just kept it to myself." Alarm bells rang in my head as I watched her, a choked laugh leaving her. "Why doesn't he like me, Cruz? I'd do anything he asked of me, even risk my own fucking life, and he continued to throw it back in my face. I just wanted to be part of your world."

"What did he do, baby?" I asked in a low voice, taking her hand and giving it a gentle squeeze. "I'm not mad at you if that's what you're worried about."

"You will be. I lied to you."

"About what?"

"I didn't sneak out to break into Rory's house behind your backs. Stone told me it was training, and he took me there and said I had to get in and out within ten minutes with a painting. If I'd told Skeeter that Stone had sent me in there, the crews would've gone after all of you," she finally admitted, my blood running cold.

"Stone sent you in there?"

"Yeah. He didn't tell me it was Rory's house, or I never would've gone in. I thought he was finally taking me seriously, so I didn't question it." That explained why the cameras were out that day, Stone had fucked with them to hide the evidence that he'd left with her.

"They could've killed you, Penn."

"Yeah, and if I'd told them your organization was involved, they could've killed you instead," she said tightly, and I was going to beat the shit out of Stone for putting her through that.

"I'll handle it. Did he do anything else?"

"No." I got to my feet and started stripping off, earning a dirty look from her. "What are you doing?"

"Pretend to be mad at me, but you know I had no idea about any of this, so I'm getting into bed. How did you end up here anyway? Zavier and Ander are helping you?"

"They bought me," she said casually as if it was no big deal.

"Excuse me?" I bit out as I kicked my black jeans off.

"Well, it wasn't real, but Dad thinks it is. Zavier can explain it better than I can."

"I'll deal with him tomorrow too," I grunted, sliding under the covers once I was in nothing but my boxers. She came to me willingly as I put an arm out for her to snuggle into me, and I was careful of her injuries as I held her.

"Don't fight with Zavier. He's been the best," she said softly, jealousy burning under my skin.

"Did he touch you?"

"No, he turned me down."

"The fuck does that mean?" It was harsher than intended, but the thought of her fucking him turned me savage. "You asked him to fuck you?"

"He risked his life to save me. I couldn't think of another way to pay him back."

"Your body isn't currency, and I would've killed him if he'd taken you up on it," I muttered, burying my face in her neck. "I missed you."

"I missed you too." She tilted her head to let me kiss her soft skin, and her hands slid across my abs as she explored. "Is Drake okay?"

"Hardly seen him. He's been away on jobs a lot, and when he isn't, he's been at Beckett's mostly. He's close with her two guys."

"And Knox?"

"He's not around much either. He's avoiding Stone like the rest of us. If you want to see Drake, I can take you whenever you're ready," I promised. "Go back to sleep, we'll talk more in the morning."

"I should make you sleep on the couch," she huffed, but she snuggled into me contentedly, making me chuckle.

"Sweet dreams, baby."

Penn

I woke up to lips trailing across my shoulder from behind, my body melting as Cruz's hand slid over my hip and gave it a gentle squeeze.

"Morning," Cruz murmured as he nuzzled into the crook of my neck, and I arched back into him slightly with a sigh.

"Morning. I should kick you out," I answered lightly, a sleepy laugh leaving him.

"But you won't. I'm taking you out for breakfast."

I rolled over to face him, his light blue eyes sucking me in instantly. He had a black eye and his lip was split, but it looked good on him despite making me feel bad for being the cause of it.

"Why?"

"Because nothing's stopping me and I want to." The front door slammed and Cruz huffed, giving me a wry grin. "Sounds like your boyfriend's home."

“Fuck off.”

He snickered as I climbed out of bed and padded along the hallway to the kitchen, finding Zavier making coffee. He ran his eyes over me to make sure I was in one piece before grabbing a second cup.

“Did you have a good night?” he asked, turning his back to me to make the drinks.

“I set the smoke alarm off making dinner,” I grumbled as I leaned against the doorframe and crossed my arms. “Ander banned me from cooking.”

“He might have texted me about that,” he chuckled as he glanced back at me, raising an eyebrow just as a hand slid around my waist and Cruz’s sleepy voice spoke.

“You got one of those for me too, bestie?”

“That depends. Say sorry for last night.” Zavier gave me an amused look. “I see you had a *very* good night.”

I rolled my eyes and walked towards the table, sitting down to wait for my coffee. “Yeah, it was great. A masked man broke in and scared me half to death. You need a new security company.”

Zavier glared at Cruz who shrugged. “What? It wasn’t like you were going to give me a key.”

“For good reason. The security was supposed to keep you out.”

“That was your first mistake,” Cruz smirked, dropping into the seat beside mine and sliding a hand onto my thigh. “I’m taking Penn out for breakfast. You’re not welcome.”

“Piss on her why don’t you,” Zavier deadpanned, joining us once he’d made three coffees.

“What’s that smell?” Cruz frowned as he glanced around, and Zavier couldn’t hold back the chuckle as he reached for the burned pot that was still sitting in the sink, holding it up to show him.

"Penn tried making noodles for dinner last night and set the alarms off."

I crossed my arms with a scowl, glaring at the pot. "The instructions weren't clear! Ander said to just put it in a pot!"

"The packet literally tells you to add water," Zavier grinned, making Cruz crack up.

"You didn't add water?"

"How was I supposed to know?" I demanded, taking a sip of my coffee. "What if I never learned to read?"

Cruz smirked, leaning closer and draping an arm over the back of my chair. "You can sext me, so you can read noodle instructions. You never did buy those lacy lingerie sets, did you?"

"I've been a little busy," I grumbled, and Zavier snorted.

"Yeah, cremating instant noodles."

I flipped him off and let the guys talk while I finished my coffee, side-eyeing Cruz to check him out. He looked so good in his boxers, and I wanted to run my tongue over his abs and chest like an obsessed psycho.

"You're drooling, Whitlock," Zavier teased, snapping me out of it to find both of them looking at me with amusement.

"I'm starved of good dick, sue me," I hissed, a low chuckle coming from Cruz.

"I can arrange that. If you want to crawl onto my lap right now and ride me—"

"She needs to heal first. You'll hurt her, you neanderthal," Zavier huffed, giving me a pointed look. "Take your antibiotics, and I'll clean your back and stomach."

I knew Cruz was going to argue before he even opened his mouth.

"I'll do it, keep your hands to yourself," he snapped, getting to his feet. "Where are the antibiotics?"

"Cupboard near the fridge," Zavier said dryly, giving me a

sigh. "I guess we won't be getting married or buying that condo on the beach after all."

Cruz's head nearly snapped off, he swiveled his head that damn fast. "What are you talking about?"

"Penn asked me to marry her but now you've ruined it."

"Don't tease him," I scolded, giving Cruz a cringe. "We made a deal last night that if we get to fifty and we're still single, we'll just be together so we're not lonely."

"You'll be too busy marrying me to make time for this asshole," Cruz answered swiftly, moving to search in the cupboard for my pills. "But if I have to kill Lopez and bury his body somewhere to make sure, I'll do it."

"You're not funny."

"I wasn't laughing," he deadpanned, handing me the antibiotics and grabbing me a glass of water. I took them and washed them down, and Zavier got to his feet to grab everything for my back and handed it to Cruz.

"I'll leave this with you then. I assume you'll be going out for the day with Cruz?" he asked, making Cruz snort.

"She's coming to stay with me, obviously."

I turned to face him, giving him a dirty look. "Excuse me? I'm staying here. I'm not going to the compound."

"I'll stay here then," he shrugged, and Zavier bit out a groan.

"This isn't a hotel. Besides, Stone won't just let you spend all your time here when you're supposed to be working."

"Bet," he scoffed, shooing him. "Make yourself busy so I can fix her back."

Zavier rolled his eyes but took his coffee to his room, leaving us in peace, so I pulled my shirt over my head and held it to my chest.

Cruz peeled the bandage off, and I could tell it was worse than he expected because he stayed silent as he assessed it. I peeled the one off my stomach too, letting it air while he started tending to my back.

"I'm going to kill him," he muttered under his breath as he worked, but I didn't bother replying. I had a feeling he wasn't really talking to me.

He was almost done when an engine revved outside before going quiet, and I was surprised when he knew who it was without even looking. "What the fuck is Lavaro doing here? Does he stay here too?"

"Yeah, sometimes. He was out with Riley doing car stuff last night but I don't know where he stayed," I shrugged, smiling as Ander walked in. "Hey, I didn't burn the house down."

"Not yet," he joked, moving behind me to inspect my back. "Seems like it's healing okay. It definitely looks better."

"Eyes off," Cruz grunted, making Ander scoff.

"Eat shit. It's just her back, not her pussy." He lifted a plastic bag in his hand, giving me a wink. "I bought more ice cream."

"Are you going to stick around long enough to actually eat it with me this time?" I asked dryly as he put it in the freezer.

"I'm a busy man. If you want to hang out, you'll have to come with me when I go out. We'll go to the track soon, okay?"

Cruz was fuming but I shot him a flat look. "Don't be such a jealous asshole. I'm enjoying being able to make friends."

"You have the worst taste in company," he said with a wry smile, amusement flicking through me.

"I know, right? I can't help but like you for some reason, though."

"Ha ha," he grumbled, motioning for me to turn around. I kept the shirt pressed against my chest as he cleaned and bandaged my stomach, then he blocked me from Ander's view so I could put my shirt back on.

"We'd better get going if we want breakfast," I said once he downed the rest of his coffee. "I want pancakes."

"Sounds good. C'mon, I'll help you get dressed," he grinned, taking my hand and tugging me towards the hallway, ignoring Ander's comment about him being an ass. I flicked the light on and opened my closet, Cruz's eyes running over all my clothes. "Where did all this come from?"

"Zavier took me shopping. I was happy with a handful of things, but he insisted on buying everything I looked at," I huffed, his eyes narrowing.

"He paid for it?"

"Well, it's not like I have any money," I pointed out as I grabbed a cute sundress off the hanger and held it up to inspect. "Zavier said it was Ander's money."

"I'll be paying him back, I won't have him buying my girl anything," he said stubbornly as he started pulling his pants on, his eyes burning into me as I stripped out of the shirt and shorts I was wearing.

The bra was uncomfortable against the wounds on my back when I put it on, but I kept it a little looser than usual and the bandages stopped it from rubbing as much.

"What do you think?" I asked as I did a twirl, nerves kicking in. "Do I look okay?"

"Okay? You're fucking gorgeous and you'll be lucky if I make it through breakfast without shoving everything off the table and spreading you out on it instead," he said seriously, my heart beating faster as he pulled his bottom lip between his teeth while studying me. He still hadn't put a shirt on, and his muscles flexed as he walked towards me with a heated gaze. "You're lucky I don't rail you right here for your new friends to hear."

"Stop being jealous," I replied and put my hands on my

hips, but a slow smirk spread across his lips as he dropped his arms around my shoulders, gently drawing me against him.

"I'm not jealous, I'm possessive. Which is much worse for anyone who fucks with what's mine."

A shiver ran through me at the tone, and I peered up at him from under my lashes. "How so?"

"Because I'd do anything for you. I know you might not believe me, but I'm never trusting someone's word about you again. I'll tear people apart with my bare fucking hands to get to you. That's a promise," he growled, leaning down to catch my lower lip between his teeth. I trailed my hands around his bare back, feeling his muscles bunch under my touch.

"I love you. Even though I'm mad you didn't come and find me," I murmured against his lips.

"I love you too, baby." He surprised me with a heated kiss, his tongue teasing mine as he took control, and I groaned as his fingers wound around my hair to tug my head back further. His thigh pressed between my legs and I ground against him, both of us jumping in surprise when his phone rang.

He glanced at it from its place on the bedside table, sliding his eyes back to mine. "Do you want to see Drake?"

I was struggling with my feelings, but if I could forgive Cruz, I could forgive Drake. They'd had no idea what had happened, only Stone was to blame in this situation.

I nodded, and Cruz grabbed the phone and answered. "Morning. Want to meet me at the Squashed Melon for breakfast? I have a surprise for you."

Chapter Six

Drake

"Did you even sleep?" Jett asked me as he drove through Rawson Grove, glancing at me with concern. "You look like shit, man."

"I got a couple of hours," I mumbled, rubbing my eyes. Sleep was hard to come by when I was working so much, but when I wasn't, my mind kept me awake. Knox had been texting me until three in the morning, apparently not being able to sleep either.

"We didn't keep you awake, did we?" he asked, making me chuckle.

"I think you guys could wake the dead. What did you do to her? Fuck her with your arm? She sounded like she needed help."

"If I suggested fisting Beckett, she'd probably tie me to the back of the Mustang and drag me along the highway," he shivered, finding a parking spot and killing the engine. "Did Cruz say what he wanted?"

"Nope, just that it was a surprise. You don't have to come in if you don't want to," I sighed, a grin tugging at his lips.

"Are you kidding? This smells like drama, which I love.

Besides, Beck and Maddox are out doing badass crew stuff today, so I'm only sitting at home alone bored out of my fucking mind for the next hour until my appointment. You're doing me a favor."

We walked inside together, but I stopped abruptly when I spotted Cruz sitting with Penn, my heart beating faster in my chest as a sick feeling started in my stomach. Jett ran into my back but I didn't react, not taking my eyes off her. She'd lost weight but she was smiling wide as she talked a mile a minute to Cruz, and butterflies started in my stomach as she looked my way and her eyes lit up.

"Drake!"

I was frozen in place until Jett gave me a nudge, huffing under his breath. "She looks pretty happy to see you, so get over there."

My feet finally started moving and she scrambled out of the booth, throwing herself at me and pushing any doubt from my mind as I wrapped her in my arms.

"What are you doing here?" I asked in disbelief, releasing my hold on her when she hissed out a pained breath. "Did I hurt you?"

Cruz turned in his seat with a grimace. "She's got healing injuries on her back and stomach."

"The fuck from?" I bit out, running my eyes over her. "Did you get out of the facility already? Just visiting?"

The thought of her leaving me again at the end of breakfast made me physically ill, and I frowned when Cruz motioned for us to join him at the table. "That's a long conversation. Sit so we can order breakfast and talk." He looked over at Jett, waving him over. "Stay, come meet Penn."

"You're Beckett's other boyfriend?" Penn asked curiously as we sat down opposite her and Cruz.

"Yep, technically I was the first boyfriend, Maddox is the

spare," he smirked, holding his fist out to bump knuckles with Cruz while talking to Penn. "I've heard a lot about you."

"Bad things I assume," she said with a wince, her eyes meeting mine. "I missed you."

"You left me," I said as if it wasn't obvious, not hiding the hurt in my voice. "You said you wouldn't."

Cruz sighed, motioning to her. "She didn't want to leave, bro. Stone sold her out."

"He wouldn't do that. He got shot so—"

"He was fine when Penn saw him last, I'm pretty sure the psycho shot himself to cover up what he'd done. She wasn't in a facility either."

They filled me in on everything, including the fact that Zavier fucking Lopez had bought her from her father. By the end of the conversation, I was ready to snap Stone's neck.

"And I thought my parents were assholes," Jett muttered under his breath. "Lopez has a white knight complex, he gets a kick out of saving girls."

"Doesn't he ever," Cruz grumbled, eyeing Penn's outfit as if it offended him. I thought she looked cute in the dress.

"And Beckett knew? She didn't mention anything to me when she got home last night," I mumbled, but Cruz shrugged.

"She only told us because she wanted to get a few hits in with Stone."

"So he's in a bad mood this morning?"

"No idea. I was with Penn last night, I didn't go back to the compound."

Frustration burned through me and I glared at him. "You mean to tell me you found all this out yesterday and didn't tell me? What the fuck, Cruz?"

We stopped the conversation as the waitress joined us to take our order, but he answered the moment we were alone again. "For starters, I broke into her house in the middle of the night, and she didn't want to see any of us. I convinced her to let me stay, and now we're here. She's been through a lot," he said carefully, dropping an arm around her shoulders. "I'm going to start looking for a house. She can't come back to the compound, and Lopez and Lavaro aren't happy with the idea of me staying with her in their house."

"If you're moving out, then I'm coming too," I scowled, crossing my arms. "You just want her all to yourself."

"Knox won't let you move out," he answered dryly, discomfort twisting in my stomach. Convincing him to trust her was going to be a fucking nightmare. I didn't want to lose him again, but I needed her.

"I'll figure it out. Why the hell aren't we putting Lopez in a shallow grave? He bought her, Cruz. He owns her. What the fuck is wrong with him?" I wanted to strangle the bastard.

"I've already thrown hands with him, and to be honest, he risked his damn life with that dodgy deal. I think we should just say thank you and only kill him if he tries to state ownership in the future to be an asshole," he said with a wry grin. "He's got more to lose than anyone if the truth gets out. I don't think Louis would let it slide if he found out the money was fake."

My phone rang multiple times throughout breakfast as we made small talk, but I ignored it. I wasn't ready to speak to Stone or I'd tear him apart, and the one time Knox called, he was probably only going to yell at me. It was likely he was stalking me on the cameras and saw who I was with.

Penn got up to use the bathroom once she'd finished eating, and I took the opportunity to ask Cruz about her. "Is she okay? How bad are the marks he left on her?"

He leaned forward, not wanting the entire room to hear our conversation. "They're bad. Zavier's got her on antibiotics and has been cleaning them since he bought her. I cleaned them this morning and they're healing, but I can't imagine how bad it could've been if she'd been in the basement much longer. She's self-conscious about them so be gentle when talking about it."

"What do we do about Stone?" I asked, glaring at the camera facing us as my phone rang again. "And I hope you didn't want this a secret from Knox, my phone's going nuts so I assume he's watching us."

Cruz gave a little wave at the camera, making Jett laugh. "He's going to show up and beat you up if you taunt him."

"Doubtful. He won't want to deal with Penn. Her leaving hurt him more than he lets on," I replied as Penn started walking towards us, the conversation switching to the track, giving me a moment to check my phone.

Knox: Answer the fucking phone, dickbag.

Drake: Is it about you currently stalking me?

The phone started ringing again and I rejected the call, scowling at the camera. If he wanted to be mad, I'd let him. As much as he'd be pissed at Stone for this whole thing when I told him the truth, he still wouldn't let Penn back in out of pride.

He was a dumbass like that.

My emotions were all over the place about it too, but if there was a chance I could be with her again, I wasn't going to fuck it up by getting mad about the whole situation.

"I need to go. I have a visit with Ry," Jett said as he stretched his arms over his head. "Are you staying here, Drake?"

I glanced at Cruz and he nodded. "Yeah, I'll take him home. Tell Ry we said hello."

"Will do. See you later. Nice to meet you, Penn," Jett replied with a smile before leaving, and Penn frowned.

"Who's Ry?"

"Ryder is Beckett's twin. He put himself in rehab recently," I said without elaborating as I checked my phone.

Knox: Stone's acting weird. He's given everyone the day off and vanished.

Drake: Good, now he has plenty of time to plan his funeral.

Knox: ???

Drake: I'll explain later. Meet me?

Knox: Alone?

I huffed, annoyed to be separated from Penn, but I knew he wouldn't if she was there.

Drake: Yeah. I'll be home soon.

"So you're living in the Heights?" I asked as I gave Penn my attention. "With Lopez? I'm kind of pissed Logan didn't tell me."

"No, apparently Lavaro has a place. He's been helping some girls get out of the skin trade, and it's like a safe house. Him and Zavier have been letting Penn stay there, so Logan didn't know until I went around there and threw hands with Zavier yesterday," Cruz said with a straight face. "He's lucky I didn't break his nose."

Penn scowled, giving him a dirty look. "He was helping me!"

"Asshole still could've told me. I thought we were buddies," he grumbled.

"Can you drop me off at home? Knox wants to talk, but then I'll come and find you guys again." Penn looked uncomfortable, and I quickly added, "Just drop me off on the road, you don't need to drive into the compound or anything."

I didn't want her anywhere near Stone if he'd betrayed her like that.

Cruz stood, dropping a bunch of bills on the table to cover the food. "Yeah, I can do that." He took her hand and pulled her to her feet, pressing a kiss to the top of her head. "You okay with that, baby?"

"Yeah, as long as I don't have to deal with Stone," she replied, surprising me as she reached her hand out for mine to hold. I took it, giving it a small squeeze as we walked outside, and I let her sit in the front since I was getting out soon.

It was also so I could stare at her without looking like such a creep.

Knox

I knew that bitch would suck him in the moment I saw them on the camera together. Whatever she'd told him had made him forgive her for abandoning him, and she was lucky I didn't storm into the cafe and choke her out for it.

I watched on the screen as they got in the car and started driving, Drake sending me a message.

Drake: On the way Xx

If they brought her inside, I was going to tear shreds off her for what she did to Drake. He'd been a mess ever since, and I didn't like her just popping up out of the blue. She'd probably escaped the nuthouse.

I shut the computer down and left the room, limping through the quiet compound and into the kitchen. The bite on my leg was hurting but I ignored it, too focused on the possible war that was on the way to my front door.

Leah was sitting with Sandra, and a few others were sitting at the far end with beers in hand.

We never had days off like this, it was weird.

"What's up with Stone?" Leah asked me, and I shrugged.

"Beats me." I rummaged for a beer in the fridge and grabbed one for Drake too, turning and almost running into Leah who was now right in front of me. "Jesus, what the fuck? Personal space."

"What's up with Cruz then? He didn't come home last night. Or Drake."

"Cruz was chasing shit pussy and Drake was at Beckett's. Why? They're not chained to this place, you know?" I snapped. It was a small lie, Penn's pussy was fucking heaven, but no one else needed to know that.

"Are you and Drake—"

"It's none of your fucking business, Leah. If you want to keep using your mouth, do me a favor and go and choke on Jai's cock," I threw back before she could finish her sentence, and Sandra glared at me.

"That's mean."

"News flash, I'm a *dick*. Stay out of my shit, both of you."

"Are you mad because Penn's back?" Leah asked flatly, annoyance washing through me.

"How do you even know that?"

"Knew it," she muttered before answering me. "I saw her on the cameras in Ashburn Valley yesterday. She's buddied up with Donovan and Lopez." I hadn't known that, but I didn't let her know.

"So? Cunt can do what she wants. She's with Cruz and Drake right now."

"Wait, really? They fucking forgave her? She shot Stone!" Sandra gasped.

"Like we all haven't wanted to shoot Stone lately," I said under my breath as I stalked off, heading straight to my room and popping the top off my beer. I sat on the edge of the bed and drank half the bottle, clenching and unclenching my fist as I glared at the wall.

Drake was so easily led, so if Penn sucked him into her bullshit then bailed again, I was likely to kill her. It had been a mistake to let her in, and I wouldn't make the same mistake twice.

It didn't take long for Drake to wander in, quietly shutting the door and moving towards me.

"Did you fuck her?" I asked bitterly, making him snort.

"No."

"Good."

I pulled him onto my lap so that he was straddling me, noticing his entire body relax. Affection was definitely his love language, Penn had been right about that at least.

"Stone lied to us about her," he said softly, holding my gaze as I dropped back to look up at him, my feet still on the floor.

"Don't let her fool you. She's the liar, not Stone."

"He sold her out," he continued, and I went to roll my eyes until he added, "Lopez and Lavaro saved her. She's pretty beat up and skinny. Apparently, her father whipped and starved her before selling her in the skin trade."

"That doesn't explain Stone getting shot."

He shuffled on my lap, placing his palms on my chest with a sigh. "Penn swears he was fine when her dad dragged her away."

"And you believed her? C'mon, babe. She's crazy, remember?" I grunted, taking the front of his shirt and tugging him down over me with a smirk. "I missed you."

It had the effect I'd hoped for, his face softening and a dopey smile pulling at his lips. "I missed you too."

I lifted my hips to grind against his ass, sliding a hand around the back of his neck to keep him close. My shoulder ached, but nothing was going to stop me from touching him.

"Since we all have the day off, I say we spend it in bed. Get naked for me."

"I'm going out tonight," he blurted out, making me frown.

"Where?"

He tried to sit back, but I didn't let him, not wanting him to escape me. "Penn's. Cruz is staying with her, so I told them I'd join them later."

My grip on his neck tightened, anger pooling in my stomach. "You mean for the entire night? I've hardly fucking seen you, Drake. You said you were coming home tonight."

"That was before I knew—"

"So she's more important than me?" I demanded, guilt filling his eyes.

"No, I—"

I shoved him off me so that he was on his stomach, and I laid over his back to pin him in place. "No. You said you'd be home to spend time with me tonight. You bitched and complained about me needing to be more affectionate, but then you can bail when it's convenient for you? Fuck that. You're staying here tonight. See her tomorrow. If she's not going to run away again, it won't be a problem, right?" I snarled, his body deflating in defeat.

"I guess."

It shouldn't have stung, but hearing his tone hit me right in the chest. He didn't want to spend time with me, he only cared about seeing her.

"You know what?" I snapped, climbing off him and grabbing the beer I'd brought in for him, popping the top and taking a large swig. "Go. Fuck off and be with her."

He rolled over to face me, distress written all over his face.

It shouldn't have made me feel better, but it did. "What do you mean?"

"You want her instead of me? Be my guest."

He didn't get up, crawling towards me. "No, I don't mean it like that."

"I've seen you, what, three times in the last two weeks?" I scoffed, shaking his hand off as he reached for me. "She comes back into your life after bailing on you, and all she has to do is smile to get you chasing her like a dog?"

"She's really messed up, I just—"

"Then go. Get the fuck out!" I shouted, not caring if anyone heard me at this point. Everyone knew we were fucking, they just knew better than to ask about it.

"I'll stay with you tonight and see her tomorrow," he promised, trying to touch my cheek, but I swatted his hand away. "Please, Knox. I love you. I'm sorry, you're right. I told you I'd spend time with you tonight, so I'll make plans with Cruz and Penn for another night."

Little prick had turned me into a fucking softie because I calmed and let him climb onto my lap again, and he took the beer from my hand to place it on the bedside table.

"I love you too," I said gruffly, sliding my arms around his waist. "You need to stop taking those jobs. I know you've been avoiding Stone, he's a dick, but you're also avoiding me. I don't fucking like it."

"I know," he mumbled, pressing closer as I palmed his ass. "Cruz is moving out."

"What? Did he say that?" I asked with surprise.

"Yeah. Penn obviously can't be here with Stone, and Cruz won't let her live on her own."

"And you?" I asked bluntly, making him shrug.

"I don't want her alone either."

He didn't say he was going to move out, I wouldn't let him, but I could tell he was thinking about it.

I raked my fingers through his hair and tugged, forcing him to look up at me. "Are you going to be a good boy for me?"

He nodded, grinding on my lap and leaning forward to kiss me. One of my hands snaked between us, sliding up his chest until I could wrap my fingers around his throat to pull him the rest of the way. I kissed him hard, my free hand holding him in place as he squirmed against me, and when he slipped a hand between us to palm me through my pants, I let him.

"How do you want me?" he breathed, my dick hardening more at his want to please me. He was so good at doing what I wanted.

"On your knees, baby," I ordered, power pulsing through me as he scrambled from my lap to do as I'd asked, kneeling between my legs. "Take my cock out." I lifted my hips so he could tug my pants down to free my length, his eyes sliding to mine to await instruction. "Put that naughty little mouth on me."

He didn't hesitate to push me down his throat, a wet gag leaving him as he worked hard to please me. It was like he could hear my thoughts, going harder and deeper when I needed it, and slowing slightly to drag it out when I became closer to release. My fingers threaded through his hair, and for a second, I wondered if he knew just how much power he actually had over me. Sure, I was in charge and he was on board with that, but no one made me feel like this.

Other than Penn.

Frustration moved through me at the thought of her, and I pulled Drake down harder on my dick, a startled choke leaving him. I did it again and again until I was sure he was going to pass out, my cum finally hitting the back of his throat as I held him in place, only letting him go when he started pushing against me for air.

Loud gasps filled the room as he dropped his butt to the floor to catch his breath, his confused eyes on me as I took a moment to get my shit together. He didn't call me out for being rough, he was used to it, but I could see the concern on his face. He knew something had just set me off, and I hated that he could read me like that.

"Don't let her back in," I said quietly, my stomach clenching as he averted his eyes.

"It's not that simple."

"Why not?"

"She was never just some girl, Knox. I can't unlove her."

I wanted to shout at him, shake some sense into his thick skull, and tell him I was all he needed, but I knew how hard it was to let her go. I'd been struggling for a month now.

"I know, babe."

Surprise flickered across his face and I sighed, leaning forward to grab his arm to pull him down onto the bed with me, knowing he was feeling vulnerable and needed comfort.

I think I needed it too.

Chapter Seven

Penn

Drake: I'll have to see you tomorrow. I promised Knox I'd be home tonight and he's in a mood.

Disappointment flared inside me as I read the text later that day, and Cruz wrapped his arms around me from behind to read over my shoulder as we stood in the kitchen.

"It's probably a good thing he's spending time with Knox. They've hardly seen each other. The best way to stop Knox from losing his shit at you is to not make him feel threatened in his relationship. He's trying really hard to give Drake affection so I think Drake made the right call to stay home tonight."

"You just don't want to share me," I replied dryly as I sent a quick reply to Drake to let him know I understood. I honestly didn't want to get in between their relationship, so I had to respect Drake's decision.

"Is it that obvious?" Cruz chuckled, his lips trailing across the curve of my shoulder and neck. "Do you think Lopez would be pissed if I railed you right here in the kitchen?"

"Go for it, but I have this entire place rigged with cameras so you'd be putting on a show for me," Zavier said slyly as he walked in. "Lavaro would definitely add it to his spank bank."

"Please don't fight," I groaned as Cruz's hands dropped to my waist and gave me a gentle squeeze.

"Don't worry, baby. I won't fight with him. I'm just going to kill him a little."

Zavier grinned, ruffling my hair and ignoring Cruz's warning growl. "He's so easy to rile up. You're like a little sister to me, you're pretty safe from my dick. Can't speak for Lavaro though. He's been looking for a rebound."

"That doesn't make me feel any better," Cruz deadpanned as he stepped back. "You're a sick fucker, Lopez. You'd probably fuck your sister if you had one."

"Doubtful, asshole." Zavier turned to me, a serious look on his face. "Have you taken your antibiotics?"

"Yes. Have you met Cruz? He's like a hovering mother hen," I scoffed. "What are your plans tonight? Did you want to—"

"We're busy," Cruz cut in bluntly, giving Zavier a fake smile. "Go play with your girlfriend."

"She's not my girl, man. Lay off," Zavier snapped.

"Well, go play footsies with Logan or something."

"You know this isn't your house, right?" Zavier grumbled as he started walking towards the hallway.

"Kick me out then, I dare you," Cruz replied as he followed him, giving me a few minutes of peace. I unlocked my phone and flicked through my apps, trying to remember how to use them all. Texting was confusing, but the internet? Way worse.

Zavier and Ander had shown me basic stuff, but Cruz had been showing me how to do so much more. My brain struggled to keep up with all the information, but I could tell he was passionate about technology from the way his face lit up as he talked.

Facebook confused me more than anything, and I scrolled through my notifications to find a friend request from Drake and another from Jett. My profile was extremely private, Cruz had made sure of it, so I only wanted to have people I trusted having access.

My finger hovered over the accept button for Jett's, and I jumped when Zavier spoke from behind me. I hadn't heard him come back.

"I'll give you some advice on girls, especially the raging psychopathic ones. If you don't have Beckett as a friend on there, don't add her guys. Beckett knows her guys won't stray for other pussy, but she'd probably kill you for having the audacity to add them anyway."

"He added me. Why would she be mad?" I frowned, and he raked a hand through his hair, a duffle bag slung over his shoulder with his free hand.

"Seriously, you need some girls in your life. They'll teach you girl code that I don't even understand, and it will save you from getting your ass beat. Trust me, girls are territorial, and they have no problem throwing punches over it. Find Beckett's profile and add her. If she accepts it, then accept Jett's."

"Girls are weird," I huffed as I accepted Drake's and clicked on the search bar to type in Beckett's name, making Cruz chuckle as he popped up beside Zavier.

"That's nothing. Beckett's killed people over her guys before."

My eyes widened and Zavier scowled. "Dude, not your business."

"What? You think I'll sugar coat shit for my girl? Fuck that. I want her to know how unhinged Beckett can be so she doesn't take any risks. You might want to keep secrets from your girl to keep her safe, but I don't roll like that. I'm loyal to Penn over everyone else. No matter what."

"Your boys come first."

"Not a chance."

Warmth filled me at his declaration, and even Zavier looked surprised.

"This just got serious. I'm going to go since you're so insistent on me leaving. Don't let Penn cook," Zavier stated, and I scowled.

"What if I'm hungry?"

"Cruz can cook," he replied dryly. "Call me if you need me."

I said goodbye and let out a squeal as Cruz snagged my wrist and tugged me against him the moment Zavier left, being mindful of my injuries. "Get naked."

"Excuse me? We can't. Apart from my wounds, the cameras—"

"Zavier was being an ass, there's no cameras inside," he said flatly, steering me towards the couch. "And if you ride me, nothing will be touching your back or stomach."

"What about Ander?"

Cruz already had his shirt off, my eyes dropping to his chest and abs.

"Ander's in Stoneleigh with Riley. Do you need help?" he asked as he motioned to my clothes, a smile tugging at my lips.

"I know how to undress myself."

"Doesn't look like it to me." He shoved his pants down his legs and dropped his naked butt onto the couch without hesitation, patting his thigh. "Jump on."

"How do you know where Ander is?" I pulled my dress over my head, his eyes instantly going to my boobs. I'd taken my bra off when we'd gotten home, so I was completely exposed to him. "Are you sure there's no cameras?"

"Baby, if you think I'd let anyone see you like that, I'm

not being possessive enough. You're mine. Zavier fucking Lopez doesn't get the privilege of laying eyes on your gorgeous body. I know Ander's in Stoneleigh because I tracked his phone."

"Do you have a condom? I got the implant thing, Jade gave it to me, but it takes—"

"I wouldn't risk it anyway with the antibiotics in your system," he cut in, grabbing his wallet from the pocket of his pants and pulling a condom out. "Why are your panties still on?" I giggled at the look of confusion on his face, and I slowly pushed them down my legs, making him groan as he stroked himself. "Don't tease me. I'm going to bust before you fucking touch me."

"Be a good boy and wait," I said playfully as I tossed my panties at his chest and stepped closer to him. He caught them, placing them beside him as he rolled the condom on and grabbed my waist to help me onto his lap.

His thumbs moved up and down on my hips affectionately as he kissed my throat, his voice full of heat. "Should I make you sit on my face first to warm you up?"

"Trust me, I'm warmed up," I murmured, his hand sliding between my legs to see for himself. He easily pushed two fingers inside me, his thumb toying with my clit lightly as he thrust in and out.

"If your back wasn't so sore, I'd lay you down and fuck you through the goddamn floor," he mumbled in my ear, my thighs tensing as he kept teasing me. "Lift up." I got up on my knees, combing my fingers through his hair as he removed his fingers and grabbed his hard dick, rubbing it across my opening. "You want my dick, baby?"

"Always." I lowered myself over him, taking my time as he stretched me. "Jesus Christ."

"I prefer God, but whatever gets you off, I'll roll with it," he chuckled, sliding his hands to my ass to gently pull me forward a little, making me gasp as my clit rubbed against his pubic bone. "I love the noises you make for me."

I rolled my hips as I dropped my arms around his shoulders, leaning down to claim his lips with mine. He let me stay in charge of the pace as I fucked him, his hands giving me encouraging squeezes every so often.

When he let out a whimpered groan, I almost came. It was the hottest thing I'd ever heard.

His fingers dropped between us to rub my clit, his voice tight. "Come with me. Fuck, Penn. I—"

"Me too," I choked out as I moved faster, my movements faltering as the tingles started. Cruz grabbed my hips and started thrusting up into me frantically, sending both of us over the edge. I clung to him as he fucked me through it, my body shaking as he slowed but continued to thrust into me. "Oh my God, stop!" I begged, my thighs locking up as I tried to shut my legs, which was impossible since I was sitting on him.

"I can't feel my body," Cruz murmured against my neck as I leaned into him.

"I'll feel it for you," I panted, a huff of laughter leaving him.

"If your limbs work after an intense orgasm, you're faking it, and I need to work harder."

I leaned back, peering down at him with a small smile. "I never need to fake anything with you."

"Good to know." He gently swatted me on the ass, lifting me slightly. "Let's clean you up so we can snuggle and watch a movie."

I got to my feet, enjoying how his eyes roamed my body like it was the only thing in the world that could hold his attention. He stood too and disposed of the condom before guiding me along the hallway to the bathroom, running the water until it was warm.

He carefully peeled off the bandages, inspecting my back. "Is the water going to hurt?"

"It stings but I need to keep it clean. We'll just have to make sure it's dry before we add more ointment," I replied, glancing over my shoulder to look in the mirror, disgust swirling in my stomach at the sight. It was never going to be the same again.

"Get that look off your face," Cruz growled, grabbing my chin to force my eyes to his. "You're not damaged or ruined. You're fucking gorgeous, and those marks on you change nothing. I don't know how I manage to keep my hands off you in public. I want to be inside you twenty-four-seven."

"You're a real romantic, you know that?"

"Only the sweetest words for my baby," he winked, leading me into the shower, being mindful of my back and allowing me to step under the spray myself. It stung like I'd anticipated, but it wasn't excruciating.

"Do you think Drake's okay?" I asked after a few moments, making Cruz frown.

"Why wouldn't he be?"

"I know it's hard to believe, but Knox is a dick, so if he's in a mood, he'll take it out on Drake.

And since Drake knows the truth about Stone, I'm also worried he'll do something stupid to him."

"Drake can handle his brute of a boyfriend, and it's not stupid if Stone deserves it," he shrugged. "Don't worry about them, okay? Everything's going to be fine."

I appreciated his positive attitude, but I also knew things were going to get messy before they got better.

Stone

It was late, but my eyes were glued firmly to the computer

screen. The compound was quiet, but that was probably because everyone was avoiding me. I couldn't blame them, I was an asshole.

The house in the Heights was quiet too, and it seemed Cruz and Penn were there alone. Zavier had left earlier and hadn't returned, and I knew Ander was in Stoneleigh because I'd spotted him on one of the cameras. Since he was with Riley, I knew they'd be out causing trouble for hours.

It took a bit of effort, but I hacked into Ander's computer, the webcam turning on and giving me access to the rest of the room. I could only just see part of the living room, but I had a good view of Cruz and Penn curled up on the couch asleep together. She was facing him, tucked against his front as he had a protective arm draped over her.

I thought they were both asleep until Cruz's arm lifted off her and he flipped the bird in my direction, making me cringe. He must have noticed the light on the computer to say the camera was on.

I exited out of it and scrubbed a hand over my face, jumping when Knox spoke from behind me. "Fucking knew you liked her. You need to work at your flirting skills though, man. Sending her home isn't how you play hard to get."

"Don't sneak up on me, you dick," I spat, and he raised an eyebrow. I could tell he wanted to punch me but he was holding himself back which worried me more. Knox was predictable when he was mad, he hit things and moved on, but this was new and I didn't fucking like it.

"I'm a dick? Big words for the resident asshole." He dropped into a chair beside mine, kicking his legs up on the desk to watch me. "Was it worth it?"

"What are you talking about? I thought I was doing the right thing and getting rid of her at the same time. If I'd have known—"

"Your brother would be ashamed of what you did," he said

flatly. "Ezekiel never would've sent a woman back to a monster just because he didn't like her. Especially if his best friends were in love with her. The fuck is wrong with you?"

"Don't bring my brother into this," I warned, a snort leaving him.

"Why not? You need a reality check. Drake's devastated, and it will be a miracle if you see Cruz again. You didn't just sell her out, Stone. You tore your entire family apart."

"Once everyone's calmed down, things will be fine." I was lying, I knew it wasn't that simple, but Knox's next words turned my blood cold.

"You know Cruz is done with you, right? This compound? The Thieves? All of it. He's getting a place with Penn, and that means Drake's likely to go with them. Now I have a decision to make."

"You'd leave too? For her? You've all gone soft," I said tightly, not surprised when he sat up and punched me in the cheek. He didn't curse or scowl at me, he was void of emotion and was eerily calm.

"I'd leave for *him*. You destroyed anything I had with Penn, but do you really think I'd stay here if Drake left? When everyone realizes this place is crumbling, they'll all jump ship and leave you alone in your big castle of deceit. Have fun being the King of nothing."

"Before she came along, you never would've let Drake leave. Just tell him to stay."

"That's because I didn't realize how incomplete Drake felt before she got here. Don't you see what she does for him? I don't like sharing him, but she chases the shadows away that have been in his eyes for so fucking long. He needs her gentle touches and her soft heart because it's his love language. She taught me to give him some of that, but it's not who I am and he deserves so much more than I can give him. That's how you should've seen things before making her disappear. Your brothers loved her, but since you didn't, you decided she had to go." He stood, walking towards the door and glancing over his shoulder. "I love you, bro, but I'm in love with Drake. I don't want to choose between you, but I will if it comes down to it. You're going to be really fucking lonely if that happens."

He left me sitting in silence, and I clenched my fists on my lap. They couldn't leave me. Without them, I'd have nothing.

Chapter Eight

Drake

I woke up to the feeling of lips on my neck, and I let out a content sigh as I leaned back into Knox and his rough palm slid over my hip.

"Morning. Is that a gun in your pants or are you—" I was suddenly on my back with Knox's body pinning me to the bed, my words cut off as he kissed me hard. It was unexpected but not unwanted as I groaned, my dick hardening against his as he ground against me.

Once he'd scrambled my damn mind, he leaned back and peered down at me, amusement flickering in his eyes. "Morning."

"You're in a good mood. Why?" I asked suspiciously as I tried to slow my heartbeat.

"Can't I be in a good mood just because I woke up next to you?"

"This is a dream. You're being nice, so there's no way this is real," I joked, my breath stalling as he kissed my chest, making his way lower at a slow pace. My abs tensed as his stubble grazed my skin, and I became deathly still as his tongue teased me just below my navel. Knox would never put my damn dick in his mouth, I knew that, but this was a lot further than he'd usually go.

He held my gaze as he moved even lower, past the brick in my pants and down to my inner thigh where he bit me sharply, making me yelp in surprise.

"I love how needy you get for me," he murmured, dipping his fingers below the waistband of my boxers. "How you beg me with your eyes to have my wicked way with you."

A whimper escaped me as he slid his hand into my boxers to stroke me, my hips lifting desperately for more. He continued to kiss and bite my inner thighs, his breath fanning across my balls as he moved higher.

My fingers threaded through his hair, and I had to force myself not to yank his mouth towards my dick. He'd shut this shit down so fast, and I wasn't ready for that. He'd pushed his boundaries for me, and I wasn't surprised when he moved back up my body to kiss me, stroking me faster. I cried out as I came hard, my cum soaking my boxers, and Knox slowed his hand, making me jerk as he ran his thumb over the tip to tease me.

"I'll always choose you," he said quietly, the words taking a second to sink in. I tried to catch my breath, but it was hard when his thumb kept running over my slit every so often.

"What are you talking about?"

"If you go, I go too." He climbed off me, grabbing his shirt from the floor to hand it to me. "Clean up. Today's going to be a shit show."

"What do you mean? You can't scramble my brain then have a serious conversation, man. I don't know my name right now, let alone understand sentences," I huffed, and despite him rolling his eyes, the corners of his mouth tipped up in a smile.

"Shower. Breakfast. Shit show. In that order."

I started cleaning myself up with the shirt, frowning at him. "What shit show? Has something happened?"

"Just a feeling I have."

He didn't elaborate so I didn't ask, both of us going for a shower and getting dressed for the day before wandering into the kitchen. It was quiet despite being busy, and my eyes landed on Stone who was silently glowering in the corner with his morning coffee. Knox took my waist from behind and steered me towards the food, ignoring people's looks. He was getting braver with publicly touching me, and it caused butterflies to flutter in my stomach.

He took a tray for me and started filling it with fruit, and he even grabbed some toast and avocado. I'd been eating terribly lately thanks to all the drama, so knowing he was in tune with me enough to know what I needed made me stupidly happy.

He handed it to me before piling his own tray up with greasy eggs and bacon, sitting as far away from Stone as possible. I thought he did it for me until Stone scoffed. "Seriously, man? Cold shoulder?"

"Come join us if you want. I'm itching to fucking hit you again," Knox grunted, not caring about people hearing him. I glanced between them with confusion, noticing the bruise on Stone's cheek. If they'd come to blows, what had they been fighting about? And when?

Knox had gone to sleep with me so they hadn't had time to fight.

"Did you hit me over your boyfriend or the princess' pussy?" Stone asked dryly, my fists clenching. After everything, he still wanted to disrespect Penn?

I stood, sick of him being such an asshole to everyone just because he could. He didn't have to like Penn, but that didn't give him the right to dictate everyone else's feelings for her.

"How the fuck do you think you're still in charge here, Stone?"

"I'm the boss, dumbass."

"Of who? You treated everyone like shit, Cruz fucking left, and you somehow still think you're in charge?" I snapped, Leah cutting in before I could keep going.

"What do you mean, Cruz left?" she asked quietly, her eyes flicking between us. "What's going on?"

Stone suddenly ran out of words to say, but I was so done with him.

"Penn never shot Stone and ran. He delivered her to her father and she's been locked in his basement for the past month. She's probably only alive right now because Lavaro and Lopez saved her. Cruz is done with Stone, he's moving out." I took a deep breath, turning my gaze back to Stone. "I'm fucking done too. Fuck with me all you like, but not my girl. She could've been raped and killed, but you don't give a fuck about that, right? As long as she's not here. Her father sold her in the skin trade, and I'm always going to blame you for that."

Murmurs went around the room as Stone glared at me, and Knox stood beside me, crossing his arms. "I'm done too."

Stone's face hardly showed emotion, but I saw the panic flair in his eyes. He had no one to blame but himself.

"If you want out, then you'd better make new living arrangements," Stone said coldly before finishing his coffee and standing, his eyes on Knox. "You sure this is what you want?"

I glanced down as fingers linked with mine firmly, my eyes flashing back up to Knox's face as he held my hand tighter.

"It wasn't a hard choice, trust me," he answered, tugging me towards the door. "C'mon, babe. Let's clear out."

We walked out, leaving people whispering behind us, and I wasn't surprised when Stone stomped after us. He'd show more emotion in front of us without an audience, but I wasn't expecting anger.

"Are you seriously leaving? If you need to throw a tantrum, take a week off and—"

"So now that no one's around, you'll negotiate?" I bit out, beating Knox to it. "You were more than happy for us to leave a second ago."

"You know I can't stand down in front of the Thieves or they'll walk all over me. I have to treat you the same as I treat them," he gritted out, and Knox scoffed.

"Since when? Everyone knows you favor us with jobs and that you bend the rules for us. You fucked up. Admit it."

"I know I fucked up!" he snapped, holding his arms out wide. "How else can I say that? I wanted her gone, and when her father said she was sick, I thought I was helping her and it was just good timing! If she was sick, then all the stories about her past were bullshit and—"

I shoved him, letting some of the anger leak out. "If Lopez and Lavaro hadn't gotten to her in time, she'd currently be tied to some rich asshole's bed. Her father *sold* her, Stone. Do you understand that? It was just a miracle that the guys were on a rescue mission for one of the other girls and managed to save Penn, too."

He cleared his throat, holding my gaze. "I should've asked earlier, but is she okay?"

"No, and you lost the right to ask about her." I didn't elaborate, swinging my fist back and punching him in the eye. He didn't even try to block it. "If you go near Penn, I'll fucking kill you. If you see us in the street, keep walking. You don't know us and we don't know you. Understood?"

"Guys, just stay and—"

"I'm done talking. Everything that comes out of your mouth are lies anyway. She told Cruz about you sending her into the Donovans' house to rob it, too. You can't pretend you didn't want to wish her harm when you knew sending her in there was going to get her killed. She's our fucking girl, Stone. I'd never do that shit to you if you let your brick walls down long enough to let someone in, even if I didn't like her. I'd just be happy for you and get over it."

"She was a liability," He said calmly, but his voice wavered a fraction, telling me he didn't believe it.

"We're all a fucking liability! What about that time Cruz hacked into the police station in the Heights to steal evidence against me because I was stupid and forgot to put gloves on? He then continued to break in alone to make sure all the hard copies were burned, too. Or recently, when Knox broke into that Kingslake house alone and got bit by the damn dog? Everyone does stupid shit, but we just figure out how to get out of the mess and move on. We don't throw each other out when it gets hard, we're supposed to be family." I started hitting him, angry tears burning my eyes with every hit. "Fuck you, Stone. You ruined everything!"

Strong arms wrapped around me and pulled me back, Knox's voice soft in my ear as I tried to fight him off. "Leave him. I'll take you to Penn, okay?"

"You'll be nice to her?" I asked tightly, not surprised when he hesitated before replying.

"I didn't say that, but I won't choke her out or anything."

"The sacrifices you make for me," I deadpanned, glaring at Stone who was now leaning against the wall, wiping blood from his lip. "I mean it, asshole. Stay the fuck away from her."

"Knox," Stone blurted out, desperation lining his tone. "Can we talk about this?"

Knox didn't even acknowledge him, dragging me further down the hallway until we reached his room where he locked us inside.

"Pack," he grunted, giving my hand a squeeze before

pulling out our duffle bags from the closet and tossing one at me.

"Are you okay?" I asked carefully, knowing he was hiding his emotions. This wasn't as easy for him to do as he was making it out to be.

"Pack," he repeated without looking at me, ending the conversation.

Knox

Drake packed a bag for Cruz, grabbing anything sentimental in the process. Cruz's guitar was one of them despite him not playing much anymore. We crammed everything into the car, and we were just pulling out of the garage when Leah ran towards us and stopped right in front of the car, causing me to slam on the brakes.

"Leah! If you want to meet Jesus, that's a good way to go about it!" I snapped as I rolled down the window. She moved to the side once she knew I wasn't going to floor it, her eyes on Drake.

"Give Penn my number. I don't blame her if she doesn't want to talk to me, but let her know I'd like to see her."

Drake nodded, lost in his own thoughts and not really paying attention, and I let out a sigh as I eyed Leah. "I'll tell her."

"Thanks. Are you guys really leaving?" she asked softly.

"Yeah. Maybe you guys should do the same," I murmured. "We need to go. We'll see you around, I guess."

"You will," she promised, stepping back and letting us leave.

I didn't force Drake to speak on the drive to the Heights, giving him some time alone with his thoughts, but I did send a quick message to Cruz to let him know we were on the way. I knew where to go, I wasn't going to lie and say I hadn't stalked Penn a little too, but Drake didn't call me out on it as we pulled up out front.

Cruz's car was parked out on the street in front of me, leaving the driveway clear for Ander and Zavier.

"Take your bag inside, I'll grab the rest," I offered as I climbed out, opening the back door to grab his bag and hand it to him. "I'll be in soon."

"I'll take Cruz's too, it's fine," he answered, seeming in a better mood now that he was so close to Penn. "Remember to be nice."

I rolled my eyes and grabbed my bag and Cruz's guitar, locking the car before following Drake towards the front door. It was unlocked, so we let ourselves in.

"Hey, baby," Drake murmured as he dropped the bags on the floor and moved into the kitchen to where Penn was sketching at the table while Cruz made coffee. Her face lit up when she saw him, my heart skipping a beat when her eyes slid to me. I didn't miss the small head shake from Drake, warning her to leave me alone, but she ignored him and got to her feet, heading straight for me as I leaned the guitar against the wall and dropped my bag beside it.

I scowled as she threw herself at me, my traitorous arms going around her without hesitation. I could feel the bandages through her shirt, and a sense of pure rage washed through me. This was Stone's fault, but it was also ours.

Why hadn't we chased after her?

I raked a hand through her hair, tilting her head back carefully but with a firm grip. "Are you okay?"

"I am now that you're here," she said quietly, and I had no hope in hell of staying away from her. Not now when she was looking at me like I could chase her demons away with mine.

"I hope you know I'm going to hack your sperm donor to

pieces," I replied, refusing to call him her father. He'd lost that privilege when he'd hurt her.

"I know." Her eyes were full of peace with that idea, which only enraged me more. It must have been horrific if she was okay with him being murdered. Maybe she didn't realize how serious I was.

I stepped back before I could grip her too tightly and hurt her, needing space that she willingly gave me, and Cruz gave me a nod as he handed me a coffee. "Hey. I'm a little surprised to see you."

"As if I'd let Drake leave without me," I grumbled, motioning to the bag of his belongings on the floor. "Brought your stuff."

"Thanks. You grabbed my guitar?" he asked with surprise, and I gave him a look as if he was stupid.

"Of course we did. That thing means more to you than anything."

Penn watched us as she took in the conversation, but she didn't ask about the guitar. If Cruz wanted her to know, he'd tell her when he was ready. My emotions switched from anger, hurt, then to worry as I watched Penn with Drake, her tiny body seeming even smaller now that I was able to get a good look at her. There was no way I could get her under me right now, I'd fucking break her.

Her eyes flashed up to me as Drake talked her ear off, and I could only hold her gaze for a second before looking away.

"Come with me," Cruz said quietly, giving me a nudge and sending Penn a reassuring smile as he led me along the hallway until we got to a bedroom. It smelled like her, and it didn't calm the anger bubbling below the surface. "What's wrong?"

"Have you looked at her? We did that. I've spent a month hating her for leaving, when she was trapped with that asshole being abused. Why the fuck did we believe Stone over her?" I bit out, making him shrug.

"Because we've always listened to him. Why would we question him now?"

"We should've," I hissed. "How fucked up is she? Drake said she's hurt really badly."

He blew out a breath, frustration taking over his expression. "She's on antibiotics for the infection and she needs the wounds cleaned and dressed regularly. I hate to say it, but if Lopez and Lavaro hadn't found her, she'd be dead I think. Especially if someone else had bought her."

"Are you *sure* she wasn't raped or assaulted?" The thought caused rage to wash through me, but it simmered slightly as Cruz shook his head.

"Not that I can tell. She said no one touched her like that, so I'm going to believe it."

"You fucked her already, didn't you?" I deadpanned, amusement flickering in his gaze.

"I missed her, sue me. Did you know Stone's been spying on her? Unless it was you being a creep by watching us through the computer camera last night."

"I caught him spying on you guys," I muttered. "The fuck are we going to do with him, man?"

"I'm going to kill him. Figured I'd let him watch his world fall down around him first, though," Cruz replied bitterly, but I knew he wouldn't. He was mad, but Stone had been his best friend for a long time now. "Are you here because you want Penn, or to give her shit? She's been through enough, Knox. Please be nice."

"I've been fucking nice," I scowled, a sigh leaving him.

"For now. Have you been cleaning your leg properly?"

"It's fine."

"Jesus Christ, show me."

"Cruz—"

"Shut the fuck up and show me," he warned, squatting in front of me to lift my pant leg. "For fuck's sake, asshole. This is the same bandage I put on it for you. You haven't checked it?"

"I've been preoccupied with everyone else's bullshit," I said through clenched teeth, pulling my leg back when he tried to unravel the bandage. "Dude, leave it. It's fine."

"You could lose your leg, you dumbass. Stand still."

"You're a pain in the ass," I bit out, and Drake chuckled as he walked in, leaning against the doorframe as Penn stood beside him.

"You're an actual pain in my ass every night. Pretty sure you fucked my chest cavity through my ass last night."

"Don't act like you weren't begging me for more," I grumbled, my muscles tensing as Penn moved closer to squat beside Cruz, her soft hand moving to my leg as she inspected the wound.

"What happened?" she asked quietly, her concerned eyes flicking up to mine. She looked so good at my feet like this, and I almost fisted her hair and demanded her to choke on my cock.

"Don't worry about it," I snarled instead, defiance shining in her eyes as she gripped my leg firmly, her finger pressing against the wound and making me hiss out a breath.

"Tell me."

Cruz snickered, getting to his feet. "He went on a job alone the other night and got eaten by a Doberman. He hasn't been looking after it since I got here. I'll be back, I need to raid the cupboards for bandages."

"Bathroom cupboard," she replied absently, staring at my leg. Her touch softened again, but her posture went rigid as I spoke.

"Since you've seen mine and feel the need to inspect it, show me yours."

"Oh, you don't—"

I grabbed her arm and hauled her to her feet, grabbing the back of her shirt to shove it out of the way. I glared at the bandages covering her back, taking the corner and peeling it back to reveal angry slashes across her skin. I peeled it back even more, hating that she tried to flinch away from me. She was ashamed, it rolled off her in waves.

She had nothing to be ashamed of, she was gorgeous.

Drake was eyeing me cautiously, waiting for me to say something cruel because normally I would. I'd spent the past month wishing death on this girl, but I'd do anything to keep her the fuck away from the Devil now.

I fixed her bandage and shirt, turning her to face me before taking her chin in my fingers.

"It's cute that he thought he could break you. If I can't, he can't."

"He did break me," she whispered, my grip tightening on her chin.

"No, he didn't. Do you know how I know?" She shook her head, waiting for me to continue. "Because you're here and you look like a queen." Her eyes watered and I scowled. "Don't be a little bitch. Why are you getting emotional on me? You—"

Her arms wrapped around me as she burrowed into my chest, her voice quiet. "I'm allowed to be a little bitch, asshole."

"Only when you're in my bed. You get the same rules as Drake," I chuckled, loving how she tried to get even closer to me. "You like that idea?"

"I like making you lose control. Do you know how much power comes with that?" she asked, peering over at Drake. "Right? I bet you love it too."

He grinned, moving towards us to kiss her temple. "Whether I have Knox's monster cock in my ass, or you bouncing on my lap, I will always feel powerful. You guys are fucking hot and you're both mine."

Cruz joined us and Penn instantly snatched the bandages and ointment from his hands, dropping to the ground. "I can do it."

When I didn't argue with her, Cruz shrugged. "As long as it gets done. I'm going to clean up a little so Penn's new big brother doesn't kick us all out, then I think we should do something fun."

"A gangbang?" Drake offered, making me scoff.

"I don't want to see Cruz's dick."

"You won't, it'll be buried in our girl," Drake laughed, dodging me as I took a swipe at him.

"Stay still!" Penn scolded. "Can we go to the track or something? I need to make friends with girls. There's too much testosterone going around here, and Zavier's terrible at teaching me girl code."

I stopped moving, letting her continue cleaning and rebandaging my leg, but I rolled my eyes. "Zavier doesn't understand girls at all, but you won't find the type of girls you're after."

"Why not?"

"Because you'll end up hanging around Luna who's timid as a mouse and hasn't had enough friends to understand the meaning of girl code, Riley who thinks like a guy and not a girl, or Beckett who doesn't play by any code. Who the hell do you think you'll become BFFs with?"

"I like Beckett when she's not beating me up."

"She doesn't do besties, other than Lopez or Zane Evans," I grunted, a small frown taking over her face as she looked up at me.

"Rage's son? From the Kings' Crew? Why is Beckett friends with him? Isn't he unhinged or something?"

"Yeah, just like Beckett," I deadpanned, fixing my pant leg when she was done. "Trust me, stay away from Zane."

"Fine. All of you get out so I can get changed," she huffed, crossing her arms as she stood and none of us moved. "Are you deaf?"

"Nope," Drake grinned, running his eyes down her body. "Strip, baby. I'm waiting."

Normally, she'd strip without hesitation, so seeing her cringe and cross her arms more tightly, pissed me off. Her father had done that.

I reached out and forcefully but carefully pulled her shirt over her head, stepping against her and placing my hands on her bare waist as her cheeks turned pink.

"C'mon, I don't date weak bitches, so show me how strong you are."

"We're dating?" she asked with surprise, and I could feel Cruz and Drake staring at me with amusement. I wasn't going to let them embarrass me. I wanted her, so I was claiming her.

"Yeah, Whitlock, and I fucking hate whiney, needy girls, so toughen up a little so we can go."

"Yes, Sir," she smiled, my dick hardening.

So much for staying mad at her.

Chapter Nine

Penn

I clung to the fence as I watched Beckett race, a gasp leaving me as the purple Mustang started sliding on the corner. Cruz chuckled, moving behind me and sliding his arms around my middle. "She's doing it on purpose, don't worry."

"Don't worry? Her tires are losing traction!" I hissed as she barreled towards the next corner, her car going sideways again. "How is she not crashing?"

"Beckett is a phenomenal driver. She's the best driver I've ever seen. If she can show off her drifting skills, she will."

"Can you drive like that?"

"I can control a drift, but I don't have even half the skills that Beckett does. C'mon, let's go meet her at the finish line," he grinned, taking my hand to lead me to where a small crowd had gathered. Drake and Knox were already there with Maddox and Jett, and Jett gave me a fake pout.

"Why won't you accept my friend request? I thought we were buddies now?"

"Do you want her to die?" Cruz asked dryly, keeping me close. "Lopez has been teaching her girl code."

"Why does he care about that? He doesn't care about bro

code when he's running around with everyone's girlfriends. If Beckett's not running riot with Evans, she's with Lopez. A real bro would get a new bestie and leave my damn girlfriend alone," Jett huffed, and Maddox rolled his eyes.

"What are you complaining about? They occupy her when she's in a mood so she doesn't beat us up. Pick your battles, man."

"You like it when she gets rough with us," Jett argued, motioning to Drake. "Knox throws you around and you love it. It's like that, but with tits in my face."

I zoned them out as they bantered between themselves, my eyes on Beckett as she sped towards the finish line. Her competition was way behind so it was obvious who was going to win.

I pulled away from Cruz as she screeched to a halt by the crowd, making my way towards her with a smile. She assessed me for a moment as if trying to figure out whether to be nice or not, then she opened the door and climbed out, giving me a nod.

"Hey. I'm a little surprised to see you here."

"The guys wanted to come. I was hoping Ander was here, he promised me a ride in his car," I grumbled, her eyes sliding towards the guys as she replied.

"He's here, but if you think your guys' egos would cope with you being in Lavaro's car playing passenger princess, you're mistaken. If you want a ride, you're better off asking one of the girls."

"How about you?"

She chuckled, giving me her attention again. "I'm not part of your little pony show. Maybe you need to convince Cruz to get a proper race car, it's not like he can't afford it."

Arms slid around my waist from behind, Cruz speaking with amusement. "I have enough dangerous hobbies. Besides, I'm currently out of work so I don't want to start splurging on sports cars."

"The fuck do you mean you're out of work?" she asked slowly.

"We walked out on Stone. Moved out and quit."

"Damn, you really like this girl," Beckett muttered, eyeing me differently. Almost like she was curious but with an untrusting edge to it.

"We love her, and Stone figured that out the hard way," he replied flatly, and before I could say anything, I was suddenly slammed down on the ground with Cruz laying over me. "Stay down!" I didn't understand until I heard the distinct sound of a gunshot, panic swarming through me. I jumped as another shot fired, Cruz's hold tightening on me. "I've got you, baby."

Screams rang out around us but I couldn't see from down here.

"Get behind the car!" Beckett ordered from beside us, and Cruz didn't hesitate to take his weight off me so I could move, but not enough to leave me uncovered as we scrambled to safety.

"Where's Drake and Knox?" I blurted out, peeking around the yard now that we were behind the car. "Cruz, where—"

"They're with Maddox and Jett still. I can see them behind Maddox's car," Beckett answered calmly, pulling a gun from nowhere and leaning around the side of her car to assess our surroundings. "Stay with Cruz."

"Where are you going?" I asked in a shrill voice, amusement flashing in her eyes.

"To kill whichever motherfucker thought they could shoot up my turf." She took off, and Cruz pulled me against his chest more, kissing the top of my head.

"Trust me, the Devil doesn't want her in his kingdom any time soon because she'd try to take over Hell, she'll be fine."

"What if it's someone my dad hired? What if—"

"We'll figure it out. Whoever it is just started a war with

the crews, so they won't be able to stay hidden for long," he assured me, the bullets going silent now that Beckett was chasing them off.

I clung to him, but I pulled away when wetness soaked into my shirt. I wasn't bleeding, but blood rapidly spread across Cruz's shirt by his waist. "Oh my God. Did you get shot?"

"It's fine."

"It's not fine!" I choked out, my hands shaking as I grabbed the bottom of his shirt to pull it up, finding a bullet wound. Blood seeped out, leaking down his side and soaking into his pants to form a large wet patch. "What do I do? Fuck."

"You don't do anything."

I pulled my eyes up to his face, and despite his crooked grin, I could see the pain he was trying so hard to hide. He was hurting, and it was probably a bullet meant for me.

Tears burned my eyes as I stared at all the blood, but Drake was suddenly beside me, pulling me back into his arms.

"It's okay, we'll fix it," he murmured as Knox knelt in front of Cruz to inspect the wound. "Are you hurt?" When I shook my head, he sighed. "Let me look anyway."

"Where's Beckett? Is she okay?" I forced out through the panic, his lips kicking up into a smile.

"She's off being a badass as usual. She's with Maddox. Now, let me look at you." He moved back to lift my shirt slightly, checking my stomach and sides, and he sucked in a sharp breath when he got to my back. "You'll feel that later."

"Was I shot?" I squeaked out, drawing Cruz's attention as he quickly ran his eyes over me. I could tell he wanted to come and check for himself, but Knox growled at him to sit still.

"No, but your back's bleeding." He peeled the bandage back, his warm hand sliding around my hip to keep me in place. "You've reopened some of your cuts."

Cruz cursed, apology in his eyes. "I'm sorry, baby. I just had to get you on the ground. I didn't mean to hurt you."

Knox scowled, glancing at me before looking back at Cruz. "She's fucking fine. Reopening old injuries is nothing compared to ending up dead, dumbass. You're fine, right, Whitlock?"

"Yes," I nodded, letting Drake fix my shirt before pulling me against him again.

Beckett and Maddox finally joined us, Beckett jerking her chin at Cruz. "You good?"

"Yeah, I'll live," he replied, using Beckett's car to get to his feet. "Did you catch them?"

Maddox's fists clenched by his sides as he kept an eye out, but he shook his head. "No sign of anyone. I called Mom and she told us to all head to her house. They've called a meeting."

"Anyone else hurt?" I asked softly, and Beckett sighed.

"Luna caught a stray bullet to the arm, one of the Kingslake car club guys got one in the shoulder, and we have a dead Ashburn Valley High School kid. Whoever did this doesn't seem to have a target in mind, they just wanted to cause destruction."

"I think it's my dad," I blurted out, a frown tugging at her lips.

"Why? He sold you, he has no reason to hunt you down. Besides, you weren't targeted, it was an openfire kind of situation. Has he reached out to you with a threat or something?"

"No, but he could still try, right? What if he finds out the sale was bullshit?" My eyes widened at the thought and I scrambled to my feet. "Has anyone heard from Zavier or Ander? What if—"

"They're both with Riley and Luna. They're fine," she promised, motioning to her car with a scowl as she pulled her phone out to text someone. "I just got this fucking car fixed from the last asshole that put holes in it. Ugh."

Cruz grunted, pressing his hand against his shirt where the wound was. "I don't mean to be a bother, but can we go before I bleed out?" Alarm filled me and he quickly added, "I won't, I'd just like to leave so I can fix it. Sorry."

I moved closer to him, taking his free hand. "Want me to call a cab home while you have your meeting or—"

Beckett snickered, tilting her head at me. "You're coming too. Mom wants everyone there."

"She probably just wants to kill me," I grumbled, making her laugh.

"If a Donovan wants you dead, you'd be dead. Trust me. Hurry up, Jade's waiting to stitch you up, Cruz."

"Shouldn't she be tending to Luna?" Cruz asked, but she shook her head.

"Luna just has a surface wound. Her mom can handle it. You guys get going, I'll wait here for the cops. We'll have this dealt with in no time."

We all split up to our cars, leaving Beckett behind, and I curled against Cruz in the backseat as Knox drove us towards the Donovans house. I didn't like the idea of being back there, but I had a feeling there was no way to get out of it.

Stone

"They're going to flip the fuck out and you know it," I grunted as I flicked through computer screens, glancing over my shoulder at Hunter Rivera. "Cruz could've handled this."

"Cruz is currently in my kitchen being stitched up from a bullet wound, Drake's fussing over Penn too much to focus, and Knox is better with his fists than a computer. You guys might be at odds right now, but our agreement is still with your organization," he replied with a shrug. "No one's going to start a war in our office either."

"I think you underestimate how pissed they are with me," I deadpanned, turning back to the computer. Hunter had called, demanding my immediate attention, but I hadn't known until I arrived that Penelope and the guys were also on the way here. This wasn't going to end well, but I was also glad I got to see them with my own eyes. Especially Penelope. I couldn't just change my mind about her, not with the amount of hate I felt towards her out of habit, but knowing how badly her father had treated her made me want to check on her myself. "You know my face is fucked up from your devil spawn, right?" I grunted, making his mouth twitch with the ghost of a smile.

"My sweet little Beckett did that? From what I heard, you're lucky it's not worse."

"Us guys should stick together, you know?"

"You fucked up, I'm not siding with you. Just be grateful it wasn't Rory. She's been stabby lately."

"Opposed to how she usually is?" He smacked the back of my head, the warning more playful than anything.

"My baby's spicy, just how I like her. Keep searching through footage. There has to be proof of who shot up the track tonight."

"You guys have a lot of enemies," I offered, his eyes narrowing.

"So do you. The track is where a lot of people hang out. They could've been after Lopez, Lavaro, us, you, or even Penn. For all we know, one of the Crestford Academy kids have a drug debt, or some of the Blackwater boys have beef with someone from the Heights. Logan probably fucked someone's girlfriend again," he huffed, making me snort.

Logan was worse than Drake had ever been, and that was saying something. I couldn't tolerate it when those two got together to hang out, it was the worst experience of my fucking life.

"Very true. I guess if someone wants to take out anyone in power around here, they're all connected to people at the track in one way or another," I nodded, scanning the computer screen for the person responsible for the gunfire.

It was like they were a ghost.

I went through private home footage in the area, quiet streets, and known meeting spots for dodgy deals. There was nothing here to show anyone suspicious coming or going.

The door opened and Skeeter walked in, giving me an annoyed look. "Anything?" He really hated it when his crew called upon my guys for help. Diesel could hack into almost anything, and Hunter was good too, but it was faster when we did it. We had the technology to scan faces and comb through smaller details. What took me five minutes would take them all damn day.

"Nothing. If people hadn't gotten hurt, I would've assumed it was just some asshole pranking everyone by using a speaker or something," I replied, clicking back to the footage of theirs from the track where the gunfire first started. I saw the exact moment Cruz was hit, and if he hadn't grabbed Penn and shoved her to the ground, the bullet would've hit her instead.

"With so many people around, any shoe prints are likely to be gone or compromised, and I can't tell from this footage which direction the damn bullets came from," I scowled, leaning back in my seat. "Unless someone saw anything out of the ordinary, you've probably got a dead end. My guess is you have a sniper on your hands, and they were nowhere near the track in the first place or we would've found them."

"This is out of the fucking ordinary," Skeeter bit out, pushing a tattooed finger firmly against the screen. "Who the fuck has enough balls to shoot up our property? Hendricks' kid got shot, for fuck's sake, this person wants to start a war."

"I don't think she was a target. I think they fired a few

random shots. Maybe a gang initiation?" I suggested, Skeeter's lip lifting into a sneer.

"We'd know if someone new was trying to set up around here. We have most of the local towns covered by crews already and at the moment, we're all at peace with each other."

"Worth looking into."

"This isn't my first rodeo, kid," he replied tightly, dropping down onto a chair at the large table in the middle of the room. "This isn't just some rookie. Everyone fears the crews."

Hunter sat beside him, leaning his forearm on the table. "Have we cut off any of the junkies? Maybe someone's coming down from their high and they're pissed that they can't get more? You know how fucked up their heads get on the come down."

"They'd just get their drugs from Blackwater. Only person we've cut off though has been Ry," Skeeter said quietly, obviously not wanting me to hear it, so I pretended I didn't as I clicked through random footage. I'd never had much to do with their son, he wasn't really friends with my guys and he wasn't a member of any of the crews.

From what I'd heard, he'd gotten fucked up on drugs and assaulted Luna Hendricks, which was the entire reason for his rehab stint. I was a little surprised he was still breathing.

They spoke in hushed voices for a while, but I glanced up as more people joined us and I heard Cruz's voice. "You've got to be fucking kidding me." He was glaring at me, but I slid my gaze to Penn as she stood beside him. She looked fucking awful, a wall of guilt slamming me in the chest when I realized just how skinny she actually was, her skin pale and her eyes untrusting as they glanced around the room for danger.

I'd done that to her. She wasn't safe in this house because of me, and she looked like death because I'd convinced myself her father was only looking out for her.

Knox's large figure stepped in front of her, blocking my view as he glared at Hunter. "Why the fuck is he here?"

"Stone's the boss, right?" Hunter asked dryly, giving them the side-eye. "Our business is with him."

"Enjoy it while it lasts," Cruz grunted at me, sliding an arm around Penn as she peeked at me from behind Knox. "You're only useful because of that technology. What happens when I take it away from you?"

"It's my fucking tech," I growled, his eyes narrowing.

"It's mine, actually. Who coded everything? Created the scanning software? Who has all the fucking passwords?" he warned, making me realize he was one-hundred-percent serious about shutting this shit down on me. "You might run the Thieves, but your fancy tech belongs to me."

I went to argue but Rory walked in, her eyes sliding around the room. "Sit the fuck down. The Kings and Reapers are almost here and I want answers before they walk through the door. Who the fuck—"

"We don't know," Skeeter grumbled, motioning to me. "Computer boy over here can't find any evidence of a shooter, other than the fact that people got shot."

"Excellent," Rory deadpanned, dropping onto a chair as everyone else sat too. "Hendricks will want answers since Luna got hurt."

"I can't give you answers that I don't have," I replied tightly, turning to face them all from my spot at the computer, looking right at Penn. "I'm sorry, I didn't—"

"Don't fucking talk to her," Drake snapped, shoving to his feet, but Penn grabbed his wrist firmly.

"Don't." It was so quiet I barely heard it, but she wasn't looking at me now. "We're not here for that."

"Finally, one of you boys found a girl with a brain," Rory scoffed, running her eyes over Penn skeptically. "Well, sort of. The last incident proves she's still a little stupid."

"That wasn't Penn's fault," Cruz said bluntly, his eyes on me as he spilled the truth without a second thought. "We've recently found out Stone set her up. He wanted her gone, and he knew you'd make that happen if she was found here uninvited. She would've done anything to get him to accept her into the Thieves, and he took advantage of that."

The room became deathly silent, and I was surprised when Hunter spoke flatly. "If I were you, I'd leave before it's not an option, Stone. You've got five seconds."

Terror spread across Penn's face, and I didn't want to traumatize her more by letting her witness me being torn apart, so I got to my feet and left without another word.

Cruz

I pulled Penn onto my lap as Stone left, trying to soothe her panic while ignoring the pain in my side from the stitches. I was a little tipsy thanks to Jade forcing whiskey down my throat in an attempt to numb the wound, but my focus being on Penn was working way better. As much as I was pissed at Stone, I hadn't really thought about the consequences of throwing him under the bus like that. I was so angry with him, but they could've killed him right in front of us.

Penn wouldn't cope with that, and I wasn't sure if I would either.

"How long have you fucking known?" Rory asked coldly, giving me her full attention. "Or did you always know?"

"It's new information. Penn didn't want anyone to know in case you guys went after us for it as a whole. We'd never do that to you, Stone was acting selfishly out of spite," I answered calmly, but inside I was freaking out. What if we still ended up killed?

Penn had lied about it too, so had I just put a target on her head?

My arms tightened around her and Rory noticed, her expression softening the smallest amount. "I'm not going to hurt her. You know we'll have to deal with Stone though, right?"

Penn flew out of my lap before I could stop her, landing hard on her knees as she fell at Rory's feet. "Please, don't kill him. It was my fault. He—"

"How the fuck was it your fault?" Rory bit out, but she lost all anger as Penn kept babbling, my heart breaking for her.

"He was mad at me, I kept annoying him, and if I'd just gone home, it wouldn't have happened. If I hadn't made him so mad—" She really believed it was her fault?

"Get up," Rory murmured, and when Penn didn't move, I stood and walked towards her.

"Come on, baby. Get up from the floor."

"It was my fault!" she screamed, making me wince at the volume. If she didn't calm down she was going to put herself in a panic attack. Between the shooting incident, me getting shot, and her being in a room with Stone, I think it was all a little too much for her.

"Drake, take her upstairs," I sighed as I pulled her against my chest. "I'll fill you in later."

Rory kept watching us as Drake joined me and took Penn into his arms, gently guiding her from the room.

"She's weak," Skeeter muttered, assessing me. "Are you sure she's a good fit for you guys?"

Annoyance hit me, but Rory beat me to it.

"She's not weak, she's fucking traumatized. She'll grow stronger now that she has people around to support her. Asshole," she huffed, having no problem smacking him in the back of the head like he was a naughty child. His eyes flared with anger but Hunter smacked a hand down on the table to get their attention.

"Handle your shit later, guys. For now, we need to figure out who shot at our fucking kids tonight."

Skeeter scowled and leaned back in his chair to light a cigarette, my fingers twitching as the smell hit my nose. Stone had forced the entire organization to quit smoking months ago thanks to some dumbass leaving a cigarette butt at a house we'd broken into, and it had been a messy issue with the law.

Maybe that was all Stone needed, a goddamn cigarette.

"Put that out. We quit," Rory ordered, but Skeeter shrugged.

"I'm stressed and like one sometimes."

"You're about to be even more stressed if I have to take it from you."

I swore all they did was argue.

One by one, other people joined us until the room was full, and I wasn't surprised when Archer Hendricks exploded a few minutes into the meeting. "What the fuck do you mean you don't know who did it? Some asshole shot my little girl!"

She wasn't little, she was a grown-ass adult, but I didn't dare say that out loud.

"Whoever did it had a plan. This wasn't a last minute decision," Knox grunted. "They remained hidden, had a quick escape, and—"

"No one's talking to you!" Archer snapped, and Rory rolled her eyes.

"Can you not make enemies out of my contacts?"

"This is crew business. They don't need to be here."

"No, they don't, but they're also willing to assist us to help bring down whoever took shots at our kids. You need to play nice with others, Hendricks."

He snorted, giving her the stink-eye. "That's rich coming

from you. You're usually the first to take a stab at anyone outside your circle."

"Yeah, well, I've been working on it. It's called personal growth," she said bitterly, dramatically making quotation marks with her fingers as she said it. "It's riveting."

I smothered a grin behind my hand, noticing a few others doing the same. Rory would never change and she knew it.

By the end of the meeting, we'd gotten nowhere, and the only productive thing that happened was Rage and Rory didn't try to kill each other for once.

Chapter Ten

Penn

"What's your problem?" Beckett muttered as she walked into the kitchen to find me freaking out at the dining table, sliding her gaze to Drake who sat beside me. "Did Mom scare her? Or was it Skeet? It's always one of the two."

"There's been some development on Penn breaking in," Drake mumbled, rubbing the back of his neck as he eyed me. "Stone set her up. So now he'll be punished, and Penn's freaking out."

"You assholes fucking lied to me?" she bit out, narrowing her eyes on me. "I asked you if you'd been ordered to break in and you said no."

"Stone was the only one who knew," I choked out. Stone didn't deserve my sympathy, but I didn't want him to die. "I didn't want anyone getting hurt."

"Hey," she scowled, fisting my hair. "Stop whimpering like a little bitch, stand up, and don't cower. I thought you were stronger than this."

"Donovan—" Drake started with worry, but she smacked his shoulder.

"Don't coddle her. That shit gets people killed in our

world and you know it," she snapped, turning her attention back to me as she let me go. "Well? Stand the fuck up, Whitlock."

I stood, taking some deep breaths as I tried hard to get my shit under control. "The guys didn't—"

"Don't tell me what didn't happen, tell me what did."

"Stone wanted me gone, and since I was so eager for him to accept me, I didn't question it when he told me to get in the car and go on a job with him," I said with a shaky voice, clearing my throat when she raised an eyebrow at me. "He parked down the street then told me I had ten minutes to get in and out with a painting or he'd leave me behind. He claimed it was how he trained everyone, so I did as he asked."

"So you didn't bother to question whose house it was?" she grunted, her face softening a fraction when I replied.

"No. I just wanted him to see me as one of his team members. I knew he didn't like me, but I didn't realize he wanted me dead."

Beckett was silent for a moment as she considered her options, finally giving me the stink-eye. "Girl, you need to grow some fucking balls. You don't need anyone, you got through life on your own and you survived. Only let those in who have your back. Stone's a walking red flag, and you'd have to work miracles to make him see you as anything more than the dirt on his shoe. He's an asshole."

"If you have to punish him, punish me instead. I was the one who—" She didn't let me finish my sentence before grabbing my throat and yanking me against her angrily.

"Don't you dare. He didn't give a shit about you when he sent you into this house to die, so don't take the fall for his bullshit. Whatever trauma bond you have with him needs to stop. You want people to respect you? Don't hide behind men who have a power complex. You think my mom is feared because of the guys in her life? No. She's feared because she personally gave everyone a reason. You think I scare people because of my guys? Jett screams when the house creaks because he thinks there's a ghost, and I've killed more people than Maddox. I even stabbed *him* once." She let me go, her voice lowering. "Women learned to survive in our world by taking the power into their own hands. Trust me, you'll feel safer the day you can defend yourself than if you cowered behind a man to protect you. When that day comes, people will respect you."

Drake chuckled, tilting his head with amusement. "Aw, I didn't know you were such a motivational speaker, Donovan."

"Shut the fuck up," she snarled, wiping the smile off his face.

"Yes, ma'am."

She scowled at him and waved a hand in my direction. "Teach her to defend herself before someone takes her again. Maybe next time she can save herself instead of waiting for one of you idiots to do it."

"I know some stuff," I said quietly, cringing at the nervous tone and speaking louder. "I just lack technique. I can throw a punch but once someone has me, I can't do much. I used to go to the gym in Stoneleigh to train, so once I'm healed—"

"Nothing's stopping you from going to the gym to build strength. Don't over do it, you still need to get your weight back up, but small things make a huge difference. I know Lopez is being a tyrant about nutrition, but it's for a good reason. Drake's a health nut when he wants to be, so sit down with him and work out a meal plan that will work well with a small fitness routine. You've had time to indulge in comfort food, but it's time to get serious. Those guys you want to be with? It means getting shot at regularly, violence, being targeted because women are seen as the weak link. If you want to be in their lives so badly, it's time you start preparing for that."

“What’s going to happen to Stone?” I asked, holding her gaze as firmly as possible. “He fucked up but—”

“Stop. Listen to what you just said. *He fucked up*. Leave it at that and don’t worry about him, he’s a grown-ass man who made his own choices. Now he needs to face the consequences,” she said bluntly. “I need to go and fill everyone in on the cops and the clean-up. Penn? Be your own savior.” She walked off, leaving me staring after her, and Drake chuckled as he pulled me against his chest.

“Damn, didn’t know she was so passionate about your safety.”

“She’s not, she’s just sick of my whining,” I deadpanned, not thinking for a second that Beckett Donovan was all of a sudden my new bestie.

It didn’t take long for Cruz and Knox to join us, Knox silently running his eyes over both of us while Cruz slid an arm around my shoulders and kissed my cheek. “Hey, you okay?”

“Yeah. Beckett was being nice to me in her own weird way and now I’m kind of scared,” I joked, making him grin.

“You’ll be having slumber parties in no time.”

“Doubtful,” I scoffed. “She thinks I need to start strength training now.”

“We can talk about that later. Right now, we need to go. Things have a tendency to turn nasty at Donovan get-togethers, and I don’t want you here when it happens. People get shot at these things,” he grunted, steering me outside. “Once we get home, I’ll run you a bath. Are you hurting?”

“A little,” I admitted, sliding my phone from my pocket to find multiple texts.

Zavier: Are you okay? Donovan said Cruz got shot.

Zavier: I know you're alive but can you please reply so I'm reassured.

Zavier: Whitlock, answer me.

Cruz grumbled about Zavier being a pain in the ass, but I quickly typed out a response to stop him from worrying.

Penn: Sorry, I've been at Rory's and didn't know you'd messaged. I'm just heading back to the house now.

Zavier: Me and Lavaro are staying with Riley and Luna. Luna's freaking out that whoever shot those bullets will come back for her, so Riley convinced us to play security for the evening to calm her.

Penn: I've got the guys so I'll be fine. Stay safe.

He didn't reply so I put the phone away, letting Cruz maneuver me into the backseat.

The drive home was quiet, other than Drake tapping away at his phone screen. I was more than happy to sit in silence.

Seeing Stone had brought too many emotions to the surface, and I did well to contain them. I wanted to talk to him, to find out the exact truth about why he'd handed me back to my father, but I didn't want to do it with an audience. The guys were likely to tear him apart too. Knox kept glancing at me in the rearview mirror, but I averted my eyes to look out the window. I didn't want him thinking I wanted to talk about tonight.

Cruz winced as we got home and he climbed out of the car, not being able to hide his discomfort.

"You go to bed," Knox ordered, pointing at him. "Take pain meds with you in case you wake up through the night."

"I'm fine, I'm helping Penn—"

"I can run a fucking bath and deal with Penn's back. I'll bring her to bed when she's done," he argued, looking at Drake sternly. "You can make sure he stays there."

"I'm only allowing you to boss me around because it makes my dick hard," Drake grumbled, sliding his worried eyes over me. "You'll be okay with Knox?"

"Kind of hoping he chokes me out and puts me out of my misery," I muttered, pulling a smirk from Knox while the other two glared at me. Cruz dropped a kiss on my lips, cupping my cheek affectionately, and tried to relax his expression.

"Fine. I'll see you when you come to bed."

Drake kissed me too before ushering Cruz to the bedroom, leaving Knox to steer me into the bathroom. I watched him fill the bath, raking my eyes over him while I had the chance.

"Did you talk to Stone before you left the compound?" I finally asked, his eyes flicking over his shoulder with a scowl.

"Yes. He seemed surprised I'd leave with Drake. Don't worry about him, he dug his own hole."

"In his defense, I'm a little surprised you left too. When I first met you, you wouldn't have."

"I wouldn't have let Drake leave in the first place," he grunted, turning the taps off before walking towards me. "It's not too hot or it would've hurt your wounds. Arms up."

I hesitated before doing as he asked, letting him strip me and remove the bandages so I could climb into the bath. He sat on the edge, making me frown. "You aren't joining me?"

"Do I look the type to laze around in the bath? Besides, I should keep my leg wound out of the water," he answered. "Lean forward so I can see your back properly."

"It's stinging," I sighed as I leaned forward, his fingers gently poking at the tender skin.

"I'm not surprised. They're definitely healing though."

"Can I ask you something?"

His eyes flicked up to mine with annoyance. "You'll ask it anyway, so sure, why not."

"Do you have any family? I don't really know much about any of you, but I've noticed family isn't something you talk about."

"The Thieves are my family. Anyone before them doesn't matter," he said with a shrug. "Most of us grew up in the foster system when we weren't in juvie."

"Why'd you get locked up?"

A small smile tugged at his lips, and I could tell he was running through memories by the way his eyes became unfocused. "Jacking rich pricks' cars in Crestford. It was such a rush."

"So you've always had sticky fingers?" I chuckled, and he seemed to snap out of memory lane because he scowled at me.

"And you've always been nosey."

"I just want to know you better since we're dating," I grinned, kneeling and turning to face him. "I might not know a lot about being social, but I'm pretty sure it's normal for partners to know things about each other."

"I'm not a fan of that," he bit out, but vulnerability flashed in his eyes. "Can I ask you a question?"

"Anything."

"Why are you so worried about Stone after everything he's done to you?"

I wasn't expecting a question like that, hesitating for a moment as I scrambled for an answer. Explaining myself was hard because deep down, I knew my feelings were ridiculous. Stone was a monster, one that needed to go.

"I don't know," I finally answered, getting comfortable before speaking again. "You guys saved me, even though you and Stone hated me at first. I want to hurt Stone because his betrayal cut me deep, but the thought makes me want to throw up. He only acted on impulse because he was freaking out. Haven't you done something like that before? If you had to hurt someone you cared about to save Drake, would you?"

"Do you hear what you're saying right now? Stone handed you over to your father, who fucking sold you. You could be dead right now, and Stone's reason was just to make you go because he didn't like you. That's insane," he snapped, my eyes dropping to the water as I fiddled with my hands on my lap.

"He thought he was protecting you."

"No, he was controlling a situation that he hadn't approved of. We don't need protecting from a fucking Kingslake princess, believe it or not," he said sharply. "He was just scared because he saw us all falling in love with you and there was nothing he could do to control it. We always came to heel like good little dogs for him, but you changed things. You weren't a job, so his word didn't mean shit. He didn't like that."

"Why couldn't he love me too?" I asked softly, my voice breaking. "I would've done anything he asked of me, I proved that, but—"

His arm shot out like a snake, his fingers curling around my throat firmly as he forced me to look at him. Rage filled his eyes, his voice sharp. "Don't. Stone doesn't deserve someone like you."

"Why not? You treated me like shit and you still got me," I threw back, not surprised when he hauled me out of the bath. My wet feet slipped on the floor but he kept me tightly in his arms, my eyes widening when he stopped in front of the mirror.

"I got you because I fucking earned it and can admit I love you. Look at what he did to you and tell me he deserves what we have."

"Knox—"

"Look!" he barked, sliding a hand around my throat to

keep me in place, forcing me to stare at the wounds on my stomach. "He's the reason you got hurt, and if Lopez hadn't been at your father's house that night, you'd be either dead, or wishing you were. You would've been beaten, raped, and passed around old rich dudes until they got bored with you. Then if you survived, you would've been sold to someone else to go through it all over again."

"He didn't know!"

"He had no right to make that choice! You're ours, not his!" he snarled, fumbling with his pants with one hand without letting me go. "You're mine, Penelope. He might be my brother, but you're my girl, and he knows I love you."

Tears burned my eyes as I shook my head. "You don't—"

"I do," he breathed in my ear, stroking himself against my ass. "I love you."

"I love you too," I choked out, trying to turn around to face him but he held me firmly by the throat, sliding his fingers between my legs from behind to tease my pussy. I squirmed, his hold loosening a fraction as he chuckled.

"You want my cock, Whitlock?"

"Please," I breathed, a groan leaving me as he pushed two fingers inside me.

"Please, what?"

"Please fuck me."

"Cruz and Drake will hear you screaming for me," he warned, but I didn't give a shit. They all fucked me, it wasn't a secret.

"So? When does that stop you any other time?" I snapped, gasping as he bit my neck hard, replacing his fingers with his dick as he slowly pushed inside me.

"Look at yourself," he murmured, thrusting in and out of me as he watched me in the mirror. "You're gorgeous." My cheeks heated as I met his gaze in the reflection, making him quirk an eyebrow. "You've done more filthy shit than see yourself naked before. Look, Penn."

My eyes drifted to myself, his fingers flexing around my throat as my hands reached for the sink. I needed something to hold onto.

"Take your shirt off," I asked, not liking being the only one of us who was exposed. "And can we go faster?"

He smirked, releasing my throat to pull his shirt over his head, his hands moving to my waist to bend me over slightly. "Hold onto the sink tightly then."

I did as he asked, bracing myself as he started picking up the pace, and it didn't take long for him to be slamming into me. Curses spilled from my lips as I held on, the sound of our skin slapping together getting louder and louder until my legs shook, and I almost collapsed as I came so hard my vision dimmed, Knox following me a moment later.

We stood there panting for a moment until he stepped back, making me cringe at the feel of his cum sliding down my thighs. "Please tell me I can clean up and I don't have to sleep in it."

That earned me a grin. "I suppose you can clean up. I'd prefer to watch Drake lick you clean, but since neither him or Cruz came to investigate, I bet they're both asleep already."

I sat on the toilet, not caring that he was there as I started wiping myself clean. "Don't think for a second that that distracted me from anything. I still want to know more about you."

"I'm Knox Carnell," he answered. "I'm twenty-four. You're Penelope Whitlock and you're twenty-two. Your birthday's the first of December. Now we know each other."

"That's cheating, you found out about me by stalking me, and I already knew all of that about you," I huffed, standing to grab a towel to dry off.

"Cruz Lennox is twenty-four too, and Drake Curtis is twenty-six," he replied with amusement, handing me his shirt.

"I knew that too. We're not all going to fit in my bed, so how's this going to work?"

"That's why we're sleeping on the couch together so I don't have to give you back to them."

"Nicely played," I snorted, making him shrug.

"They would've done the same thing to me."

Knox

I put the TV on, but we didn't take much notice of it as Penn got comfortable on my lap once I'd put ointment on her stomach and back and rebandaged the wounds. She sat sideways across my lap, curled against my chest under a blanket she'd found in the cupboard. It didn't take long for her to fall asleep, and I didn't dare move her. I could sleep like this if I had too.

My lips skimmed her temple as I stared at the TV, but I was aware that the webcam light had turned on. If Stone wanted to be a creepy fuck, he could. He'd only hurt himself by watching us all move on without him.

"Hey," Drake mumbled as he walked out of the dark hallway, his eyes instantly running over Penn. "Is she okay? Why didn't you come to bed?"

"You're delusional if you think we'll all fit in there," I said quietly as he sat beside me, and surprise registered on his face as I lifted my arm for him to curl into me too. Penn's legs were in the way, so I carefully lifted them, placing them over his thighs as he snuggled into me.

"Cruz is in a pretty deep sleep thanks to his pain meds. He didn't wake up when you two were screaming the house down," he chuckled, resting his head on my shoulder as he watched our girl's face.

"Penn's upset about Stone not wanting her," I grumbled, giving him my attention. "She can't figure out why he hates her, and it's bothering her. Why's she so desperate for his attention? She has us, and he's never given her a reason to like him."

"He's like a wounded animal, and we all know how women love to take those home to fix," he replied with a sigh, frowning when he noticed the computer. "You know the webcam's on, right?"

"Yep. Let him look and see what he's missing out on."

"I think this is as relaxed as I've ever seen you," he grinned.

"I'm hardly relaxed. We need to find a place to live since we can't live here forever, and I'm constantly wondering when something bad is going to happen again. What if someone really was after Penn tonight? Pretty sure Cruz took a bullet that was meant for her."

The thought freaked me out a little. We had to keep our eyes open at all times, and as much as we were used to that, I didn't want that kind of life for Penn.

"If her father found out about the dodgy sale, he would've gone after Lopez and Lavaro first. I don't think he'd try to kill her, he'd want her back to resell. Shooting up a property that's run by the crews is stupid, and I don't think even Louis Whitlock's that dumb," he offered.

"Maybe it was just a random attack?"

"Possibly. I'll check in with Beckett later to see if they've heard anything," he nodded, taking the edge of the blanket and pulling it over himself. "I think Beckett's right, though, and we need to train her. We can go with her to Stoneleigh to check out the gym."

"I did a quick online check of the place. It seems to have a good reputation, but I won't trust anyone there until we go ourselves. Tomorrow? We can pay for her to use it so she doesn't owe anyone shit. She used to give people information as payment, but there's no way in hell I'm allowing that to happen."

"Me either. Sounds like a plan."

I watched him silently for a moment before leaning over to give him a kiss. "I love you."

"I love you too. You're being really nice tonight," he said almost nervously, his face softening when I let out a huff.

"It's nothing. I said it to her, so I feel like I need to say it to you, too."

"I really love seeing this side of you. I mean, I love the grumpy side, but this side looks good on you too. Is she making you feel warm and fuzzy?" he teased.

"Don't be a dick."

"Sorry."

"No you're not," I chuckled, peering down at her. "She keeps asking me questions about my past. I don't like people getting personal with me. I told her why I was in juvie, and my last name and age. She doesn't need to know about foster care though, right?"

He shrugged, snuggling closer as his eyes closed. "She's had a pretty fucked up childhood, so ours won't faze her. Maybe you'll bond over it. Relationships need trust, so if you can't trust her with things that make you feel vulnerable, that's a red flag. You're either all in, or you're out. Don't play with her, okay?"

"I don't even like you knowing, so how can I be comfortable with her?"

"Just tell her. Let her fuss over you, and then you can fuck afterwards, and you'll feel better. She's a good listener, Knox. Trust me."

By the time I replied, he'd fallen asleep.

"But she'll look at me differently."

Chapter Eleven

Cruz

I woke up alone, wincing as my wound burned. I could hear the TV quietly playing from the living room, so I popped a few pain pills and grabbed my phone before making my way out, pausing in the hallway as I noticed the three of them sleeping on the couch together. I'd never seen Knox so content, and I was a little surprised he'd tolerated Penn sleeping on him all night. He wasn't usually the cuddly type.

Drake stirred, blinking against the light that was peeking through the curtains, his eyes landing on me. "Morning."

"Morning. Did you guys seriously sleep like that all night? You'll wreck your necks," I chuckled, moving towards the kitchen. "Coffee?"

"Can you add some cocaine or something?" he joked, pulling himself away from them to join me. "How are you feeling?"

"Like I got shot," I grumbled.

"We're going to head to Stoneleigh today to check out the gym if you want to come."

"Sounds good. We can check in with Beckett while we're out, too." I checked my phone, sending a text to Luna. I knew she was fine, but I worried about her. She was one of my best friends, and ever since Penn came into my life, I'd neglected her.

Cruz: You alive, Hendricks?

Luna: I appear to be. You?

Cruz: I'll let you know once I have coffee.

She sent back a bunch of laughing emojis, and I put my phone on the counter to finish making the coffee.

"Leah wants to see Penn," Drake said as he sat at the table. "She wanted me and Knox to give Penn her number, but with all the drama, we haven't. Do you think we should?"

"Penn and her got on like a house on fire. If Leah's genuine, then I think that's a good idea. Our girl needs some friends," I answered, placing a mug in front of him before grabbing two more, carrying them into the living room and placing them on the coffee table in front of the couch. I leaned down, dropping a kiss on Penn's cheek. "Hey, baby. Made you coffee."

She stirred, blinking up at me with confusion. "Huh?"

"Coffee," I chuckled, motioning to the cups. She grumbled but nodded, sitting up and giving Knox a small shake. I left her to wake him, going back to the kitchen to join Drake.

"Stone was spying on us again last night. We need to move the computer," he sighed.

"Do you think I should've kept it to myself last night about him being the one who sent Penn into Rory's house?" I asked quietly. "I'm pissed at him, but fuck. He's going to get killed."

"He made his choice, man. If they found out later that we all knew and hadn't told them, we'd all get buried."

"I need to talk to him."

"Is that a good idea?" he asked dryly, sipping his coffee and eyeing me over the brim before continuing. "You'll only come to blows."

"I think we need to."

He chuckled, shaking his head slightly. "Ezekiel would take shots at all of us for what we've done to his organization. He would've liked Penn, though. She keeps Stone on his toes and gets under his skin."

"He would've appreciated her enthusiasm. Probably would've turned her into a thief within weeks."

"He'd hate how involved we are with the crews. We were ghosts until Zavier dragged us into that shit," he grumbled as if he didn't get a kick out of crew drama regularly, smiling when Penn walked in with Knox close behind. "Morning. Are you guys ready for a fun-filled day of—"

"Keep your peachy bullshit to yourself," Knox grunted, dropping into a chair beside us, leaving Penn to sit beside me. I ignored their usual morning banter, turning to Penn and sliding a hand over her thigh.

"Did you sleep well?"

"Surprisingly, yes," she replied, putting her hand in mine. "How about you?"

"Pain pills knocked me the fuck out."

"I missed you," she said softly, holding my gaze. "It was weird not having you beside me."

"Well, I'm calling dibs tonight," I grinned, lifting her hand to kiss her knuckles. "Have your coffee. I'll rebandage you before we go."

"Knox said we're going to the gym? Am I training today?" she asked, and I shook my head.

"We're checking the place out and sorting out payment today. If we think it's safe enough, then training can start this week. Take it easy though, okay?"

Her whole face lit up with excitement, and I could've

watched her all damn day. She was gorgeous, especially when she smiled like that.

She downed her coffee before heading to her room to get ready for the day, the rest of us doing the same thing once we decided it was time to get moving.

Penn

Excitement bubbled inside me as we pulled up at the gym in Stoneleigh, the guys on full alert as they looked around. The place was run-down, but it felt like home to me. I climbed out, ignoring Knox as he told me to wait, hearing him curse as I headed for the front door. It had been months since I'd been in here, but nothing had changed.

"I told you to fucking wait," Knox bit out behind me, but I was too focused on the familiar face I'd spotted.

"Owen!" I squealed, his head lifting to find me as he finished speaking to the man lifting weights beside him. He trained a lot of people here, me included, and he'd been one of the only people to give me the time of day.

He smiled, ending his conversation before moving towards us, holding his arms out wide. "There's my girl! Where the fuck have you been? I was starting to worry."

I threw myself at him, hugging him tightly and ignoring the burn from my wounds as he hugged me back. "Long story."

Knox growled, and Owen raised an eyebrow as he stepped back. "New friends?"

"Oh! This is Knox, Drake, and Cruz. They're—"

"Her boyfriends," Cruz said bluntly, looking Owen up and down with a frown.

"Boyfriends, plural? Damn, girl. You must be having fun

in the real world. Daddy let you out?" Owen chuckled, giving the guys a once-over, too.

"Doubtful. He sold me."

His eyes narrowed and he tugged me against him, his attention on the guys. "These assholes bought you? You can stay with me if you need, I'll—" Knox was definitely about to tear him apart, so I quickly replied.

"No, a friend of mine bought me to keep me safe. These guys really are my boyfriends."

Knox stepped forward, grabbing my bicep and yanking me into him with a scowl. "Don't touch her or you'll lose hands."

"I worry about her, it's nothing personal. I know how rough she's had it, and I've been trying to keep her safe," Owen answered, his expression softening as he smiled. "I'm glad she has more people looking out for her. You need to feed her more though, she's too skinny."

"We're aware," Drake said dryly, scanning the room. "What kind of security do you have? We can't have our girl here unless it's safe."

"Walk with me," Owen said brightly. "I'll show you."

Knox and Cruz followed, but Drake took my hand to stop me from following them. I frowned, turning to find him assessing Owen cautiously. "What's wrong?"

"I don't like him."

"Give him a chance. I've known him for years and he's never hurt me. He took me home some nights because he was worried about me walking around alone in the middle of the night, he's sweet," I explained, giving his hand a squeeze. "I think you guys would be good friends if you tried."

"Don't get your hopes up," he grumbled, letting go of my hand to drape an arm around my shoulders.

The guys grilled Owen for over an hour before seeming satisfied, the three of them standing off to the side to murmur amongst themselves while I stood back with Owen, amusement on his face. "They're intense."

"You have no idea," I chuckled, motioning around the room. "I thought you got the green light to hire help? It's pretty busy in here." He was basically an unofficial manager since he'd been here for so long, but he definitely needed help.

"One of the guys helps out a lot. He keeps the place clean, and I deal with all the paperwork. You sure you're doing okay?"

"I'm the happiest I've ever been. The guys look after me, and I've made a few friends, too, which is nice. I don't have to sneak around anymore either, which feels weird."

"You should've run to me, Penn. You know I would've kept you safe," he said quietly, reaching out to ruffle my hair like he always did. "I've always got your back."

"I'd still be locked in my tower if the guys hadn't found me. I didn't run, I had to be rescued," I huffed. "These guys took me the first time, then when Dad found me and dragged me home, he sold me. Luckily, it worked in my favor, or I'd be dead by now. I had a nasty infection that I'm still fighting off."

"You're hurt?"

"Dad whipped me, and it broke the skin," I explained, turning to lift the back of my shirt. "My friend got me medical help, so it's healing now." His fingers peeled the bandage back a little, and he sucked in a sharp breath.

"Jesus, Penn."

I went to speak, but Cruz was suddenly there, putting my shirt back in place and tucking me under his arm. "C'mon, Donovan's waiting for us."

Owen gave me the side-eye. "You're making friends in high places."

"Hardly. She spends most of her time wanting to beat me up," I deadpanned. "I'll see you soon."

He smiled, giving me a nod. "You will. You're paid up for a

year, so come and go as you please. You know the code to get in. It was good to see you."

"You too," I replied, giving him a wave as Cruz led me outside with Drake and Knox trailing behind us.

"He wants to fuck you," Drake said flatly once we were in the car, his eyes firmly on the door as if Owen was going to chase after us.

"He already did," I answered, all of them turning to glare at me as I got comfortable in the backseat. "What?"

"You didn't think to mention that before?" Knox scowled, a frown tugging at my lips.

"Why does it matter? It was just sex, and it was a long time ago. It wasn't a relationship or anything."

Knox was fuming, but Cruz sighed. "We really need to teach you better social skills so you read people better."

"I'm good at reading people, I grew up in a pit of snakes. It's not my fault you're insecure and think he can take me from you," I sassed, pulling my phone from my pocket, trying not to react when I noticed an unknown number had texted me. I knew exactly who it was though.

Unknown: Can we talk, Princess?

The guys would tear Stone apart if he went anywhere near me, so I deleted the message and put my phone away.

"I'm not insecure," Knox grunted, and I raised an eyebrow.

"Really? You freaked out and hate-fucked me because you and Drake—"

"Bite me, Whitlock."

I rolled my eyes, snuggling into Drake as he moved across the seat to sit closer, and Knox drove us out of Stoneleigh in silence, apparently done with being social.

Nerves hit me as we pulled up at Beckett's house to find

multiple cars in the driveway. I'd never been here before, but I knew she lived with Maddox and Jett.

"It's just them here," Drake said quietly when he noticed me freaking out a little, and he took my hand to steer me towards the front door. Cruz let himself in, and we followed behind, my muscles relaxing as I spotted Zavier leaning against the kitchen counter. He grinned, pulling me in for a gentle hug.

"Hey. Are they looking after you?"

"We just went to the gym in Stoneleigh. They met my friend, so now they're feeling territorial and grumpy," I whisper-yelled, making Knox snort.

"You're lucky I didn't go back in there and pummel him into the ground."

Zavier chuckled, stepping back. "Noted."

Beckett stalked out, my eyes going wide when she came straight for me, and confusion washed over me as she plucked my phone from my pocket. "Unlock it." I wasn't going to argue with her, giving her what she wanted, but I relaxed when she continued. "I can appreciate you being a pal and not adding my guys on social media apps, but Jett's driving me insane with his whining. Be besties, text about the weather, I don't care. Anything to make him stop. He can't believe his boyfriend's girl won't even try to get to know him."

She pulled her own phone out and accepted my friend request, surprising me when she added her number into my phone before handing it back.

"Thanks," I mumbled, guessing by the amused look on Drake's face that he was the apparent boyfriend, but she was already over it and moving onto another subject.

"We still don't have any leads on the shooting. It's one of many that are unresolved, and my parents are starting to get pissed. We figured the shootings we've had at Devil's Dungeon were unrelated, putting it down to some wannabe crew, but now we aren't too sure. It's been quiet for the past month with Penn gone, but now we suddenly get shot up again? That can't be a coincidence."

"Wait, you think this is because of me after all?" I squeaked, making her roll her eyes.

"We aren't sure, but we didn't have a single issue in your absence. Mom's looking into your father, but so far, he's still content that you've been sold, and he has no idea that the money was fake. He's an arrogant piece of shit."

"If he found out, he'd get someone to kill Ander and Zavier, right?"

"Your daddy runs in a corrupt crowd with a lot of connections, but our connections are better. Zavier's pretty known to be in our circle now, and as much as I hate to admit it, Ander isn't someone to be fucked with either. Only an idiot would target them."

My eyes flashed to Zavier who gave me a crooked grin. "Don't worry about me, Whitlock. I've got friends in high places like Daddy Whitlock. Exhibit A." He motioned to Beckett, and she rolled her eyes.

"One day, we'll say no, and you'll be screwed."

"No, you won't. You like me too much."

"Want to bet?" she chuckled, but it was obvious she was teasing. Maddox joined us, offering to shoot Zavier right now to save time, but Jett bound out, throwing himself at Drake dramatically.

"You're here! Are you staying tonight? Maddox! The TV is mine tonight, I have a date with my boy!"

Beckett snickered, giving me a look. "I know you're probably used to sharing him already, but you'll have to get used to their bromance. It's embarrassing."

Drake put Jett in a headlock and ruffled his hair, the pair of them ending up wrestling on the floor, and Cruz pulled me back to avoid me getting rolled into while Knox scowled down at them. "Knock it off. How old are you, five?"

"And a half!" Jett whined, making Drake cackle as he tackled him again. Knox cursed at them, and Cruz acted like they weren't even there as he turned his attention back to Beckett.

"I'll have to meet up with Stone this week to discuss the future of the Thieves. It might be his company, but it's my tech. I refuse to work with him after what he did to Penn, I don't trust him."

"Maybe remind your girl he's a piece of shit, because she thinks she's the problem," Beckett muttered, eyeing me as my face fell from the mention of his name. "I really think you need to get her some counseling. She definitely has Stockholm Syndrome."

"Fuck off," I said without thinking, amusement flickering in her eyes.

"I was wondering where your balls were."

"Stone was just mad and—"

"I'm not having this argument with you again," she cut in. "Focus on strength training and learning to defend yourself. No offense, but Night Thieves business isn't your concern. Don't lie awake at night stressing over it." That was easier said than done.

"You guys have just become immune to normal emotions around death. I don't like anyone getting murdered, let alone someone I know," I huffed, her eyes sliding to Knox.

"You'd better fix her or she won't last long."

I squeaked as Knox plucked me from Cruz's hold, dropping an arm around my shoulders.

"She'll get used to it. She handled her first dead body better than Drake did. Next time, I'm hoping she doesn't throw up, though."

"Next time?" I asked with annoyance, but they ignored me. I didn't want to deal with more dead bodies.

"Bring her to the cage fights. That should get her used to violence fast," Beckett suggested, a snort leaving Maddox as he studied me, his voice low and gruff.

"She'll piss her pants in five minutes and be crying before anyone even hits the ground. Face it, your girl isn't made for our world."

"Excuse me?" I spat, my eyes going wide when he lazily pulled a gun from the back of his pants and aimed it at me. Pure panic filled me as he stared me down, Knox growling behind me.

"Don't be a dick. There's a difference between seeing dead bodies, and being the dead body."

Maddox didn't lower the gun though, stepping towards me until the barrel was against my forehead. "You show all your emotions on your face. That's dangerous. Do you think I'll shoot you?"

"A little bit," I croaked, my eyes darting to Beckett but she watched silently, letting him give me his fucked up lesson.

"Good, because you should always assume the person holding the gun wants you dead," he continued, my eyes squeezing shut as he pressed it harder into my skin. "Open your fucking eyes and don't shy away from my gaze, Penelope."

I had no idea why none of my guys were stepping in to stop this, but I forced myself to look into Maddox's emotionless stare, swallowing hard. "Now what?"

"I don't want to see a single flicker of fear on your face. Stand up straight, stare me down, and put a mask on. Your enemies will always get a sick sense of satisfaction out of making you cry. Don't give it to them. If you're going to end up dead, die with fucking dignity, and never on your knees." I tried hard to do as he said, but the second he removed the safety, the click made me flinch, and he looked at Knox who hadn't moved from behind me. "Toughen her up, man. She'll only become a target otherwise, and it's the quickest way to bring you all to your knees."

"I'm aware," he replied dryly. "Now get that gun out of her face before I make you."

Maddox's lip lifted into a dark smirk, but he stepped back and tucked his gun away again. "Maybe you should all go back to the compound where it's safer. I don't think Stone would fuck with her again, but there's a lot of people out there that will."

Knox scoffed, but Cruz shook his head. "I won't have her near him. We'll find a house and rig it with as much security as possible. It'll be fine."

I didn't mind the idea of going back to the compound. It felt safer than the house we were currently in, and we were harder to sneak up on. The thought of being in a confined space alone with Stone made me feel a little wary, though.

"I think—" Knox didn't let me finish.

"We're not going back, Whitlock. If Stone comes anywhere near you, I'll kill him."

"That's a little dramatic."

His fingers threaded through my hair, jerking my head back to look up at him. "I won't fucking lose you again. Do you understand?"

To anyone, Knox's expression held anger and frustration, but I saw the pain he hid behind the mask. He was terrified of something happening to me, and this was as close to putting it into words that he could manage.

"I understand, baby," I whispered, his eyes softening at the term of endearment, but his lip lifted into a snarl as if he was disgusted by it.

"Good. Stop being such a pain in the ass, and let us handle

shit, okay?" He turned to Cruz, annoyance on his face. "Are you guys going to hang out here for a while?"

Cruz sighed, giving me a wary glance before replying. "Yes, why? Are you leaving? I'm sure someone can take me home later."

"Yes, I'm leaving. Whitlock's coming with me."

I frowned, glaring up at him and crossing my arms. "Excuse me?"

"You fucking heard me," Knox snapped, and Beckett waggled her eyebrows at me.

"He needs to remind you he's full of that alpha-male bullshit. Take advantage of his ego. You're about to get railed with a purpose."

"I'm not—" Knox scruffed the back of my neck, steering me towards the door before I could finish my sentence, a scoff of outrage leaving me. "Hey! I want to stay here! If you want to be a grumpy piece of shit, that's your problem!"

"Shut the fuck up and get in the car, Whitlock," he threw back, slamming the door and cutting off the amused chuckles from the others, forcing me in the direction of the car. Once he'd shoved me into the passenger seat, he made his way around to the driver's side and climbed in, giving me a scathing glare. "Like it or not, but I'm going to fuck you until the only name you remember is mine. Got that?"

"No. I'm not in the mood," I lied, his hand roughly forcing its way down the front of my pants, a dark chuckle leaving him as he swiped his fingers through the wetness between my legs, pushing two inside with ease.

"Liar. Do you like fighting with me, babe? Does the thought of me using your pussy like a fuckdoll get you off?"

"Knox—" I tried to sound angry, but it came out breathless and desperate, making him grin as he removed his hand from my pants, cleaning his fingers with his tongue before speaking.

"Secret's safe with me. I was going to tell you to warm yourself up on the drive home, but I don't think you need to."

"Asshole," I muttered under my breath, a snicker leaving him as he finally started the car and backed out of the driveway, heading towards home.

Chapter Twelve

Knox

Penn didn't understand how fucked up everything was. Stone was dangerous and could try to cause her harm, especially now that she was the reason his world was falling down around him. In his eyes, anyway. In reality, he had no one to blame but himself.

Now, I had to worry about Owen too. He came across as nice, but I didn't like the guy, and neither did Cruz or Drake. He wanted our girl, I saw the jealousy in his eyes when we'd touched her.

I was being a dick, but between my possessive bullshit and my fear of losing her, I was close to the breaking point. Luckily for me, Penn saw through my asshole behavior and after two minutes of driving, her hand slid onto my thigh, giving me a small squeeze to let me know she understood.

We drove in silence the entire drive back to the Heights, and I'd hardly shut the door behind us before I was on her. She squeaked into my mouth as I kissed her, my fingers yanking at her shirt impatiently, needing to dominate her and remind her that she was mine. I was being too rough, I knew that, but she didn't complain as she let me angrily jerk the material over her head before going for her pants next. My shirt tore as I wrestled it off, tossing it aside blindly as I grabbed her throat to force her lips to mine again.

She was consuming me, and the fact that I was oblivious to our company proved it.

"Getting a good look, Lavaro?" Penn murmured against my lips, and it took a second for me to register her words before I pulled away to scan the room, finding Ander leaning against the kitchen counter with a beer in hand, amusement on his face.

"If you were a good friend, Whitlock, you would've kept your mouth shut and kept going."

"Eyes off!" I barked, making Penn scowl as I shielded her small body with mine, glaring at the cocky asshole across the room. "Why the fuck didn't you say anything?"

"Why would I? I don't have any morals. Besides, this is my fucking house, not that any of you seem to remember that." As much as he was being a dick, his eyes remained on mine and he didn't make a move to come closer. He was winding me up on purpose.

Penn slapped at my shoulder, not giving a shit as she walked around me to speak with Ander. "You're never here."

"Don't act like you didn't know I was here," he chuckled, shamelessly dropping his eyes down her half naked body before returning to her face. "I was starting to think it was a silent invitation." Before I could react, he continued, looking away from her. "Unfortunately, I have no interest in joining the Penelope Whitlock fan club. It seems it's already a little crowded."

She rolled her eyes, crossing her arms and making her tits almost pop out of her fucking bra. I was close to strangling her.

"Are you staying tonight? Because if you are, don't expect to get any sleep."

"I actually have somewhere to be." He glanced towards the hallway as a familiar woman with black hair wandered out, and I didn't miss the way she cringed at seeing us as he spoke to her. "You ready to go, babe?"

"Yep." She basically ran out the door, and Ander chuckled as he followed, giving us a salute.

"Have fun, kids." He shut the door, leaving us alone, and Penn turned to me with surprise.

"Who the fuck was that?"

"She's his comfort pussy," I snorted, starting to steer Penn towards the bedroom. "Blake used to illegally street race with him. They dated, but they broke up when she had to focus on her sister's future. Apparently, they can't keep their pants on around each other though. Stop thinking about Ander's love life. Finish getting naked for me so I can fuck your brain cells out." Penn didn't even try to remove her bra, so I reached around and unhooked it, dropping it in the hallway just before we reached her bedroom, my fingers dipping below the elastic of her panties to tug them down.

She squealed as I pushed her down onto the bed, kicking my pants off and climbing over her. My mouth dropped to hers as I slid a hand between her legs, and she gasped softly as I pushed two fingers inside and began to fuck her with them.

"Don't come until I tell you to," I warned, brushing my thumb over her clit and making her groan.

"Can't we play that game another time?" she whined, my dick hardening at her needy tone. "I'm going to come the moment you start fucking me."

"Be a good girl for me," I grunted, a shudder rolling through her as I nipped at her neck. "Do as you're told."

She let out a sound of frustration but she nodded, struggling to contain herself as I rubbed her clit faster until her legs started to shake, then I pulled my hand away and slapped her pussy, making her jerk. "Hey!"

"As much as I want to fuck you like this, roll over. Your stomach is healing faster than your back, and this is going to be rough," I replied, not waiting for her response before flipping her over. "Keep your legs shut for me."

"Wait, what?" she asked with confusion and tried to roll over to face me, but I straddled her thighs and leaned over her to kiss her neck, my teeth sharply biting into her soft skin and making her yelp.

"Don't question me." She was soaked, and I slid my cock between her legs, clenching my jaw as I started pushing inside her, her closed legs making it impossibly tight.

"Fuck," she cursed, dropping her face into the pillow as her fingers fisted the blankets.

"Remember, don't come," I repeated, pulling out before slamming back in again, her cry of surprise bouncing off the walls and making me even harder.

Penn's pussy was heaven, and I intended on making this last as long as possible.

I fucked her hard, her curses not even in English at this point, but when she started trying to scramble away from me, I knew she was close.

"Don't fucking come," I snapped, a desperate plea leaving her.

"I can't hold it, Knox, please—"

"No!" I growled, fucking her for a few more seconds before pulling out completely. I'd managed to train Drake to basically come on demand, so I knew I could teach Penn the same thing. She whimpered at the loss of my dick, lifting her butt a little to try and entice me. I slapped my palm against it, admiring the pink tinge as it rose to the surface of her skin. I did it again, a groan leaving me. "Fuck, I could spend all damn day marking you."

"How about you make me come, then I'll let you do whatever you want to me?" she begged, wriggling her butt. "I was so close."

I slid between her legs again, pushing deep but not moving once I was there, her pussy clenching around me as she desperately squirmed against me, chasing her release. I put more of my weight on her, stopping her movements.

"You'll come when I say so," I said softly in her ear, slowly pulling back and sliding back in again, giving her enough to drive her crazy, but not enough to get her off. "I want you dripping with my cum so badly."

"You're killing me," she panted, her fingers tightening in the sheets as I went a little harder. Just as I reached the pace she wanted, I stopped again. "Knox!"

"Come with me. I want to feel you milking my cock as I fill you up," I replied, reaching out to tangle her hair in my fist and sitting up without dislodging myself from her pussy.

"You'll let me come?"

"You have to hold off until I say you can," I answered, my hold on her hair tightening as I pulled her head back a little more. "Can you do that for me?"

"Yes."

"Good." I loved teasing her and Drake, both of them going crazy before I let them finish, but I loved making them come even more. Making someone lose control of their body was a powerful thing, and it never escaped me that both of them trusted me enough to do as I pleased, even when I was being a raging asshole.

I fucked Penn hard again without warning, her gibberish curses filling the room, and I knew she was struggling to stop herself from coming within seconds. I was close too, but not yet.

"Now?" she asked tightly, her thigh muscles bunched as she fought herself.

"Not yet."

"I can't—"

"Not yet!" I gritted out, slamming into her three more times before the familiar tingle started in my balls, my thrusts becoming erratic as I let go of her hair to grip her waist instead, probably hurting her but not caring. "Now, baby."

Her pussy strangled me as we came together, my ears ringing from the intensity, but I could vaguely hear her screaming my name. I kept fucking her, prolonging it as long as I could before I collapsed against her back, our rapid breathing being the only sound in the house.

Cruz

"I feel like divorced parents who have shared custody of a child," Beckett grumbled as she parked in front of our house in the Heights. Drake had insisted on spending the night with Jett, the two of them yelling at video games together while being three sheets to the wind.

"I'm sorry, but he definitely gets his behavior from his mother," I replied dryly, making her snort.

"Fuck off, Lennox." She glanced at the house, a sigh leaving her. "I'm sorry for Maddox pointing a gun at your girl, but you know he had a point. She wears her thoughts all over her face, and she's a huge target."

"Yeah, I know," I mumbled, not moving to get out of the car. "She's even less safe away from us though, and I'm too selfish. She's changed us, Donovan. Knox has never been so open to his feelings before, and Drake's not hurting anymore. She's managed to repair the damage between them and make Knox understand his emotions."

"And what did she do for you?" she asked curiously, no teasing in her tone. "Has she changed you?"

"If any woman could tie me down with a family, it would

be her. I could imagine having kids with her, you know? She's not just a pretty girl who I like getting naked, she's *the* girl. The one that doesn't compare to any others."

"What happens if the others don't want the same? Knox doesn't seem like the type to enjoy kids running around and getting into all his stuff."

"You'd be surprised. You saw his possessive bullshit tonight. If he had the chance to knock her up, he would." I didn't want to bring up the fact that he was infertile, but I'd bet he'd do it if he could.

She let out an amused huff, watching me in the moonlight. "You'd be a good dad. Maybe wait until people have stopped shooting at us though."

"I have zero intention on adding *baby daddy* to my resume this week, but thanks for your input," I deadpanned, reaching for the door handle. "Thanks for the ride."

"Hey," she said softly, making me pause as I turned to face her again, discomfort written all over her face. "We're holding off on dealing with Stone so you guys can do whatever it is you have to do first. After that, I can't promise anything. I know you're pissed at him, but I also know you still love him. He's been your family for a long time. I just wanted to give you a heads-up."

"I appreciate it."

"Cruz," she murmured, her eyes softening even more, making my throat tighten. "Mom hasn't come to a decision on how to deal with him, but he's likely to end up dead. I don't want it to go that far, but—"

"He made his choice," I cut in, not wanting her to feel guilty. "Do me a favor though? Please make it quick." I swallowed, hating that tears burned my eyes. "And if you can avoid doing it in front of—"

"Jesus," Beckett said on an exhale, raking a hand through her hair. "We might be monsters, but we're not that cruel to gun him down in front of you. Mom might be satisfied with beating his ass up for a week in the basement before letting him go, I'm not sure, but I promise I'd never do that to you. Get inside to your girl and make sure Knox didn't fuck her to death."

A small smile tugged at my mouth as I opened the door and stepped out, turning to look at her. "Penn might be scared of a lot of stuff, but she knows how to handle Knox in the bedroom."

"Make sure she hasn't suffocated him with a pillow then," she laughed, waiting for me to say good night and close the door before she drove off, leaving me to walk inside alone.

The house was quiet, and I grinned as I noticed the clothes dropped on the floor, Penn's bra randomly in the hallway by her bedroom. I peeked inside, finding Knox wrapped around her from behind, both of them sleeping peacefully.

I stripped off, sliding into bed beside her, her eyes fluttering open. "Cruz?"

"Yeah, baby. It's me. Drake's staying at Beckett's, so he'll be back tomorrow," I murmured, loving how she instantly draped an arm around my stomach. Knox mumbled in his sleep and rolled over, so I tugged her closer, snuggling into her. "Go back to sleep."

She hooked a leg over my waist, pressing her naked body against mine. "I missed you."

"Missed you too," I whispered, placing a kiss on her neck. She squirmed, my dick jerking to life as her pussy grazed it. She let out a sleepy moan, rubbing against me and making me chuckle. "Didn't Knox give you enough?"

"He did."

"So you're just wanting to cover my dick in his cum for the fun of it?" I teased, sliding a hand between us to grab the brick I was now sporting, running it backward and forward across her pussy.

"That feels good," she said sleepily, a groan forming as I rubbed the head against her clit, spreading Knox's cum over it. She was probably sore from him since it was likely they'd had multiple rounds while having the house to themselves, so I carefully eased myself inside of her, taking it slow.

"I need to find a condom." She felt so good without anything between us, but Beckett's teasing rang loudly in my ear about having babies in the middle of a shoot-out, reminding me to be cautious. "The last thing we need right now is to knock you up."

"I like it like this," she mumbled, tilting her face up to kiss me, my brain short-circuiting as she rolled her hips slightly. "Just pull out when you come."

"You have way too much trust in my control," I scoffed quietly, not wanting to wake Knox.

A gasp left her as I continued to thrust slowly in and out of her, and my lips found hers in the dim room, swallowing the small sounds she made for me. We didn't pick up the pace, happily grinding on each other slowly until she came quietly, whimpering into my mouth as she tried hard to stay quiet, and I followed a moment later, exhaustion washing over me instantly.

Penn was practically asleep in my arms, but I gently shook her to get her attention. "Penn?"

"Hmm?"

"Go clean up. I forgot to pull out," I murmured, her eyes opening to peer into mine.

"Shit."

"C'mon, I'll help," I said softly, sitting up and gently pulling her into my arms, not giving a fuck as her wet pussy rested against my abs. Once I'd carried her into the bathroom, she sat on the toilet and cringed, rubbing her tired eyes.

"We have to stop doing this until I'm off my antibiotics

and the contraception has time to kick in," she mumbled, peering up at me. "I don't want to trap you with babies."

I scoffed, grabbing a cloth from the cupboard and running water over it in the sink, cleaning myself up. "We're the ones who can't pull out. We'd be trapping you."

"Yeah, because I try really hard to escape you," she deadpanned, grabbing toilet paper to clean herself up. I rinsed the cloth, using it between her legs once she'd wiped most of the cum away, then I steered her back to the bedroom and climbed in behind her, placing a kiss on her shoulder as I spooned her.

"Sweet dreams, baby."

She mumbled a response, but she was asleep within seconds.

Penn

Waking up between Knox and Cruz was strange. I was used to being between one of them and Drake, but not just the two of them. Knox was wrapped around me like we shared a damn body, and Cruz was staring at me with a soft look on his face from the other side.

"Uh, morning?" I mumbled, his lips kicking up into a smile.

"Morning. Sorry, you looked so peaceful, I didn't want to wake you."

"So you decided to stare at me?"

"I was trying to distract myself from waking you up with my dick in your pussy," he chuckled, a grunt coming from behind me as Knox tightened his hold on me.

"Not a chance in Hell. What's the time?"

"Eight," Cruz answered, dropping a kiss on my cheek before rolling over to climb out of bed, completely naked. "I'll make coffee."

"Or we could go back to fucking sleep," Knox grumbled, tugging the blankets around us tightly and burying his face in my hair. "Your boyfriend's a dick."

Cruz snorted as he left the room, and I giggled, pushing his arm off me enough to roll over and face him. "Yeah, it's something they all have in common."

"You're a dick, too," he muttered, his mouth curving into a smile. "I need to go to the compound today. If Cruz wants to come, you'll have to stay here alone. Is that okay?"

I frowned, my good mood shifting slightly. "Why? Nothing will happen to me when I'm with you guys."

"You were with us last time and you were taken. I'm not risking it, and there's no reason for you to come anyway. Sketch or something," he answered firmly, dismissing me as he climbed over me to get out of bed.

"Excuse me?" I bit out, following him closely and not caring about my nakedness. "I'm not a dog, asshole."

"I'm aware. Dogs do as they're told." He yanked a shirt over his head, pulling some jeans on before heading along the hallway towards the kitchen, and I yanked Cruz's shirt over my head to follow him.

"Hey! I'm talking to you!"

"You won't change my mind, Whitlock," he replied, Cruz's brow creasing as we took our argument into the kitchen.

"What happened?"

"I'm going to the compound this morning. If you're coming, she's staying home alone," he said casually, accepting the coffee Cruz handed him. "She's not too happy about it."

I crossed my arms, waiting for Cruz to jump in to defend me, so I was surprised when he didn't. "Sounds fair. It's not safe for her there anyway."

"You're ganging up on me now?" I hissed, making Cruz blink at me as if he didn't understand my complaint.

"It's common sense, babe. You're safe here, and there's no reason for you to come. We need to talk to Stone."

"You're both cut off from the goods," I said flatly, and Knox rolled his eyes at my dramatics.

"It's cute that you think you can stop me from getting into your pants."

"I don't consent."

"I don't give a fuck." He stood over me, his intimidation not working like it used to. Knox wouldn't hurt me, and he fucking knew it. "Just stay home and stop being a brat."

"I can do whatever I want. I'm not a prisoner anymore, and I'm not being hunted. Nothing's stopping me from walking out that door once you guys leave," I said sweetly, his jaw clenching.

"Why did you wake up and choose to be a cunt today? Cruz and I both fucked you enough last night to keep your attitude at bay for at least a few days."

"Time out, can I at least have my coffee before playing referee for you two?" Cruz snapped, not looking amused in the slightest. "Penn, can you just stay home? Did you forget we all got shot at the other night? I *did* get fucking shot." That calmed me slightly as I glanced at his bare side.

"Have you cleaned it?"

"Have you cleaned yours? Take your antibiotics," he said sharply, sipping his coffee more aggressively than necessary as he slid one towards me. Knox backed off, giving Cruz the side-eye.

"Can you put pants on?"

"No." Well then.

We lapsed into silence as we drank our coffees, and Knox grunted something about going for a shower before stomping off, leaving me with Cruz.

"Are you really going to run off just to be difficult?" he

asked with a sigh, frustration burning inside me as I lifted my gaze to his across the dining table.

"I've spent my entire life being locked away. Ander and Zavier gave me a fresh start, but so far, all I've done is hide in this fucking house. Why can't I go to the gym? Or make friends? Maybe—"

"You want to have some girl time?" he asked lightly, making me pause to listen to him. "Leah wants to apologize to you for being a shitty friend. If you hang out with her, I won't worry."

"I get to go out?"

"Don't say it like that," he groaned, walking around to drape his arms over my shoulders, kissing my neck. "I don't mean to control you. I'm terrified of you being taken again or someone hurting you. Everyone's on edge thanks to this shooting, so we need to play it safely. So, do I tell Leah to clear her schedule?"

"I'd like that," I nodded, downing the rest of my coffee before standing. "I need a shower."

"With Knox? You're brave," he chuckled, giving me a kiss. "He's not even mad, he's just worried. Go tell him you're going out with Leah so he stops having an angry wank or whatever it is he's doing in there."

"Guys hate-fuck themselves?" I deadpanned, a smirk spreading across his face.

"We don't need a particular mood to jerk off." I had a feeling he was being serious.

I headed into the bathroom, not caring about disturbing Knox, and he gave me a dirty look as I pulled the shirt over my head and joined him. "Get out, Whitlock."

"Make me," I threw back, his fingers instantly going around my throat as my back hit the wall, causing me to wince.

"Don't tempt me," he warned, pressing against me and making me shiver.

"I'm going to catch up with Leah, so you can stop glaring at me about me running off on my own," I said breathlessly, his grip loosening a little as he eyed me.

"At the compound?"

"Doubtful. You and Cruz won't like that," I said flatly, his hand dropping to his side as he relaxed.

"Good. Stick to her like glue." He tugged me under the hot spray, sliding his hand between my legs gently and making me suck in a sharp breath. "Sore?"

"A little. The second round was rough," I grinned, his fingers carefully sliding across my pussy as he started washing me.

"I'm not sorry."

"Good. I wasn't complaining," I murmured, standing on tiptoe to kiss him. "I love you, barbarian attitude and all."

"And I love you, even when you're a bitch," he grunted, but his tone was teasing.

I let him wash me, and by the time we were done, Cruz was banging on the door demanding a shower himself.

Chapter Thirteen

Penn

"If she needs to go for some reason, call me and I'll come and get you. Don't come to the compound," Knox said firmly as I leaned against the side of the car, both him and Cruz standing in front of me as we waited for Leah to arrive. We were in Ashburn Valley, standing in the parking lot at Harley's bar, and they'd been giving me rules ever since we left the house.

"I know. Harley and Alex are both working today, right? I'm safe here, so stop stressing," I mumbled, Knox scowling.

"You're so stealable. Even Drake managed to steal you from your fucking castle, and he's a terrible thief."

"Is not," I scoffed, knowing Drake had just as much skill as the rest of them.

Leah parked beside us, and she almost knocked me over as she flew out of the driver's seat and threw her arms around me. "Please forgive me! Are you okay? Did—"

"Take it easy," Cruz warned, tugging on her arm to pull her back a little. "She's still recovering. I assume you all heard about the shooting at the track?"

Her face flushed with embarrassment for her outburst, but

she nodded. "Yeah, Stone's been glued to his desk scouring through hours worth of footage, but he still hasn't found anything. You got shot?"

"I've had worse," he replied, motioning to me. "Keep an eye out, and don't leave her alone. We have no idea if the shooting was random or targeted. Our money is on it being targeted, but we have no idea who the target was. If you get the feeling you're being watched, leave and call me or Knox straight away."

"Yes, boss," she huffed, hooking her arm through mine.

Knox eyed me for a moment in silence before blowing out a breath. "Promise me you'll stay with Leah."

"I promise. Go, we'll be fine," I smiled, standing on tiptoe to kiss him. The worry on his face softened a fraction, and he stepped back, letting Cruz in to kiss me, too.

"I love you," Cruz murmured, and I couldn't stop the grin from spreading across my face even if I'd wanted to.

"I love you too." I turned to Knox, batting my lashes at him. "You too, asshole."

"Fuck off," he grunted as he walked around to the driver's side of the car, opening the door and glancing over the roof at me. "Love you too."

Cruz gave me a wink before climbing into the passenger's seat, and once they'd left, Leah gave me the biggest smile. "You have Knox saying sweet shit? You must have a golden pussy."

"He seems to like it," I chuckled, starting to walk towards the bar. "C'mon, I'm starving."

Once we were seated, Leah took my hands across the table and gave them a squeeze.

"I'm so sorry I didn't fight for you. Stone really had a good story to make you out to be the villain, and it was hard to ignore the fact he'd been shot. I can't believe he lied to everyone and hurt you like that."

I sighed, shrugging slightly. "He was mad, and my father convinced him I was crazy."

"He shouldn't have gone behind everyone's backs, though."

"I know. I want to talk to him, but the guys won't let me near him, especially not alone. I'm so mad, but I have a lot I want to ask him."

That made Leah snort as she leaned back, letting go of my hands. "You won't get much out of him. He won't take his eyes off his computer, and when he does, it's to get alcohol. He's a mess. I don't think he's noticed that people are leaving."

"I'm worried about him," I admitted, not meeting her gaze. "I know he fucked me over, but that doesn't mean I want him dead. He's pissed off Rory, so I know they won't let it slide."

"You're too good for those guys," she said softly, giving me a small smile as I glanced up at her.

"Why do you think that?"

"They're assholes," she chuckled, but her expression was warm. "Knox has never looked at a girl like he looks at you, none of them have. Drake and Cruz respected their one-night stands, unlike Knox, but they still didn't care about them."

"To be honest, I've never cared about my hookups either. Sex is just sex, there's no need to attach emotions to them," I stated.

"I don't know how the four of you even found your emotions if that's how you all look at it," she snorted, glancing up as Harley joined us. His eyes were trained on me, but despite the serious look on his face, he sounded pleased to see me.

"I'm surprised to see you here without your guys."

"I had to beg, trust me," I grumbled, his posture relaxing.

"At least they know where you are. What can I get for you?"

I considered piling up on pancakes, but I knew Beckett's suggestion of nutrients was important so I sighed. "Can you make me one of those avocado toast thingies with poached eggs and spinach? I definitely want coffee, too."

"You've been hanging around Drake too much," he chuckled, turning to Leah. "And you?"

"I'll have the same," she replied, waiting for Harley to leave before raising an eyebrow at me. "You're on a health kick?"

"A nutrients kick," I corrected, leaning forward on the table with my elbows. "Beckett thinks I need to start strength training carefully while I recover from my injuries and lack of a proper diet. I'll heal faster if I eat and sleep properly, so I'm trying to make better choices. Besides, I actually like the weird shit Drake eats, I just prefer a pile of sugar."

"Drake loves sugar, he just likes to take control of his diet when he's stressed. Not because he has a problem with food, but because if he's following a plan, he remains focused," Leah said, making me pause. I knew that, but I was surprised anyone else had noticed. "What? I've known the guy for years and see his patterns. When Knox is feeling out of control, all he does is fuck Drake. Well, you too now, I guess. Cruz is a little harder to read when he's out of control because he goes quiet. He likes being alone to clear his head."

"And Stone turns into a raging asshole?" I joked, a cringe lining her features.

"Yes, but he also overthinks and ends up putting himself in a tizzy. He controls everyone around him, so when we start to pull away and ignore his orders—"

"He panics and makes princesses disappear because he convinces himself it will make things return to normal," I mumbled, pulling my phone out as a message came through.

Stone: Stop ignoring me. Say you'll meet me to talk.

I didn't want to play into Stone's bullshit, but I was worried the guys were going to show up and murder him.

Penn: Cruz and Knox are on the way to you right now to talk. Trust me, I don't want to be there.

Stone: Tell Leah if she keeps avoiding jobs, she's fired.

Leah was staring at her phone, angrily typing a message herself, so I quickly glanced up at the security camera in the corner as if I'd see Stone watching us through it.

Stone: Admit it, you like me watching you.

Penn: You wanted me gone, so stop acting like you miss me. You did this.

Stone: I can admit I fucked up. Stop pretending to hate me.

I pushed my phone into my pocket with a huff, looking up to find Leah's gaze on mine. "Are you okay?"

"Yeah, just a lot of spam messages lately," I lied. "I'm surprised you could come see me on such short notice. Did the tyrant give you the day off?"

She chuckled, putting her phone down on the table. "No. I'm supposed to be in Crestford with Will, but Jai went with him when Cruz said you wanted to hang out."

"Aren't you worried about Stone kicking you out?" I asked, a little surprised by her answer.

"If he keeps up his bullshit, we'll all leave anyway. We have plenty of money saved, most of us could retire comfortably if we invested properly. Do you actually understand the money your guys have? They'd probably put your father to shame."

"I don't care what money they have, I need to find a job

once I'm healthier so I can rely on myself. Not that the guys seem too keen on the idea," I sighed, giving Harley a smile as he brought our food over. He seemed busy and didn't stick around, leaving us to enjoy our meal in peace.

"Don't take this the wrong way, but they're just worried you'll get hurt because of how easy you are to manipulate," Leah said with a cringe. "You're missing a lot of social skills that we rely on to stay alive in our world. I mean, you jumped into your kidnappers' car and willingly left with them. What if they'd raped and murdered you? Did you even question their intentions?"

"Of course I did. I was desperate to escape Dad's, so I chose to leave and thought I'd escape from them too. I didn't plan on sticking around," I chuckled dryly, taking a forkful of food and shoving it into my mouth. The food here always tasted good, Harley and Alex had a good business going on.

"I've seen you around the guys when they're being assholes. You want to please them, and it's how Stone keeps fucking you over. You blindly trust him all because he says to. You can't do that, Penn," she warned quietly.

"I just want to be normal," I mumbled, her face softening with pity. "I want to earn my own money, and live independently. I want to learn to drive, and do my own groceries. Giving someone control over my life has caused nothing but pain, and I refuse to allow it to continue happening. I love the guys, but if they love me, they'll teach me to rely on myself."

"They will, just take small steps. Focus on healing, then I'll even help you look for a job, okay?"

"You'll help me?" I asked with surprise, earning a look as if I were crazy.

"Of course. You're my friend. You going to tell me about the filthy shit your guys do to you yet?" she teased, amusement filling me.

"Do you really want to know?"

"Definitely. I'm nosey."

Knox was the only one who seemed to give a shit about people knowing the nicer details about him, so I shrugged. "Knox fucks like he has something to prove. He likes to keep all the control which I'm completely fine with. Cruz and Drake both like to change things up. Sometimes it's hard, other times it's sweet. Like last night, Cruz got home late, and we just ended up having some kind of sensual, slow-grinding sex while Knox slept beside us."

Leah sighed dreamily, her food forgotten as she watched me. "Who's the most romantic?"

"They all have their own way of romance," I answered, not liking the idea of comparing them.

"Jai's romantic with one of the girls he fucks, but he's not like that with me. I don't know what to think. We agreed to be casual, and I still want that, but he's only having a fling with her, too. I don't understand why he doesn't do sweet stuff for me, you know?"

"I don't know much about dating, but I do know a lot about casual sex. The more casual it is, the less drama can come from it when it's over. You work with Jai, he doesn't have to bullshit you into his bed. He probably doesn't care about hurting the other girl later when it ends, but he still has to see you at work and you're also good friends. That changes things," I offered, making her nod.

"I guess that makes sense. Jai won't even let me sleep in his room," she said lightly, but I could hear the hurt in her tone. She was way too into him to keep their relationship casual.

"It's okay to want more with him. I think you two would be good together," I said carefully, thankful when she gave me a grin.

"I appreciate what you're doing, but it won't work. Neither of us want to commit to one person."

"Me either," I smirked, taking another bite of food before adding. "But that's why I've got three holes."

She laughed, checking her phone and texting for a few minutes while finishing her food. I jumped when the office door slammed and Harley stalked out, raking a hand through his hair as he cursed quietly. Alex followed him out, the pair of them speaking in low voices, but I caught a few words about someone quitting and Alex had to leave.

"Uh, is everything okay?" I asked loud enough for them to hear me, and Harley scowled.

"It's fine. I had someone coming in this afternoon to help in the kitchen, but they bailed."

"Like, a chef?"

"Kitchen hand. Dishes, clearing tables, that kind of thing," he answered, his eyes assessing me as he understood where my questions were going.

"I can help. I'm a hazard around food, but I can clean stuff. I'll just have to convince the guys to leave me alone here," I shrugged, Alex giving me a grimace.

"You don't have to do that. I hear you don't get out a lot, so don't waste your day slaving over our sink."

"I want to. I'll be looking for work eventually, so the experience would look good on a resume, right? I'm glad to be out of the house, I don't mind working," I said confidently, waiting for Alex and Harley to have a silent conversation with their eyes before Harley blew out a breath of relief.

"Finish your food then I'll show you the kitchen. Leave your guys to me, I'll handle them. We really appreciate your help, thank you."

"Just give me a glowing reference when future employers call you, then we're even," I beamed, starting to shovel my food in, making Leah sigh.

"You're bailing on me?"

"Don't act like you're miserable about it. I can see you're

itching to go and deal with whoever you've been texting," I mumbled around my food, making her cringe.

"You noticed that? It's just—"

"It's fine, really. We can text now and meet up another time."

We finished our food and Leah headed off to her car, leaving me to follow Harley into the kitchen where he handed me an apron to protect my clothes.

"I don't know how much you know about hospitality cleaning, so I'll give you a quick rundown. Scrap any food scraps into that trash can." He pointed to one near the sink before continuing. "Then rinse everything and stack it in the dishwasher." He showed me how to put the rack into the dishwasher and how to work it, then he moved further along. "Once it's finished, open it back up and be careful of the steam. We wash in boiling water. Since it's so hot, everything dries within seconds almost, so all you have to do is put everything away. All the plates and glasses are on the far wall, and utensils go in that bucket to be polished."

He gave me a quick tour of everything so I knew where the kitchenware items went, then he left me to start on the dishes while he went back out to the register to serve some customers.

Cruz

Being back at the compound was fucking with my emotions. It was home, it had been for a long time, but I couldn't live with Stone again, that much was obvious when I put my fist through his face the second he opened his mouth to speak.

"Nice to see you too," Stone grunted, not seeming surprised by my anger. "Where's Drake?"

"Not here," Knox grunted from beside me, his eyes on Stone. We all glared at each other for a moment before Stone let out a huff of annoyance.

"Why are you here?"

"We need to discuss Thieves business, and I want to know what the fuck is wrong with you," I answered, making him frown.

"What do you mean?"

"The Psychos—"

"I mean the other thing. You want to talk about Penn?" he inquired, dropping into his desk chair to look up at me. "What's there to tell? You won't listen anyway, you'll only punch me and storm off."

"Why did you fucking ruin everything?" I asked, my voice dropping in volume. "We were fine until you went rogue. She trusted you, man. You know the Psychos and Devils have to deal with you, right? They haven't let this go."

"I'm aware."

"You're going to get yourself killed," I gritted out, clenching my fists as his face remained blank. "Do you even care, Stone?"

"Do you?" he threw back, holding my gaze. "You sound worried for me. Is this a welfare check?"

"I'm pissed at you, but I don't want you six feet under," I muttered, surprise registering on his face as I dropped into the chair beside him, raking my hands through my hair. Knox leaned against the wall, crossing his arms.

"We have a business deal with the crews, so what do we do about that? The tech is Cruz's, but the business is yours. We need to figure this out."

I didn't expect Stone's answer, and I had no idea how to handle it. "The deal still stands. If you're willing to allow me to have access to the tech, then you can take over that side of things. Kind of like different branches in the business."

"I won't work for you. Penn almost fucking died because of you," I said sharply, his face remaining serious.

"I don't want her dead. I was looking into her father's business more, and—"

"Don't act like you give a fuck now!" Knox snapped, cutting him off. "And stop spying on her through the computer camera. It's fucking creepy."

"Just let me talk to her!" he shouted, losing his temper and making me frown. I'd never seen him so damn desperate, and for some reason, I felt bad for being a dick to him. Knox scoffed and stalked off, apparently done with the conversation, but I kept my eyes on Stone as he let his walls down enough for me to see the pure guilt and self-loathing inside. "Please, Cruz. I didn't know he was going to hurt her like that or sell her off. I forced myself to believe he really was worried about her because it was fucking convenient, but I never—"

"You didn't just put her at risk, but you betrayed me, asshole," I said quietly, stopping his rant. "No matter what was happening, you should've spoken to me, and we could've looked into it together. Why didn't you talk to me?"

He had the decency to look a little ashamed, and more of the anger left me as he blew out a breath. "You guys were so caught up in her that I figured I had to handle it alone. You guys are my family, and I'd do anything for you to keep you safe, even if that meant being the bad guy. I was wrong about her though, and I just want to have the chance to explain it to her. I'd die for you, Cruz, you're my brother. The thought of her father tearing through everything we built got to me, and I wasn't going to allow that to happen."

"You should've talked to me," I repeated, shaking my head a little as I pulled my phone from my pocket as it started to ring, panic washing over me as Harley's name crossed my screen. He'd only call if something was wrong. I answered, getting to my feet. "What's wrong? I'm on my way."

Stone stood too, confusion on his face, but I paused my escape as Harley chuckled in my ear. "You have it so bad. Nothing's wrong, I just wanted to let you know that Leah has left, and Penn is staying here with me. She's currently elbow-deep in my sink doing dishes."

"Why the fuck is she doing your dishes? I'll come and get her."

"Leave her be. You've got a girl who wants to pave her own path in life, so if allowing her to do a little work makes her feel good about herself, let her. She said something about getting experience for her resume," he answered lightly, but I could hear a tone of warning, too. "You know she's safe here, so give her some leeway, or you'll lose her. Come get her at eight."

"Eight? You'd better fucking pay her," I gritted out, his carefree attitude vanishing.

"Of course I'll pay her. Just leave her alone, let her work, and you'll see her later." He hung up before I could reply, and I scowled as I shoved my phone back into my pocket.

"What's wrong?" Stone asked, not being able to stop himself from letting some of his worry slip.

"Apparently, Penn is working for Harley and Alex for the rest of the day," I grumbled, a flicker of amusement flashing across his face.

"I hope she's not cooking. I hear she burns noodles."

"Me either." I stopped, eyeing him with annoyance for managing to get me to have a conversation with him about her.

"Move back in, man," Stone said when he realized I wasn't taking off. "I won't touch Penn. She's welcome to come back."

"What happens when we get shot at again?" I snorted, crossing my arms. "You'll only send her packing to protect us."

"Why would we get shot at again?"

"Zavier bought her with counterfeit cash. Louis will eventually notice, surely, and then things will go to shit," I stated, giving him a pointed look.

"He's a fucking idiot. Why would he do that?" he hissed.

"Because he didn't want to see her sold to some sick, middle-aged man who was going to tie her to the bed and rape her until he got bored and likely kill her. It seems Penn has formed a good friendship with him, too. And Lavaro," I muttered, walking from the room in search of Knox, Stone following behind.

"Aren't you worried about him? What if she wants to be with him too?" Stone asked casually, making me chuckle.

"He could've had her by now if he wanted her. He's stated he doesn't."

"Humor me."

I turned, finding him studying my face for an answer. "Penn isn't in an open relationship with us. If, for some reason, she wanted to be with him too, we'd have to sit down and talk about it. I personally don't want to share her with anyone else, and neither would the others. I don't mind Knox and Drake being with her because she's repaired damage between them that she didn't cause, and she turned us into better people. Zavier's got a boner for Raven anyway, so why are you asking me this shit?"

"Just wondering," he shrugged, looking away from me.

We found Knox in the kitchen talking to some of the other Thieves, his face unreadable as he spoke to me. "Ready to go?"

"Sure. We don't need to get Penn until eight, though. She's working for Harley today, apparently." I still didn't like the idea of her working, I had enough money to keep us afloat for a long time, but I had to respect her desire for independence.

"You're kidding me. He's making her slave away in his fucking kitchen—"

"No, she wants experience for her resume. He said he'll

pay her, so we have to leave her be. You know how much it will mean to her," I sighed, his face scrunching with frustration.

"Sometimes, I wish she was a fucking princess."

"No, you don't. You like her exactly how she is because her defiance gets you off," I teased, making him grunt.

"Whatever you say."

Stone watched our interaction longingly, but I had to stop feeling sorry for him. He could've had this with us, but he was so fucking stubborn that he lost the best thing that could've happened to him.

Penn would've worshiped him if he'd let her.

Stone

The moment Cruz and Knox left, I locked myself back in the office alone, pulling up security footage of Harley's. It wasn't too busy, Alex at the register serving someone while two other tables were filled with people already eating, and my eyes locked onto Penn as she made her way out of a back room with a tray. I watched as she collected dirty plates and glasses from a table, taking them into the kitchen to clean. I switched cameras, finding Harley cooking as he spoke to Penn. The audio sucked and I couldn't hear anything, but she was grinning at whatever he said.

She was fucking gorgeous, my damn dick had always known that, but something flipped inside of me from her smile. I'd never seen her so happy before. Princesses didn't like to work, so I really had been wrong about her.

That made me feel even fucking worse for how I'd treated her.

I spent two hours watching her before Zavier walked through the door at Harley's with Beckett, the pair of them sitting in a booth at the back. Harley gave them a wave to let them know he'd seen them, then he ducked into the kitchen before emerging again with Penn who appeared nervous.

Harley handed her a pen and notepad, letting her take their order, and she looked so proud of herself. Beckett studied her as she walked away, saying something to Zavier that was probably rude. She really didn't trust Penn.

Zavier, on the other hand, was grinning and talking with his damn hands, more than happy about Penn working too. She seemed right at home as she moved in and out of the kitchen, getting more confident as Harley let her take more orders, and I scrubbed a hand over my face with a sigh. Most women would lock themselves away after what she'd been through, but she was trying so hard to stay strong. I admired her for that.

I wasn't surprised when Knox, Cruz, and Drake eventually wandered in and sat at a table, spending the rest of Penn's shift there. It wasn't like I could scoff at them, I'd watched most of her shift on my computer like a fucking weirdo. This was the kind of bullshit Drake would do, not me, but I continued to search her out in footage whenever I was at my desk.

I turned it off when they all went home, sitting there in silence for a little longer. I'd lost my family, friends, and for some reason, I was pissed off that I'd fucked it up with Penn too. I had other things to worry about, though, like the fact Beckett's family was likely to come after me and put me in a hole.

Sending Penn into Rory's house had been stupid, and it had ruined a good business relationship with the crews, as well as made me lose literally everything I cared about.

Knox had been right, my brother would be disgusted with me.

Chapter Fourteen

Penn

For the following week, the guys took me to the gym in Stoneleigh and helped me with some strength training, and Drake had organized a proper meal plan for me to follow. Knox and Cruz turned their noses up at most of it, but I'd never tasted food so good before.

My back and stomach were healing a lot better now, too, and I was completely off my antibiotics and bandages. I felt really good, especially since Harley had asked me to help out a second time at the bar. I'd loved working there, and I kept glancing at my bank account that Zavier had set up for me, giddy with the fact I had my own money in it. It wasn't much, but it was mine, and I'd worked hard for it.

The guys had backed off a little and didn't glue themselves to me either, which made it a lot easier to keep tabs on Stone. I'd overheard Knox and Drake talking about how the Psychos were likely to kill him, so instead of ignoring Stone's random messages, I kept replying. That way, I knew he was okay.

Like today, for instance, when all three of the guys were out doing stuff that I hadn't questioned, leaving me home alone.

Stone: You know I can see you, right?

That made me pause as I stared down at his recent text while I tidied up the living room, glancing around at the windows as if he was going to jump out at me.

Stone: Don't you own your own clothes?
You're always in their shirts.

Penn: Where are you? The guys will kill you if they find out you've been creeping around the house.

Stone: Who said I was there?

My eyes flicked around the room in confusion, another message coming through as I started walking towards the kitchen.

Stone: Cold.

I stopped, walking the other direction.

Stone: Warmer.

I had no idea how he was watching me, Zavier said there were no cameras inside the house, but now I was worried he'd lied. Stone could hack into them if there were any, so that would explain how he could see me without being here.

Penn: Don't play games with me, asshole.
How are you seeing me?

Instead of answering my question, he kept playing his stupid game.

Stone: Colder.

I let out a huff of annoyance, walking towards the couch and stopping when he messaged again.

Stone: Hot.

My eyes darted around the space, landing on the computer with a frown. I hesitated before walking up to it, noticing a little green light on.

Stone: Such a smart girl.

"Can you hear me?" I asked out loud without taking my eyes off the computer, a message coming through on my phone a moment later.

Stone: Yes.

"How long have you been spying on me?" I demanded, sitting in the chair to glare at the computer. Had he been watching me and the guys this whole time? I almost dropped my phone as it rang, and I stared at it for a moment before hitting answer and holding it to my ear. "You're going to get in more trouble."

Stone chuckled, the sound going straight to my traitorous pussy. "Thought you liked walking on the wild side, Princess? Bad boys aren't your thing anymore?"

"You betrayed me," I said softly, staring at the computer since I knew he could still see me.

"You'll get your revenge soon. The Psychos aren't going to let me walk around untouched after I fucked them over," he answered, not seeming bothered by the fact he had a target on his back. Frustrated tears burned my eyes but didn't fall, and his voice softened. "Are you crying?"

"It's all my fault. If I'd just left you alone—"

"Don't fucking blame yourself," he bit out, and I swiped at my eyes when I felt a tear finally run down my cheek. "Penn, that was all on me. I never should've tricked you like that, I almost got you killed."

"But I—"

"You're not to blame for anything," he promised. I'd never heard his voice so gentle before, and I couldn't help but clutch the phone a little tighter.

"I don't want you to die because of me, Stone."

"I'm sorry about all of it," he said instead, hesitating before continuing. "How's your back?"

It was strange talking to him so casually, but part of me loved being able to. "Healing."

"Don't overwork yourself at the gym. Yesterday's session was too much for you," he warned, surprising me a little.

"You were spying on me at the gym too?"

"I'm always spying on you," he chuckled, but it sounded hollow. "I feel better knowing I can keep an eye on you. I can't figure out who shot up the track the other week, so you need to only trust the guys."

"What made you change your mind?" I asked.

"I was wrong. You're not using my boys, and you're not the crazy chick your father made you out to be. I believed him out of convenience, but I shouldn't have. Meet up with me."

"The last time I went off alone with you, you handed me over to my father," I said dryly.

"I know you won't, but you can trust me this time. I had no idea how bad it was for you when I handed you over, or I wouldn't have done it in the first place. Shit, Penn. I could've gotten you raped and killed."

"I don't trust you, and I won't meet up with you," I said sternly, proud of myself for stopping my voice from wavering. I wanted to see him, but my luck, I'd end up going for a ride in the trunk or something.

"I guess I can respect that. Looks like Drake's on the way home, so I need to go."

"How do you know that?"

"I see everything," he answered. "Bye, Penn."

"Bye," I murmured as he hung up, my eyes sliding to the light on the computer as it turned off. My stomach twisted with confusion and guilt as I thought about Stone. I couldn't tell the guys, but I didn't like keeping secrets from them either.

I got up and put my phone in my pocket, making my way into the kitchen just as Drake got home, a warm smile tugging at the corners of his mouth as he found me. "Hey, baby. Cruz and Knox are handling something with Beckett, so they'll be home later. What have you been up to?" He slid an arm around my waist and pulled me close to drop a kiss on my lips.

"Just hanging around the house," I said quickly, his brow creasing slightly at my tone.

"Are you okay?"

"I'm fine." I felt stupid. It wasn't like I'd snuck out and fucked Stone behind his back, but it felt like it from the way the guilt ate at me. "What are your plans for the rest of the day?"

"I was hoping to take my girl to the beach," he grinned, burying his face in my neck. "But now I'm considering spending the rest of the day in bed with you."

"You'll take me to the beach again?" I beamed, loving the idea of spending the afternoon there. We hadn't been back since he'd fucked me for the first time, but I'd spent a lot of time thinking about it.

He swatted my butt and stepped back, giving me a wink. "If it's quiet, maybe we'll have time for a quickie there."

"Can we swim?"

"You know how?" He seemed surprised, making me giggle.

"Well, yeah. Emily taught me. We had a massive pool, and I wasn't locked away when I was younger."

"You don't talk about her much," he observed, and I shrugged.

"You guys don't talk about your lives before me either."

"We'll have to change that," he promised, taking my hand and giving it a squeeze. "Go get ready. I'll find some towels."

"Drake!" I squealed as he tossed me over his shoulder, making his way towards the water.

"My girl wanted to go swimming, so I'm giving her what she wanted," he teased, not slowing his steps.

"Don't you dare!"

"Sorry, can't hear you!" he laughed, ignoring the strange looks from an old couple who were having a picnic close by. I kicked and squealed the entire way, my breath catching in my throat as I was suddenly surrounded by icy water. I sputtered as I surfaced, flailing to get my feet on the sand below me.

"Asshole!"

"You love me," he chuckled, taking my hand and tugging me into him. I went without a fight, threading my arms around his neck to soak in his body heat.

"I do," I smiled, giving him a quick kiss. "You're lucky I left my phone in the car."

"I like seeing you like this," he murmured, and I tilted my head slightly.

"Like what?"

"Like you're free. You aren't constantly looking over your shoulder with your guard up."

"That's because I know I'm safe with you," I replied without hesitation, his face softening.

"I'll always protect you."

I went to speak, but he consumed me with a kiss, the cold water lapping at my skin as he set me on fire. I wrapped my legs around his waist as his hands slid down to my ass, keeping me close as I kissed him back.

"We can't fuck here," I groaned, pulling away to glance towards the beach where the elderly couple still sat, noticing a few other people walking along the beach further along. "We have an audience."

"You love an audience," he teased.

"Yeah, but only your friends because they can fuck me too," I deadpanned, his dick jerking against me.

"We are so having a gangbang."

"Good luck convincing Knox to rub balls with Cruz," I chuckled, swimming backwards away from him to float along the surface.

"Tell me about your sister," he said randomly, and I hesitated before replying.

"Emily was my best friend. She's the reason I learned to sneak out, she taught me how she did it. She loved bad boys." I paused, laughing lightly. "She'd probably high five me for bagging you guys. Either that or beat me up to keep you all to herself."

"Where's she buried? I'll take you to see her," he offered, my mouth curving into a soft smile.

"Kingslake Cemetery. Dad never liked it when we went to see her, so he stopped taking me."

It was quiet for a few minutes before Drake spoke. "I had shit foster parents. The crazy religious kind who only helped kids to make themselves look good. I was practically just a slave for them. I did all the cleaning and had to learn to cook to avoid getting my ass beat."

"When did you get out?"

"When I got locked up at sixteen. Set their house on fire," he smirked, but I could see the sadness he hid behind the humor. "Their *god* dealt with them a month later. Car accident, very messy."

"And then you met the guys in juvie?"

"I'd already been in there for a year when Knox got his ass thrown in for carjacking. Cruz was never supposed to see the light of day again when he was convicted, but Ezekiel got him out alongside Knox. He came back for me after Knox told him how I easily escaped my cell to sneak around at night. I guess I seemed like a good investment," he laughed. "Stone was always in and out, but it was just to scout out potential thieves. He'd be in there for a month or two, then vanish, then a few months later, he'd be back. His brother had a lot of pull with the warden. I think he blackmailed him, but I'm not sure. I never asked."

I swam towards him, my voice quiet. "What happened to your real parents?"

"Overdose. I was born addicted to heroin if that tells you how loving they were," he said casually, giving me a small smile. "I know your dad's a piece of shit, but what about your mom? I know she took off, but what was she like?"

"She wasn't maternal at all. I honestly hardly knew her, she didn't spend much time with me. Estelle raised me, not Mom," I said dryly, accepting his hand as he pulled me closer as I shivered.

"Let's get out and get warm," he murmured, and I hadn't even noticed how cold I was.

We walked hand in hand back to the car to grab towels, then we headed to our spot on the rocks to sit and watch the view in the sun to dry off.

"Mom never wanted us," I said as if we'd never stopped

the conversation, resting my chin on my knees. "She only did it because it's what rich families do."

"I don't know anything about being a parent, but I know what not to do," Drake grunted, laying back to close his eyes. "I'm surprised all of us turned out to be good people thanks to our awful upbringing."

"Who said anything about us turning out to be good? I'm a damaged brat and you're a professional thief," I pointed out, earning a grin from him.

"You're hardly a brat."

"Ask Knox, he'll tell you," I giggled, squealing as he pulled me down beside him and wrapped his arms around me. "Hey!"

"It's cute when you act like you don't want my hands on you but then make no attempt to escape," he mumbled into my neck as he kissed across my skin, his hand slipping between us to dip into my shorts. I gasped as he didn't hesitate to push a finger inside me, his teeth grazing my neck as he chuckled. I ground against his hand, running my fingers through his hair to jerk his head back so I could kiss him.

Sex with Drake was always spontaneous, and I fucking loved it.

"Ride me," he whispered against my lips, waiting for me to nod before pulling back from me to remove his shorts and shirt, leaving the wet material on the rocks beside us. I pulled my shirt off but left my bra on, kicking my shorts and underwear off before straddling his lap. "Dammit, my wallet's in the car."

"You keep fucking me without a condom anyway, don't worry about it," I huffed, not wanting him to move, and he raised an eyebrow.

"Are you sure?"

"Yes. I'm off my antibiotics, and I have the thingy in my arm. Fuck me raw," I replied, a groan leaving him as I reached between us to start stroking him, lining myself up with the head.

"Keep talking like that, and I'll come before I'm inside you."

"You guys all love dirty talk." I sank over him, taking my time to avoid hurting myself. Knox had ridden me hard before bed last night, so I was still a little tender. "I love how your cock stretches my pussy as I—"

"You're killing me," he said tightly, making me gasp as he grabbed my hips and rocked me forward, his dick pressing deep inside me. "I need to get you off first."

"How did we go from talking about our parents, to fucking in public?" I panted as his fingers pressed against my clit, rubbing small circles on it as I rolled my hips.

"You didn't know? We're a little fucked up. Blame our parents," he murmured, rubbing faster until my fingers dug into his shoulders and he had to take over, moving my hips how he wanted as I came, a loud whimper leaving me that only got louder the more he moved my body. "You sure you want me to come inside you?" he asked, and all I could do was nod as he kissed me, keeping a firm grip on my waist as he let out a moan.

I slumped against him as he became still, his arms staying around me as he left kisses across my shoulder.

Drake

"Are you done being a creep?" I asked dryly, Penn's head lifting from my neck to look around in time for Knox to step out from his shitty hiding spot. I loved the way Penn instantly relaxed when she saw him, not caring that he'd been watching us.

"I kept a lookout, you're welcome," he grunted, running

his eyes over her as he moved closer, offering her his hand. She took it without a second thought, letting him pull her to her feet. I groaned, getting a good view of her pussy as my cum started leaking out of her.

"Why is that so hot?"

"Because you're a perv," Knox deadpanned, not giving a shit as he grabbed my wet shirt off the ground and started cleaning her up. "Are you okay? You usually only come here when you need time to think." It took me a second to realize he was still talking to me.

"Yeah. Penn loves it here, and it's quiet. Figured I'd bring her here to relax."

"It is pretty quiet here," he agreed, glancing at her wet clothes before sighing and pulling his shirt over his head. "Get your bra off." Her eyes widened as she glanced around, but he blocked her view with a scowl. "Do you honestly think I'd let anyone see your tits? Take it off. You'll get sick if you stay in wet clothes, and even though your back is healing now, I'm not risking a soggy fucking infection."

I chuckled, raising an eyebrow. "A what?"

"Shut the fuck up," he snapped as he flicked his gaze to mine before looking back at Penn. "Go on. Take it off and put this on."

She reached around to unhook her bra, dropping it onto the ground beside her with a scowl. "Happy?"

"Immensely," he said flatly, holding the shirt up for her to slip her arms into it. I didn't miss the way his eyes heated at the sight of her wearing his shirt, and something settled in my chest at knowing just how much he cared for her. He'd always wanted her, despite his shitty way of showing it, but he cared about her now in ways that he hadn't before.

"Why are you here? Not that I'm complaining," she smiled, not giving a shit that annoyance washed over his features as she threw her arms around him, stretching to slide her hands around the back of his neck to attempt to tug him down for a kiss. "Did you guys get everything sorted with Beckett? Where's Cruz?"

His annoyance vanished after a second, and he leaned down to give her the kiss she'd silently asked for. "Tracked your phones to see where you'd gone. Cruz is hanging out with Riley and Luna having girl time." He scrunched up his face, making me chuckle.

"He's painting his nails and gossiping?"

"You know how much he secretly loves it," Knox grunted, giving Penn a reassuring look when she frowned. "He's got a soft spot for Luna. Not in a romantic way, but a little sister kind of way. Riley isn't exactly the girly type, so Cruz humors her and lets her paint his nails and shit."

I expected Penn to get uncomfortable, but she laughed. "I'm not surprised. Luna mentioned girl time once, and I was very confused. That makes sense."

"He's not into her or anything," I clarified, not wanting to leave any room for doubt, but she gave me a grin.

"I know. Riley would beat his ass if he tried anything, and I don't know if you noticed, but he's a little obsessed with me. I'm not worried about him going anywhere he shouldn't."

Knox took her hand and started walking back towards the beach, leaving me to scramble to put my wet shorts back on and bundle the rest of the clothes up in the towels, and I trailed behind them as I watched their interactions. He always looked so grumpy, but his expressions were softer, and his hand never left hers.

Knox never held hands, but it was something he seemed to be doing a lot lately. He wasn't as affectionate as me, but he also knew it was my love language, as well as Penn's, so he was trying.

That meant everything to me.

We were within view of the cars now, and just as I caught

up to them, my car exploded, sending pieces of it flying. The sound was deafening, my ears ringing. Knox instantly reacted by shoving us both to the ground, trying to keep Penn shielded by his large frame while still keeping a firm grip on my arm as if I was going to charge towards it and get myself hurt. It was just a car, nothing special, but if it had been a few minutes later, we would've been sitting inside it when it had exploded.

What if she'd run ahead of us and climbed in? Or if I'd wandered to the car to get my fucking wallet for that condom earlier?

My stomach twisted as her scared voice reached me, the ringing in my ears starting to fade.

"What the fuck?" Penn choked out with wide eyes, glancing at me as I watched what was left of the car burn. I reached for her shaking hand to try and comfort her, not wanting her to have a panic attack when we were so vulnerable here out in the open.

Someone screamed from the beach, and I heard the sound of a child crying somewhere, too, but no one was hurt from what we could see. Luckily, the flying chunks hadn't hit anyone.

"I think we found out who was the target at the track," Knox grunted. "It can't be a coincidence that everywhere Penn goes, something gets shot at or blown up."

"Who would be after her though? If it was her father, he'd be going after Lopez and Lavaro," I pointed out as Penn released my hand and I slowly got to my feet, inspecting the area around us for trouble. No one was around, so the explosion had been caused by something being planted on the car either before we got here, or while we were swimming.

Knox got to his feet, too, while encouraging Penn to do the same, keeping her close as he scanned our surroundings for danger, too. She pressed even more firmly into his side as the fear on her face increased. "Why would someone be trying to kill me?"

"I don't know, Whitlock, but we'll find out," Knox promised, steering her towards me. "Stay with her while I check my car."

"It might explode!" she shrieked as she reached for him, but I held her against me and kissed the top of her head.

"Knox knows his weapons, babe. That includes explosives."

"But what if—"

"I'll be fine," he said firmly as he made his way towards it, starting to inspect the vehicle the moment he got there.

There was a reason Knox handled so much of the protection details, he knew his shit. I couldn't lie, my dick got ridiculously hard every time I saw him in his tactical gear, too.

"The only person who'd be pissed at you would be Stone. Maybe—"

"It's not Stone," she bit out sharply, surprising me with her anger. She pulled back from me, crossing her arms with a scowl. "He learned his lesson, and he feels like an ass, not to mention he's too busy running from blood-thirsty crews right now to give a fuck about me."

I studied her for a moment before speaking, my voice low. "How do you know that?"

"I just do. You saw him at the Donovans that day, he was upset that I'd been hurt thanks to his actions. There's no way he'd blow up your car to kill me, let alone risk you."

It made sense, and I relaxed a little at the thought. She was right, Stone wouldn't risk me, even if he was out to get her.

Knox waved us over once he was finished, his voice gruff. "Mine's fine. Which makes me think it's definitely Penn who's the target."

"Why can't people just leave me alone? I just got used to

being free again!" she hissed, sympathy filling his eyes as he brushed damp hair back from her face.

"We'll get them. I think we need to call in a favor with Beckett, though. We have manpower, but they'd have better contacts. Our resources are only helpful if there's an online presence, and there's no security here for us to breach. If someone tampered with the car here, we won't be able to find proof."

I nodded, keeping my eyes on Penn. She looked pale, defeat written all over her pretty face. If anyone thought they could cage my girl, they had another thing coming. "Let's get home. I'll call in help to clean up this mess."

"You know we'll have to speak to Stone, right? He'll have to handle the cops," Knox muttered, making me sigh.

"Yeah. We'll stop there on the way home, and we can call Beckett when we get there, too. I'll text Cruz to let him know what's happened. Give me your phone."

He handed it over, murmuring something to Penn as she shuffled even closer to him. I let her sit in the front, it was obvious she didn't want to let go of Knox's hand. At least with him comforting her, it meant my hands were free to start organizing new bank cards and identification.

Chapter Fifteen

Penn

Knox headed into the compound the moment we arrived, leaving me to sit in the car while Drake climbed out and paced on the phone. Cruz had freaked out about the car being blown up, and the two of them were having a pretty big discussion about it.

I waited for fifteen minutes before opening the door, giving Drake a pleading look. "I'm going to piss my pants. How much longer is this going to take?"

"Knox could be a while. Him and Stone are currently on a call with the Psychos," he answered, holding the phone away from his ear. "Can't you hold it?"

"I'll be fast."

"Pee in the bushes," he said seriously, making me snort.

"Stone's busy with Knox, and I know where the bathroom is. If I sneeze, it's all over for this car seat and my dignity," I deadpanned, his lips twitching with amusement.

"Fine. I'll come with you."

"Jesus Christ, Stone's not going to murder me in the bathroom, and if he tells me I can't use his toilet, I'll guilt trip him with him selling me out. I'm fine," I snapped, climbing out and shutting the door. "I don't need a babysitter in there."

"Be fast," he warned, returning to his conversation while eyeing me as I made my way across the yard. I knew the code now, so I let myself in through the front door and scampered through the quiet compound, shutting myself in the bathroom and relieving my bladder. Best tinkle I'd ever had. Five stars.

Once I'd washed my hands, I opened the bathroom door and started walking along the hallway, a hand suddenly darting out to cover my mouth as I was pulled into a room, the panic only lasting a second until I was surrounded with the scent of Stone's cologne. When I didn't fight him, he removed his hand and I turned around, his calculating eyes assessing me. He didn't speak, and I let out a huff.

"What? I needed to pee. Surely you're not going to get mad because I used your bathroom."

"I know. I'm not mad. I've been trying to get you to come and see me all week, if I'd have known a nice toilet would've convinced you, I would've offered it sooner," he said dryly.

"If I'm not back outside in a minute or two, Drake will—"

"I'm not trying to hold you hostage, I only need a minute," he bit out, some of his frustration seeping through. "I just wanted to apologize to your face. I'm fucking sorry, Penelope. I wanted you gone, but I didn't want you hurt, not really."

"I can't do this with you," I tried to say firmly, but my voice cracked a fraction, and I took a step back from him, which only put me further into his room. Not that I could get past him to escape anyway.

"I fucked up," he said calmly, moving towards me but keeping his hands where I could see them. "I know I can't take back what happened, but I just need to know that you're okay."

"Do I look okay?" I laughed bitterly, motioning to myself. "People are trying to blow me up and shoot me."

"I'll find them and make them pay," he growled, and I flinched when he took my face in his hands. "You don't have to believe me, but I've got your back, okay? You never deserved my hate, and I'll keep saying sorry until one day, maybe you'll believe me." I didn't move, holding his gaze as he stepped closer, one of his hands leaving my face to rake through my tangled, damp hair. "If you need me, just call."

"Stone—" I lifted a hand to push him away, but my fingers gripped his shirt as if to keep him close.

"Let me," he murmured. "Can I see your back? The guys said it was bad. Is it healing?"

My body leaned into him, but my brain screamed at me to get away, and finally, my feet started moving to put some distance between us. "You're not allowed to give a shit now. It was your fault to begin with. You didn't mark my skin with your hands, but you might as well have when you handed me over to him. You don't know what it was like in that dark basement. He didn't let me bathe once in the entire month, you know? I got a sponge bath when he decided to sell me, but that was it. No fresh clothes, nothing to eat or drink other than stale bread and water that he made me lick off the fucking floor. He treated me like an animal, and then he whipped me and degraded me, all while I had hope that the guys would show up and save me."

"Penn—"

"I'm not finished," I bit out, surprised when he clamped his mouth shut and let me continue. "The day he decided to sell me, he dragged me out of the basement and through the house I'd always called home. He let his friends say cruel things to me, inflicting fear into me that I'd spend the rest of my life being raped and used. You have no idea what it's like to feel paralyzed by fear. It's a rich man's world, Stone, and women hold no place in it. They bid on me. Shouting out prices as if I was nothing but cattle. Do you know how terrifying and humiliating that is?"

"I know the fear you felt," he said softly, remorse all over his face.

"No, you don't. You're a man in a man's world," I scoffed, and he shook his head slightly as he finally turned towards the door, opening it and speaking quietly.

"I do, Penn. Maybe one day you'll give me the chance to tell you about it. Remember to keep your eyes open and make mental reports wherever you go. That shit will keep you alive." He walked off, leaving his bedroom door open for me to leave, and I quickly shut it as I headed back outside, almost running into Drake as I swung open the front door.

"There you are. What took so long?" he demanded, no longer on the phone as he glanced around behind me.

"I had to shit," I lied, taking his hand and pulling him towards the car. "Is Knox done yet?"

"I haven't heard from him."

"I'm getting hungry." I just wanted to get the fuck away from here before I did something stupid like go back inside and ask Stone what the fuck he'd been talking about. Then we'd both get in trouble.

"Once we're home, we can shower, and I'll make you some food. Promise," he smiled, kissing my cheek and leaning against the car, pulling me between his legs. "I'm sorry today went to shit. I was really enjoying spending time with you."

"Me too. Thanks for taking me out," I replied, standing on tiptoe and giving him a kiss as his hands slid around my waist to grab my ass through Knox's massive shirt.

"Anything for my girl."

His hold on me tightened as I heard the front door open, and I glanced over to find Knox and Stone walking out together. Knox didn't look happy to see me out of the car, but

Stone's eyes were glued to me as if he hadn't just been right in front of me having a conversation.

"Drake," Stone greeted gruffly, stopping in front of us and giving me his usual bored expression. "Penelope."

"Get in the car, baby," Drake said tightly, making me scowl.

"No. It's Stone, not the fucking Grim Reaper. He's not going to shoot me right in front of you."

I didn't miss the way Stone's mouth twitched with the ghost of a smile, his voice calm. "I'm not going to waste bullets when we might need them."

"I see you're still as charming as ever," I replied, also acting like I hadn't spoken to him recently. Guilt stabbed at me, but it was better this way.

"And I see you're still a pain in the ass," he chuckled, but his tone was softer than normal. "I don't know why the guys are flipping out so much. It's obvious you're fine."

Knox growled and stepped between us, warning in his tone. "Don't talk to her. We appreciate your help, but leave her alone."

"She's a big girl and can handle her own shit," Stone replied flatly, turning his attention to Drake. "I've been going through all the footage I can from the shooting at the track, and I can't find shit. I tried to see if anything stood out today, but whoever's after Penn isn't leaving much of a trail. Looks like we have a pro on our hands."

"A hitman? Do we have contacts in the area that we could ask about it?" Drake asked, but I shook my head, replying before Stone could.

"Friends or not, a hitman won't disclose a business deal he has with someone else. If the person paying them loses their anonymity, the hitman will lose their reputation. Why don't you know that?"

"Exactly. Drake does know that, you've just fucked all of

his brain cells out." He gave Drake the side-eye before adding, "I'll ask around for information, but I don't like our chances. If it's a pro, they'll be like a vault and there'll be no trail to follow. If by chance they're an amateur, we might get lucky. I'll do some digging."

"Thank you," I said on an exhale, and he gave me a nod. Knox and Drake went on alert as Stone stepped closer, and he snarled.

"Jesus Christ, I'm not going to hurt her." He pulled two phones out of his pocket, handing one to Drake and offering one to me. Drake tried to snatch it, but Stone pulled it back, leveling him with a glare. "Not for you. It's for her."

"Get back in your lane, dick," Knox bit out, but Stone ignored him, offering me the phone again. If he'd wanted to hurt me, he would've done it by now, so I stepped forward and extended my hand, taking it from him with a small smile.

"Thanks. I can pay you back."

"This is me paying you back. Not that it covers much of it," he said seriously, stepping back before the other two could start throwing hands. "Eyes open, Penelope." He turned and walked away, making Drake clench his fists.

"Was that a fucking threat? Did he threaten her?"

"No, you psycho. Get in the car. You're the one being crazy now," I scowled, and I swore I heard Stone laugh as he stepped into the compound.

Stone

I shut myself inside, watching them leave through the window. Penn had looked back before getting into the car, and my dick jerked in my pants at the thought of having her attention. She hadn't even fought me when I'd shoved her into my room once she realized it was me, so I knew there was hope in fixing things with her.

Once I'd watched the car vanish into the distance, I walked into my bedroom and locked the door, dropping down onto my bed with a sigh. It was always so quiet around here now, especially without Drake's antics.

I was surprised when a message came through on my phone from Penn, my heartbeat rising a fraction as I read it.

Penn: Thank you. Keep me in the loop? I'm going to talk to Zavier about Kingslake gossip to see if he can find out anything.

Stone: Will do. Let me know if he finds anything.

I didn't expect her to reply, but my phone buzzed in my pocket a minute later.

Penn: Sure. Maybe we can meet up and talk about what we find later in the week. Then you can finish the conversation we were having before?

Telling her the truth about my past wasn't something I'd ever intended on doing, but the words had spilled from my lips before I could stop them earlier. Cruz knew about it, but that was it.

Stone: I'll think about it.

I dropped my phone beside me on the bed, staring up at the ceiling for a moment. Penn had only been wearing Knox's shirt, and I wondered if she was wearing panties under it or not. She hadn't been wearing a bra, that much I knew. Since they'd been at the beach and her hair was still wet from swimming, I assumed her panties were with the rest of her wet clothes. That thought alone made my dick strain against my zipper. I really needed to get laid, it had been way too long.

I wracked my brain as I tried to remember exactly when I'd fucked someone last, drawing a blank. Surely it wasn't more than a couple of years ago, but time had been blurring into one lately, so I wasn't too sure.

My palm ground against the bulge in my pants, frustration hitting me when it wasn't what I needed. What I did need was Penn on her knees for me, but that wasn't happening, so I admitted defeat and unbuttoned my pants, shoving my hand inside to wrap around my length. I pumped slowly at first, but the more I thought about Penn, the faster my movements became.

Her amber eyes flashed through my mind and I groaned, coming embarrassingly fast and soaking my boxers. I withdrew my hand, scowling at it as if it had a mind of its own, and I cleaned up with a shirt off the floor. My quick tug hadn't sated anything though, and I'd needed a second one in the shower twenty minutes later.

My dick's newfound obsession with her was ridiculous.

Cruz

Penn had been exhausted when she'd gotten home, wanting to shower alone and eat before lying down in bed for a nap. Which made grilling the guys so much easier.

"Is she okay, or should one of us be with her?" I asked quietly from my spot on the couch, glancing between Drake and Knox.

Knox shrugged, but Drake sighed. "She was acting a little weird at the compound. She took forever on the damn toilet, but she didn't mention anyone giving her shit, and Knox was with Stone, so maybe it's just in my head."

Knox's head swiveled around to face him, a scowl on his face. "You let her inside alone?"

"She had to pee. The only person in there that's out to get her is Stone, and you were with him. What's the big deal?" he huffed.

"Stone was gone for a while when I was on the phone to the Psychos."

"What was he doing?" I frowned, earning a dirty look in return.

"I don't know, I didn't give a shit. I thought Penn was safely strapped into the car with Drake."

We were quiet for a moment before I raked a hand through my hair and leaned forwards. "How was Stone acting?"

Knox snorted, placing an arm behind his head and dropping the other around Drake as he curled up against his side. "Like he always is. They spoke outside when we left, but it didn't seem like they'd seen each other beforehand. Stone was being a dick but less than normal, and Penn sassed him and got mad when we told her to get back in the car. If he was bothering her, I think she would've called him out in front of us." I wasn't too sure about that.

Penn was hurt by Stone's behavior, but she was freaked out about him getting killed. She'd kept her mouth shut about him before to keep him safe, so I wouldn't put it past her to do it again.

"Keep an eye on him, that's all we can do. I'll ask her when she wakes up if he bothered her when she went inside. Any news about Drake's car? Footage? Anything?"

"Nope," Knox grumbled. "Stone couldn't find shit because there's fuck all security around Lightning Cove. He's looking into it more, though."

"He probably fucking did it," Drake muttered, his eyes closed as he rested his cheek against Knox's chest. "I suggested it at the beach, and Penn flipped out at me."

"She's got to stop protecting him," I sighed, checking my phone in hopes of a message from Stone with answers, but the screen was blank.

"I think she really does have a trauma bond with him or something like Beckett says. She claims to hate him, but when push comes to shove, she panics and takes his side," Knox stated in a low voice, his eyes on the empty hallway as if to make sure Penn didn't sneak out and hear him.

"We're the ones who took her. Stone avoided her for most of it," I pointed out.

"He fucked with her the most, though, and kept letting her in just to stomp on her again. It's like they were in a weird trust cycle, and now she can't get out of it."

"Harley mentioned letting her help out from time to time at the bar to keep her busy. He's really impressed with her," I said, changing the subject, and Knox sighed.

"I don't like that idea."

"She's safe there, and it's giving her a purpose. I think it's a good idea," I said calmly, knowing he wasn't going to be on board.

"I say we keep training her and bring her into our thing," he answered, a snort leaving me.

"What thing? We don't have a thing."

"Sure we do. I think Stone's idea of us splitting the thieves like a franchise is a good one. He gets to feel like he's the fancy CEO, I get to shoot at people, and you get to keep playing with computers. Drake's happy as long as we're all happy too, but you have to admit, he likes being a thief, and he's damn good at it when he's focused."

"And you think Penn should be a thief? What changed

your mind?" I chuckled, giving him a teasing grin. "You hated the idea before."

"That's because I didn't trust her. I do now, and she's a fast learner. She can go on smaller jobs with us until she finds her footing."

"And what if she doesn't want to be a thief and prefers working at Harley's?"

"Then we burn the bar down, simple," he said seriously, but he smiled after a moment, giving it away that he was joking. "If she really wants to work there, we'll talk about it, but I don't like her out of our sight."

"Take a page out of Stone's book and stalk her," Drake mumbled, sounding like he was about to fall asleep. "I swear he spies through the computer every fucking night."

He wasn't wrong. The light had been on most nights to say he was watching us.

I stood, walking towards it and yanking the cord from the wall, turning with a satisfied smile. "Problem solved. Next issue? I'm on a roll now."

Knox snickered, but his eyes closed, apparently tired from today's ordeal, too. Drake mumbled a response, but I didn't hear what it was, his breathing slowing as he fell asleep, and I put my hands on my hips in disbelief as Knox started snoring softly a moment later.

"Unfuckingbelievable," I huffed with amusement, moving in front of them and getting zero reaction. "Seriously? We were having an important conversation."

I glanced towards the hallway when I heard a noise, realizing it was Penn when I heard it a second time. It had been a few days since she'd had any nightmares, but after the day's events, I wasn't surprised it had brought one out of her.

My feet were silent as I padded along the hallway to her bedroom, peeking inside to find her curled up in a tight ball, panicked whimpers leaving her as she breathed rapidly. I closed the door, not wanting to wake the others up, then I slid into bed beside her, and pulled her back flush with my chest to wrap myself around her.

"Penn, baby? Wake up. You're having a nightmare."

Her body tensed tighter, but after a second she relaxed against me, her whispered voice reaching me. "Cruz?"

"I've got you," I murmured, placing a kiss on her neck. "Go back to sleep."

"Where's the others?"

"Napping. They fell asleep on the couch. I'll stay in here with you," I promised, relieved when she dozed off again without a fuss. She needed the rest.

My eyes drooped after a few minutes of lying in silence, so I wasn't surprised when I eventually drifted off to sleep, too.

Chapter Sixteen

Penn

"Why the fuck didn't anyone call me?" Zavier bit out as he stomped into the kitchen the next day, moving towards me with concern and ignoring the guys as he took my face in his hands and started inspecting me. "You're alright? Beckett just told me someone tried to blow you up yesterday."

"Calm down, big bro, I'm okay," I teased, but I was grateful for his worry. He reminded me of Emily sometimes with how protective he was. She'd like him, and she'd be so grateful for everything he'd done for me.

"Beckett said you have no idea who's after you, but you're assuming it's connected to the shooting?" he questioned, sitting in the chair beside me at the dining table. My phone buzzed in my pocket but I ignored it, knowing it was Stone. He'd been texting me like a psycho all morning, not that I really minded. He'd been hunting through hours of footage from Stoneleigh and Kingslake, trying to help find whoever had tried to kill me yesterday.

So far, it was all a dead end.

Cruz scowled at Zavier for sitting beside me, but he gave him a run down on the entire day we'd had and what we already knew, which was fuck all. Drake placed a plate in front of me with a massive omelet that was packed with tomato and other random healthy shit, my mouth watering as I started digging in, and I hadn't been paying attention to the conversation until I heard Stone's name mentioned.

"They're going to kill him, man. He seriously fucked up," Zavier said, my head snapping up to stare at him.

"What?"

Cruz gave him a dirty look, but Zavier sighed, leaning on the table. "Stone. Psychos voted, and he's fucked." Nausea rolled through me at the thought, and I itched to call Stone to warn him. Did he know? Would they surprise him and drag it out? "Penn?" Zavier frowned, but I pushed back from the table and ran to the bathroom, fumbling with the lock before leaning over the toilet and throwing up my breakfast. I vaguely heard knocking on the door, but my ears were ringing, everything sounding so far away.

I couldn't let him die.

"Baby? Open the door," Drake said softly, but I ignored him and pulled my phone from my pocket, dropping it twice as I clicked on the messages from Stone. It was all updates on his lack of finding anything, so I quickly typed out a message, needing to know if he was okay or not.

Penn: Are you okay?

Drake knocked on the door and said my name again, but I blocked it out as I waited for Stone to reply, the minutes dragging until my phone buzzed.

Stone: Yes. Why?

Penn: You need to go, Stone. Trust me. Please.

He didn't reply straight away, my heart sinking when he did.

Stone: They'd better not do it in front of you or I'll come back and gut them all in their sleep.

Penn: That's not fucking funny.

Stone: It wasn't supposed to be.

"Move, I'm kicking it in," Knox growled from outside the door, and I quickly put my phone in my pocket and flushed before swinging the door open. I walked past them without a word, finding Zavier in the kitchen sporting a freshly split lip.

"I'm sorry," he cringed, and I dodged Cruz as he reached for me.

"Who hit him?" I bit out, motioning to Zavier. "You claim you don't keep shit from me, so why can't Zavier be honest with me? I have a right to know."

Cruz eyed me silently for a moment before replying. "You don't need to know that shit."

"Like fuck."

"Penn, he dug his own hole, now he—"

"He's sorry!" I snapped, jabbing a finger against his chest. "Why isn't that enough?"

"Knox," Cruz warned, two seconds before I was yanked back from Cruz, and my back was shoved against the wall. Knox looked furious, putting his face in mine.

"Sorry doesn't fucking fix it, Whitlock. This has nothing to do with you, and everything to do with the fact he fucked over two of the crews. It's because he sent you in *there* that he's getting his ass handed to him, not because he put you at risk. I don't care how many times he says sorry, it won't change anything."

"Get off me!" I shouted, but he held firm, his expression

softening the smallest amount.

"You really think things will just go back to how they used to be? Babe, he's only feeling guilty now because he lost us, not because he's actually feeling bad about what happened to you. Stone doesn't let people in, he didn't even let us in one-hundred-percent, but we were his family. That's why he's sorry."

"Get off me, Knox!" I repeated a little more hysterically, shoving at his chest when he didn't move.

"Jesus Christ, move, asshole," Drake huffed, grabbing Knox's wrist and tugging him back a step. "Let her fucking breathe." I slid down the wall and tried to catch my breath, jerking when a hand touched my arm, and I found Drake kneeling in front of me. "Hey, breathe, baby. You want them to go away?"

I nodded, thankful when everyone seemed to leave the room, and I relaxed a little once I didn't have everyone's eyes on me. My head was a mess, I shouldn't care about Stone's fate, but he needed someone on his side.

Drake stayed in front of me, but he didn't try to touch me, waiting me out until I reached for him.

"Did Stone bother you yesterday when you went into the compound? Knox said Stone snuck off for a while, and he didn't think anything of it because he thought you were with me," he asked gently, and I shook my head.

"He didn't bother me." Not exactly a lie, but I still hoped that Stone had wiped any footage of our interaction.

"Okay, just wanted to check."

He got comfortable beside me, dropping an arm around my shoulders to keep me close, and we sat in silence for ages until Cruz joined us. He squatted in front of us, giving me a small smile. "Hey, will you be okay with Drake for a few hours? Hunter's called me to help with a faulty camera, and with everyone getting shot at lately, we want to go out in pairs at the minimum so no one's alone. Lopez is having a shower then heading out to see if he can find any information about the explosion."

I nodded, grabbing his wrist when he tried to stand and leave, not wanting him to think I was mad at any of them. They could be distracted then and get hurt. "I love you."

"I love you too, baby. We'll be fine," he said, knowing my concern as he dropped a kiss to my head, turning to Drake. "Stay in the house. If someone's hanging around, call us. Don't deal with it alone."

"Sure thing," he replied, bumping knuckles with him before watching him leave, nudging my shoulder gently. "You want to watch a movie with me?"

"Okay," I nodded, letting him help me to my feet before leading me into the living room to find it empty. Drake picked a movie, but I wasn't really paying attention to it.

"Hey," Zavier murmured as he walked in half an hour later, giving me a look of apology. "You okay? I'm not very sensitive with my words. I'm used to girls like Beckett and Riley around me, and Raven doesn't really give a shit about anyone outside of our circle, so I didn't even think—"

"I'm okay. I'm glad you told me," I replied quietly, a smile spreading across his face.

"I'll call you if I find out anything about who's after you. Be careful, okay?"

"You too," I said firmly, noticing Drake was sleeping beside me. After everyone's napping yesterday, we'd all thrown our sleep schedules out, and despite it being early, we'd all been awake for hours.

The moment Zavier left, I pulled my phone out to find another text from Stone.

Stone: Are you worried about me, Princess?

Penn: Believe it or not, but I don't wish death upon you.

Stone: What are you doing right now? Someone unplugged the computer so I can't spy on you.

I glanced at the computer, noticing the plug on the floor.

Penn: Watching a movie. Drake's asleep and everyone else went out. What are you doing?

It felt weird texting with him, but my leg bounced anxiously as I awaited a reply. Every time he went quiet, I panicked that he was bleeding out or something.

Stone: Watching the security outside your house.

Penn: Why?

Stone: To make sure you're safe.

Butterflies fluttered in my stomach, and a moment later a photo came through of his desk, multiple screens all showing different angles of the house.

Stone: I meant what I said. I've got your back.

Penn: Is it stupid that I almost believe you?

Stone: I think it's good that you can trust after you've been burned. Means you're not as fucked up as you think you are.

I considered putting my phone away, but I wanted to take advantage of him talking to me.

Penn: Tell me a secret.

I wasn't expecting his answer.

Stone: I came in my fucking hand three times over you in the last twenty-four hours.

I stared at the message, not knowing how to reply. Was he teasing me? He had to be.

Penn: Doubtful.

Stone: Why would I lie? Your turn. Tell me a secret.

My brow creased as I read the message a second time. I didn't really have any secrets, they knew everything about me.

Penn: I like that you watch me.

Stone: Noted.

Drake shifted, and I slipped my phone into my pocket quickly, and I tried to tell myself I was doing nothing wrong, but it was hard.

He sat up and blinked at me, giving me a dopey smile. "Hey, was I out long?"

"Not really."

"Good. Sorry." He scrubbed a hand over his face. "I'm not made for sitting around the house, it puts me to sleep."

"We could go out. Surely someone would come and get us," I stated, an idea popping into my head. "Maybe we could go to the gym?"

"I suppose. Let me wake up a little first," he grunted and pulled his phone out. "I'll check with the guys. One of their cars would be here, so we can just take that."

I walked off to get changed, not surprised when I returned to find a sour look on Drake's face.

"We need an escort. Jai and Will are coming to get us, and they'll hang around the gym until you're finished. I did request that they bring Leah and Sandra. We'll go in one car, and another will follow."

"Just be glad we're allowed," I huffed, finding my shoes while we waited for backup to arrive.

Drake

I let Penn and the girls workout together while I hung out with the guys, wanting to give her some space. I knew she'd eventually flip out at us for smothering her, and I could tell she was agitated by the constant security.

"How have you guys been? It's been a while," Will asked as he leaned against the wall, his eyes firmly on Sandra.

"Would be better if we could leave the house without someone attempting to murder any of us, but apart from that, things are good. Is Stone still being a drill sergeant?"

Penn's laughter rang out from across the room, and I smiled as she bantered with Leah about something. Having friends was important to her, so I was glad she had some girlfriends to hang out with.

Jai snorted, drawing my attention. "Stone's acting weird. Pretty sure he's got a secret girlfriend or something."

"We're talking about the same Stone, right?" I asked dryly, and Will grinned.

"Yeah, he keeps smiling at his phone, and it's freaking me out. At least he's not yelling so much anymore. He's been setting up jobs in the office and stating how many people need to go, then usually leaves us all to figure it out. We've been making bank lately without any stress."

"I don't think he knows any girls. None that would tolerate his bullshit anyway," I replied, narrowing my eyes on Owen as he walked over to the girls to help Penn adjust the weights. "Hey! Don't add more, she's not recovered enough yet!"

Penn huffed, her voice whiney. "The light stuff isn't doing shit."

"Did you think you'd be toned in a week or something? This is going to be months of slowly building strength, babe. If you go too hard too fast, you'll only get hurt and fuck up your progress," I warned, Owen giving me a strange look.

"She can handle this, it's not much."

"Just because she can, doesn't mean she should."

He muttered under his breath but didn't argue with me, and Jai let out a low whistle. "Who's that guy? He's got balls."

"Owen. Penn's known him for years. She used to sneak out of Kingslake and come here to train with him. As you can imagine, it's really hard to be nice to him when he's such an idiot," I replied quietly. "We've run checks on him and nothing flagged as a problem, much to our annoyance."

"He's got a major hard-on for her by the looks," Will commented as we all watched him interacting with her, and I didn't let him know they had history. It wasn't their business.

"So, you have no idea who Stone's been talking to?" I asked, changing the subject. "No one's been hanging around? For all you know, it's Leah."

Jai glared at me. "It's not."

"How do you know? You two aren't exclusive."

"C'mon, man. Leah can't stand him half the time," he pointed out, making me grimace.

"Yeah, and Knox hated Penn for a while, but he still found time to fuck her."

"I hate you," Jai grunted, his gaze going back to Leah as

she ran on the treadmill, Sandra on the machine beside her as they talked amongst themselves.

For the next hour, I had to tolerate Owen gluing himself to my girl. I didn't like it, but I trusted her, and it wasn't like he could try anything with me watching them. Causing a scene would only make her mad at me.

"I'll just shower, and then we can go," Penn panted as she walked up to me, sweat coating her skin and a flush on her cheeks.

"Nope, do that at home," I answered, tugging her against me. Public bathrooms weren't safe. I couldn't go in there with her without making other women uncomfortable, and I didn't have any of our scanning devices on hand to make sure there weren't any hidden cameras.

"Are you serious?" she scowled, but Will nodded, giving Sandra a look.

"You too."

She rolled her eyes but didn't argue, knowing we were right. The girls had been with the Thieves for a long time now, so they knew the dangers that others were oblivious to.

"You just want to fuck in the shower," Penn deadpanned, a smirk taking over my face.

"Aw, how'd you know, baby?"

Her lips twitched but she fought the smile, trying to act mad. "You're a pig."

"I know." I gave her a kiss, trying not to get annoyed when Owen joined us, obviously overhearing our conversation.

"The girls are perfectly safe here in the bathroom."

"They can do it at home," I answered, tucking Penn against me while holding his gaze. "But thanks."

His brow creased in confusion but he nodded. "Okay, sure. I guess I'll see you guys next time then." He turned to Penn, his confusion being replaced by a smile. "I'll text you later."

"Thanks for helping me," she said warmly, sensing my shifting mood from his friendliness, and started to tug me towards the door.

Jai and Leah seemed to be in a heated discussion by the time we got back to the cars, so I volunteered to go in Will and Sandra's car with Penn to give them some privacy.

"What are they fighting about?" Penn asked softly as we slid into the backseat, making Sandra sigh.

"Leah thinks he's getting too clingy. It doesn't feel too casual right now."

"I don't understand what the problem is though. Why wouldn't she like that?" Penn asked, glancing at me with a frown. "I love it when you guys are clingy."

That made me chuckle. "No, you love it when we smother you. You hate it when we're clingy because you feel cornered."

"Yeah, but I'm traumatized. Why doesn't Leah want clingy, though?"

"All the thieves came from messy home situations. Leah's no different, and neither is Jai. You'll have to ask her if you want answers because even if I knew, I wouldn't tell you, no offense," I smiled, grabbing my phone to check it, surprised to find one from Knox.

Knox: Take Penn home then come to Harley's.

Drake: Why?

Knox: Psychos and Devils are dealing with Stone. Cruz needs you, man, but he doesn't want Penn to know just yet.

I swallowed, glancing at Penn who was looking out the window. She'd be hurt, but we couldn't risk her trying to get involved, which she would. I'd been with Stone and the guys for years now, and knowing he wasn't going to be breathing by the end of the day tore something inside my chest. He'd fucked us all over, but he was family.

Drake: Okay. Tell him I'll be there soon.

"I need to go and help the guys with something. Will you be okay at home by yourself for a few hours?" I asked once my phone was in my pocket, her eyes finding mine as she smiled. It looked forced, telling me she didn't want to, but she wasn't going to tell me no.

"Is everything okay? Cruz and Knox?"

"They're fine, they just need another set of eyes and asked me to tag along."

"I'm a big girl, I don't need a babysitter," she teased, her attention going back out the window.

"You cool to drop me off in Ashburn Valley?" I asked Will, knowing it wasn't going to be a problem before he even answered.

"Sure thing. Do you need more backup?" he offered, but I shook my head.

"Nah, it's nothing serious. Thanks, though."

I almost blurted everything out when we arrived at the house, and Penn tried to bail from the car without even speaking to me. I grabbed her wrist, stopping her escape. "Hey, I'm sorry. I promise I'll be back soon. Don't be mad at me," I murmured, and she rolled her eyes.

"I'm not mad at you. I was just hoping you'd hurry before the guys run into trouble. All three of you better get back to me safely," she replied tightly, and I realized she was worried about us getting hurt.

"I promise." I gave her a quick kiss before letting her slide from the car and shut the door, a sigh leaving me as she practically ran into the house without a backwards glance.

Yeah, she was pissed about being made to stay home.

Chapter Seventeen

Penn

My heart slammed in my chest as I got inside and yanked my phone from my pocket, panic clawing at my insides as I called Stone. I knew the guys had been trying to look out for me, but I couldn't believe they were just going to allow Stone to die. I'd glanced down at Drake's phone for a second without even really meaning to, the words hitting me like a punch to the guts.

"I'm starting to think you like me," Stone drawled as he answered, but he turned serious when a sob left me. "Penn? What the fuck happened?"

"You have to run. They're coming for you, I saw messages," I choked out, almost tripping as I made my way into my room to get changed into some sweats and a hoodie. I felt gross in the gym gear and really needed a shower, but a change of clothes would have to do the job for now.

"You need to stay out of this before you get yourself hurt," he warned, but his voice was strained with a hint of fear. "How did you find out?"

"Drake just lied to my face. Knox messaged him and said the Psychos are dealing with you. They're not even fighting for you!" I snapped as frustration washed through me. "How could they just—"

"Because I deserve it, that's why," he cut in. "Running won't fix anything. They'll only track me down later, even if it takes ten years."

"But—"

"I appreciate you calling, but leave it be, Penelope," he whispered, hanging up without another word. If no one was going to save him, then I had to.

I wiped my eyes as I quickly moved back through the house, praying no one was watching the cameras as I left the house and started running, my legs already tired from the gym. After five minutes, a car pulled over and wound down the window, the woman seeming worried as she assessed me. She appeared to be close to my age but her eyes showed how exhausted she was.

"Are you okay?"

"I need a ride to Rawson," I blurted out. "Please, my friend's in trouble."

"Jump in," she nodded, pointing to the passenger seat. I thanked her as I did as I was told, buckling myself in as she took off towards Rawson Grove, thankfully not asking anymore questions and being more than happy to drive in silence.

My leg bounced nervously the closer we got to the compound, worry starting to seep in at the thought of what I might be about to walk in on. Were the crews already there? Was Stone still okay? Was I too late?

"Are you in danger?" the woman finally asked, snapping me out of the thoughts in my head. "Are you running from someone? I'm heading to Mount Mercer if you need somewhere to hide. I just bought a little house up there, so you're welcome to stay with me."

It took me by surprise, genuine kindness was hard to come by, especially from strangers.

"Not today," I tried to joke, but it fell flat. "But thank you for the offer, uh?" I had no idea what her name was.

"Maeve. You can call me Mae, though," she smiled softly as she tucked her auburn hair behind her ear.

"I'm Penn," I replied, pointing to the familiar street up ahead. "Can you drop me off there?"

"Of course." She pulled over, giving me another smile. "It was nice to meet you. I hope your friend's okay."

"Me too, thank you!" I exclaimed as I bailed from the car and took off towards the street, my feet pounding the pavement as I headed towards the gate to the compound. It was locked, and I let out a sound of frustration as I considered climbing it but not knowing if they had some kind of electricity security to help keep people out.

My phone rang and I pulled it out to see Stone's name, and I answered immediately.

"What the fuck did I tell you, Penelope? Get the fuck out of here!" Stone barked, but I ignored him.

"Let me in!"

"Go home!"

"Let me the fuck in Stone, I mean it!" I shouted, reaching for the gate but he let out a growl.

"Stop, you'll hurt yourself. Hang on." The gate beeped and opened for me, and I forgot all about Stone on the phone as I started running towards the compound, the front door opening before I reached it. Stone looked pissed as I tore inside, grabbing his arm tightly.

"We need to get you out of here. Shit, someone needs to check the cameras to see if they're on the way yet. They—"

"Stop," he ordered calmly, taking my face in his hands when I kept babbling. "Penelope, I said stop."

Tears streamed down my face, and he wiped them away with his thumb gently, my voice cracking as I spoke. "Why couldn't they just beat you up or something? People don't need to play God and kill others who wronged them. I was the one in their house, not you. Why aren't they coming after me?"

"You didn't know, that's why. Stop blaming yourself for the sins of others," he said quietly, locking the door before steering me towards the office, shutting us inside. I hadn't seen anyone else around, so a lot had either left, or were in their own rooms.

"That doesn't matter. It should be me getting punished," I argued, but I stumbled as he scruffed the front of my hoodie, dragging me into him with a growl.

"I don't want you here. It won't change anything, the only difference is that you'll leave here fucking traumatized. I'll still be leaving in a body bag. I deserve it after what I did to you, so stop trying to save me. You can't."

"You don't deserve it!"

"Yes, I fucking do!" he snarled, getting in my face. "I wanted nothing more than your forgiveness, but this is bullshit. I haven't earned it, and I had so much more planned before getting anywhere close to deserving it! Don't be a pushover, Penelope!"

An alarm sounded to let us know there was an intruder on the property, and concern filled his eyes as he released his hold on me. "Go out to them. They won't hurt you, but you can't be in here when they do it."

"No. If they want to kill you, then they can do it in front of me. I'm not fucking leaving you to die scared and alone," I threw back, fear flickering inside me as a loud bang echoed through the compound. They were definitely inside now.

I tried to force my tears away as I backed up towards Stone, the door flying open to reveal Hunter who instantly cursed at the sight of me. "Jesus Christ. What are you doing here?"

"You can't kill him," I bit out, refusing to look away as they started filtering into the room. Inside, I was terrified, but I wasn't about to run and leave Stone on his own. This entire thing had gotten out of hand all over a stupid break-in, and it needed to stop.

Stone tried to move around me but I moved with him, making him snap. "Get her out of here. She doesn't need to see this. Don't do it in front of her, please. I've given her enough fucking trauma."

Skeeter rolled his eyes and lifted his gun, aiming it at Stone without hesitation, but I tried to make myself as big and tall as possible, covering every inch of Stone that I possibly could.

"I can shoot through you if you wish, Whitlock," Skeeter warned, but Rory stepped beside him and scolded him to put it down. He ignored her though, walking towards me with a blank look on his face, placing the barrel of his gun against my forehead. "Move, or I shoot."

This was ten times more scary than when Maddox had done it, but I tried hard to remember what he and Beckett had told me, keeping my breathing even and forcing my body not to shake from the fear. I held his gaze, knowing I was doing well to contain my terror when a small flicker of surprise flashed across his face.

"Don't fucking touch him," I said firmly, feeling Stone's hand rest on my waist.

"Penelope, I swear to God," he murmured, but there was no anger in his tone. I tensed when more people joined us, not surprised to find Beckett and Maddox present, but it was a surprise when Cruz, Knox, and Drake stepped into the room looking ready for a fight. I thought they were here about me, but they all seemed confused to see me.

"What the fuck are you doing here?" Knox bit out, glaring at Drake. "You said you didn't tell her!"

"I didn't!" Drake insisted, appearing hurt when he looked at me. "How did you even get here? You—"

"Someone had to come and help Stone. It should've been you," I hissed, Cruz stepping closer with his eyes on Skeeter.

"You'd better lower that from my girl's head."

"Or what, Lennox? You going to shoot me?" Skeeter sneered, but he was already lowering his hand. "Control your fucking girl, and this shit wouldn't happen."

"Says the one dating a psychopath," Cruz deadpanned, walking towards me. I jerked back into Stone further, but confusion took over when he stood beside me and crossed his arms, staring down the roomful of gang members. "We're not here for Penn, we thought she was safely at home. We're here to stop you from killing Stone."

"This is ridiculous," Skeeter spat, but Rory made her way towards us, holding my gaze.

"You'd seriously die over this asshole? Do you remember what he did to you?"

"I did that to myself," I answered sharply, and she raised an eyebrow for me to continue. "It's not a secret that I lack the ability to know when someone's bullshitting me in some situations. I should've known to question Stone the day I broke into your house, but I blindly trusted him because I thought he'd accepted me. If someone tried to kill one of your guys, wouldn't you die for them too? Even if they were the one in the wrong?"

"Penn—" Cruz started, but Rory glared at him.

"Shut it. Penn is quite capable of talking for herself. Don't interrupt her."

Nerves kicked in as she gave me a nod, and Stone's fingers brushed my back gently, giving me the strength I needed to keep going.

"Stone's an asshole, he fucked me over, and he fucked you over, but can't you meet in the middle with a punishment? Why does death have to be the answer? Punish him so he can learn from this. If a lonely little rich girl wandered into your family's lives and started interfering with shit, wouldn't you try to make her disappear out of fear? What if he'd been right, and I was just having some fun with a bunch of bad boys, then got scared and ran home to my father? I knew enough to tear the organization apart. He wasn't trying to fuck you over that day he told me to break into your house, he was only thinking of a way to make me vanish from his life," I explained, her eyes narrowing.

"You think he should live after handing you over to your father?"

"I think he deserves a second chance. Everyone does," I confirmed, ignoring the dirty look Knox threw at me as he and Drake moved to stand beside me, too, showing their support even if they didn't like it. "Beat him up or put him to work, but please, don't kill him. I love when you take down bad guys who rape and abuse women and children, that kind of crime deserves death because there's no coming back from it, but Stone just made a mistake."

"You're a smart girl, Penn, but I really don't understand what you see in him," she replied, flicking her sharp gaze to Stone who'd been silently waiting for the verdict. "You'd better roll out the red carpet for that girl and kiss her feet, she just saved your life." Skeeter threw his hands in the air and stalked off with annoyance, but everyone else stayed put. My shoulders relaxed as fatigue took over, but I stood straight when she added, "You're not escaping punishment, though."

"What will you do to him?" I asked softly, but she was done being nice to me, her eyes not leaving Stone.

"None of your concern. You've done your community service for the week by keeping him alive. Count your blessings and get out of here. He'll probably wish he was dead by the time we're done, though."

I turned to face Stone with worry, but he gave me a nod. "Go. They'll keep their word. I don't want you here when they do it."

"But—"

"I need you to go," he said firmly, cutting me off and reaching out to take my hand, giving it a squeeze. "I'll be fine." Drake tugged me back from him as Cruz warned him not to touch me, but Stone didn't give a shit. His eyes remained on me, the ghost of a smile tugging at his lips. "Thanks, Penn."

I nodded, letting the guys drag me from the office, and I just knew I was going to be getting the talking-to of the century when we got home.

Stone

I stared at Penelope as the guys took her from the room, a weird feeling bubbling in my chest. She'd stood in front of a gun to keep me safe, even though I'd done nothing but hurt her.

"Do you believe her yet?" Beckett asked as she moved to stand beside me, and I was under no illusion that she was a friend right now. She was simply filling in time until Penn was out of the compound so they could hurt me without her within earshot.

"I don't know how to begin making it up to her," I answered, turning my attention to her. "I don't think she'd appreciate a severed head from her enemy like you would."

She smirked, tilting her head to the side. "I don't know. Where does she stand on murdering her father? Maybe she'd appreciate that one."

"I don't think she'd be upset if someone killed him, but I

don't think she'd like it to be done by the hands of someone she knows," I replied dryly, taking my phone from my pocket and placing it on the desk. I didn't want it broken when they beat me up. I wasn't born yesterday, so I knew Rory's warning about me wishing I was dead by the time they were finished punishing me would be accurate. I could take a beating, but this wasn't going to be a few punches and kicks, this was really going to suck.

"Girl's like Penn just want your time and attention. If you really want her in your life, that's all you've got to do," Beckett said in a low voice, nudging my shoulder. "And good dick, but you two have had so much tension and frustration built up, you probably have nothing to worry about."

"I don't want—"

"Don't fucking lie to me, asshole. You've got a major hard-on for that girl these days. It's okay to want her, but you really have to prove yourself. She's growing on me a little, so fuck her over one more time and you're dead." Hearing that was almost amusing coming from her, but I nodded.

"She's grown balls. I think you'd have to wait your turn if I fucked with her again."

"Bet you came in your pants when she stood up to Skeet and Mom like that, huh?" she chuckled, patting me on the back.

"I thought they were going to kill her, my dick was flaccid as fuck," I grunted, bracing myself as Hunter wandered over with a grim look on his face.

"You're about to be out of action for a few weeks, I hope you know that."

"I know."

"I really don't see why she thinks you're worth saving."

"Me either," I mumbled, taking a deep breath. "Let's get this over with."

Didn't have to tell Beckett twice.

Cruz

It was hard not to explode at Penn. None of us talked the entire ride home, and Knox stomped out to the backyard to avoid strangling her the moment we arrived.

"You could've died today," I said as calmly as possible, but she still flinched at the anger lacing my tone.

"You might say this is all Stone's fault, but his death would be on my conscience for the rest of my life. I can't live like that, Cruz. Yes, Stone fucked up majorly, but that doesn't mean—"

"I know, baby," I sighed, pulling her against my chest and wrapping my arms around her, kissing the top of her head. "That's why we went there to try to talk the crews out of it."

"You should've had his back from the start," she whispered, peering up at me. "Whether he was wrong or not. He's your family."

"I'm not going to argue with you right now, but I can't forgive him for hurting you."

"I know," she answered, tightening her hold on me. "Did you see how badass I was, though?"

"Pretty sure Knox is outside abusing his dick over it, yes," I chuckled dryly, glancing over at Drake who was eyeing her with uncertainty. He'd been so sure she was going to sit at home on her own, but she'd lied right to his face. In her defense, he'd lied to her, too.

I gave him a pointed look, and he managed to relax his features a little, then he took a breath to calm himself before stepping closer to sandwich her between us.

"You scared my dick off, babe. You're lucky Skeet didn't kill you. He doesn't tend to give a shit about our business arrangement, let alone your relationship to us," he murmured against her neck. She turned to face him and I stepped back, giving her hand a small squeeze.

"I'm going to check on Knox."

She nodded, tugging Drake down onto the couch to snuggle while they talked, and I wandered out the back door in search of Knox, not surprised to find him sitting on the porch with a cigarette between his lips.

"Where the fuck did you get that?" I grunted, dropping down beside him.

"I always keep some on me for emergencies." He took a long drag before silently offering it to me, but I shook my head.

"I know I won't stop if I have any."

"Suit yourself," he shrugged, popping it between his lips again and looking out across the yard. "I'm so fucking pissed with her, man."

"Me too. Fighting with her won't change anything, though, it will only make her resent us. Tell her you're upset, you're allowed to be, but don't blow up like I know you want to. Just admit she scared you, and that's why you're mad," I suggested. "Look, I think we need to—" Smashing glass stopped me mid-sentence, a panicked scream coming from Penn inside just before the sound of gunfire hit us. We were on our feet in seconds as we ran inside, finding Penn on the floor by the couch with Drake covering her. All the windows were shattered, bullet holes through the door and the walls. Car tires screeched outside as the shooter sped off, and I instantly moved towards the couch, kneeling beside Penn and Drake.

"Were you hit?" I couldn't see any blood, but a few bullets definitely went through the couch.

"I'm okay," Penn said in a shaky voice as Drake moved back to help her into a sitting position, her eyes raking over us for damage. "We can check the cameras, right? We can get their license plate information off it and—"

"Little hint about the criminal world, they're not afraid to remove the license plate," Knox muttered, helping Drake to his feet since I had Penn. Drake scrunched his nose up as he got a whiff of Knox's cigarette-scented shirt, but he didn't say anything.

"You might recognize the car or something, though, right?" she insisted, and she had a point.

"First, let me call Lopez and break the news to him that his and Lavaro's safehouse just got hit in a drive-by," I sighed, pulling my phone from my pocket. It rang before I'd even unlocked it, Zavier's name popping up on the screen. It could've been a coincidence, but I knew it was likely that he'd seen it on the cameras. "We're fine," I said the second I answered, a rush of air leaving him straight away.

"Thank fuck. Did you recognize the car?"

"We haven't seen the footage yet. Knox and I were in the backyard and Drake was on the couch with Penn. The house is kinda trashed, dude."

"I don't give a fuck as long as you guys are alright," he replied, the sound of a car door slamming in the background. "I'm on the way over. I can't get hold of Beckett, or I'd get her to come too."

Penn grimaced as she must have heard what he said, knowing the reason behind Beckett's silence before I even spoke. "Beckett's with the Psychos and Devils at the compound. Stone's being dealt with."

"Shit, I'm sorry. Does Penn know?" he asked quietly, making me snort.

"Penelope is aware. She convinced them to beat him up instead of killing him."

"How the fuck did she manage that? Beckett said they were pretty set on killing him."

"She got there before they did and got between Stone and

Skeeter's gun," I answered flatly. "We arrived to find them having a standoff."

"Your girl's a baddie. I hope Stone appreciated it, or I'll kill him myself," he said brightly, and I could hear the grin in his voice.

"It was *reckless*."

"She's fine, right? Pat her on the back and move on. I'll see you soon." He hung up before I could growl at him about being an asshole, and I knew Penn had heard what he said by the way she was trying not to smirk.

"Don't try to be cute. I'm going to spank you later for doing something stupid," I scolded, her smirk widening.

"Please?"

"Go pack your shit. We can't stay here now. I'll check in with Beckett later to see if they have somewhere we can stay," I sighed, rubbing my temples. She wandered towards the bedroom but she glanced back at me with a thoughtful look.

"Why don't you ask Stone if—"

"No," I bit out, and she rolled her eyes as if I was being crazy. I turned to Drake, finding Knox lifting his shirt to check him over for injury. "You sure you're okay?"

"Yeah. I think we need to worry about her, though," he answered, letting Knox literally strip him to his boxers, knowing he'd worry unless he saw proof that there were no bullet wounds.

"Why do you say that? Is she hurt?" I demanded, intending on chasing after her, but Drake shook his head.

"No, but I don't like how protective of Stone she's being. She always seems to know what's happening with him despite not seeing him. Isn't that a little strange?"

Knox was finally satisfied that Drake wasn't shot, so he handed his clothes back and joined the conversation. "You think he's blackmailing her or something?"

"Or something," he confirmed, pulling his shirt over his

head. "Finding shit out is kind of our thing, so keep your eyes open."

"You want us to spy on her?" I hissed quickly, and he quickly shook his head.

"No, don't go through her stuff, just take notice of little things like when she's out and she goes to the toilet for too long or something. Maybe he's meeting up with her and threatening her, maybe he's even paying her to protect him. He knows she's a good shield because no one will hurt her."

"That won't work for everyone. Skeeter would've had no problem shooting her to get to him today," I muttered, but Knox shrugged.

"I don't think he would've. Penn might have pissed him off by breaking into his house, but she's innocent in all of this. He spends a lot of time saving women and children from danger, and as much as he'll attempt to scare her into doing as she's told, I don't think he'd actually hurt her."

"We'll figure this shit out later. Right now, we need to get all of our things together and find somewhere to stay. Preferably off the grid," I sighed, glancing around the room at the mess. "The fuck did they use? A machine gun?"

"I didn't poke my head out the door to ask them, my bad," Drake deadpanned, scowling as Knox swatted the back of his head. "And don't think I can't smell cigarette smoke on you, asshole."

"I'm not hiding it," he replied, walking towards the bedroom. "You guys can handle Lopez when he arrives, I'll handle Penn."

Zavier would barge in and go straight for Penn anyway, so it wasn't like we needed to deal with him.

Chapter Eighteen

Penn

Zavier fussed over me for ages, trying to convince us to all stay with him at Raven's house, but it was already too crowded there and we didn't want to risk his friends. Whoever was coming for me would track me down way too easily there.

Zavier had finally gotten hold of Beckett, but she said they didn't have any vacant houses right now. Most of theirs were currently occupied with abused teens or foster kids who'd turned of age and wanted their own space.

"I know where we can go," I said as I tried to wrack my brain for the address. "Seventy-seven Sale Street."

"In Briar Falls?" Cruz asked with a frown.

"Yeah. It's Estelle's house. She wouldn't turn me away," I confirmed, not wanting to take drama there, but knowing she wasn't connected to us to leave much of a trail.

"What if this is your Dad's doing? Can you trust her?"

"With my life," I nodded, motioning to Zavier. "If it was Dad, surely he'd be gunning down Zavier and Ander."

"I think it's a good plan," Zavier nodded.

"What about this mess?" Cruz asked, but Zavier shrugged.

"Ander and I can't keep people here, too many people

know about it now, so it's not safe anymore. We'll fix it and get rid of it. He has other safehouses anyway."

Guilt hit me, and I cringed a little. "Sorry."

"Don't be, this shit happens sometimes. We can't always keep the girls we help hidden. I'm considering pulling back and letting Lavaro work with Beckett or something. They have better connections and money between them. I need to focus on keeping my family safe, and I can't do that when I'm getting involved with this sort of thing. I saw how fucked up things got when Raven found out about Reid and Logan illegally street racing with Lavaro and Riley, and I don't want to be next," he said with a shiver. "Not to mention she could get hurt with what I'm involved in."

"That's a good idea. Stay away from me until this all dies out," I smiled, but he just laughed.

"You're different. You're my little sister, remember? You can never escape me now."

"You're being weird," Cruz muttered, but my heart melted a little. I loved the guys, they were it for me, but Zavier had become family, and I appreciated all his help.

"You're the best brother in the world," I murmured, hugging him and flipping Knox off from across the room as he cursed at Zavier. They could get over it.

We loaded the cars and I took one last glance back at the house, leaning back against Drake as he wrapped his arms around me. "You okay?"

"Is it weird that leaving here makes me feel homesick already, but leaving Kingslake wasn't even a blip on my radar?" I asked, sliding my gaze towards the others who were talking quietly with Zavier closer to the house.

"You might have lived in that castle your whole life, but it was never a home, baby. Time doesn't make a home, the people in it do."

"Is this how it felt to leave the compound?"

"It still feels like that," he confirmed, opening the passenger door for me. "In you get. You go with Cruz, and I'll ride with Knox."

I gave him a kiss, sliding in to wait for Cruz who was slowly making his way towards me, and he said something to Drake before getting into the car and giving me a smile. "You sure Estelle won't mind?"

"If she does, we're no worse off than we were before I suggested it. She'll let us stay at least tonight to figure out where to go next," I answered.

"Have you told her we're coming?" he asked as he backed out of the driveway, waving to Zavier before driving along the road with Knox and Drake behind us.

"I don't have a way to contact her. She told me to let myself in if she wasn't home. She's probably still at Dad's."

"I don't think she meant you could bring a bunch of thieving hackers with you," he teased, reaching out to take my hand.

"She'll be fine with it." She'd love them, I had a feeling. All she'd wanted was for me to find happiness, so if these guys meant everything to me, they'd mean everything to her, too.

I'd never been to Briar Falls before, so I stared out the window as Cruz drove, my eyes taking in the gorgeous green landscape. It was a small town, mostly ranches and small cottages with surrounding porches and white picket fences, and my nose pressed against the window as I tried to get a better look at the small creek running through some trees.

Cruz chuckled, his fingers squeezing my thigh gently. "What's got you so entranced?"

"It's so pretty here," I replied without moving, my eyes scanning over a field as we passed it, horses running along the fence line and making me smile.

"It's peaceful, too. What number were we looking for?"

"Seventy-seven Sale Street," I confirmed, glancing behind

us to make sure Knox and Drake were still following. Drake gave me an energetic wave, and I relaxed at knowing we were all okay.

"Looks like this house," Cruz murmured as he slowed, my eyes turning to the house we'd stopped in front of. It was a cute, white cottage with a white picket fence, exactly the type of home I'd always pictured Estelle living in.

We climbed out with our bags and Cruz's guitar, waiting for the other two to do the same, then we headed towards the house and let ourselves through the gate. We tried knocking on the front door, but I wasn't surprised to find her not home, so we went around the back, and I found the hidden key under the pot, letting ourselves in.

Once we'd taken our shoes off, we walked into the kitchen and placed our things on the floor. The kitchen had dishes piling up, making me frown. Estelle was a perfectionist at Dad's, so I was a little surprised to see clutter in her own space.

"I've got it," Cruz murmured, dropping a kiss to my lips as he steered me towards Drake and Knox. "You guys hang out in the living room."

Drake rolled his eyes, patting my butt as he stepped around me. "I'll help you. Penn can snuggle with Knox for a little bit. Pretty sure he's sick of my company thanks to that car ride."

Knox grunted, giving him a dirty look. "You think? You can shove *I spy* up your ass."

"You know what I'd prefer up my ass—"

"He's all yours," Knox deadpanned, giving Cruz a look before taking my hand and steering me into the next room, pulling me down onto the couch with him. I got comfortable on his lap, snuggling into him as he let out a content sigh. "Nice and quiet."

"You thought you'd get peace and quiet with me?" I joked, earning a dark smirk.

"I can make you quiet, trust me."

"Not here," I scolded, swatting his arm and making him laugh.

He tightened his hold on me, kissing my neck. "You sure?"

"Positive. Have some control."

"That's rich coming from you."

"I've been training. I can fight you now," I grinned, but I kissed his cheek affectionately.

"I'd let you win, baby," he promised, closing his eyes and running a hand up the back of my shirt, brushing his fingers across my scars. I didn't like them, but I loved that Knox did. He called them victory scars, because it was the last war I'd ever have to fight, and I'd done it alone.

It made me feel like a badass.

Before long, we'd both drifted off to sleep, the sound of Cruz and Drake talking in low voices while plates clinked in the sink being the perfect lullaby.

Knox

"Estelle's home," Drake murmured as he peeked out the window, and I gave Penn a gentle nudge to wake her up. I hadn't slept for long, but I wanted her to sleep as long as possible. Cruz stood from where he was sitting on the floor, smirking as Penn grumbled at me to go away. "Baby, it might be best if you greet Estelle. We're likely to scare the fucking shit out of her if we're who greet her at the door."

She huffed, sitting up to rub her eyes. "You like breaking into houses any other time, but you're scared of a random woman?"

"I don't want to scare her because she matters to you," he corrected, and that woke her up. She got to her feet just as the front door opened, and a woman's firm voice reached us.

"Who's here?"

"It's Penn," Penn answered, a woman entering the room a moment later. She had short, hazel hair, and the look on her face relaxed me completely. She looked at Penn like a mother would with her own child, holding her arms open to invite Penn in for a hug.

"Oh, sweet child. It's so good to see you."

"I missed you," Penn choked out as she wrapped her arms around the woman and held on tightly, her voice wavering slightly with emotion.

I moved to stand beside Cruz and Drake, drawing Estelle's attention as she replied. "I missed you too. Who do we have here? They're handsome."

Penn's face flushed a little as she turned to us, and it was cute to see her so nervous. "This is Knox, Drake, and Cruz. My boyfriends."

"The boys who abandoned you?" she asked lightly, but I could tell she'd beat us up with a wooden spoon if she got close enough.

"They didn't know what had happened," Penn answered quickly. "Stone, the psycho, shot himself and pretended I'd attacked him. Made it seem like I'd wanted to leave. Cruz even broke into Dad's house to try to find me, but he didn't know I was in the basement. They thought I was in a facility because I was crazy."

Estelle's eyes studied us hard in silence before she stepped closer, a surge of panic washing through me when she opened her arms at me. "Well, I'm glad they came to their senses. Don't be a stranger, we hug in this house."

Cruz and Drake smothered snickers, and Penn cringed. "Ah, Estelle? Knox isn't exactly the touchy-feely type."

"Nonsense," she scoffed, my body going rigid as she trapped me in her hold. "He's just shy."

The hug was terrifying, mainly because I couldn't tell

her to fuck off like I would've with anyone else. It would mean the world to Penn if Estelle liked us, so I tried to relax, giving her an awkward pat on the back. "It's nice to meet you."

"You're a sweet boy," she answered, hugging me a little tighter for a moment before letting go and moving onto Drake who happily hugged her back, Cruz being just as accepting when it was his turn.

"Thank you," Penn whispered as she took my hand and gave it a squeeze, my face softening as I looked down at her to find the brightest smile on her pretty face.

"Anything for you," I murmured, kissing her forehead. Estelle eyed us but didn't say anything, ushering us into the kitchen to make coffee, but she paused when she saw how clean the room was.

"Who cleaned up?"

"Drake and Cruz," Penn said proudly, knowing I was still a little uncomfortable, so she pushed me down into a chair and perched herself on my lap. "We were hoping to crash here tonight if you have room. Our house kind of got, uh, shot to pieces."

Estelle gasped, the coffee forgotten as she looked us all over. "No one's hurt? Who tried to hurt you?"

"That's what we'd like to know. Someone's stalking me, but they're like a ghost."

"What happened to those boys who saved you?"

"That's whose house we've been staying at. They've got their own families to worry about, and I'm fine now that I have these guys," she smiled, patting my cheek. "Knox usually scares anyone off with his resting bitch face."

"Fuck off," I grunted, trying not to wince once I realized what I'd said, but Estelle laughed, turning to finish the coffee.

"I'm not surprised if he's grumpy. You're a handful, Penelope. They deserve an award."

Penn was quiet for a second before speaking. "How's Dad?"

"Being a stain on society as usual. He's at a private poker game tonight out of town. Enough about him, what have you been up to?"

"I've been working a little," Penn said proudly. "It's not much, but Harley from Harley's Bar in Ashburn Valley lets me help in the kitchen sometimes. I made real money from it, and it was all mine."

"A job?" Estelle asked with excitement, bringing cups of coffee over with a smile. "Tell me more. I want to know everything."

They talked for ages, and the more Estelle talked, the more I liked her. She asked us questions about ourselves, too, swiftly changing the subject when it was obvious she'd asked something too personal, and that made me relax even more. I could see why Penn looked up to her as a parent figure so much.

"How about you all sit outside and light the fire pit? It's a lovely evening. I'll cook some dinner and let you know when it's ready," Estelle suggested after a while, and Drake frowned.

"We can help. I can't speak for Penn, but the rest of us are good cooks."

"Hey!" Penn huffed, but Estelle gave her a knowing look.

"You're unteachable. There's no way your cooking skills have improved."

I grinned, kissing Penn's cheek to soften the blow as I answered. "Penn burned instant noodles and set all the alarms off once because she didn't know she had to add water to the pot. Trust me, she's probably gotten worse."

"Sounds about right. She put a tin of beans in the microwave once and blew it up," Estelle said with amusement, getting to her feet. "I mean it, go light a fire. Relax."

Penn got to her feet and let Drake drag her outside as she giggled and pretended to curse him out, and I was surprised when Cruz grabbed his guitar from the living room. He shrugged like it was no big deal, but he rarely played in front of people.

We wandered outside to find Drake attempting to light the fire, and I nudged him out of the way with a shake of my head. "Move, your survival skills suck."

"I can light a fucking fire, asshole. It's not hard."

"Just sit down before you hurt yourself," I grumbled, pointing to a bench close by, grateful when he did as he was told. Penn's eyes were glued to Cruz and the guitar as he sat on another bench opposite Drake's across the fire, and I motioned for her to sit with him. Drake could get over it. If Cruz intended on playing anything, he'd prefer Penn beside him while he did it.

I quickly started the fire and sat beside Drake, dropping an arm around him to let him lean into my side. As much as I'd never been an affectionate person, this shit was growing on me. Cruz stared into the flames for a while in silence, but he eventually picked the guitar up and draped it across his lap. Drake relaxed into me more as Cruz's fingers started plucking at the strings. He was a little rusty, but the gentle strumming soothed me as I closed my eyes, soaking in the peace surrounding us.

Penn was fascinated by it, her eyes bright as she watched him play, and I had to admit, it was good to hear him playing again.

Cruz

I never thought I'd play in front of a woman. It was something I held close to my chest that only my closest friends knew about. This guitar was more than just an instrument, but Penn was more than just some woman.

"My foster mom gave me this as a gift," I said quietly as I kept playing, Penn blinking at me as she tried to process that I'd said something. "She was the only person in my life who I'd ever call a parent."

"Was?" she finally whispered.

"She was killed in a home invasion. My foster brother's biological junkie dad found him and tried to take him. Ethan had told us a lot of stories about his dad, and Mom promised him he'd never have to see him again." My chest went tight at the memories, and I swallowed past the lump in my throat, focusing on the sounds coming from the guitar. "I was in juvie for stealing millions of dollars from some old rich fucker in Kingslake. I'd been trying to help Mom since I knew she was struggling, but I didn't cover my tracks properly and ended up getting arrested. I was fifteen. Mom and Ethan's visits always gave me something to look forward to in there, but when they didn't show up that day, I just knew something was wrong." I could feel Drake's eyes on me, but I didn't look at him. He knew how long it had taken me to calm down from being that angry, bitter little boy. Having him and the guys in juvie had definitely helped, but it had been a long road. They'd seen me at my weakest, and even though Knox and Stone acted like they didn't give a shit, they looked out for me when I was lost in my grief.

"What happened to Ethan? Did his dad take him?" Penn asked with wide eyes, her hand sliding onto my knee to comfort me.

"He was beaten pretty badly, but he managed to get away. We lived in a quiet neighborhood, so the cops had already been called and his dad was arrested. Ethan got placed in another foster home after that, and we're still in contact. He lives further south, so we don't really hang out anymore. He just finished college."

"I wish I could've met your mom," she smiled softly, shuffling closer. "Did she teach you to play?"

"She knew basic stuff, but when it was obvious I needed more, she had someone come and give me lessons. I tried to convince Ethan to play too so we could form a band, but he wasn't a fan of that idea," I chuckled, the look on his face still clear in my mind as he'd scrunched his nose and looked at me like I was a psycho.

"What was his thing? Did he like sports? Art?"

"He's always been into fast cars and bikes. He's a bit of an adrenaline junkie. Mom would be so pissed to know he got his bike license, let alone how he rides it." We lapsed into a comfortable silence, the only sound being the guitar, and Knox cleared his throat before speaking, surprising me.

"My foster dad used to beat me all the time when I was younger. I was only taken away from him when I ended up in the hospital with a broken arm and ribs from falling off the swing at school. They found all the bruises I'd been hiding under my shirt and called child protection services."

I'd heard a little about Knox's past, but not a lot. Drake was the only one who knew all the dark details.

"Thank fuck you got out of there," Penn answered, not hiding the sadness in her voice. "Did they find you a better foster home?"

Knox didn't reply, and Drake gave him a gentle nudge. "You can tell her, babe."

I looked away from them, focusing on the guitar and acting like I wasn't there. Knox knew I'd hear him, but it was obvious he was only opening up for Penn, not me. I wasn't expecting what he said next, and I did well not to react.

"My new foster home was worse. I was ten, and I spent the next five years there being sexually assaulted until I got locked up for carjacking. The foster mom appeared to be the sweetest woman on earth, but it was all an act. She ignored the kids once she got them into her care, letting her husband do what he wanted with us. One of the girls was eleven when she killed herself, and I just knew he was hurting her in the same ways he was hurting me. They put on a big act about how she'd been bullied at school and they'd been trying to help her, which meant I was still stuck there with one other boy. He was only seven, and at this point I was thirteen. I tried to keep him safe, but in doing so, I only made myself a bigger target."

"He raped you?" Penn choked out, intending on getting to her feet, but Knox snapped at her.

"Don't fucking coddle me over it. It was eleven years ago, I'm over it."

She flinched at his tone, and I lifted my eyes to his across the fire. "She cares about you, man. You could've just said you didn't want to be comforted. You know she'll respect your space."

"Fuck off, Cruz. This has nothing to do—"

"Yes, it does. She's my girl too, and you're being a dick. It's okay to not want affection, but just say it nicely," I cut in, placing the guitar beside me to slide an arm around Penn. He stood and stalked off, and Drake put his hand out to stop Penn when she went to follow. "Leave him, baby. I'll make sure he's okay. Trust me, that took a lot for him to tell you, but he doesn't want you making a fuss about it or pitying him."

She nodded, watching Drake wander off into the darkness, and she let out a sigh. "Why do I always fuck things up with him?"

"Hey," I frowned, tugging her onto my lap so that she was facing me, not that I could see her expression properly now that the flames were behind her. "You know he's not the type to share personal things, so now he's just freaking out a little. It probably didn't help that I was here, he's never told me much about his past either."

"I just want to take it all away for him," she whispered,

resting her forehead on mine. "To take all the pain away from all of you."

"I love you for that, but you can't, baby. It's part of us, we just learned to live with it. Knox hides his under anger, Drake hides his under his jokes, and I hide mine by helping others. It's never going to go away, but it fades a little more each day. You help soothe it just by being here, I promise."

"You help soothe mine, too," she murmured, her lips pressing against mine as she gave me a slow, lazy kiss.

Chapter Nineteen

Penn

Knox had politely eaten dinner at the table with us after he'd left the firepit, but he'd excused himself and asked where he was sleeping, making my heart sink. Estelle had shown him the guest room, not batting an eye as Drake followed Knox into the room as they'd said goodnight. Cruz and I had slept on the couch, neither of us getting much sleep.

He'd stayed awake to keep an eye out the window for threats, and I'd been awake worrying about Knox.

"Morning," Estelle chirped as she wandered into the kitchen at seven, finding Cruz and I already sitting at the table with coffee in front of us.

"Morning," I yawned, Cruz mumbling a good morning too. Estelle chuckled, giving me the side-eye.

"I see you're still not a morning person."

"I didn't get much sleep," I admitted, her eyes narrowing on Cruz.

"Do I need to separate you and the horny boys?"

"Jesus, Estelle. I'm not going to fuck in your house," I snorted, and Cruz grimaced.

"Yeah, I have no plans on doing anything under this roof."

"Keep it that way," she hummed, making herself a coffee as she continued. "I leave in half an hour, but you're welcome to stay."

"Maybe I should go with you and visit Daddy. Me showing up might put him in an early grave," I suggested sweetly, sipping my coffee. She tutted me, hiding her amusement.

"Don't say things like that, karma is always listening."

"I think karma owes me one at this point," I grumbled, checking my phone to find a message.

Owen: Hey, are you coming by today?

Penn: Not today. House got shot to shit.

Owen: Are you okay? Where are you? I'll come to you.

Penn: We're all fine, but we need to hide out for a little while. It's safer if you don't know where we are.

Owen: That makes sense. Call me if you need me, okay? Be careful.

I sent a smiley emoji back, glancing up to find Cruz's eyes glued to my phone with a frown on his face. I turned the screen to face him, not caring if he read the messages. "Owen's just checking in."

"Don't tell him shit," he replied firmly, not caring about Estelle hearing our conversation. "He might be your friend, but you can't trust him right now. For all you know, the person who's after you might go to him and threaten him for information."

"Should we hide him too?" I asked with panic, but he shook his head.

"No. You guys don't hang out outside of the gym, so I

don't think that will happen. It was just the worst-case scenario. The only people that matter are under this roof."

I knew he was right, so I didn't argue.

Estelle sat with us while she had her coffee, then she hurried off to work, giving me a hug on the way out, leaving us alone. It wasn't long before Knox and Drake wandered out, Knox leaning down to drop a kiss on my cheek.

"Sorry." He looked highly uncomfortable, so I gave him a smile.

"For what? Going to bed without me? You should be." My teasing tone caused him to relax, and he dropped down onto a chair beside mine while Drake made them both coffee.

"I'm not good with words, but I shouldn't have gotten angry with you last night."

"It's okay. I was just worried I'd upset you somehow. Thank you for telling me," I replied, tilting my head back as Drake moved behind me to bend down to give me a kiss.

"What's the plan for today?" Cruz asked, and Knox shrugged.

"We need to go over the footage from yesterday to see if we can figure out who owns the car involved in the shooting. Maybe you or Drake should reach out to Beckett and see if they know anything. Penn can check in with Zavier."

I perked up, turning to him in surprise. "I get to help?"

"You're doing me a favor by dealing with that asshole," he grunted, but his mouth curved into a soft smile. "Maybe once you're done, you can help us go over some footage."

"I get to work on this with you guys? Like, you'll give me jobs to do?" I was going to hyperventilate with excitement soon, and Drake laughed, draping his arms around my shoulders and nuzzling into my neck.

"Yeah. Let's face it, you're not going anywhere so I think we can trust you."

"I get to be a thief?" I squeaked, tears burning my eyes and making Cruz grin.

"We think it's time. People are already shooting at you, so there's no harm in you being all in I guess. Besides, teaching you the tech side of things isn't exactly like throwing you into a house to rob."

"I was good at that when you took me to that house in Crestford! You said so!"

"Keep eating and training like you are, and you'll be robbing the rich in no time," he teased, getting to his feet. "I'm going to take a shower. I'll be back out soon."

Knox's hand slid onto my thigh as if to stop me from following him, and I waited for Cruz to vanish along the hallway before speaking.

"What's wrong?"

"You're not really going to visit your dad, right? I heard you mention it to Estelle earlier," he said quietly, taking my hand and giving it a squeeze. "I don't want anything to happen to you again."

"I don't think I need to. I wouldn't get anything out of it," I answered, sliding my eyes to Drake. "Right?"

Drake nodded, giving me a wink. "I don't think so, but if you do want to go back, I'll come with you to take more shit. He has a lot of nice stuff."

"If you'd listened to me when you kidnapped me, you could've cleared out the fucking safe," I deadpanned, grabbing the empty cups off the table and rinsing them in the sink. "Without starting an argument, has anyone checked on Stone to make sure he's alive?"

That had kept me awake for half the night, too. He'd been radio silent, and that made me nervous.

"Beckett said they left him breathing," Drake offered, the worry in my stomach only getting worse.

"That sounds hopeful then," I muttered, slipping my phone from my pocket to quickly send a text to Stone.

Penn: Please tell me you're alive, asshole.

I put it away, tidying the kitchen while I waited for his response. It never came, my panic growing by the minute. Cruz wandered out, and the guys got set up at the table, but I excused myself for a shower, too, needing to stress in peace where the guys wouldn't notice.

I tried calling Stone three times once I was alone in the bathroom, but he didn't answer, so I messaged Leah.

Penn: Are you at the compound? Have you seen Stone?

Leah: Jai tried to speak to him this morning through the bedroom door but Stone told him to fuck off. Why?

Penn: I was just checking if he was alive.

Leah: He's well enough to be a dick if that helps. I miss you.

Penn: I miss you too.

I put the phone on the sink and stripped off, stepping into the shower and ducking my head under the hot spray, closing my eyes and letting the water run down my face. I vaguely heard the door close, and I wiped a hand over my face to get the water out of my eyes, finding Knox standing in the middle of the room. I held my hand out and wiggled my fingers at him, encouraging him to join me, and he held my gaze as he pulled his shirt over his head before pushing his sweats down.

"You good?" I asked as he stepped in behind me and

threaded his fingers through mine, his forehead dropping to the back of my head.

"No."

"What can I do to fix it?"

"You can't," he mumbled, his hand tightening in mine. "It just numbs it."

"What does?" I turned to face him, sliding my arms around his neck.

"Being with you." His jaw clenched as he said it, and I thought he was going to take off until he blew out a breath and relaxed his muscles a little. "Deep down, I know I can trust you, but part of me is freaking out about you telling people or seeing me differently. Tell me I can trust you, and maybe I'll believe it."

"I swear, I'll never tell a soul," I promised, stepping closer to him to press my lips to his chest. "Please tell me he's dead."

His mouth curved into a smirk as he wrapped his arms around me. "Anonymous tip got his house searched a few years ago. Found some damning evidence on his computer and phone which got him a one-way trip to a prison cell. Bikers, gang members, and even the scariest of psychopaths don't tend to take too kindly to child abuse, so neither he nor his wife lasted long."

"Good," I nodded, giving his chest another quick kiss before turning back to the water to finish showering. I thought that was all he'd come in for, but then he spoke again.

"What's bothering you? We all noticed you slink off with something on your mind."

"I'm just a little overwhelmed, that's all. I just needed five minutes alone," I answered, not bringing up Stone and risking starting an argument. His arms slid around me, and he sighed.

"Fine, don't tell me. If you need something to take your mind off whatever it is that's bothering you, feel free to blow me."

I snorted, glancing over my shoulder at him. "I'm not doing anything in Estelle's house. She's the only parental figure I respect."

"I was just trying to help," he shrugged, his hand sliding down my stomach to dip between my legs.

"Knox."

"Just shut up," he chuckled, teasing my clit and biting my neck a little harder than I expected, making me hiss out a breath. "This will help both of us forget about the world's bullshit for five seconds," he murmured, and despite his dick pressing firmly against my butt, he didn't try to go further.

The hot water ran down my body, and I moaned as my head fell back against his chest. This was going to be over really fast, the temperature of the water making everything so much more sensitive.

"Put your fingers inside me," I groaned, grinding against his hand but needing more. He obliged, sliding two inside me while continuing the slow torture on my clit with his thumb. My thighs were tense enough they'd likely ache later, and I bit the inside of my cheek to stop myself from making embarrassing noises that the others would definitely hear. His free hand slid up my chest towards my throat, but he didn't squeeze hard, he just splayed his fingers out and increased the pressure a little as if to remind me he could one-hundred-percent snap my neck if he wished.

"Once we're set up in our own house again, me and the guys are going to fucking worship you, Penn. You won't be able to move for a month. You'll have all three holes stuffed with our cocks, begging for our cum like a good girl."

"You play dirty," I panted, crying out as he worked his hand faster between my legs, my orgasm just out of reach.

His fingers suddenly tightened around my throat, his teeth nipping at my ear as he chuckled. "Dirty words for a dirty fucking girl. Come all over my hand, baby. Scream so the guys know what we're doing in here."

I shook my head but my body betrayed me as a startled scream left me the second my climax hit, the hot water making it stronger as he kept fucking me with his fingers. His hand left my throat to wrap around my waist as I slipped, steadying me so he could continue his torment.

He finally stopped and my body slumped in response, not bothering to lift my head as the door creaked open.

"Is this a party?" Drake asked cheerfully, but Knox rinsed me off and turned the water off, helping me out before answering.

"No. I just wanted to say sorry for being a dick last night."

"Can you say sorry to me too then? You hurt my feelings when you kept telling me to fuck off," Drake grinned, handing me a towel as I shivered. "We think we found the car that was involved in the shooting. We're going to go and investigate."

"I assume I'm not part of the we?" I huffed, a grimace taking over his face.

"Uh, could you stay here? We still need to go over footage for more details, so it's not like you're not helping. You could keep going through them and—" I wanted to argue, but if they were going to start letting me be involved with jobs, even if it was searching through security footage, I'd bite my tongue. Maybe if I impressed them or found answers, they'd start taking me on the more risky jobs.

"I can do that," I smiled, and he gave me the strangest look.

"Like, you'll stay here and go over the footage without arguing?" he asked, a laugh leaving me.

"Well, the footage is important, right? Maybe I'll crack the case on my own and get to rub it in your faces?" I turned to Knox who seemed amused by the conversation. "Then I can be the boss and tell you all what to do because I figured it out without help, which makes me pretty skilled."

"Okay, baby. You keep thinking that," Knox answered dryly, patting the top of my head. "Will you be okay alone? I don't want to split up, but—"

"It's secluded out here and we're off the road a little. I'll hear cars on the gravel before they can do anything, and I noticed Estelle has a basement. I'll keep my phone on me and hide if anything goes wrong, I won't take risks," I said seriously, eyeing his naked body as he snatched my towel and quickly dried himself, giving Drake a few moments to check me out.

Knox wandered across the hall to the bedroom completely naked, and Drake happily took the towel he left behind to help me dry off.

"I can stay behind if you need me to," Drake offered quietly, but I shook my head.

"I'd prefer that you three stayed together. If someone follows you, you have better chances of seeing them early if you have more eyes on the lookout. Text to check in, though, so I know you're okay," I asked, giving him a quick kiss that made his face light up.

"I can do that. No offense, but I'm taking five minutes to be selfish and make Cruz be a lookout while Knox rails me. A man has needs, and this chastity house is killing me."

"We'll have a sex party when we get a place, I promise," I giggled, squealing as he swatted my ass before hauling me against him.

"Good, because I want this ass gripping my dick," he murmured, my breath catching as he slid his fingers along the crack of my ass, his teeth grazing my neck. "I'll be a lot more gentle than Knox, trust me."

"You do know I've done anal before, right?" It wasn't that

good the few times I'd done it, but that didn't mean the guys wouldn't make sure I enjoyed it with them.

"Yeah, but anal with Knox is a little different. Take it from someone who's been fucked in the ass by him for years," he replied before stepping back to grab my clean panties. "Here, get dressed so you can say goodbye to Cruz. I'll show you what we were doing with the footage before we go too."

He helped me get dressed before taking my hand and leading me out to the kitchen, finding Cruz and Knox going over something on an iPad. Cruz motioned for me to join them, and he pointed at a laptop on the table.

"Crash course in technology. Keep it plugged in and the battery won't die. Don't click anything that says delete or—"

"I'm not an idiot," I huffed, making Knox grunt.

"Can't be too careful, baby."

I flipped him off before turning my attention to Cruz as he showed me everything I needed to know, handing me a piece of paper. "I also wrote down a basic list for you in case you forget. Don't go anywhere on your own, even if you find something worth looking at. Call us and we can check it out, okay?"

"Okay," I agreed, reaching up to grab the back of his neck and tugging him down for a kiss. "You guys have to check in with me too, though, so I know you're alright."

"Done. And if anyone starts snooping around here—"

"I'll be sure to hide and call you," I nodded, giving his arm a gentle squeeze. "I've got this."

His expression softened and he smiled, kissing the top of my head. "I know you do, baby. I love you, be safe."

"I love you too," I answered, giving them all one more quick kiss each before they left, leaving me alone.

I felt like a professional as I flicked through footage, managing to connect to other devices that weren't already accessible to me. Some had huge security walls but some didn't even require a passcode which was stupid.

My phone rang, and I smiled when Leah's name popped up, answering instantly. "Hey, girl."

"I'm only doing this because I know you care about him," she said quietly, the sound of a car engine in the background. "So don't rat me out to your guys, or they'll kill me."

I stood, worry starting to soak into me. "What's wrong? What are you doing?"

"Stone's not good. He hasn't come out of his room, and we saw the security footage of what they did to him. He really needs a fucking hospital but he won't go, let alone accept any of our help. He might listen to you."

"He won't even answer my messages or calls, so how am I supposed to do that?" I sighed, my ears pricking as I heard a car outside. The guys were still busy, and Estelle had hours left of work.

"Don't be mad, but I know the guys are out, and I tracked you. I didn't want to risk you telling me in case someone was watching you. I know it's putting you in danger if you come with me, but—"

"I'll be out in two seconds," I answered, hanging up and running to the back door to grab my shoes, locking up as I left. It was stupid, the guys had told me to stay in the house, but if Leah had called me and gone against the guy's rules about Stone staying away from me, it meant he was worse than she said. There weren't any security cameras around here, so the guys wouldn't even know I'd left if I didn't stay gone for long and only got out of the car at the compound.

Leah gave me a small smile as I dove into the passenger seat. "I don't want to get you in trouble, but I don't know what to do. If he hasn't come out, it means he's not even cleaning the wounds. It was fucking bad, Penn."

"I'm glad you called me," I answered, leaning over to give her a quick hug. "It's good to see you."

"You too. You're looking good," she grinned, reversing out of the driveway and heading towards Rawson.

"I feel better than I did."

"I can tell."

We chatted as she drove, filling me in on the monkey-sex she'd been having with Jai, and I was surprised when she said they'd decided to try dating after all. I was happy for them because I thought they were great together. I had a feeling she'd been avoiding it out of fear, but she could trust Jai, they'd been best friends for a long time.

The compound was quiet when we arrived, but Jai stormed towards us the second we opened the front door. "What the fuck is she doing here?" I was a little taken back by his anger, but he quickly calmed down and cringed. "Shit, I'm not mad to see you, Penn, but there's no way the guys let you come here without them. You don't need the drama this will bring, and neither does Leah."

"I'm just going to check on him. I won't stay too long, the guys are busy for hours so I'll be home before them," I explained, starting towards Stone's bedroom. "I'll see if he'll let me in."

Leah gave me a thumbs up, turning to Jai to argue some more, but I blocked them out as I left the room and made my way along the hall to Stone's bedroom, hesitating before lifting my hand to knock. The bed creaked but he didn't reply.

"Stone? Let me in," I said firmly, his voice reaching me a moment later.

"Penelope, go home."

"No."

"For fuck's sake, leave!" he barked, but the usual anger was gone, making me frown. I tried the handle just in case, but I wasn't surprised to find it locked.

"Please? I'll go home once I've seen you."

"I don't want you to see me like this," he said more quietly, his voice sounding like it was closer to the door.

"I'll stand here all damn day and night if I have to, but then the guys will show up and cause a scene. I'll leave once you let me in and I can—" I didn't get to finish before the door opened to reveal his swollen, bruised face, a small gasp leaving me. "Jesus, Stone. You need medical help."

He limped back towards the bed, so I stepped inside and closed the door behind me, moving across the room to sit on the side of the bed.

"It'll heal on its own. You're worrying for nothing," he mumbled, wincing as he tried to get comfortable. "It's not as bad as it looks."

"Fucking bullshit," I bit out, reaching out to touch his face, but he pulled away. "Let me look at you. This cut needs cleaning."

"Why do you even give a shit? You shouldn't. You kept me alive, but now you need to stop putting yourself in danger for me."

I scowled, giving him the stink-eye. "Don't chase me down and beg for forgiveness, then get annoyed because I let you in a little. You stink, so you're going to get out of bed, have a shower, and tend to these cuts and bruises. Got that?"

He blinked at me with confusion for a moment before the faintest smile tugged at his lips. "You think you can boss me around now?"

"I saved your life, so you can do me a favor and get in the bathroom." I stood, crossing my arms to glare down at him. "Come on, don't make me drag you."

"You're not watching me shower," he said flatly, but he

started easing himself out of bed, slowly making his way towards the closet.

"Grow up, it's just a dick," I threw back, his eyes narrowing on me from across the room.

"Penelope—"

"Stop arguing with me. Get in the bathroom now so I can check you over, make sure you're clean, then put ointment on the damage. *Then* I'll leave."

He muttered under his breath about me being a pain in the ass, but he grabbed an armful of clean clothes and followed me out of the room, snarling as he noticed Leah peeking around the corner at the end of the hallway. "You're dead to me!"

"Love you too, boss," she replied brightly, giving me a wink before ducking out of view. Stone tried to shut me out of the bathroom, but I barged past him thanks to his current weak body, pointing towards a stall. "Go on. Strip off, and let me see the damage."

"If you wanted to see my dick, you didn't have to romance me," he deadpanned, stepping into the stall and letting me slip inside before locking the door, trying to pull his shirt over his head but struggling.

"Just accept my help without giving me attitude," I scolded, stepping closer to help him out of the shirt. He tried to step back from me at first, but he was obviously in a lot of pain because he let me strip him after a half-assed argument about it. His body was black and blue, bruises covering his ribs and chest, and when he turned around, his back and shoulders were no different. He jerked as I reached out to touch one on his back, but I followed him and slid my palm down his side where his ribs were.

"These are bad," I murmured, my brow creasing as I explored his beaten skin. "They have to be broken."

"They are," he mumbled, turning to face me, giving me a

moment to inspect the bruises on his chest more. "Now that we've cleared that up—"

"Shut up and get in the water," I said, cutting him off before he could attempt to kick me out. He rolled his eyes, but he did as he was told, turning the taps on and stepping under the spray. My eyes drifted over him as he turned his back to me, and I couldn't help myself as I took a peek at his dick as he turned a little.

"If you're going to stare at my dick, at least wash it for me," he grunted, my eyes flashing up to find him watching me.

"I was just seeing if my assumption of you having a pin dick was right," I joked as he turned his face towards the water, gently cleaning it before stepping back to answer me.

"If you think you can hurt my feelings by attacking my dick, you have another thing coming. I'm very comfortable with my body, and I know for a fact that there's nothing wrong with the size of it. Nice try, though." His hand dropped to his dick, and I held his gaze as he washed himself, taking his time like an asshole. He finally decided he was clean, and I handed him a towel once he'd turned the water off.

"Are you going to be a good boy and let me put ointment on you without causing a fuss?" I asked lightly, surprised when he nodded.

"Yeah. Thanks," he said quietly, drying himself as I slipped from the stall to find ointment in the bathroom cupboards. He stood still as I smothered him in it, making sure everything looked good before bandaging a few that were worse, then I grabbed his clean boxers and held them out by his feet. "Step into them."

"I can dress myself, Penelope."

"You'll hurt yourself," I replied, his dick almost smacking me in the face. "Just step into them and stop being difficult."

He huffed but did it, letting me do the same for his sweats

before I helped him into a shirt. Once he was done, he gave me an unsure look. "Uh, thanks for this."

"Stop moping in your room. You're the boss, so man up and run this shit. Work with the guys, get this business back up and running properly, and gain back the respect you've lost. The guys miss you, but they're too worried about me getting hurt again to let you back in. Prove to them that they have nothing to worry about," I said softly, going completely still as he stepped closer and put his arms around me, hugging me carefully to avoid hurting himself. I had no idea what to do, but I slowly hugged him back, relaxing into his hold.

"They have nothing to worry about. You're one of us, I know that now," he murmured, not moving back from me. "Thank you for being what they needed. I've never seen them like this before. You fixed the jagged edges between Knox and Drake, you've given all of them a kind of peace that they didn't even know they needed, and you gave Cruz something he'd been craving for so long."

"If you weren't such a stubborn bastard, you could have peace too. You're not so bad when you're not screaming at people," I teased, making him chuckle as he finally stepped back to look down at me.

"I wouldn't burden a woman with my charming personality, but it's cute that you think it's possible."

"You're not hard to look at, Stone. Well, when your face doesn't resemble stomped on grapefruit. If Knox can find two people to tolerate his bullshit, you can find at least one," I grinned, bending down to grab his dirty laundry and towel. "C'mon, let's get fresh sheets on your bed and get some food into you. Then I'll go. You'd better text me back when I'm trying to reach you, though, or I'll storm back in here and fuck you up."

"I don't mind," he answered with a straight face as I led him out of the bathroom and back to his bedroom, making sure his room was back in order and his bedding was fresh before steering him into the kitchen to make sure he ate something. I'd been gone longer than anticipated, and the guys would freak if they got home and I was gone, so I really needed to get going.

"I'll see you later?" I asked once Stone was settled back in bed, a gentle expression on his face.

"I'd like that. Let me know when you're back in the Heights?"

"About that," I said with a cringe, his eyes narrowing to slits.

"Did something happen?"

"Um, someone did a drive-by. We're staying at Dad's housekeeper's place in Briar Falls."

I jumped as he jerked forward, a curse leaving him as he clutched his ribs while glaring up at me. "What the fuck? Why didn't anyone tell me? Was anyone hurt?"

"No offense, but you're not really in the cool kid's club right now. In my defense, I assumed you knew because you love stalking me. I guess you've been a little preoccupied getting beat up, though. Then again, if you'd replied to my fucking texts—"

"Penelope, don't get smart with me." He tried to get out of bed, but I stepped closer and forced the blanket higher up his body, giving him no choice but to lay back.

"We're all fine, no one was hurt, I promise. Please lay down and rest so I can go before the guys get back and notice I'm gone," I begged, the fight leaving his eyes.

"Text me when you get there. No exceptions," he said in a low voice.

"Of course."

I hated leaving him, but I'd done all I could, even managing to force-feed him pain meds, so I left him to sleep it off and hoped he'd look after himself a little better now.

Chapter Twenty

Penn

Leah dropped me off before the guys got home, and I made sure to send a text to Stone. He didn't reply, but at least he couldn't say I hadn't stuck to my end of the deal.

Over the next week, I managed to check on him a couple of times, thanks to Leah sneaking me out when the guys got busy.

"We can't go out. I'll either get shot at, or the guys will see me with you and murder us both," I hissed as Stone dragged me out of the compound towards his car. His face was an awful shade of yellow and green as the bruises started to lighten, and the swelling had gone down a lot. I frowned when he opened the driver's door and motioned for me to get in. "Stone, I can't drive."

"I know, that's why I'm teaching you. We won't leave the yard. Trust me?" he asked, and for once I paused to think about it. He'd been grumpy all week with me because of my fussing, but he hadn't hurt me or put me in danger. I genuinely believed he wanted to repair the damage he'd caused.

"Yes," I finally replied as I slid into the driver's seat,

surprising him. He closed my door and wandered around to the passenger seat to climb in, instantly handing me the keys.

"Okay, take this and put it in the ignition. Make sure the gear shift is in neutral first." I blinked at him with confusion, and I could tell he was frustrated, but he did well to remain calm. "Put your hand on this. See that pedal? It's called the clutch. Push down on it with your foot, then you can move the gear."

I did as I was told, and for the next ten minutes, he made me repeat it without the car even being on. I switched between gears, struggling with a few that were at weird angles.

"Why is this so hard?" I huffed, making him roll his eyes as he rested his hand on top of mine.

"Release your death grip. It'll shift easier with less force. That's better, now feel how much pressure I'm using." He easily moved through the gears with a light push of his hand, encouraging me to do it myself again and smiling when I managed it. "See? Now, put it back in neutral and push the clutch in so we can start the car."

"Won't it start moving?"

"The emergency brake is on and it won't do shit in neutral, so it's fine."

I followed his instructions, panicking when he asked me to take the brake off and put it into first gear. Somehow I managed to do it without a problem, but once he asked me to gently use the accelerator as I slowly took my foot off the clutch, the car jerked forward and turned off, panic filling me.

"Did I break it?!"

"No, it just stalled. How about we work on finding the right spot with the clutch first? Start again and put it in gear, but instead of using any gas, just slowly lift your foot off the clutch until the car starts creeping forward, then hold it there."

The first two times I stalled again, but the third time I

managed to get the car rolling forward, my face lighting up as we slowly crept along the driveway. "Oh my God, I'm driving. How do I stop, though? The emergency brake?"

"When you want to stop, just push the clutch in again. We'll just focus on this today so you can figure out the clutch and steering. We'll add gears and speed another time," he smiled, my heart hammering as we got closer to the end of the driveway by the gate. "You have lots of room to move here, so just turn the wheel without moving your foot. The car will turn and won't go faster. Go back the way you came from."

"I'm driving," I kept repeating as I turned the wheel, my heart hammering as I got close to some shrubs, but Stone leaned over lazily and helped turn the wheel a little more without saying anything.

We spent an hour doing that, and I felt really comfortable steering by the end of it.

"Who knew the princess could drive?" Stone teased as he locked the car once we'd climbed out, an unusual carefree look on his face. "You already drive better than half my team. We'll make a getaway driver out of you for sure."

"Why did you want to teach me to drive?" I asked as he opened the front door to let me inside, my curiosity getting the better of me.

"I know it's something you've been wanting to do, and I've been thinking about what would happen if you're out with one of the guys and they get hurt. If they can't drive, you're stranded and could end up taken. At least if you know how to drive, you can get away. Also, then you can come and see me whenever you want," he smirked, leading me towards his bedroom where we'd spent most of the week. One of the days I just sketched at his desk while he napped, then two days ago we watched a movie and ate a bunch of snacks. Each time he let me check his injuries, which were thankfully healing.

I had to leave, I'd been here for almost two hours today,

but I quickly tended to Stone's wounds like I always did, freezing when he stepped into me once I was finished.

"Penn—"

"What are you doing?" I squeaked out, flinching when he raised his hand. His face fell a fraction, and I eyed him warily as he slowly reached out to cup my cheek, the affectionate touch taking me by surprise.

"I'd tear this world apart with my bare hands to keep you safe," he whispered, flicking his eyes between mine. "You might think I'm still a monster, but the difference is, this time you're the one holding my leash." My heart hammered as he kept staring at me, my hand absently resting on his stomach as if to push him away, but I didn't. He leaned closer, dropping his head until his lips almost touched mine. "I'll do anything to make you realize how much I want you, Penn."

"No, you don't. You're just feeling guilty," I said breathlessly as I continued to hold his gaze, my heart melting as he replied.

"No, I'd do it because I'm falling in love with you, even though I'm trying really hard to fucking fight it." When I didn't move, he leaned a little closer until his lips brushed mine, and I closed my eyes without a second thought. I kissed him back hesitantly at first, but once he knew I was okay with it, he deepened the kiss and walked me backwards until my legs met the mattress. I fell back, but he leaned down to keep kissing me, my hands running over his bare back as if I hadn't been touching him all week thanks to his injuries.

"Fuck, we have to stop," he growled as he tried to pull away, but I wrapped my arms around him with a frown.

"Says who? Do I not look willing enough?"

He chuckled, but it sounded hollow. "I already hurt the guys by hurting you. I can't fuck you behind their backs too."

My eyes widened and I groaned, letting him climb off me to drop beside me. "Shit."

"I know, babe," he mumbled, raking a hand over his short hair. "What the fuck are we doing?"

"I need to go," I blurted out as I got to my feet, but he snagged my hand to stop me escaping.

"I'll take you home. If the guys haven't noticed Leah stealing you all week, they won't know I took you home. I'm sorry, I shouldn't have kissed you," he apologized, but I shook my head.

"You can't take me home, and I kissed you back, so it's my fault, too."

"I don't think Leah's back yet, so let me take you," he insisted as he pulled a shirt over his head, and he wasn't wrong. I couldn't wait much longer for Leah to return from lunch with Jai.

"Fine, but just this once," I warned, letting him lead me out into the living room where chaos erupted.

The front door slammed open, and Jai ran in, Leah's bloodied body in his arms. "He killed her, he fucking killed her," he kept repeating, Stone instantly pulling my face into his chest to block my view. I tried to fight him off, but he only held me tighter.

"Who? What the fuck happened?" he demanded.

"I don't know! I had to use the bathroom after lunch, so Leah said she'd meet me in the car. When I got out, she was dead in the passenger seat. There's no smashed glass or anything, so she wasn't trying to fight them off. They must have snuck up on her. Fuck, I don't—"

"Get her into the office. I'll be in once I've gotten hold of Cruz," Stone ordered, tears blurring my vision as I pulled back just in time to see Leah's lifeless body being carried away, a bullet hole right between her eyes.

"Don't look, Princess," Stone growled, stepping in front of me more to force my eyes up to his as he pulled his phone from his pocket.

"I can't be here when Cruz gets here," I managed to choke out, reality hitting me suddenly. "I'm not supposed to—"

"I'm calling him to come and get you. I don't give a fuck if he's mad at me. You're an adult, and I didn't drag you here. Let him be mad, but right now, he'll push it aside to be there for you." He kept talking, but I wasn't really listening, my ears ringing as I stumbled slightly. "Penn! Snap out of it!" he bit out, clicking his fingers in my face. "You're going into shock, but I need you to focus."

"This is my fault. If it's the same guy who's after me—"

"Jesus Christ, it's not your fault. Baby, look at me. Shit, no, not you, Cruz. I need you at the compound." He tucked me against him and kissed the top of my head, but I barely felt it.

Leah was dead because of me.

"I don't have time to fucking argue with you, man. Leah's fucking dead, and Penn's going into shock. Get your ass here so I can deal with this without worrying about your girl. Bring Drake and Knox if you can, Jai thinks it was the person who's been stalking Penn," Stone continued, hanging up before wrapping his other arm around me. I was suddenly lifted off the ground as he carried me to his room, tucking me into bed and murmuring that he'd be back in a second.

My phone was ringing in my pocket, but I ignored it as tears fell. The shooter must have seen her driving me around all week and recognized her. I squeezed my eyes shut as the sound of Sandra screaming somewhere in the compound hit me all of a sudden, hard sobs threatening to choke me as I tried to catch my breath. Arms wrapped around me and pulled me into a chest, Stone's cologne surrounding me. He must have shut the door because the sounds were a lot more quiet now once I focused on them.

"Breathe," he murmured, and no matter how much I tried, I couldn't get close enough to him. He cursed before sitting up and pulling me onto his lap, making it possible for me to wrap my legs and arms around him tightly as he stroked my back. I was probably really hurting him, but all I could think about was needing to be closer, to somehow use him to anchor me from the overwhelming grief that was drowning me.

I didn't know we had company until Cruz's face popped into my vision as he crawled onto the bed, reaching out to wipe my tears. "Hey, baby. Come here so Stone can deal with Jai."

I clung to Stone even tighter, not wanting him to leave. Now that the guys knew I was obviously sneaking around with him, they'd never let me out of their sight again. They couldn't take him away from me now.

Stone's hand slipped up the back of my shirt and he buried his face in my neck, not giving a shit that Cruz was here. "Princess, I need you to let go so I can handle this." I shook my head, making him sigh. "Look, I'll convince Cruz to let you call me later to check in, okay?"

"She's dead because of me," I whimpered, Cruz giving me a sad look as he shook his head.

"No, she's dead because some piece of shit killed her. That has nothing to do with you, and we'll figure out who did it. We can stay here a little longer if you let Stone go. He could probably do with our help anyway." I released my grip on Stone a little, knowing from the way he breathed out with relief that I'd definitely been hurting him, and Cruz opened his arms for me. "Come on, sit with me while Stone helps Jai."

I reluctantly climbed off Stone's lap and crawled to Cruz who took me in his arms tightly, kissing the side of my head and motioning to Stone that it was fine to leave. Drake hovered in the doorway, but Knox was nowhere in sight. Stone said something to Drake before shooing him into the room and closing the door, leaving us alone.

Neither of the guys spoke, they just sat with me while I cried it out, not mentioning why I was even here to begin with.

Stone

Knox was already barking orders at people in the office to go over the footage and see if they could track where the shooter had come from, leaving me to handle Jai who was falling apart right in front of me. I wasn't the type to comfort anyone, but I knew I had to try. Jai and Leah had been part of my organization for a long fucking time, so I had to make sure I did everything I could to help him through this. They might have only just started dating, but he'd loved her for a long fucking time now.

"We'll find them and make them pay," I said sternly as I pulled him in for a hug, clapping him on the back. I didn't expect him to hug me back, but I gritted my teeth through the pain as he clung to me, my body screaming in protest.

"Is this because of Penn? It has to be, right?" he choked out, catching Knox's attention from across the room.

"This isn't on Penn."

I thought Jai was going to argue, but he shook his head as he stepped back from me. "I'm not blaming her, but is it because that person is after her?"

Sandra, on the other hand, lost her fucking shit. "No, this is Penn's fault! If she wasn't so hungry for Stone's dick, she wouldn't have had Leah sneaking her over here all week! Was her pussy fucking worth it, Stone? Your little affair got Leah killed!" She shoved me, and I winced as my aching body throbbed in response. Knox was eyeing me silently, obviously waiting for my answer.

"I haven't fucked Penn," I said calmly, keeping my attention on Sandra. "I do recall that Leah was the one to bring her here last week to tend to me because all of you were sick of my shit. None of this is Penn's fault, she'd do anything for anyone, and you know it."

"I bet she would. She's been sneaking around with you when she should've been home with her boyfriends."

"This is your grief talking. Until now, you didn't give a fuck about Penn being here," I hissed, not caring about Knox hearing me. "You've happily watched her spend time with me all week just so none of you copped the brunt of my mood while I healed, so don't throw her under the bus now. If Penn had been there today, she would've stepped in front of that bullet if it meant saving Leah."

"She's a little bitch, don't fucking—"

"Do you have any idea why I'm not dead right now?" I snapped, getting in her face. "Because the moment the Psychos made it very clear they were coming to kill me, everyone went into hiding. Not Penn, though, she fucking hitched a ride here with a random stranger, then put herself between me and the barrel of Skeeter Maddox's gun. She bargained with them to keep me alive."

"Look what they did to you! She didn't keep you safe!"

"But I'm alive!" I threw back, backing her up until we reached the wall, and she had nowhere to run. "None of you were here, but *she* fucking was. You don't think she's already blaming herself? Shut your fucking mouth about Penn, or I'll shut it for you." I stepped back, glaring at Will who'd been standing awkwardly to the side. "Get your girl the fuck out of here."

Sandra tried to argue, but he thankfully dragged her out before I lost my shit with her, Jai murmuring about needing some air and walking off too. I scrubbed a hand over my tender face with frustration, trying to calm myself to avoid snapping at everyone else before making my way over to Knox, who was trying to appear busy, but we both knew he'd been focused on me a moment ago.

"You and Penn?" he asked bluntly, but he didn't seem to be too pissed at me.

"There's no me and Penn. She's been dealing with my grumpy ass all week, making sure I looked after this damage." I motioned to my face before continuing. "We've just been hanging out."

"You haven't touched her?"

"I kissed her today," I mumbled, his eyes narrowing. "It was stupid. I was about to take her home when Jai arrived with Leah."

"Did she want it?" he asked instead of losing his shit, making me cringe.

"Damn, man. I know I've been a dick, but I'm not a rapey dick. It almost went further, but I just couldn't do that to you guys. I'm sorry, I shouldn't have kissed her in the first place."

He snorted, shaking his head a little as he scrolled through the footage of the place Leah and Jai had been for lunch. "But you don't see a problem with sneaking around all week with her? If you weren't already black and blue, I'd kick the shit out of you. Don't fuck with her. Whatever mind game you're playing—"

"I'm falling for her. It's not a game," I blurted out, his head turning to face me. "She's been amazing, man. I'm sorry for not telling you guys, but I didn't want her to stop talking to me, and I knew you'd stop it if you found out."

"Once we're done dealing with this shit, we're continuing that conversation. No more fucking lies, you got that?" he demanded, hope filling me. If he wanted to talk about it, maybe there was a chance they'd let me back in, and I could see Penn more.

My eyes landed on his screen and I frowned, leaning closer as I watched someone with a hood over their head approach

Jai's car. They leaned an arm against the open door for a minute, seeming to talk to Leah with ease, telling me she knew them.

She barely saw it coming as he suddenly pulled a gun out and pressed it against her forehead, pulling the trigger without hesitation before closing the door with his arm and walking away.

"She knew him," Knox observed, mirroring my thoughts. "I don't recognize the hoodie, though, and you can't see his face. If it's even a guy."

"Follow their tracks. They have to look up at some point," I suggested as I pulled my phone out. "I'll call this in with the cops. We'll pay them off and give them some information so they start looking too. Leah doesn't deserve an unmarked grave. We need to do this the right way so she gets a proper funeral."

Knox nodded, focused on the task at hand as I stood and called my contact from the Rawson Grove Police Force.

Cruz

It was late by the time Knox and Stone were done raking through hours worth of footage. The shooter's trail ran cold in Pine Valley, thanks to the lack of security there. It was mainly a forest with cabins, and if you trespassed out there you'd just get shot. No security required.

Stone and Knox were finishing up with the cops, giving us a little longer before we'd have to wake Penn and get her home. She'd thankfully fallen asleep after an hour of trying to keep her calm, and Drake curled up in bed with her while I got up and sat at Stone's desk, finding a couple of drawings there. I lifted one, seeing Penn's name written neatly in the bottom corner, a small date on the back to say when she'd drawn it. It was from almost a week ago.

I pulled out my phone and logged into the security system here, going through days worth of footage to find Penn had been coming here for more than just today. Today, Stone had let her drive his car around the yard. She'd gone to Stone to teach her?

I frowned, going back a couple more days to find security footage of her coming inside and beaming at Stone as he teased her about something. Most days, they went into his bedroom, which I didn't have access to. I contemplated whether to confront him about it, but I ended up hacking into it, surprised to find them just hanging out or her helping him with his wounds.

Until today's date, when they'd been making out like horny teenagers. I should've felt hurt, but the more I watched their interactions, the more relaxed I became. There was no way he was luring her into anything, he was acting like he did when he was just around us. He was content and just being himself. Sure, he got grumpy in a few clips, and I could see they were arguing in a couple, too, but the way he'd kissed her? Stone didn't just kiss girls for fun. It confirmed his feelings were real by the way he looked after her today. He'd tried hard to shield her from Leah's body when Jai had arrived, and he'd tried hard to soothe her when she'd started freaking out.

The door opened, and I switched out of the footage, finding Stone and Knox in the doorway. Knox moved inside and brushed Penn's hair from her face, giving her a nudge. "Time to go, Whitlock."

She stirred, seeming confused for a moment before her eyes wandered to the doorway to find Stone standing there with his arms crossed. Panic flared in her eyes and she shook her head. "Can't we stay here?"

"I think we need to talk about a few things in private,

don't you?" Knox grunted, Stone's eyes sliding to me. I didn't say I'd gone through the footage, but I hadn't bothered to cover my tracks, so if he went looking, he'd see that I'd snooped. Considering he'd been sneaking around with our girl, I doubted he was going to argue with me.

"Please?" Penn begged, her voice cracking as she turned her sad eyes to Stone again. "Stone, don't—"

"I'm not throwing you out," he murmured, not moving closer. "You're all welcome to your old rooms here if you want to crash tonight."

Drake's brow creased, but Knox snorted. "I suppose you want Penn to sleep in here? Not happening."

"No. She can have her own room too if she wants," he replied, Penn relaxing a little the more he talked. "Then we can have a long conversation in the morning over breakfast. I think we need it."

Penn glanced at me, and I knew dragging her home tonight would just upset her for no good reason, so I nodded. "Okay, we'll stay. Let Estelle know not to expect us, or she'll worry."

"I'll call her once I've gone to the bathroom," she smiled, sliding from the bed and padding into the hallway, Stone giving me a look before he followed her without a word. From the way Knox didn't react, he already knew something, too, but Drake scowled.

"What the fuck does he—"

"Leave them," Knox said before he could finish his sentence, making Drake's mouth drop open.

"You're okay with Stone following her to the bathroom? Have I fucking missed something?" He turned to me for backup, finding me not looking bothered either. "Seriously? You're cool with it, too?"

"Apparently, our girlfriend's been sneaking over here to

play doctor with Stone all week," I murmured, Knox letting out a dry laugh.

"He kissed her."

"Yeah, I know," I said on an exhale, Drake's eyes almost bugging out of his head.

"What the fuck? Why didn't either of you tell me?"

Knox gave him a dirty look. "Sandra lost her shit today and spilled a lot of information, but Stone also told me some, too. I don't know how Cruz found out, though."

Drake turned to me, and I held up my phone. "I started going through the footage here when I found some of Penn's drawings on the desk."

"So, how we thought Stone might have been blackmailing her—"

"Yeah, I think she's been keeping tabs on him and not the other way around," I confirmed, getting to my feet and stretching. "From what I could see, it's been innocent until today."

"He's falling for her. He told me," Knox said quietly, his face scrunching with annoyance. "I want to punch him, but I also don't."

"Let's leave this for tonight. We're all tired, and our nerves are fried from Leah. Sleep on it, then come back with a fresh mindset first thing in the morning," I suggested, grimacing before adding, "I think Penn's going to want to sleep in here with Stone, though."

"Absolutely not," Drake scowled, but I blew out a breath and raked a hand through my hair.

"She's beat, bro. If he's going to be what she needs to sleep tonight, I think we should let it slide. It's Stone, not a stranger."

"We're just going to forgive him now?"

"No, but he's not going to hurt her."

Drake didn't look convinced, but he kept his mouth shut

when Penn walked back in, not bothering to hide that she was holding Stone's hand, tugging him into the room behind her.

"I'd like to sleep in here. I don't want to upset you or anything, but I just—"

"It's okay, we figured you might," I said quickly, her entire body almost sagging with relief.

"Really?"

"Yeah, baby. We'll see you in the morning," I smiled, moving towards her and giving her a quick kiss.

"But then you'll be on your own. Knox and Drake have each other, but you—" It was cute how she worried. Before I could reply, Stone spoke.

"You can crash in here, too, if you want."

"You hate people in your room," I pointed out, making him snort.

"And you probably hate me sleeping in here with your girl, so I think I can compromise."

That seemed to satisfy Drake once he knew Stone wasn't going to be alone with her, so I nodded. "Yeah, okay. Thanks."

Knox and Drake said good night, kissing Penn on their way past, then Stone shut the door and led Penn towards the bed. It was weird seeing him so gentle with her.

She started stripping her clothes off, making him frown.

"What are you doing?" he questioned, managing to keep his eyes on her face.

"She likes to sleep naked most of the time," I chuckled, finding amusement in the panic flaring in his gaze. "Want me to sleep in the middle?"

Penn gave me a look that said she was confused by how calm I was being, but Stone's eyes finally dropped to her naked chest as she unhooked her bra and dropped the material, his muscles tensing.

"Princess, if you sleep next to me like that, we're both getting in trouble."

"Find some self-control," she said lightly, making him scowl.

"Find some fucking pants."

I snickered, stripping to my boxers before sliding into bed. "How about I eat your pussy and make him watch, baby? Make him beg for it."

Stone gave me a look of surprise, but Penn rolled her eyes. "How about I fuck myself, and both of you suffer?"

"Who's suffering? Sounds good to me," I said as I waggled my eyebrows, patting the bed beside me as she kicked her panties off. "Now get in and cover up before Stone comes down his damn leg and embarrasses himself. He hasn't seen boobs in years."

"Shut the fuck up," Stone demanded, stripping to his boxers, too, before sliding in on her other side. It didn't take him long to shuffle closer and slide an arm around her middle to spoon her, and Penn sighed contently as she snuggled into my chest.

I pretended to be asleep when Stone murmured good night to her once she'd drifted off, and any hidden concern about his intentions with her became soothed as I fell asleep, too.

Chapter Twenty-One

Penn

I woke up in a daze. My eyes hurt from all the crying I'd done last night, and I had a little bit of a headache forming. A groan left me as I buried my face in the warm chest in front of me, and it took a moment for me to realize who it was.

"Hey," Stone mumbled sleepily, his arm tightening around me as he pulled me closer. Warmth was at my back, and I vaguely remembered Cruz coming to bed with us.

"What's the time?" I whispered, keeping my eyes closed.

"Early. Sun's only just coming up," he answered, his fingers skimming across my bare back and causing me to shiver. They trailed over the raised scars but I didn't shy away. I shuffled closer and dropped my leg over his hip, making him chuckle. "You're pushing it, Princess."

I peered up at him, finding amusement all over his face. It was nice to see him so relaxed, and I couldn't help myself as I rubbed against him a little. "Oh? How so?"

"I'll fuck you right through this mattress, Cruz be damned," he warned, sliding his hand down to my ass and giving it a firm squeeze.

"No, you won't."

He smirked, his hand moving towards my pussy, but he paused when Cruz spoke from behind me. "You're just going to fuck my girl in front of me? No shame?" I went to roll over to face him but he moved against my back more, keeping me in place. "And you're just going to let him?"

"I—" I jerked as Cruz's fingers suddenly pushed into my pussy from behind, a gasp of surprise leaving me.

"If you're going to let him touch you after everything he's done, make him fucking work for it, baby. He doesn't deserve to come in that premium pussy just yet," he murmured in my ear, Stone's brow creasing with confusion. It sounded like permission, but it also sounded like he was forbidding it. I was confused, too.

I squirmed as Cruz kept pumping his fingers in and out of me, Stone's cock like a brick in his boxers, and just as I started to reach for it, Cruz bit my shoulder with a growl. "He doesn't get to come. Only you do."

"You know I fucking hate riddles, asshole. Can I touch her or not?" Stone bit out, getting annoyed with the conversation. Would it be rude for me to beg Cruz to let him? Cruz's lips found my neck and I moaned, Stone's eyes flashing to mine to watch my reactions.

"You want Stone to make you come, baby?" Cruz murmured, pushing his fingers a little deeper and making me cry out. "Do you think he deserves it?"

"I fucking deserve it," I snapped, getting frustrated as he kept the slow pace. "Are you trying to get me off or wash your fingers in my pussy? Go faster."

"So demanding," he snickered, pulling them out and forcing them into my mouth without asking. Stone's eyes darkened as I held his gaze, sucking on Cruz's fingers greedily.

"Cruz, I swear to God—" Stone gritted out, and Cruz finally sighed.

"You don't get to come, so I don't know why you're so—"

He didn't get to finish before Stone's mouth was on mine, tasting me as his tongue swept into my mouth. "But sure, she's all yours, man," Cruz added dryly, but I barely heard him as Stone's hand moved between my legs and he pushed his fingers inside me. He didn't bother taking his time, pushing me over the edge as fast as he could and swallowing my cries as he continued to kiss me. I thought that was it, but he shoved the blanket off me as he pushed me onto my back and made his way down my body, apparently wanting to get me off again. "Fuck, Stone—"

"Shut the fuck up, you deserve it, remember?" he growled, not waiting for a reply before shoving his tongue into my pussy. Cruz chuckled in my ear, kissing my neck as his fingers toyed with my nipple, making me arch my back.

"I don't think you're getting out of bed any time soon."

I was probably hurting Stone with the grip my thighs had on his head, but if it hurt, he didn't say anything. He didn't give a fuck about how loud or messy he was being as he noisily licked and sucked on my clit, his fingers pushing deep inside me to tease my G-spot. His hair was too short to grip onto, so I couldn't yank him away as he brought me closer to a second orgasm.

Cruz's fingers fanned around my throat lightly as he kissed me, my body exploding and causing me to almost fly off the damn bed, but Stone kept hold of me as he kept tonguing my clit again and again until it was almost painful, uncontrollable shakes racking my body from the delicious torture.

He finally stopped, crawling up my body to look down at me. His dick was hard against my sensitive pussy, but he stuck to Cruz's rule and didn't attempt to push the boundaries. His lips dropped to mine in a slow, lazy kiss, and I somehow managed to lift my arms off the bed to wrap them around his neck, keeping him close.

"I hope you're both relaxed enough now because this

morning could get messy," Cruz murmured, climbing out of bed and making me pout.

"Don't you want me to deal with that?" I asked, pointing to his tented boxers. Just because Stone wasn't allowed to come, didn't mean Cruz couldn't.

"As much as I'd love to feel you choke on my dick right now, I think we need to get up, make coffee, and sit down for a long conversation," he answered, grabbing my pants off the floor and tossing them at me.

We quickly got dressed, and I was well aware of Stone's eyes burning into me the entire time, and as soon as Cruz opened the door, I was almost bowled over by Drake. I was pretty sure he'd been listening to us.

"Good morning, baby cakes. I missed you," he groaned, kissing the crap out of me then pausing before leaning back. He raised an eyebrow, his voice full of teasing. "Why do you taste like your pussy?"

Knox was leaning against the wall in the hallway with his arms crossed and a blank look on his face, but from the hickeys on Drake's neck, I knew they'd had a good time alone, too.

"I got hungry," I joked, but Cruz wasn't about to keep a secret.

"I shoved my pussy-coated fingers in her mouth, and Stone ate her for breakfast before kissing her. That's probably why."

Knox's eyes narrowed, and even Drake managed to look annoyed. "You let him—"

"We'll talk about it over coffee," Cruz said firmly, dropping an arm around my shoulders and steering me towards the kitchen. It was pretty quiet, a few people wandering around aimlessly with breakfast and coffee, but it wasn't bustling like it used to be. Grief hit me at knowing Leah wasn't about to walk in with her cheerful laughter, and Cruz pressed a kiss to my temple, instantly noticing the change in the air around me.

"You go sit with Drake. I'll get you some coffee and food."

"I'm not—"

"Just something small," he said gently, not letting me get away with skipping breakfast. Drake took my hand and tugged me towards the table, pulling me down onto his lap while eyeing Stone across the room as he followed the other two towards the food and coffee.

"Promise me he's not being a dick."

"He's had a personality transplant," I smiled, drawing his attention as I kissed his cheek. "Look, I don't want to upset anyone, but Stone—"

"I'm not mad at you," he said seriously, making me pause. "I'm just worried about you. I'm struggling to forgive him for fucking us over too. I don't know how you've managed to forgive him."

"He's shown a lot of remorse, but this week it's been different. He's let his walls down and really let me in. I don't mind the other side of him when he's barking orders and being a dick, but it's nice to see him relax. Not to mention he's trying really hard to make up for his mistakes with orgasms today, apparently," I grinned, a sense of relief filling his eyes.

"That's good. As long as he respects you, then I'm okay with it. I'm mad at him, but he's my family. Part of me is really happy he's let you in because when he's not being a spiteful asshole, he's one of the most loyal guys around. If he's serious about you, then he'd stand between you and a fucking tank if he had to."

"If a tank's coming at us, I don't think Stone could hold it back with the power of his bare hands," I teased, making Drake smirk.

"You'd be surprised what his love for you can do. When he wants something, the man can swim through set concrete."

Cruz and Knox joined us, sliding plates in front of us as I moved to sit beside Drake, and Stone sat opposite us next to Cruz.

"Okay, no one swing at me until I'm finished," Stone said gruffly, making Knox snort.

"We'll see. Start talking."

Stone's eyes met mine and he blew out a breath, launching into a detailed explanation of everything that had been happening. Between the texts, secret meet-ups, and the kiss, it was a lot, and I was surprised when he made it to the end and no one had thrown a punch. Cruz and Drake weren't fazed by any of it, but Knox still seemed a little unsure from beside me.

"You seriously want to let him in? He literally shot himself and pretended you did it. He's a dick," Knox grumbled, and I gave him a sweet smile.

"So are you."

"I don't like you sometimes," he grunted, but his mouth curved into a small smile as he tried to hide it behind his coffee cup.

The rest of breakfast passed by without anyone losing their temper, but I sensed tension when Stone opened up a new subject. "You don't have to, but if you'd like to move back here, I think it would be a good idea."

"I bet you do," Drake muttered, but Stone rolled his eyes.

"Think about it. Someone's after Penn, and it's obvious they don't care who gets used as collateral damage in the process. The compound has the best security possible, there are more eyes here to keep watch, and you'll have access to the best weapons and tech in one place. It's not just Penn's safety I'm worried about, it's yours, too. You don't have to like me right now, but you're still my brothers, and I love you. Not that I'm good at proving it." He said the last part more to himself than to us, but Cruz's expression softened a little as he studied Stone.

"It's going to take a lot for me to trust you again, man," he finally answered, and Stone nodded.

"I know. I owe your girl my life, and I won't forget what she's done for me."

"Our girl," Cruz said dryly, giving me an amused glance. "Pretty sure she's yours too."

"Maybe," Stone mumbled, not seeming too sure on what I wanted. "Regardless of where I stand with Penn, I really would like you all to move back here."

"I'd like that," I said softly, startling as Drake let out a loud whoop and got to his feet.

"We're moving home, baby!" He took off, screaming it through the compound to make sure everyone knew, and Knox barked at him to shut up as he stomped after him, the rest of us laughing at the familiar antics.

Stone

I was being pathetic. I couldn't keep my damn eyes off Penn, and I got fucking butterflies like a damn girl whenever she glanced over and smiled at me.

"I hate to tell you this, but your emotions are showing," Cruz whisper-yelled from beside me as we watched Drake and Knox attempt to teach Penn some more shooting skills in the gun range. She needed to be able to defend herself if one of us weren't there, and I wasn't surprised to see her skills were somehow worse than before. She really did suck at it. It probably didn't help that the last time she was down here, I'd locked her in and turned the lights off.

I was impressed that she'd even agreed to step foot in here.

"Eat shit," I muttered, my eyes trained on her as she took another shot. I knew it would miss its target before she even fired the bullet. Her stance was all wrong and she kept looking back at me, repetitively distracting herself. "Jesus Christ, you make this look so fucking hard," I bit out after the millionth failed attempt, ignoring Cruz's warning to be nice.

I stalked over to her and shoved Drake out of the way, moving her body how it was supposed to be, then I wrapped my arms around her from behind and helped her position the gun correctly.

"You're a shitty teacher," she whined, making me scoff.

"I'm the second best shot in this entire organization, so shut up and pay attention."

"Who's the first?"

"Knox. Now stop talking, focus, and hit some targets. I won't put you on jobs until I know you can do basic targets successfully. Relax your arms more, you're as stiff as a board," I ordered.

"Me too," Drake mumbled under his breath, rearranging his dick in his pants as he watched Penn. I understood what he meant, Penn looked good with a gun in her hand.

Knox smacked the back of his head and scolded him for being distracting, but Cruz said nothing, standing back and letting me take over. He knew I was a good teacher because I'd learned from my brother, who'd trained all of us.

She managed to hit a target, but I didn't let her celebrate, keeping her in place and speaking in her ear. "Now, do it again. Hit five in a row, then you have something to be excited about."

She didn't argue, which was nice for a change, hitting three before missing the fourth, then starting all over again. It took half an hour, but she finally hit five in a row, so I dropped my hands from hers and gave her a small smile. "That's better. Now you can celebrate."

She threw herself at me and gave me a kiss, hugging me way too tightly for my healing body to handle, but I let her because any touch from her was worth it. "Thank you! I'll be on protection details in no time!"

Knox gave me a look that said exactly what I was thinking. There was no way she'd ever go on those jobs. We could easily turn her into a thief, but she'd have to let us get our way with the tactical team.

We started making our way up the stairs, and I jerked in surprise as Penn's hand slid into mine, cringing when I saw the dejected look on her face. At first, I thought she was just upset that I'd pulled back from her, but then I realized she was freaking out about being locked in here again.

I took her hand and gave it a reassuring squeeze, maneuvering her so that she was a step ahead of me. I didn't want her doubting me, so if I put her ahead of me, she didn't have to worry that I'd lock her in here. Her entire body relaxed, and she let my hand go to make it easier to walk up the stairs, but once we were outside, she laced our fingers together again as we walked towards the compound. A few of the lingering Thieves gave us curious looks, and just as I went to bite their heads off, Penn spoke.

"It's okay to let people know you're happy, you know? I can feel your anger from the way you're trying not to grip my hand and failing."

I glanced down at her, finding her amused eyes on mine. "I'm not angry."

"You look murderous. Relax, who gives a shit if people see you holding my hand?"

Knox was stalking ahead, but even he had Drake's hand in his hold, ignoring the looks people threw at him. If that asshole could get over the public affection bullshit, then I could too.

Cruz sidled up to me, his phone pressed to his ear. "Can I trust you with Penn? Rory wants to look over the footage from yesterday. They're trying to piece together the shooting at the track still, and they're hoping this will help."

I wanted to be offended, but I had no right to be. He was allowed to worry about leaving her with me.

"We'll stay in the compound. Don't go alone, take some guys with you," I warned, and he quickly replied to whoever was on the phone, saying he'd be there soon with Knox and Drake. That meant he trusted me a little, right?

Knox had argued about leaving Penn alone with me, but Drake managed to convince him it would be fine, giving me a pointed look that said he'd kill me if I made him look like a liar.

"Go. Penn can pick a movie, and we'll just hang around here, I promise," I encouraged, wanting to be alone with her. I wanted to get her naked again, even if I couldn't fuck her. Cruz knew exactly what I was thinking, though, his voice quiet as Penn let me go to kiss the other two goodbye.

"You only take it as far as she's willing to go. Don't be a dick if she gives you blue balls."

"She can turn them purple if she wants, as long as she gets those clothes off," I muttered, laughter leaving him as he clapped me on the back, making me wince as pain spread through me.

"Yeah, you've got it bad. We'll be gone for at least an hour. Use the time wisely. And Stone?"

"Hmm?"

"I'm glad you finally let her in," he replied with a small smile before moving towards the others, and I couldn't help but watch them silently for a second. We'd always been a family, but Penn made it feel even better somehow. I couldn't explain it, but my boys were so damn happy, and I loved that.

Once they were gone, I took Penn's hand and led her to my bedroom, locking us inside. She raised an eyebrow, tilting her head slightly in question. "What are you doing?"

"Apologizing again. Get naked so I can say sorry," I demanded, scowling when she didn't move. "I meant now, Princess, not next week."

"I bet your balls are starting to hurt," she said offhandedly, and I let out a sigh of frustration.

"Babe, just get naked so you can sit on my face."

She moved towards me, pulling her shirt over her head as she went, her bra and pants going next until she was only in her panties. I let her help me get my shirt off because that honestly still sucked to wrangle on my own, and I almost came when she dropped to her knees in front of me and started unbuckling my belt.

"My face is up here, Penelope. Sit on it," I deadpanned, but she ignored me and yanked my jeans and boxers down, my dick more than happy with the attention she was giving it. Thanks to the one-sided foreplay this morning, I was already leaking pre-cum, and I had to put my hand out to brace against the door as she wrapped her fingers around my shaft and licked the head slowly. This was going to be the fastest blow job in history.

I cursed as she finally pushed me down her throat, working her hand in tandem with her mouth, and I tried hard to keep my hand out of her hair but it didn't last long.

"Fuck, baby." My thighs shook slightly, telling me I was definitely going to embarrass myself in a second, but I'd prefer to be quick with this and take my time once I got inside her pussy. I made the mistake of looking down at her, and the moment her pretty amber eyes met mine, I was a goner. My balls tightened and a sound between a whimper and a growl left me, my load spilling into her mouth as she swallowed every drop I gave her.

My legs were like jelly as she released me, getting to her feet as if we were done. I'd never be done with her, not now.

I kicked my jeans completely off, taking her hand and

pulling her towards the bed. My dick was already growing hard again, and I wasn't going to waste the time Cruz had given me. He could've taken Will or literally anyone else, but he'd taken Knox and Drake for me so I could have this time alone with her.

"Can I fuck you?" I asked, pushing her back onto the mattress to yank her panties down, shoving her legs open. "Holy fuck, you're dripping. You liked sucking my dick?"

"I'm surprised I didn't come, to be honest. I love that you aren't afraid to make noises in the bedroom," she grinned, reaching for me so that I was lying over her. "Don't you need recovery time or something?"

"Does it feel like I need it?" I chuckled, grinding my dick against her pussy.

"You're clean?"

"Yes. I got tested six months after the last time I had sex. And that was more than a year ago." I hadn't expected her to let me fuck her bare, and my dick hardened even more somehow at that thought. "You're not on anything, though, right? I need to pull out?"

"Jade put that implant thingy in my arm a while ago. I'm covered," she promised, taking my hand and pressing my finger to the inside of her arm so I could feel it. "See?"

"You want me to come in you?" I asked because I wanted to do this right. I didn't want to fuck it up when she was offering me so much. I'd learned before that assuming things was dangerous.

"Please."

I dropped my lips to hers, not caring that my taste lingered on her tongue, and I lifted one of her legs over my shoulder before fisting myself, dragging the head up and down her slit to coat it in her juices. A soft sigh left her, and something shifted inside of me at knowing just how content she felt under me right now.

She trusted me, and I'd make sure she never regretted that.

I eased inside of her, taking my time to savor the feeling of her pussy tightening around me the deeper I got, groaning into her neck as I bottomed out. I'd never fucked someone I cared about before, and it sounded stupid, but it felt different. I noticed every sound she made, wanting to force more from her, and I found it felt better for me. Not just because there were no barriers between us, but because it was with her.

I pulled out almost all the way before thrusting back inside, her hands instantly going to my back as if to dig her nails in but she held back. She was so wet, and I picked up the pace and went harder, her nails finally biting into me as I found the right rhythm.

"Fuck, harder," she moaned, telling me exactly what she wanted which made my job a whole lot easier. I slammed into her, pushing her leg back by her head and leaning down to bite her neck, her voice cracking as she cursed. She was close, so I licked my fingers and slipped my hand between us, rubbing her clit and being rewarded with my name being screamed loud enough for anyone in the compound to hear.

I fucked her through it, ending up pinning both her legs to the side as I pushed her into a second orgasm, her release leaking out of her and setting me off too. I slammed a little too deep, making her wince, but she rolled her hips as I stilled with concern, my dick jerking inside her as I filled her up.

"Sorry," I panted, brushing my fingers through her sweaty hair. "I didn't mean to hurt you."

"I'm okay," she promised, not letting me escape as she kept a tight hold on me. We laid like that for a few minutes, and I freaked a little when I pulled out of her to find her bleeding.

"Shit. I was way too rough." My cum leaked out of her, a tinge of red mixed with it, sliding down her ass and onto the bed. "Let me—"

“Hey, Knox fucks hard too. They can’t get mad at you,” she scolded, a spark of anger hitting me.

“I’m not worried about them beating my ass, I’m worried that I fucking hurt you.” I climbed off the bed, grabbing my shirt off the floor to clean her up, the blood seeming worse against the white material. It wasn’t a lot, but that wasn’t the point.

“Hey,” she said softly, my eyes darting up to hers to find her watching me. “I’m fine. Will you shower with me?”

“Yeah, Princess,” I murmured, giving her a quick kiss. “C’mon, let’s get you cleaned up. Then we can put a movie on in the living room and wait for the guys to get back.”

She gave me a gorgeous smile, and I knew without a doubt that I was completely in love with her.

Chapter Twenty-Two

Drake

"I CAN'T BELIEVE you left her alone with him," Zavier grumbled as he walked beside me towards the compound, Beckett deep in conversation behind us with Cruz and Knox. We had no idea who the mystery shooter was, but we knew it couldn't have been anything to do with Penn's father, not if Leah had known them.

"It's like he's flipped a switch. He's stupidly obsessed with her. Like, his eyes turn into hearts when he sees her," I chuckled, walking a little faster. I couldn't lie, I'd been nervous about leaving them alone, too.

We walked inside, and I was a little surprised to find Stone on the couch watching a movie, Penn curled up on his lap as she napped peacefully. Stone's arms tightened a fraction when we approached, but I wasn't about to wake her up.

Cruz grinned as he moved closer. "What did you do? Fuck her into a coma?"

"Something like that," Stone grumbled, not happy about the audience. "Find out who the shooter is?"

"Negative," Knox sighed, dropping onto the couch beside him, tucking Penn's hair behind her ear in an excuse to touch her. “It can’t be connected to her father, though. Leah knew them, so unless the rich prick managed to convince someone in our circle to betray us, it can’t be him.”

Penn stirred, blinking against the light as she peered up to find Zavier smiling down at her.

“Hey, Whitlock. Got yourself another boyfriend? You’re going to give your big brother a heart attack.”

“Hey,” she mumbled sleepily, sitting up and rubbing her eyes. “What are you doing here?”

“I wanted to see you. Blink twice if Stone’s holding you against your will,” he joked, and Beckett snorted.

“You’re ridiculous. Get yourself a girlfriend and leave everyone else’s alone.” Penn’s eyes widened at the sight of Beckett, but Beckett just scoffed. “I’m not here to harm your new toy. That’s water under the bridge, right, Stone?”

“Sure,” Stone deadpanned, his hands moving to Penn’s waist to keep her in place. “Already forgotten about it.”

Knox got sick of playing nice and slid an arm around Penn, yanking her onto his lap. Stone looked ready to punch him, but he decided better of it and stood, learning to share like a good boy.

“Who the fuck is smart enough to stay hidden from us? Even when Penn’s father sent people to drag her ass home, they were easy to handle. This person is stupidly qualified or something,” he admitted, and Beckett shrugged.

“The dumbasses that went after Penn before were idiots, that’s why. If this person is trained, it would explain how they remain hidden. For all you know, they’re right in plain sight, and they’re just hacking into shit like you do. They’re probably just covering their tracks.”

That made me frown. “Do we have any rogue Thieves? It could be why they’re so good at hiding. They know how we work internally.”

“Everyone’s accounted for,” Stone answered.

"No one has a grudge against her?" Zavier asked, and Knox shrugged.

"Sandra's a little pissed, and Jai could have motive despite claiming he doesn't blame Penn for Leah's death, but both of them would only count as of yesterday. This has been going on for weeks."

Penn's circle wasn't that big, so it was likely to be a targeted attack to spite her father.

"Hey. What if they're trying to injure and kidnap Penn in hopes of a ransom? That would make sense, right?" I offered, and Cruz slowly nodded.

"I guess that could be it. The Whitlocks are the richest family in Kingslake. Maybe people think he's kept her hidden to keep her safe?"

"What about Owen?" Knox muttered, earning a glare from Penn.

"Leave him alone. You just hate that he's nice to me."

"No, I don't trust him, that's all."

"He used to patch me up and feed me when Dad wasn't so discreet with his abuse. It's not Owen," she insisted, but he rolled his eyes.

"Maybe your father paid him to keep tabs on you? For all you know, your sense of freedom was controlled."

"If that was the case, Owen wouldn't have fucked me. Dad thought I was pure, it's the only way he could've married me off," she pointed out, all of us scowling in response and making her scoff. "You insecure assholes."

Beckett chuckled, giving her a grin. "And guys say us girls are the whiney ones in a relationship. They can't handle a hit to the ego, they complain for years about it afterwards."

"I don't know why they're so worried. Why would I stray? They have such charming personalities," she said dryly, smirking when we glared at her. "And big dicks. That helps, too."

"Girls are weird," Zavier mumbled, giving me the side-eye. "They claim we're crude, but I know way more girls who talk absolute filth. Your girlfriend is one of them."

"There's no shame in being sexually open," she smiled sweetly, batting her lashes at me. "Right, baby?"

"Don't make me jizz in my pants in front of guests," I grinned. "But you're in our bed tonight, so you can do it later."

Cruz gave me an irritated glance, not seeming happy with that idea. "Why's she in your bed?"

"I called dibs."

"It doesn't work like that."

"Does now," I answered smugly. Beckett was over the conversation, and she walked around to grab Penn's wrist, tugging her to her feet.

"I need to talk to you." When we all took a step in their direction, Beckett snorted. "I'm not going to murder her. Fuck off and let the girls talk." They headed towards the office, and my eyes went to Stone to find him watching Penn like a psycho. His eyes tracked her every movement, but instead of glaring at her, his face was softer with concern.

"I guess you two had a good bonding experience?" I asked, his eyes snapping to mine. His face hardened as he went to get defensive about it, but I waved it off. "I'm not giving you shit, bro. If she was sleeping on you, that means she trusts you, and you weren't a raging asshole while we were gone."

Zavier dropped down onto one of the couches, giving Stone a flat look. "I don't know how you managed that. If I get one whiff of bullshit coming from you, I'll gut you."

Instead of arguing, Stone nodded. "Yeah, I know. Thanks for getting her out, Lopez."

Zavier didn't know how to respond to that, so he just nodded back.

I stumbled as Knox grabbed my hand and yanked me

down beside him, a teasing smile tugging at my lips. "Aw, does my grumpy love muffin want a snuggle?"

"Shut up and take what I offer," he muttered, but his arm snaked around me to keep me close. His mouth kept saying he hated every second of affection, but his actions proved he was enjoying it just as much as I was.

I had no idea how Penn had rewired his brain, but I wasn't complaining.

Penn

"You're a dumbass," Beckett grumbled as she shut us in the office, but she didn't look mad. "Getting between Skeet and a target is never a good idea." I went to defend myself, but she put a hand up to stop me. "I'd have done the same thing for Jett or Maddox though."

"I love what your family does. I've idolized you all for years, hoping that one day you'd take out all the men my father's connected with. I know the skin trade isn't just run through them, but it could save at least one person from being taken and sold."

She eyed me silently for a second before tilting her head. "I could take out your father if that's what you want. I can do it fast or drag it out. Ask your guys, I like to play with someone before killing them."

"I *want* him dead, but I don't know how I'd feel afterwards. I don't want to resent anyone later, and I'm worried I will. I know Knox would tear him apart if I asked," I cringed, surprised when she patted me on the shoulder.

"That's not a bad thing. I can't wallow in my emotions like that, but you're allowed to. You're human, Penn, and most people would be upset if their father was killed. If he becomes a problem for you later, we can go and threaten him.

Once he knows you're protected by the crews, he won't do shit to you."

"Why do you even want to protect me? You hate me," I scoffed.

"I don't hate you. Still don't particularly like you, but I do respect you. Anyone who can stare down my dad like you did deserves that, at least. Stone's only alive right now because of you, and I hope he knows that. Loyalty is hard to find, so he'd better not take it for granted again. You impressed Mom too," she said as she dropped down into a chair, crossing her legs. "It takes a lot to impress her."

"I'm really sorry about breaking into her house," I said softly, sitting in a chair beside her. "I just wanted to belong somewhere, and I wanted so badly for that to be here. Stone's approval meant everything to me, and I thought I'd gotten it, so I didn't question it."

"I saw the way he looked at you when I dragged you in here. I don't think you have anything to worry about now."

"They're finally going to train me properly to be a thief," I said with a grin, and she raised an eyebrow.

"Make sure they teach you which houses are off-limits while they're at it," she deadpanned. "I heard you got yourself a job at Harley's."

"I just helped out a few times," I shrugged, but she let out a sigh of annoyance.

"Harley told the guys he'd put you on regularly. They didn't tell you? If you want it, it's there for you."

"I got a job?" I asked with surprise, my excitement turning to anger when I realized what she said. "Wait, the guys knew?"

"Oops, maybe I wasn't supposed to say anything," she said with the face of pure innocence, and I got to my feet and stomped out of the office, hearing her snicker behind me. Stone frowned when I stormed into the living room, Zavier and Cruz seemed amused, Knox rolled his eyes, and Drake darted across the room to get away from me, letting out a fake squeal.

"I didn't do it! Don't hurt me!"

"Who was going to tell me Harley offered me a job?" I snapped, and Cruz winced.

"We were hoping to deal with the stalker first. He knows what's going on, so there's not a time limit on his offer."

"You still could've told me," I pouted, surprised when Stone stepped forward and slid an arm around my waist. Being touched by him was a whole different feeling from the others. It wasn't better or worse, just different. It was like he needed to touch me all the time now, and I loved that.

"If you want to work, we can figure it out. I'll come and keep an eye out if you need. Maybe after a few more driving lessons, you can go for your license and drive the car to and from work, too."

Everyone looked at him like he'd grown two heads, but my anger melted. "You mean that?"

"Yeah, Princess. We know what your independence means to you. We were just talking about some of your training. How would you like to break into Daddy's house?" he murmured, my eyes widening.

"My dad's house? What for?"

"Whatever the fuck we want," he chuckled. "You know the layout and the security, so it's kind of like a test run. We'll make sure he's not home. Only if you're comfortable with the idea though, I'm not going to force you to go back there."

"Hell, we can burn the place down if you want," Drake laughed as he walked over, deciding it was safe to approach me. I couldn't go that far, Estelle needed that job, but taking some of his prized paintings was a good way to say *fuck you* to Dad.

Beckett wandered into the room with a sigh, motioning to Zavier. "We've got to bounce."

"Is everything okay?" Cruz asked as he went to follow, but she chuckled.

"Yeah, Riley and Logan got drunk at Devil's Dungeon, and I've been asked to take them home. I'll grab my sister, you can deal with your bestie, Lopez."

"Ugh," Zavier groaned, ruffling my hair on his way past. "Reid said he was going with them to drive. He must have stayed home with Rae." Stone growled about him touching me, but Zavier flipped him off and added, "Be nice to my sister!"

"She's not your fucking sister, you freak!" Stone barked, making him laugh as he and Beckett walked out the front door.

I nudged Stone, giving him a fake scowl. "Leave him alone. He saved me, so if he wants to pull the big brother card—"

"He can eat my dick," Stone deadpanned, making me smirk as I ran a hand over his groin, palming him through his pants.

"I bet he won't do it as good as me."

His fingers went to my hair and he pulled, forcing my face up to look at him. "No one does it as good as you." I flushed from his compliment, and his grip on my hair loosened as he dropped his lips to mine for a quick kiss. "I'm going to get some things organized for your father's house if you're on board? The guys are going to take you to Estelle's to get your things. Once you get back, I'll fill you in on the plan."

"We're doing it tonight?" I asked, feeling both nervous and excited.

"Yeah, if he's not home. We know everything about the house since we've been there before. We just need to keep an eye out for people and anything new he might have installed. What time does Estelle usually finish work?"

"I think she was due home a little after dinner. I'll text her to let her know we're picking up our things so she doesn't get home to an empty house if we're gone before she gets home."

"Good idea. Keep your eyes open," he said seriously, giving me another kiss before telling the guys to be careful, then he wandered off without another word. Knox watched him with a frown, but Cruz had no issue voicing his thoughts.

"Damn, baby. Did you give him the hoover three-thousand or something? Whatever you did, keep doing it. That was the most pleasant conversation I've seen him have in a long time."

"I finally reeled him in with my cursed pussy, or whatever it was that he called it," I joked, taking his hand and giving it a squeeze. "Come on, let's go get our things. I'm even getting my own bedroom."

"Why bother? You'll never be in it," Knox smirked darkly, butterflies taking flight in my stomach as he continued. "Because here? I don't give a fuck who hears us. We don't have to be quiet, we can fuck you all day, every day."

"Why would you say that on the way out the door?" I huffed, and Cruz grinned as he tossed a set of keys to Knox.

"It's okay, baby. I'll make you come while Knox drives. If they're claiming you tonight, then I get you today."

Knox cursed at him and stomped off, and Drake gave me a wink as he followed, leaving me to trail behind with Cruz.

I expected Cruz to shove his hand down my pants once we were in the car and on the road, but he grabbed my sweats and tugged them off completely, making me squeal as he yanked me across the seat so that I was lying back against the door. "What are you doing?" I hissed, but he ignored me and knelt between my legs, spreading me open. My head smacked against the door as I jerked the moment he pushed a finger inside me and started sucking my clit, discomfort hitting me thanks to my tender pussy. "Can you be a little gentle?"

He paused, lifting his head to frown up at me. "I'm

surprised you're walking to be honest. I've got you." He leaned over me, kissing me so tenderly that I completely forgot I was mad, his fingers lightly skimming my clit and making me shiver. "How about I just use my mouth on you instead of my fingers?" he asked quietly, waiting for me to nod before he moved back into position, a breathy curse leaving me as he slowly teased and sucked on my clit.

"This is bullshit," Knox grunted, eyeing us in the rearview. "You'd better kiss it all better, because I have zero intention of taking it easy later when I get her between me and Drake."

He was so full of shit. I knew he could be gentle, and with how open he was becoming with Drake now, too, I knew I could convince him to take it easy for a night.

Drake's eyes were glued to what Cruz was doing to me, and I loved how he reached out to give me his hand. Hard and fast was great, but there was something really good about slow and sensual, my body burning with need as Cruz slowly built my climax.

"I'm going to crash, and you'll both die because you don't have your fucking seatbelts on," Knox bit out with frustration, trying so hard to keep his eyes on the road but failing.

"You look so hot," Drake groaned, ignoring Knox's complaints. "Fuck, you're so close, aren't you?"

"Yes," I panted, my muscles bunching as my body fought the sensations building inside me. My hand tightened in Drake's as he kept mumbling dirty words to me, and my other hand went to Cruz's hair as a choked moan left me, my back arching as pleasure washed over me. Cruz kept rolling his tongue around my clit, and I jerked from being overstimulated.

"Fuck," I mumbled when he finally stopped torturing me, satisfaction in his gaze as he helped me sit up.

"Better?"

"Definitely," I murmured, leaning over to lick his pussy-coated lips. He kissed me, sharing my taste as his hand wandered up my shirt, but I almost went flying as the car braked suddenly, Cruz's eyes whipping up to Knox's in the rearview.

"What the fuck, man? Be careful."

"Put your fucking seatbelts on and you wouldn't have to worry," Knox said flatly, making Drake snicker. Knox was such a sour puss when he wanted to be, but he did have a point.

Knox

We tidied the house once we'd packed our things, and I made sure to leave some bills on the dining table to help Estelle. She hadn't accepted any money from us but had cooked for us every night when she got home from work, on top of letting us stay for a week. Electricity and water wasn't free.

Estelle texted Penn to let her know she was working late, which threw our plans of breaking into Penn's father's house tonight out. Apparently, he was hosting a party, so the place would be crawling with people. We'd have to do it tomorrow instead, but it also meant we could plan a little better.

I could tell Penn didn't want to leave, she'd enjoyed being here, but she also knew we were putting Estelle in danger by staying. The compound was safer, and everyone in it was trained in case of an attack.

"We need a bigger bed," Penn said casually on the car ride back to Rawson Grove, making me snort.

"The fuck for?"

"So I can sleep beside all of you instead of having to make a schedule," she answered, snuggling into Cruz more in the backseat. "And it means we won't fall out while having wild monkey-sex."

"It's going to be a while before I'm happy to look at Stone while we tag team you, Whitlock."

"I'm patient," she grinned, pulling her phone out to text. Drake was in one of his annoying moods, flashing me a devious smirk.

"How about some road head, big guy? I know you secretly love it when Penn watches us. You finish faster."

"Pass."

"Is it because of Cruz? He doesn't mind. Right, bro?" Drake asked as he turned in his seat, and Cruz chuckled.

"Pretend I'm not even here. I'm getting used to you two having spontaneous fuck sessions. How about you pull over and let me drive? I'd do that for you since I'm a good buddy."

"No road head!" I barked, narrowing my eyes when Drake sighed.

"Fine. Cruz? You want some road head? What's a little head between brothers, am I right?"

My hand darted out to wrap around his throat, my eyes flicking between his and the road.

"The day another man's cock goes between those lips is the day you fucking lose teeth, Drake Curtis. Do you understand?"

"Oof, yes, Daddy," he cackled, and I tightened my grip even more.

"I fucking mean it. You want to choke on dick that badly? Fine. Go ahead," I snarled, releasing him to unzip my pants and free my dick. Cruz rolled his eyes in the back, and Penn still seemed focused on her phone, so I grabbed Drake by the hair and yanked his face down into my lap. Sharing Penn with my boys was one thing, but I'd kill any other motherfucker for touching her or Drake. Cruz and Stone had zero interest in him, I knew that, but I didn't like how Drake thought he could taunt me.

The angle was awkward, and Cruz silently leaned forward

and released Drake's seat belt. Drake pushed my dick down his throat and gagged loudly, drawing Penn's attention, her phone forgotten about as Drake obediently blew me. My eyes flicked to the rearview, hating Cruz being here despite knowing he didn't give a fuck what we did, and I relaxed a little at finding his face in his phone. He wasn't paying us any attention, and even as a groan left me, he didn't glance up.

"Fuck, deeper," I growled, pushing Drake down how I wanted him, hardening more as he let out a wet gag and struggled for air. Penn shuffled forward, giving us our own time, but her hand slid up the back of Drake's shirt to offer him silent encouragement like he'd done for her earlier. Knowing she was watching made Drake work even harder, my thighs tensing as I fought to keep the car on the road.

We'd done this a lot over the past few years, but knowing Penn was watching was distracting as fuck.

Within minutes, my knuckles were gripping the steering wheel, and heat licked at my spine as I came, cursing insults and praise at the same time. My body was weak from the intensity of it, and Cruz finally glanced up, the hint of a smile on his face.

"Want to pull over and let me drive now?"

"Fuck off," I huffed, cupping the back of Drake's head and planting a quick kiss on his forehead. "Thanks, babe."

Drake's sugar-high behavior was gone, replaced with a tired one. "I think that's a record."

Penn was flushed, but she didn't mention it as she spoke, directing everyone's focus away from my dick. "Stone texted. Dad's security is literally the same. The party's started, and Ander's there rubbing shoulders with a few rich idiots."

"He's there without Zavier?" Cruz asked with a frown, mirroring my thoughts. It was dangerous to go in together, let alone on their own.

"Yeah. Stone's keeping an eye on the cameras, just in case.

If something happens, he's sending a team in," Penn replied. "I should probably go and see Owen soon, too. He's a little freaked out about my stalker and wants to make sure I'm okay."

"If you're texting him, then he knows you're fine. Why would you go to the gym now that you have access to the one in the compound?" I grumbled, fixing my pants with one hand while keeping my eyes ahead on the road.

"Because he's my friend."

I felt too damn good to argue with her thanks to Drake, so I let it go.

Chapter Twenty-Three

Penn

We spent most of the night in the office, keeping tabs on the security cameras at Dad's. I curled up on Cruz's lap for a lot of it while he showed me how to work the tablets they used to keep tabs on security while they were on jobs.

Since so many rich assholes were currently at my father's, Knox decided it was a good time to hit one of the houses they'd been watching. The man was single, no children, and lived in Crestford, meaning there was plenty of time to sneak in and get back out before he left Kingslake.

I was surprised when Stone offered to go with him, snagging Will on their way out. I assumed Stone always stayed in the office to watch over the jobs from the screens.

"We track them from the moment they leave, while also keeping an eye on the targeted house," Cruz explained, reaching around me to use the mouse and keyboard without moving me from his lap. "This is why we have so many different screens."

Drake dropped into a chair beside us, pulling up a screen of his own with little dots scattered everywhere on a map, some being out of the country. "We can also track each other through our phones. These dots are all Night Thieves."

My jaw almost hit the ground as I leaned closer. "There's hundreds!"

"We're a big organization. But it's also how we never really get caught. Different jobs, different people, it makes it a lot easier to hide. Once we got our foot in the door with the crews and more law enforcement, we could start working with clients face-to-face, though. In most cases, our clients think we're just runners, not a lot know we're the ones who actually take this stuff," Drake shrugged, zooming in on Rawson Grove. There were a shit load of dots, but my eyes went straight to the ones on the move. When he zoomed in even more, their names popped up above the dots to reveal Knox, Stone, and Will. "I'll keep an eye on these, as well as the footage of Ander to make sure he's fine, while Cruz watches the live footage from street security. He's faster at jumping between different devices than me."

"You have to hack into each camera?" I asked, watching as Cruz's fingers flew across the keyboard, his eyes glued to the screen as he followed the guys' journey to Crestford.

"A lot of them are cheap and easy to get into, which means I don't always have to manually get back in each time. My software recognizes patterns in security and auto hacks into most of them," Cruz said proudly, not taking his eyes off the screen. "Whereas others with high-tech devices need a little nudge sometimes. They scramble the pattern and it confuses my software, but it's easy for me to get into because I think, unlike the software that's running off memory."

"Why is this turning me on?" I mumbled, a smirk taking over his face as he glanced back at me.

"The same reason it turns me on when you're holding a gun. As much as I'd love to have you sit on my dick while I do this, I really need to concentrate. Sit with Drake, he'll show you how to access the trackers. We'll get you your own devices eventually, so you'll need to know how to use them all."

I climbed off him, sliding onto Drake's lap instead, his arms wrapping around me as he kissed the back of my neck. "I can watch the screen and fuck you at the same time if you want?"

"No, I want to learn. Let me help on this job," I whined, and he let out a huff.

"Trust me to find a girlfriend with life goals. Okay, while Cruz is doing that, we just keep an eye on this, and since we know exactly where Mr. Launder is, we'll keep the screen up of him partying at your dickbag dad's house so we can let the others know if he leaves. A lot of this job is just watching screens, won't lie, but it's just as important as being out there thieving shit."

He showed me the information they'd been keeping on Mr. Launder, revealing weeks' worth of his home security, pictures of him out in public, and even down to a spreadsheet of his routine. They knew his every move.

"I have no idea how you missed the fact I existed when you broke into Dad's the first time," I muttered, and Drake hugged me tightly.

"But aren't you glad we fucked up? You're having the time of your life, right?"

"Yeah, baby," I promised, twisting my head to give him a quick kiss.

The rest of the job went smoothly. Cruz fucked with the home security just before Stone and the guys arrived, and they got in without a single issue. Watching Knox and Stone move silently through the house with their balaclavas on was insanely attractive.

"Try to remember as much as possible about what's on the footage. Take note of things you don't even think are important," Drake said and tapped on the screen in question before turning his attention to the footage of Ander. He was shaking hands with my father, handing over money as a girl was dragged forward. She didn't look older than fifteen, and I was so glad that Ander was getting her out of there. No matter what people told me about him, I'd always respect what he did to help people.

"Penn? Focus. Your eyes should be on the other screen," Cruz said sternly, snapping me out of it.

"But why? Stone won't ask for a report, right? I'm not there," I said with a frown, glancing at him.

"Maybe not, but it will help you train your mind to remember bulk details. Stone's an ass, remember? He'll probably grill you the second he steps foot through the door. Keep an eye on the exits, the rooms they go in, all of it," he suggested, his eyes going back to his screens. It was hard to take note when they were all scattered through the house, but I tried my best.

By the time they were out and back on the road, I was struggling to keep details in order.

"It gets easier, I promise. Now that we're back at the compound and Stone's letting you work a little, you can sit with us when we're scoping stuff out. You'll get loads of practice," Drake assured me, kissing my shoulder.

Jai appeared in the doorway, and I frowned when I noticed how tired he was. "Have you slept?"

"Not really," he said with a shake of his head, making his way towards a computer on the other side of the room. "Every time I close my eyes, I see Leah's dead eyes staring back at me."

I climbed off Drake's lap to sit in the seat beside Jai's. He seemed a little annoyed by my presence, but I wanted to help. If my stalker had killed her, then I wanted to find them and make them pay. "I'll text Owen and see if he noticed anyone shady hanging around while we were at the gym. She came with me a couple of times, so maybe the shooter was watching us?" I offered, but he snorted.

"If someone shady was hanging around, we would've noticed. You always had one of your guys or me and Will with you. No offense, but your little bestie isn't trained to scope shit out like we are. We've been over the gym's security footage already." His shoulders sagged, and grief washed over him as he blew out a breath. "I never should've let her walk out to the car alone."

"Hey, this isn't on you," I said softly, hesitating to reach out and take his hand. He pulled back, but after a moment he took my hand in both of his with a shaky smile.

"Thanks, Penn. Maybe I should try to get some sleep after all. Leah would kick my ass if she knew I wasn't looking after myself."

"Yeah, she would," I smiled back, patting the back of his hand with my free one before he let me go and got to his feet, mumbling to himself under his breath as he walked out.

"I think he's starting to lose his marbles from the lack of sleep," Drake observed, his eyes still on the door that Jai had walked out of.

"He's grieving," I pointed out as I walked towards him.

"He's talking to himself, and he looks like a zombie," he deadpanned, glancing at the screen. "The guys are coming along the road now. That was an easy job, thank fuck."

"Can I go and meet them in the yard?" I asked, wanting to see them with my own eyes to make sure they were okay despite watching the entire thing. Cruz chuckled, giving me a nod.

"Sure, but stay back from the road. It's dark, and they won't see you. Stay by the door."

"I will," I grinned, heading out of the office and out towards the front door. I stepped outside just as headlights lit up the yard, and I waited for the car to stop in the garage before I wandered over. Stone climbed out of the driver's seat, frowning at me.

"Why are you standing out here in the dark?"

"So I could see you quicker," I answered, confusion reflecting on his face and making Knox snicker.

"She missed you, idiot," Knox stated as he walked in our direction, hugging me as he kissed the top of my head. "Everything go okay here?"

"Yeah. Drake and Cruz tried to show me as much as possible, but it was a lot," I admitted, giving Will a small smile as he went to walk past. "Hey. Jai said he was going to bed but he was talking to himself and—"

"I'll check on him," Will promised, patting me on the back in thanks before making his way inside. Knox let me go so I could approach Stone, and I worried when Stone grabbed my wrist and started tugging me towards the house. Why was he mad at me?

"Stone—"

"We can do this inside where it's safer," he scolded, relaxing his grip a little and sliding his hand into mine. "What room did Will go into after the kitchen?"

"He went upstairs to the master bedroom," I answered, Stone's steps slowing a little as he calmed more.

"Who went into the house first?"

"Knox."

"Which street was the house on?" He knew I had no fucking idea on street names, but instead of getting angry like he usually did, he kept his voice gentle. "Work on that. Get on the internet in your spare time and study local maps. When you're out, take note of signs. You'll remember it in no time."

"Maybe you can take me driving and test me on street names once I've practiced?" I suggested as we reached the front door, and Knox chuckled from behind as he kept guard at my back.

"If you drive like you cook, you've got no hope."

"I just need someone to teach me and I could do both really well," I sassed, yelping as he smacked my ass once he'd locked the door behind us.

"Stone must have the patience of a saint."

"I'm not teaching her to cook, that's Drake's issue," Stone grumbled, finally pulling me against his chest to drop a kiss on my lips. "But I don't mind teaching her to drive."

We walked into the office and Drake pounced, giving Knox a big kiss. "Hey, baby. Welcome home, let's go get Penn naked."

"She's sore, remember? Give her poor pussy a rest," Cruz joked, and Stone eyed me with a flicker of amusement.

"Did I break you or something?"

"I can handle more. Cruz kissed it better in the car today," I grinned, my arms tightening around him. "You *did* fuck your way to China through my pussy though."

Drake smirked. "I don't need your pussy, babe. I want to slide into that sweet ass of yours."

I could tell Stone didn't like the idea of the guys stealing me, and I leaned into him a little more to reassure him. I had a feeling jealousy was going to be a huge issue with him, and as much as he had to learn to share, maybe we had to start small.

"How about we all have a little fun?" I murmured, Knox scowling as Drake hung off him like a damn monkey.

"I told you—"

"You don't have to be the bread in my sandwich. I'm sure Cruz and Stone could work together."

"I want to be the bread!" Drake demanded, but Cruz shrugged.

"I don't give a shit who I'm looking at, as long as my dick's inside you, baby. If you want to get a little wild, I can team up with Bread Boy over here." He jerked a thumb in Drake's direction, and Knox huffed.

"I don't like that idea."

Stone groaned, raking a hand over his short hair. "How about you guys fight about this a little longer while I put Penn into a sex-coma by myself? But Knox, Cruz rubbing balls with Drake isn't going to make them horny for each other."

"Like you'll be able to sit back and watch them fuck her without wanting to tear their limbs off," Knox argued, and I held up my hands in the shape of a T, signaling a time out.

"How about I choose? Cruz and Drake can get their sandwich, but Stone and Knox can boss them around. If Cruz is okay with that?" I turned to find Cruz chuckling.

"I don't mind being told what to do, not that Stone deserves bossy privileges."

"Fine, Knox is the boss and—"

"I think the fuck not," Stone barked, but I jabbed a finger against his chest, silencing his argument.

"Do you want to go to bed alone then? I want you all to stuff me full of cum, so either get on board, or go to bed," I ordered, annoyance flashing across his face.

"Fine, but I'm not doing anything stupid."

With that settled, I started walking towards my bedroom, knowing they'd follow. It was so good having my own space again, but Knox was right, I'd rarely sleep in here.

The door had hardly shut behind us when Drake started stripping me in record time, and once I was naked, Knox ordered me to sit on the edge of the bed before he sat in the chair in the corner.

"Gotta warm her up first. Stone?" Stone eyed him with murder in his gaze as Knox continued with the hint of a smirk. "Crawl to her and eat her pussy."

"I'm not fucking crawling," he snarled, but Knox narrowed his eyes.

"Prove you'll do anything for her. Fucking *crawl*."

Stone's angry gaze slid to mine, and I spread my legs for

him in invitation, leaning back a little so he got a good view of me. I dipped my hand between my legs, teasing my clit with my fingers as I watched him. I could tell it had the desired effect before he even opened his mouth.

"Jesus Christ," Stone grumbled, dropping to his knees and crawling towards me.

"Slower," Knox said lightly, and I could tell Stone was going to kill him later for this. He slowed, taking his time to reach me, then he devoured my pussy without hesitation, making me drop back onto the bed with a moan while Knox continued to order everyone around. "Cruz." I had no idea what Knox wanted him to do, but after a second, a bare-assed Cruz climbed onto the bed, straddling my chest and fisting his dick in front of me.

"Open, baby." I did as he asked, gagging as he leaned forward and pushed himself down my throat. "Good girl. Tap my leg if it's too much and I'll pull back a little."

I couldn't see what Stone was doing, but I cried out around Cruz's dick as Stone changed direction with his tongue, pushing a finger inside me to curl it against my G-spot. I gagged more as Cruz fucked my mouth, testing to see how far I'd let him go as he went deeper. Saliva ran down my face as I choked again, my senses in overdrive as Stone pushed me closer to orgasm, and Cruz eased back just as I came, letting me breathe as wave after wave of pleasure washed through me.

"Drake, you're up," Knox said, motioning for Stone to move. He wasn't impressed with that idea, but he kept it to himself as he got to his feet and stalked across the room to get out of the way. I wouldn't let them toy with him too much, but for now, I'd let Knox have his way.

Cruz moved off my chest, grinning as he reached out to wipe the drool from my face. "How about you come ride me? Drake needs to prepare you anyway before he fucks you."

I didn't understand what he meant, my brain was still foggy from the orgasm, but once I was positioned on Cruz's lap with my arms around his neck and his dick deep in my pussy, Drake moved in behind me and teased my ass with wet, cool fingers.

"Sorry, the lube's cold," he murmured when I jumped in surprise, Cruz placing one hand on my waist while the other cupped the back of my head to draw me in for a kiss. I writhed on his lap as Drake started to ease his finger in and out, a groan leaving me as he added a second.

"There's no way your dick will fit in there while Cruz is in my pussy," I panted, rocking my hips slightly to try and find relief. It felt so good, but almost too much at the same time.

"Trust me, it will fit," Knox said confidently, his pants around his ankles and his dick now in hand as he watched us. "Do you want Stone to come and distract you?"

A whimper left me and I nodded, hissing as Drake added a third finger. It didn't hurt, but it was uncomfortable. Stone appeared on the bed beside us, completely naked, and I instantly reached out to wrap my hand around his length, stroking him while holding his gaze. That seemed to be his thing, he liked eye contact. He moved closer, Cruz's lips tickling my ear.

"Choke on him like a good girl, baby. Show him how badly you want his cock."

I opened wide and let Stone guide himself into my mouth, his fingers tangling in my hair as he thrust deep. I almost forgot about what Drake was doing until he removed his fingers and gently squeezed my ass. "You ready?"

Stone pulled back, but his fingers stayed in my hair as he gave me unexpected comfort. "Relax, Princess. Let him in."

Nerves raced through me as Drake's dick prodded my ass, but they all gave me words of encouragement as Drake kissed my shoulder, taking his time to avoid hurting me.

"I can't," I gasped, my fingernails biting into Cruz's shoulders as Drake pushed in a little further, my heart beating faster as the discomfort started to burn a little. "It hurts."

Drake stopped moving, his hand stroking up and down my spine affectionately. "You want to stop?"

"She can handle it," Stone said gruffly, leaning down and kissing me so hard and fast my head spun. His hand moved to my clit to tease me as Cruz started rocking into me slowly, and before long, I was begging them to make me come. Between Cruz's dick, Stone's fingers, and Drake carefully making his way into my ass, I came so hard I almost blacked out.

"I'm in," Drake murmured as I started coming down from the high, and I hadn't even noticed him pushing the rest of the way in. "You did so good, baby."

I preened at the praise, Stone's fingers tightening in my hair again to remind me he was there. I opened for him again, moaning and groaning around him as the other two worked together inside me, not surprised when Knox finally joined us. He didn't have to ask, I simply wrapped my fingers around Stone to stroke him, switching so that Knox was in my mouth on my other side. This was the hottest thing I'd ever done, and I was close to coming again just from the thought of it.

I kept changing from Knox and Stone, trying to give them both the attention they deserved, but I couldn't focus once Cruz and Drake got me close to the edge again. Stone and Knox climbed off the bed, letting the other two fuck me a little harder without risking me biting anyone's dick off, and once Cruz and Drake both came with me, Stone tugged me to lie down on the bed on my side to face him, lifting my leg over his hip as he eased into my pussy.

"You going to come for me and Knox too, Princess?" he whispered, a needy whine leaving me that made him chuckle as he thrust in and out of me, and I was surprised when Knox laid down behind me and ran a palm over my ass. I figured he'd wait until the end, but it seemed even his frustration with Stone wasn't going to stop him from rubbing balls with him.

"Breathe for me," he said gently in my ear, teasing my ass with the head of his dick, using Drake's cum as lube. "Kiss Stone like before. You looked so fucking hot."

Stone didn't even hesitate, his hand going to my throat as he kissed me deeply, continuing to thrust in shallow, slow strokes as Knox made his way into my ass. It wasn't so bad now that Drake had been in there, and I found myself relaxing into it more. Slowing down with Stone and Knox was really something else.

"Fuck, baby. Look at you," Cruz groaned, his boxers now on as he sat in the chair. "Such a dirty girl for us."

I was a panting, sweaty mess, there was no way I looked at all attractive right now, but I ate up his words like my last meal, my nails lightly dragging down Stone's back as both guys started thrusting a little deeper.

I must have blacked out for real the next time I climaxed, because the next thing I knew, Knox was tucking me into bed and saying he loved me.

Chapter Twenty-Four

Stone

I'd slept like shit. I tried to sleep in Penn's bed with the guys, but it was too overcrowded. I ended up going back to my own room, waking up after a few hours, so I gave up and headed into the kitchen to make a coffee before wandering to the office so I could start work for the day. I was a little surprised when Penn padded in at around five o'clock, the guys nowhere in sight.

"I can't sleep, it got too hot," she yawned as I pushed back from the computer a little, and she didn't even hesitate to slide onto my lap as if it had always been a natural thing between us, my arms instinctively tightening around her as I kissed her neck.

"I gave up too. Can I ask you something?"

"Anything."

"Are you sure you're okay with going back into your dad's house?" I asked quietly, a small smile curving her mouth.

"Yeah. I know what means the most to him, so fucking with him one more time could be fun. If you were me, would you do it?"

I didn't answer straight away, trying to figure out my

answer. My situation had been vastly different to hers, but it was also the same. My father hadn't loved me or my brother, we were pawns in his game too.

"My dad was part of a wannabe gang," I said quietly, speaking before I lost my nerve. "He raised us to follow in his footsteps and beat us when we refused to heel. My tenth birthday gift was a thirteen-year-old girl in a business deal. Dad wanted me to be a man, and the girl was an unwanted virgin. The business deal was that Dad got what he wanted for me, and the girl's potential buyer would agree on the deal once she was broken in. I wasn't opposed to sleeping with her until I found out she hadn't wanted it. I figured she worked with the sellers how I worked with Dad, so naturally, I thought she had agreed to the deal."

"What happened to her?" she whispered, my arms tightening around her as if to stop her from running away when I told her the truth.

"I walked into the room to find her bent over a table, being restrained so she couldn't move. They'd gagged and blindfolded her, but I could still hear her sobbing. That's when I questioned the business deal and said I didn't want to do it. He hit me so hard my ears rang and told me to man up. I had no choice but to do as I was told." I swallowed, staring at the wall to avoid Penn's eyes as I said the words. "I raped her."

"You were a child, Stone. You didn't want it either."

"Doesn't change what happened," I mumbled, finally looking at her. There was no disgust on her face, just understanding and sympathy. "She was sold to the buyer, but she ran. Girl didn't live to see her fourteenth birthday."

"Where's your dad now? What about your mom?" she asked as she teased the back of my neck with her nails, attempting to soothe me.

"He was killed in a drive-by shooting a month after my birthday. Ezekiel was fifteen, and he'd already gotten deeply involved with the gang world. He did a year in juvie, but he'd always had good connections. Mom didn't know what to do with us, and looking back, I'm pretty sure she'd been forced into marriage with Dad. She hated the criminal life, was relieved when he'd died, and when she met her new rich boyfriend, she had no problem walking away from us." I had a feeling my brother and I were the products of domestic violence and rape, but I still couldn't help but resent her for abandoning us. "Ezekiel turned a handful of criminals into what the Night Thieves are today when he got tired of being someone else's bitch six months after that, and he raised me alongside it while managing to dodge the foster system. I was in and out of juvie regularly, but after the first short trip or two, he realized the potential those kids had in there. As he got older, he started asking me to keep notes on the regulars. A lot of our current members came from juvie, and we still bring newbies in that way sometimes."

She turned on my lap to face me, curiosity in her eyes. "What made you want the guys? You don't seem to be besties with the other members."

"Cruz had my back in there, and I had his. We weren't exactly close, I didn't trust anyone other than my brother, but I had a little altercation in the yard one day and he proved himself loyal to me. Drake was a similar situation."

"And Knox?"

I chuckled at the memories, confusing her. "Knox didn't like me. Broke my fucking nose. He was a big guy even back then, and I saw the potential he had, even if he didn't like me. We all stuck together in there, but we didn't become this close until we lived together here in the compound. Our friendship was formed out of survival tactics, but it eventually grew to more of a found family." I tucked her hair behind her ear, loving how she leaned into my touch. "Then after years of building his empire, Ezekiel got wrapped up with some rich fucker's wife in Kingslake and got killed. The bitch cried rape, but they'd been banging for ages. He was so fucking in love with her, but the thought of losing her cash cow husband? She'd never walk away. She didn't know the kind of money Ezekiel had, or she would've happily jumped ship for him."

"Is that why you had a problem with me being a rich bitch?" she teased, making me snort.

"Mostly, but I've just met a lot of girls who I thought were like you, and the outcome was never good. We've had to bury a lot of bullshit over the years, and I didn't need your Kingslake princess drama on top of it."

"And now?"

I smirked, leaning closer so that my lips brushed hers. "Now, I want you on top of everything. The table, the hood of my car, the bathroom sink—"

"After last night, I think I need a day or two before we tackle the bathroom sink. I'm really tender today," she laughed, snuggling into me. "I appreciate you telling me about your family. I wish I could've met your brother. You're a dick, but he obviously raised you well for you to be able to take over this entire organization. I think he'd be proud of you, Stone."

My throat tightened and I nodded, not wanting to speak in case my voice cracked. I'd buried a piece of myself the day I buried Ezekiel, and as much as I'd never get that back, Penn was making the edges a little smoother to handle.

Penn sensed me clamming up, so she suggested we look over some maps with street names before we had breakfast. She turned so that her back was pressed against my front, my arms going around her to use the keyboard, bringing up the local map for her.

I was in the middle of giving Penn another driving lesson by the time the guys finally woke up and crawled out of bed. She was focusing on starting and stopping along the driveway, only stalling a few times now that she was getting used to the clutch. She was using the gas today, too, instead of creeping the car around, her confidence a lot better today as I gave her pointers. I only had to interfere once by grabbing the wheel when she wasn't turning enough.

A few more of these lessons, and I'd take her to get her damn permit, that was how sure I was that she'd ace it.

She stopped by the house when she noticed Cruz leaning against the wall watching us, a content smile on his face as he walked in our direction. He opened the driver's side door, leaning in to give her a quick kiss. "Morning, baby. How long have you been awake?"

"Since five. I got too hot in between you guys, and Stone was already in the office so I just stayed up," she shrugged.

"You're doing good with the driving," he noted, her face lighting up as she went on about everything she'd been doing. I watched Cruz as he paid attention, and I opened my door and motioned for him to take my place.

"Go for a lap or two with her so she can show you. Just be mindful of when she turns right to come back, she doesn't always swing hard enough on the wheel when turning that direction."

He nodded, happily jumping in, and I stood back as I watched her drive back along the driveway. I knew I had to spend the rest of my damn life making it up to her for how I'd treated her, but this was a really good start. I'd opened up and let her in, I was taking my time to teach her things that interested her, and I hoped the more time we spent together, the stronger her trust with me would grow.

Penn

The gravel crunched under my shoes as we made our way towards my father's house. We'd kept an eye on the property for most of the day, and so far, Dad had gone out and hadn't returned. It was getting dark, and all the staff were gone, so we made our way towards the place I'd been trapped in for my entire life, my heart hammering in my chest. Drake slipped a gloved hand into mine, speaking in a whisper. "Take a few breaths. You're panicking yourself, and your breathing is getting louder. Shut it all out, okay? If he comes home, we'll bail."

I nodded, giving his hand a small squeeze. My face felt hot with the balaclava on, but I was pretty sure it was mainly the spiking anxiety causing me to overheat.

Will and two other guys were monitoring the system at home, but Cruz also had a tablet in hand, keeping an eye on things himself as we reached a window and Stone eased it open. We climbed through one after the other, then the guys walked ahead to cover me as we moved through the silent house, freezing as we heard a small thud.

"I didn't think Daddy Whitlock was home," Knox stated as we moved through the house, glancing at Cruz for confirmation. "Can you see any movement on the cameras?"

"Negative. It's probably the house creaking," he answered, his eyes glued to the screen as he trusted the rest of us to watch his surroundings for him. "Drake, come with me. We'll check out the office and see if the safe code is still the same. Knox and Stone can split up to sweep upstairs, and Penn can stick by one of them. Don't go off on your own," he said, aiming the last part at me.

"Affirmative," I said with a grin, making him chuckle.

"Alright, keep your head up and eyes open. We'll meet back here once we're done."

Knox motioned me towards him, much to Stone's annoyance, but I gave his hand a quick squeeze before following Knox. Knox seemed the most trained for shit like this, so I was more than happy to shadow him to learn.

We knew my father's bedroom was empty, but I didn't roll my eyes when Knox instructed me to go in and check it. He was trying to make me feel important, and I appreciated it. It was good practice anyway.

I opened the door and scanned the room before stepping inside, checking in the closet and under the bed for movement, then I started rifling through his drawers. I paused when I found a photo of Emily, picking it up and inspecting it. She was dressed up, smiling widely for the camera, and I vaguely remembered it being taken on her tenth birthday. I was only five, so the memory was small, but I remembered the pretty dress she was wearing.

I pocketed it, moving into the hallway again, and making my way into the next room, pausing when I opened the door and saw a pair of feet beside the bed. I should've waited for Knox, but I poked my head into the room properly, my stomach twisting as I found my father lying on the floor, blood soaking the carpet and multiple bullet holes in his head.

"Dad?" I whispered, despite knowing he was gone. Grief was a strange emotion. I hated the man that was lying in front of me, but I'd known him my entire life, he was my dad.

I swallowed, trying to control the tears as I moved closer, not expecting to find another body.

A scream left me, Estelle's blank eyes staring up at me from the chair in the corner, her wrists and ankles bound to the chair. She'd been shot right between the eyes, just like Leah.

I ran towards her, tripping on one of her shoes that had been tossed aside and landing hard on my hands and knees, but I barely noticed my father's blood all over my hands as I scrambled towards Estelle.

"No, no, no. Please." I didn't know what I was begging for, there was no way she was still alive, but the words kept coming out of me as my shaking hands felt for a pulse.

Someone cursed behind me, but I wasn't paying attention, the grief consuming me and making the rest of the world vanish. I fought when someone wrapped their arms around me and pulled me backward, Knox's voice in my ear.

"Baby, she's gone. Shit, I need help in here!" He shouted the second part, holding me tightly as I kept trying to escape, but the slick blood on my hands stopped me from getting a good grip. Cruz appeared, taking in the scene and pointing towards the door.

"Get her the fuck out. Take her to her old room." I had no idea how Knox knew where that was, but he grunted a response and carried me down the hall, placing me on the bed. He held me against him as agonizing sobs left me, and he murmured words that I didn't hear in his efforts to calm me down.

At one point, he released me, and Drake took his place, Knox growling down the phone to someone. It was all too much. Losing Emily had fucked me up, but Estelle too?

I retched as images of her dead eyes popped into my head, and Drake helped me to my feet and into the bathroom just in time for me to throw up. He held my hair out of the way, rubbing my back as I cried and threw up, and I could hear him talking to someone, but I had no idea who. It sounded like Cruz, but I wasn't sure.

I had no idea how long it had been since I found Estelle, but exhaustion took over by the time Drake got me back on the bed, and within minutes, I was passed out.

Knox

I never should've let her wander into rooms alone. We had the cameras up, and it still showed the house as empty, the carnage being hidden behind fake footage. Will had no answers for me, all he could see was the same as us, but something was blocking us from changing to live feed. After a while, Will found that our footage was from almost two weeks ago.

Drake crept out of the bedroom that Penn was in, quietly closing the door behind him. "She's asleep."

"I never—"

"Jump on the guilt train later," Stone growled as he joined us. "But for the record, none of us saw this coming." He clapped my shoulder in support before motioning down the hall. "Cruz is on the phone to Beckett. We might have good connections, but the crews have better ones. We don't have Kingslake in our pockets as much as they do, and we need to call this in. Our connections get us out of theft, but the Donovans will get us out of someone pinning us with murder. We can't avoid this getting out, Louis is a huge part of Kingslake, his absence won't go unnoticed, and there's no way I'm putting Estelle in a shallow grave. She needs a proper grave."

"The cops will want a statement from Penn," I grimaced, glancing at the closed door she was currently sleeping behind.

"They'd have to get through me, and that's not happening," Stone bit out. "She needs to rest, they can bother her later."

We left Penn to sleep, waiting for backup to arrive, and within half an hour, Beckett walked in with Maddox, Slash, and Hunter. Having the two leaders of two crews was going to get this issue resolved fast, which meant we could get our girl home sooner.

"Where's Penn?" Hunter asked as he approached, and I blew out a breath.

"She was hysterical. She's sleeping in her old bedroom upstairs."

"Show me the bodies," he nodded, and I led him up to the bedroom that was currently a crime scene. "Is it just the two?"

"So far. We haven't looked for more since Penn freaked the fuck out."

"Get your guys to do a proper sweep of the rooms you haven't checked. We'll handle this mess and the cops," he promised, dismissing me as I went in search of Drake. Between the four of us, as well as Beckett and Maddox, we managed to complete the sweep in record time, and once we were back in the kitchen, Maddox joined me. I got along with him the easiest because he didn't fuck around like Beckett. She liked to make a game out of everything, and it drove me insane.

"You really have no clue who could've done this?" he asked with a frown, making me groan.

"My guess is it's Penn's stalker who killed Leah two days ago and who probably shot up the track. Then there's the whole issue of them blowing up Drake's car and doing a goddamn drive-by. We don't have an ID for the person, though, or we would've dealt with them by now."

"Are you sure they're after Penn? What if they're just going after you guys? They blew up Drake's car after all, so maybe he's the target?"

"That doesn't explain killing Penn's dad or his housekeeper," I pointed out.

"Maybe that was just to throw you off the scent?"

"We're nowhere near close to figuring out who's been causing chaos for us, so it was an unnecessary tactic to use," I sighed as Beckett joined us. "I take it you guys have no idea who this psychopath serial killer is? They've got balls if they're taking out major players like Louis Whitlock. This could make waves in the underground."

"It's not me," she said brightly, making me roll my eyes as she continued. "But we've been keeping an eye on things, and so far, nothing's standing out."

"You guys have your foot in every damn door, and we have

eyes literally everywhere. How the fuck is this person such a goddamn ghost?" I snarled, clenching my fists.

"You're not the only people who can hack technology. If the cameras are showing an empty house right now without a crime scene, then it means you've got someone with similar skills to you who's causing mayhem. Which could be why they're a ghost, they're deleting evidence and covering shit up as they go. They're probably right in front of us," she grumbled, annoyed with the mindfuck herself. "Zavier's the best for underground information, so if he doesn't know anything, no one else is likely to."

"How many more people are going to die? There's no pattern, so we can't even try to avoid more deaths until we find this asshole."

"Whoever it is had better hope they run fast when I find them," she snorted, turning to Slash. "Hey, Dad. Did we find any details from the bodies? Even the type of gun used?"

He shook his head, crossing his arms. "Nope. Whoever it is knows how to stay hidden. All the bullet wounds have exit holes, and he's taken the bullets with him. I called Rory to get a few of the Psychos to scout around the outskirts of town, the blood was pretty fresh, so you likely scared the culprit away when you climbed through the window. Penn's father was still warm."

That made me frown. "How fresh?"

"He was probably still in the house when you first found them. Why?"

"Fuck, I need to check on Penn," I said quickly, taking the stairs two at a time as I ran, a sick feeling starting in my stomach. The only room we hadn't checked since finding the bodies was the one she was currently sleeping in. If the killer had snuck in there to hide, we wouldn't have noticed.

I shoved the door open, not caring about scaring her at this point, but I was met with an empty room. We were too high up for anyone to use the window, but that didn't mean they didn't knock her out and sneak out another way while we were downstairs waiting for Beckett.

I wasted no time, running back down to the others as panic clawed at my throat, but I couldn't break now, not when my girl needed me.

"They took Penn. She's fucking gone," I snapped, Cruz and Stone already running towards the front door before I even finished the sentence, Beckett grabbing my arm and making me snarl as she stopped me.

"You guys stick to the main roads, Maddox and I will head towards the back end and meet up with Mom. We'll cover more ground that way. We'll get her back, Knox. Whoever this asshole is obviously doesn't want her dead, or he could've shot her and run. He took her, which means she's valuable to him. I'll call you if we find her," she promised, and I nodded before taking off, Drake right on my heels as we tore out into the night.

Chapter Twenty-Five

Penn

My mind was foggy as I woke up, rubbing my temples with a hiss. I had an insane headache, and my mouth tasted like ass. I sat up, blinking as I took in my surroundings, and uneasiness washed over me as I realized I had no idea where I was. Nausea hit me as I looked at the bedside table to find multiple pictures of Emily, waking me up faster.

This room wasn't in Dad's house, so where the fuck was I?

I slowly climbed from the bed, taking my time as my head swam, and I found more and more of Emily's things as I quietly opened the closet. Some of her clothes, her favorite Barbie, a stuffed bear Estelle had given her for Christmas one year. Tears pricked my eyes at the thought of Estelle, but I swallowed my emotions back as I walked out into the hallway.

Music played softly from the living room, and I glanced around to find even more photos of Emily on the walls, noticing the music was some of her favorites.

"Hungry?"

I screamed, finding Owen standing behind me with a plate in his hand, apology on his face.

"Sorry, I didn't mean to scare you. Here, sit." He placed

the plate on the table off to the left, and I tracked him cautiously with my eyes.

"Where am I?" I asked, not moving from where I stood.

"My house. Well, it's your house, too, Emily. See? I made it just how you like it," he beamed. I went to tell him I wasn't Emily, but I paused when I realized something was even more odd.

"Owen, how do you know Emily? I never showed you pictures of her or anything." I took a step back, but he followed me.

"Emily was everything to me," he explained, his eyes getting a glazed look to them as he lost himself in whatever memories he thought he had. He didn't know her, it was impossible. "We were each other's first everything. She saved me from my demons and kept them at bay. She wasn't afraid of me, not like everyone else."

I absently dropped down on the couch, not taking my eyes off him. "You dated?"

"I was going to marry her. We were so excited when we found out she was having a baby," he smiled, but rage suddenly took over as he fisted his own hair firmly and pulled. "But then he killed her and took her from me!"

My mind was still focused on the baby thing, but I managed to ask the other burning question. "What do you mean someone killed her? She killed herself."

"She'd never leave me!" he screamed, getting in my face. "She loved me! She told me every day!" His face softened a fraction when I flinched, and he reached out to cup my cheek. "I'm sorry, baby. I didn't mean to scare you. I'm not mad at you."

"I'm not Emily, Owen," I whispered, my own grief surfacing and mixing with pity for him, but it was short-lived as he slapped me. He looked eerily calm, no emotion on his face, which was scarier than his anger.

"If I can't have her, I'll have you. I can turn you into Emily, you see? Then she can be alive again. The day you walked into that gym, I just knew it could work."

"Owen," I said softly, shuffling back a little to put some distance between us. "She's gone. I'm Penn, remember? Your friend?"

Instead of getting angry again, he nodded. "I've always been your friend, right? I'm the only person that knows you properly. I'd never deceive you like those boys that claim to love you, or that girl."

"Leah?" I croaked out. "You killed her? Did you kill Dad and Estelle, too?"

"I'm going to kill all of them for you, Emily. So then we can be together," he said firmly, muttering under his breath to himself as he started to pace. "Leah was going to stop us from being together. She had to die, right? Jai said she wasn't a problem, but he lied. He lied!" He grabbed the small coffee table and threw it across the room, his emotions giving me a severe case of whiplash. "I tried to take down too many at once at the track that time, but I learned. It's smarter to take them out one by one. If Cruz hadn't shoved you to the ground, you would've gotten shot instead. I didn't mean to. You believe me, right? I'd never hurt you."

"Jai? What did Jai do?" I asked as I stood on shaky feet, trying to keep him talking as he spilled everything.

"He said he'd help us be together, but then Leah got in the way and he started freaking out! So I got rid of her before she could tell you lies about me. She doesn't understand my love for you," he scowled, clenching his fists. "Jai was distracted by her anyway. She had to go. I should've just threatened his life a long time ago, he's been good today."

"If you're only trying to help me, why did you kill Estelle? She was good to me," I whispered, crying out as he slapped me again, sending me flying to the floor as he stood over me.

"Because she lies! They all lie!"

"No she didn't! She loved me!" I sobbed, his face twisting with disgust.

"If she loved you, why did she let you be raised like trash? Why did she let your father abuse you? She could've tried to run with you, but she chose not to."

"She couldn't, that's kidnapping."

"She could've fucking run, and your father wouldn't have gone after you! He'd never let the town know all about his filthy little secret that he'd tried so hard to keep buried!" He grabbed my arm, hauling me to my feet. "You want to know why Barbara Whitlock left and never came back for you? Because she fucking hated you. You're the product of Louis' affair with the lowly nanny who cared for their little princess. I find it amusing that they promoted her to housekeeper, probably as hush money. The second Emily was killed, Barbara left because there was no longer anything in that house she cared for, including your father. I know he found out about Emily's baby and fucking killed her." Tears tracked down my face, and he pulled me close, kissing the top of my head. "It's okay, they can't hurt you now, I fixed it."

"Don't touch me!" I shouted, attempting to push him away but he held me firmly.

"Emily, stop."

"I'm not Emily!" I screamed, trying to hit him, but he pinned my arms by my sides and shushed me, stroking my hair.

"It's okay, you've had a big day, I know you're confused."

"You're confused, you psycho! You blew up Drake's car! I could've died!" I threw back, lifting my knee and hitting him right in the balls. He hunched over in pain, his arms loosening enough for me to dart away. He grabbed me, tearing my shirt as I kept fighting to get away from him, my voice hoarse as I managed to stumble away and run for the door. There was a padlock, my heart sinking as terror raced through me. I was trapped in here.

"Stone!" I screamed, slamming my fists against the door to try and draw attention. "Cruz!" I kept pounding on the door, screaming all their names until Owen yanked me away, holding a gun to my head. I froze, sobbing as he watched me through tear-filled eyes.

"Don't do this to us, baby. They don't love you, I do. I've always looked after you, haven't I? When your dad hurt you, or when you needed an escape? I never would've let you get hurt in that explosion. I'd planned on taking you, and blowing it up once Drake got in to chase after me, but then Knox showed up." He reached for my pants and I flinched, the gun pressing against my head more. "I can take it all away. I can call you Penn today, okay? Would that help? You can learn your new name later."

"Please, don't touch me," I begged, the safety clicking off on his gun and making me whimper.

"Stop fighting this. We can start fresh. I can cut that thing out of your arm, and we can have lots of babies and get married, just like we were supposed to. Take your pants off." I shook my head, but he waved the gun at me with a scowl, losing his temper. "Take them off!"

My hands shook as I reached for the waistband, nausea twisting inside my stomach as I did as he said. "Owen—"

"I love how you say my name," he breathed, pulling his shirt off while keeping the gun trained on me. "Go on, now the shirt. Put on a little show for me." He put more space between us, but I felt even more trapped as I removed my torn shirt, leaving me in nothing but my bra and panties. This wasn't the guy I'd fucked to take my mind off things, the gentle guy who'd been worried about hurting me the first time we'd had sex despite me not being a virgin. This was a psychopath who was locked in some kind of self-made reality where the past clashed with the present.

"Can't we talk about this first?" I asked quietly, trying to stall him.

"No. Take the rest off." His jaw was set hard, his patience completely gone. "Penelope, take it the fuck off, or I'll cut it off you."

"I'll never love you," I whispered, his face falling. "I love them."

He snarled, starting to pace the room again, but he suddenly shook his head, pointing the gun at me. "If I can't fucking have you, then neither can they. They don't even love you! I'd never share you with my friends like you're a cheap whore! You're a queen, you're supposed to be cherished!"

I was going to die in my fucking underwear thanks to a psychopath. What Emily had seen in him, I'd never know, but the more he talked, the more I realized she'd probably felt trapped with him, and that was why she'd chosen death. It was the only way to escape his chains.

"Just let me go."

"I can't," he said through gritted teeth, taking a calming breath as all the emotion vanished from his face again. "I'm sorry, Emily. I won't let them have you."

I squeezed my eyes shut as he steadied his aim, but they flew open again as the door was kicked in, and someone hurtled towards me. A scream left me as the gun went off multiple times, pain slicing across my arm as someone wrapped their arms around me like a shield.

Shouting filled the room, but all I heard was Stone's voice in my ear, soothing me.

"I've got you, Princess." He kept repeating it as if to convince me, but after a moment, he started leaning on me, his words slurring.

"Stone?" I asked with worry, pulling back to see how pale he was. "Stone!"

I wrapped my arms around him to try and hold him up, my hands getting covered in blood from his back. He choked, leaning on me harder as he fought to stay on his feet. He was hurt, badly.

"I love you. Even if you don't believe me," he mumbled, a loud sob leaving me.

"Don't you fucking dare! Don't you—" Cruz was suddenly there, helping get Stone on the ground.

"Baby, give me your shirt," he said in a panic as he pointed to the torn material on the ground, everything moving in slow motion. "Penn!"

I scrambled to grab it, dropping it twice before handing it to him, and he pressed it to the growing blood puddle on Stone's back. Knox dropped to his knees to help him while talking on the phone to who I assumed were the paramedics, my vision blurring as more tears poured out of me. Stone looked so cold, his eyes now closed as the guys tried to stop the bleeding.

To the world, he was going to be just another person who died because of me.

"Hey, stay with me, babe," Drake murmured, pulling his hoodie over my head and reaching down to grab my pants to help me into them just as sirens sounded outside. "I'll get you home."

"No!" I tried to yell, but my voice was half-gone and it came out raspy.

"Cruz and Knox will stay with Stone. We can get updates from them," he promised, holding me tightly as my legs gave out. I couldn't lose Stone, but from the way his body stayed completely still and his eyes remained shut, I think I already had.

Maddox appeared beside us, his voice low. "Who was he?"

I was confused for a moment, but my eyes landed on Owen's still body across the room, giving me my answer. He'd been my best friend for years when I'd had nobody, but my grief for him felt wrong now that I knew every second of our time together had been a lie.

"Penn's friend, Owen. He ran the Stoneleigh gym," Drake answered, lifting me into his arms. "I need to get her out of here."

"She needs the hospital, too," Maddox said calmly, and I could feel his eyes running over me. "She's in severe shock, Drake."

"But she—"

"She needs to be monitored properly. She could risk organ damage or die. Take her to the hospital, man. I fucking mean it."

I clung to Drake as he nodded and made his way out into the cold, night air, and he'd hardly started driving before I passed out.

Drake

I'd never been this scared before. Stone was currently in surgery, and we'd been warned to prepare to say goodbye. The bullets had hit vital organs, meaning if he did pull through, he would have a long road to recovery.

The three of us were sitting in Penn's room, anxiously waiting for her to wake up. She'd scared the fucking shit out of me when she'd passed out in the car and I couldn't wake her. As much as the Donovans had better pull at the hospital in Ashburn Valley, they managed to secure private rooms in Kingslake's hospital, which was probably what saved Stone from dying on the ambulance ride over. If they'd had to take him to Ashburn Valley, he wouldn't have lasted the trip.

My hand was in Penn's, my other in Knox's as he sat on my other side. Cruz was half asleep in a chair on the opposite side of the bed, his hand in hers as he rested his head on his arm on the mattress beside her. He was covered in Stone's blood, but he refused to go home and change. He wanted to be here the moment Stone got out of surgery.

The door opened and Cruz's head shot up, the doctor giving us a small smile as she closed the door behind her for privacy.

"Mr. Barrett is out of surgery and it went well. There was damage to his bladder and kidney, and luckily, the bullets just missed his spine. He'll have to stay here for a while and remain hooked up to a catheter, but with rest and monitoring, we expect a full recovery. You've got yourself a fighter."

I sagged in relief, but Cruz got to his feet. "Can I see him?"

"He's not awake yet. Leave him to rest for now, and I'll let you know when he's ready for visitors," she replied, running her eyes over the machines that Penn was hooked up to and checking her chart before excusing herself again.

Cruz kicked his shoes off, not giving a shit as he climbed onto the bed beside Penn and got comfortable, being mindful of her IV line and monitor. He looked as bad as they did, so I wasn't surprised when he was asleep within minutes.

"C'mon, let's go get some coffee," Knox murmured, and I shook my head.

"I don't want to leave her."

"Babe, she'll be fine. Let her and Cruz nap while we stretch our legs. We should fill Beckett in on the update too, she's probably still in the waiting room," he replied, and I sighed before untangling my fingers from Penn's to allow Knox to pull me to my feet.

He was right, Beckett was in the waiting room with Zavier who almost knocked me over when he saw me. "Are they okay?"

"Yeah, Penn's sleeping, and Stone just got out of surgery. He'll be stuck in here for a while but he should be fine," I mumbled into his shirt as he hugged me tightly in a death grip.

"Maddox said she was practically naked when you guys found her. Did he—" He didn't finish the sentence, but I knew what he meant. We'd all thought the same thing until the doctor confirmed Penn had only sustained a bullet wound to her arm and a shitload of shock, as well as a few hits to the face. There was no sign of sexual trauma.

"No, she's okay," I promised, patting his back and stepping into Knox's side.

"It was Owen all along? Did Penn say anything before passing out?" Beckett asked, dropping into a seat. "The house has pictures of Penn's sister all over the place like a fucking shrine, but didn't she die when Penn was really young?"

Knox nodded, sitting beside her and tugging me onto his lap, not giving a fuck about the dirty looks from the couple sitting across the room. "Emily was fifteen when she committed suicide. Her death records seem legit, but I can't find much of a trail between Emily and Owen. As far as Penn knew, they weren't connected. Penn met Owen because she started sneaking out of Kingslake and going to the gym."

"Maybe they weren't connected, and Owen's just a creepy bastard who was obsessed with Emily? Maybe that's why he snapped with Penn?" Beckett suggested, the idea not being too far-fetched.

"Hopefully he said something to Penn about it before we killed him," I said, itching to get back to Penn. Knox could sense me fidgeting, and he let out a sigh.

"Penn and Cruz are both asleep, but you're welcome to come and poke your head in if you want to see her."

Zavier nodded, and Beckett shrugged as she motioned for us to walk and they'd follow. She made it obvious she wasn't Penn's number one fan, but she wasn't a complete cold bitch towards her. Penn had proven she wasn't a prissy Kingslake princess, so Beckett had accepted her in some weird kind of way.

Cruz was still sleeping beside her when we walked in, and we spent the next hour just watching both of them sleep, Beckett glued to her phone in the corner. I was exhausted, too, but there was no way I could leave until Penn left with me.

I wasn't letting her out of my sight ever again.

Cruz

Beeping woke me, and I was surprised to find Zavier and Beckett here, deep in conversation about fuck knows what. I heard Owen's name mentioned and something about his death being too fast, guilt hitting me that it hadn't been faster. If I'd been one or two seconds faster with getting inside that cabin, then Stone and Penn wouldn't have ended up in the hospital.

"Hey," Drake murmured, drawing their attention to me as I yawned.

"Sorry, how long was I out?"

"An hour. Stone's still not awake, and neither's Penn," he said quietly, worry filling his eyes. "Why isn't she awake yet? Did they miss something?"

Beckett snorted, not moving from her spot across the room. "Her mind is fried and her body's exhausted. She might wake up soon, but she'll probably crash again. She's had a lot of emotional hits in a small amount of time. She was close with the housekeeper, yeah?"

I sighed, not daring to move in case I woke Penn. "Yeah, and Leah. As much as she also hated her father, finding him dead probably wasn't a fun experience for her. She talked a lot of shit about you guys taking him down, but she's not as tarnished as the rest of us. It probably hurt to see him like that more than she'd admit."

"Most likely. I have a feeling she'll come out of this a little more fucked up than you realize," she replied, running her eyes over Penn. "The girl's got balls, though. I take back everything bad that I said about her. She tamed Knox *and* Stone, the girl deserves an award."

"I'll give her whatever she wants once we're home. Pizza for breakfast? Done. Those awful energy drinks I think are toxic? Done," Drake grunted, gripping Knox's hand on his lap. "As long as she comes home."

I nodded my agreement, sliding my eyes to her beside me. She was so still, blood smeared across her pretty face and hands. They'd tried to clean as much as possible, but it was difficult when she was resting. I had no idea if it was Estelle's, her father's, or Stone's at this point.

I slid a hand across her stomach, wanting to cuddle her but not wanting to risk hurting her. She moved, my eyes darting to her face just as she blinked against the light. "Cruz?"

"Yeah baby, it's me. Drake, Knox, Beckett, and Lopez are here, too," I murmured, brushing her hair from her face. Her heart rate monitor started rising as grief and panic filled her eyes suddenly.

"Where's Stone? Is he—"

"Hey, he's okay. He's out of surgery. We haven't seen him yet, he needs the rest first, but they said he should make a full recovery," I assured her, taking her hand and giving it a gentle squeeze. "We can see him later once he's awake."

"He's alive?" she croaked, tears welling in her eyes as she squeezed my hand back, making me smile.

"Yeah, not even the Grim Reaper wants his grumpy ass. Guess you're stuck with him."

The nurse scurried in and scolded me, shooing me off the bed so she could check on Penn now that she was awake, and

Beckett pulled me into the hallway, wanting to talk in private. I didn't want to leave her, but I knew the others would fill me in on anything the nurse said.

"Mom texted me. It seems that Owen guy was a real weirdo. The cops have gone through his house and found a lot of shit. There were a bunch of dresses that belonged to Emily, and he had a diary he kept regular entries in. He was acting like Emily was still alive, talking about their future together."

I frowned, crossing my arms and leaning back against the wall. "Do you think he actually knew her or just stalked her? Maybe he killed her?"

"Doubtful. He blamed Louis." She leaned closer, not wanting her voice to carry into the room Penn was in. "He also claimed it was because Louis found out Emily was carrying Owen's child. He's either really crazy, or he had a secret romance going on with her."

"I'll drill Penn about it, but not until we get home. I need to find out how much she knows before we start throwing ideas around," I answered, thankful when she nodded.

Beckett was a good friend, but I'd fight her on it if she tried to bully her way into getting information out of Penn.

"We also found something else," she said with a sigh, pulling a piece of paper from her pocket and handing it to me. It had names and numbers on it. "Louis never came after her the first time you took her. It seems Owen had originally hired some helpers to try and take her. No idea if he was trying to kill her, though. These guys are the ones we dealt with, and he even kept notes about their failures. We found another contact he had, which is ironically one of ours. Said Owen tried to hire him months ago but the guy refused due to Penn's connection with us. I guess not all the people hired knew what they were getting into. Seems the drive-by at Devil's Dungeon that time was also connected to Owen. Hopefully, this is the end of it all. The only time we can find anything connected to Louis, was when he hired the Kings to retrieve her the day Stone handed her over."

"Hopefully, that's it then," I nodded, handing the paper back. "I'll keep you in the loop if I find out anything from Penn once we're home. I appreciate you stopping by to check on her."

"I'm only here for Lopez," she said with a scowl as we walked back into Penn's room, but we both knew that was bullshit. Zavier was more than capable of driving himself here.

Chapter Twenty-Six

Penn

Stone had woken for a short time later that day, but the nurses demanded I stayed in bed to rest. Cruz had gone to check on him with Knox, leaving Drake with me. The following morning they switched, Knox stayed with me while Drake and Cruz went and sat with Stone for a while, but I still wasn't allowed out of bed.

Finally, after being stuck in here for two whole days, they took pity on me and claimed I could see Stone, but they wanted me in here for one more night thanks to my stupid blood pressure going haywire.

Cruz pushed me in a wheelchair along the hallway as the guys wandered alongside us, and Drake opened the door to Stone's room to let us through, my eyes seeking out Stone straight away. He looked awful, but he was alive and that was all I cared about right now.

"Hey, Princess," he said sleepily, lifting a hand to reach for me, and Cruz moved my wheelchair beside the bed so I could take Stone's hand. I gave it a small squeeze, trying not to cry like an idiot, but tears fell anyway.

"Hey. You scared me half to death, you dumb idiot."

"I'd do it again if I had to," he smiled, wincing as he tried to move. Knox helped him get comfortable, and then Stone met my gaze again. "The guys said he didn't touch you. I need to hear it from you."

"Stone, we talked about this," Cruz murmured, concern flashing in his eyes. "She needs to rest, so don't throw traumatic shit at her."

"I'm not, I just need to hear her say he didn't fucking touch her," he bit out, gritting his teeth as he hurt himself again from his tense muscles. I leaned forward, holding his hand more tightly to draw his attention.

"I promise, he didn't."

Relief filled his face, but he didn't relax. "When I ran in and saw you nearly fucking naked, I thought—"

"Stone," Cruz warned more firmly, but I scowled at him.

"I'm not that fragile. If I don't want to talk about something, I'll let you know."

"Bossy," he muttered, but his eyes flashed with amusement as I turned back to Stone.

"He was stuck in some weird false sense of reality. He claimed he loved my sister and they were together. He wanted me to be her," I said quietly, my heart hurting as I added, "Apparently, she was pregnant with his baby when she died. He thinks Dad killed her, but I think maybe my sister was terrified of Owen and saw death as the only way out of her relationship with him. Maybe he made the whole thing up, and Emily didn't even know him, we'll never know."

Knox grimaced, his voice gentle. "His story checks out. The cops raked the house for information, and there's photos of Owen and Emily together. They'd met multiple times over the span of a year or two."

Stone frowned, glancing at Knox. "How was such a psycho so smart, though?"

"Crazy doesn't always mean stupid, you know?" Knox

grumbled, turning his attention to me. "Did he say anything about someone helping him?"

My heartbeat picked up, and as much as I wanted to tell them, I couldn't. Jai deserved to get his ass beat for what he'd done, but I wasn't ready to throw the Grim Reaper card at him just yet. There'd been enough death on my hands this week.

"Enough," Cruz said firmly, noticing my panic and giving my shoulder a gentle squeeze. "We can talk about all of that later. Let's just focus on getting everyone back on their feet, okay?"

Stone looked ready to argue, but he thankfully kept his mouth shut about it and changed the subject. "When are they letting you out? Apparently, I could be in here for weeks. How the fuck am I supposed to run the Thieves from a hospital bed?"

"You don't," Cruz snorted, giving him a stern look. "You rest, eat your vegetables like a good boy, and let us handle it. You know we're all capable, and we can still run things by you when needed. Both you and Penn are on bedrest until further notice. No exceptions."

Stone's nostrils flared, and I could tell he was about to explode, so I got to my feet and leaned over to kiss his cheek, silencing his attack. "It's okay, Stoney Baloney, I'll come and hang out with you so you still have someone to yell at."

"Sit down," Cruz growled, but I ignored him and kept talking to Stone.

"I know you were out to prove yourself, but you didn't have to be a drama queen and take bullets for me."

"Yes, I did, because you were willing to do the same for me." Then Stone grinned, teasing in his tone. "Kind of hoping I get unlimited sex on tap for the rest of my life now, too."

"Definitely," I laughed, giving him another kiss before

sitting back in my wheelchair so Cruz didn't have an aneurysm.

We spent an hour sitting here just talking, then Stone seemed to realize none of the guys were at the compound and sent Knox and Drake back, agreeing that Cruz could stay as my personal wheelchair pusher. Drake texted Cruz religiously for the rest of the day, and when Cruz ducked out to use the bathroom, I turned to Stone with a dirty look.

"I can't believe you'd confess your love to me like that. You're supposed to wait until we get home when everything's okay again, and then—"

"Shut the fuck up, and give me a kiss," he grunted, giving me the stink-eye. "In my defense, I thought I was a goner and couldn't die without you knowing."

"Taking bullets for me was a pretty big give away," I said dryly, shuffling onto the bed, being mindful not to hurt him as I leaned over to kiss him. He let out a curse as he tried to move over for me, and I scolded him. "I'm tiny, why the fuck do you think I need more space? Don't move."

He ignored me, gritting his teeth as he reached out to place a hand on my waist. "Did Owen tell you why he targeted those particular people? I thought maybe he'd killed your father to help you in some weird twisted way, but if he knew what Leah and Estelle meant to you—"

"He told me," I said softly, hesitating before continuing. "He said Estelle could've run with me to keep me safe, but instead, she watched him hurt me for years. I don't have any proof, but he claimed she's my real mom."

His eyes went wide. "Really?"

"Yeah. It makes some sense as to why Mom hates me but loved Emily. I was proof of Dad's affair. It wasn't even with someone of a high social status, which was probably the more embarrassing part for my family. The rich don't mingle with the help, you know how those circles can be. If Dad was sleeping with Estelle and knocked her up—"

"Then the only way she could keep you was by pretending you weren't hers," he finished, pity filling his eyes as I nodded. "I'm sorry, baby. Don't let this taint the memories you have of her. I know how much you loved her."

"I'm mad at her for not telling me, but I also get it. Dad would've kicked her out, maybe even had her killed to keep her silent. She mothered me as much as she could without making it known," I mumbled, laying down to gently rest my head on the pillow beside his. "I wish she'd told me, though, when we were staying with her."

"I know, babe. Get some rest. I love you," he whispered, my eyes closing as I kissed his shoulder.

"I love you too."

Leaving Stone at the hospital was the worst. I was still ordered to rest, but I hated doing it at home without him. The guys had organized a funeral for Estelle, and as much as I didn't think my father deserved anything, they also organized for him to be buried. All of his estate belonged to me since I was his only living relative, but most of it felt like dirty money, or it was counterfeit anyway, thanks to him never checking it, so I donated what I could to charities that helped people suffering from abuse, the fake money being destroyed.

I wish Dad was alive to hear how much counterfeit cash he had because then he'd know he'd been screwed by multiple people. It was almost a shame that he had no idea that Zavier and Ander had been my saviors, not my villains.

It had been a week now since I'd been back at the

compound, and I'd just finished having a shower and gotten dressed when I'd stepped out of the stall to find Jai in front of me. Immediate fear trickled into me, but he darted forward to clamp a hand over my mouth before I could scream, desperation in his eyes. "I'm not here to hurt you, shit. I didn't know this would get so bad."

When I stopped fighting, he slowly pulled his hand back, letting me talk. "Why the fuck did you even do it?"

"At first, it was because Stone wanted you gone, so I figured I was helping, but then when Owen started threatening other people, I tried to back out. I never wanted anyone to die," he choked out, stepping in front of me when I went to move towards the door. "Please, don't tell them. They'll kill me." My hands shook slightly as I tried to contain my panic, but it was hard when he kept getting in my face. "Penn, I'm begging you."

"How did you know Owen?"

"We grew up on the same street when I was in foster care. I tried to talk him out of hurting anyone, but that made it worse. He told me he was planning to kill your dad, which I figured everyone would be on board with, so I helped him that night. I had no idea the woman—"

"Estelle," I bit out, anger washing through me. "Her name was Estelle, and she was the nicest woman in the entire world. Apparently, she was also my mom, but you probably know that." His gaze dropped from mine, making me snort. "You're not as innocent as you want me to believe. Did you even love Leah? He killed her because of you, not me. Do Will and Sandra know how much of a fucking snake you are?"

His eyes widened and he lunged at me, covering my mouth again in a panic as if to stuff the words back down my throat. "No, they can't know!"

I lifted my hand and jabbed him in the eye with my finger, and he jerked back from me, giving me a second to escape. I'd just reached the door when Knox appeared, catching me as I barreled into him.

"What the fuck is going on in here?" he demanded as Jai tried to dart past us, but I put my foot out and tripped him, sending him sprawling across the ground. Knox let me go and bent down to grab him, hauling him to his feet by his shirt. "Did you fucking touch my girl?"

Jai's frantic eyes met mine, and I knew I couldn't straight up lie to Knox. I'd kept it a secret for as long as possible, but the truth was, Jai was never going to be able to avoid this forever, and neither was I.

His blood wasn't on my hands, I knew that now. He'd done it to himself. Even if it tore me apart to know how someone else I'd cared about had been nothing but a snake.

"He grew up with Owen," I said softly, keeping my gaze on Knox to avoid breaking down. "He's the one who got Leah killed, and how the cameras always got scrambled. He's been working with him from the start."

Murder filled Knox's eyes, but he thought better of it as he realized how much this was hurting me. Another betrayal, another dead body.

"Baby? Go to Cruz, he's in his room. Me and Drake will hand Jai over to the Psychos." That surprised me.

"You're not going to kill him?" I asked, hating to sound relieved.

"Archer Hendricks still wants his pound of flesh for Luna getting shot at the track. Hopefully, this will show him we're willing to work with the crews. As long as Jai ends up in the ground, I don't care who does it," he said in a low voice, motioning for me to walk past him. I quickly walked out, not being able to meet Jai's eyes on the way out, and I shut the door behind me once I was safely in Cruz's bedroom, finding him playing his guitar on the bed.

He frowned, putting it aside before holding a hand out for me. "What's wrong?"

"It was Jai," I blurted out as I took it and let him pull me onto his lap. He knew exactly what I was talking about without me having to say it.

"Where is he?"

"Knox is taking him to the crews to handle. Like an olive branch for Archer or something," I mumbled, burying my face in his neck. "I didn't want someone else to die, Cruz. I wasn't ready to face that yet."

"It's not your fault that the others died, you know that, right?" he said firmly, cradling the back of my head and kissing my neck. "It's because of Owen, and you were a victim of his psychotic bullshit just like they were."

"But I'm alive and they're not," I whispered, and he leaned back to take my face in both his hands, forcing me to hold his gaze.

"Only because Stone got between you and that gun. Stone's taller than you, and if he hadn't been there, you would've copped multiple bullets to the lower part of your lungs. He'll never regret the choice he made because that grumpy piece of shit loves you. You hear me?"

"I want him to come home."

"Me too, and I think the nurses agree. He's giving them hell, he's a terrible patient," he chuckled, giving me a quick kiss before turning me so that I was straddling him while facing away from him. He grabbed his guitar, placing it over my lap awkwardly. "Here. Copy my fingers."

"You're going to teach me to play?" I asked, watching how he placed his fingers on the strings before he moved so I could do it. I got it wrong so he helped rearrange where I put them.

"I won't teach you anything too fancy, promise."

I didn't realize how much time had passed as Cruz taught me more chords, but Knox and Drake were already back by the time we finished and left the bedroom. Will was in the living room, sitting on the couch with his elbows on his knees and his head in his hands. Cruz dropped down beside him, giving his shoulder a nudge.

"You all good, man?"

Will's head lifted and he met my gaze, and I could tell he'd heard about Jai already by the way the grief was written all over his face. From what I'd gathered, Jai and Will were as close as Stone and his boys, they were family, so losing him would hit hard.

"I'm so fucking sorry. I had no idea—"

"I know," I said softly, squatting in front of him with a small smile. "You're not responsible for his actions." The irony of this conversation wasn't lost as Cruz gave me a knowing look as if I should take my own advice. "Does Sandra know?"

He was quiet for a moment before shaking his head. "Sandra left last night. She's not coming back."

"Wait, what?" I murmured, a shaky breath leaving him.

"She's been wanting to leave for a while, but Leah's death pushed her over the edge. She told me to choose, and I told her I was staying. This is my home and my family is here, and despite all the chaos that's been happening here, I don't blame you for any of it. Sandra can't let shit go, so I didn't beg her to stay."

My heart hurt for him, and I was glad when Cruz dropped an arm around his shoulders for one of those manly half-hugs.

"I'm glad you stayed, bro. We'd miss your ugly face at breakfast. Besides, you'd miss watching Penn make a dick out of herself in the target room, she's our newest recruit."

"Hey! I'm not that bad!" I scolded, but Knox looked me right in the eye, his face completely straight.

"You're not that fucking good either, Whitlock."

"Bite me, asshole."

"Where do you want it?" he chuckled deeply, and I stood up straight to flip him off.

"Who's taking me to see Stone today? I'm surprised he hasn't called to throw his daily tantrum."

Drake snickered, sliding his arm around my middle to pull me close, smacking a kiss on my cheek. "He's occupied. Zavier wanted to go and harass him."

"I bet Stone loved that."

"For sure. I think Zavier's tying up loose ends with Ander before pulling back. This is the second thing in the past year that could've landed him in deep shit, and he's got to stop testing how many lives he's got. Raven would kick him the fuck out, and he's totally in love with her, so he'll put her first."

"Why aren't they together then?" I huffed, crossing my arms. "He deserves a nice girlfriend."

"Yeah, well, he won't get that from the little hellcat. Not to mention, Reid and Logan would tear his dick off if he even tried. That girl's going to die a virgin at this rate," Drake laughed. "I know Ander's friendship is already getting him in trouble too, Raven can't stand him."

"Why? He's nice."

"No offense, but you've only seen the playful Ander with the hero complex, you haven't seen the ruthless underworld player that likes to bathe in the blood of his enemies," Drake replied dryly before adding, "You're biased because of the ice cream he bought you. He's not like that with everyone, he just felt sorry for you."

My phone buzzed with a text and I pulled it from my pocket, smiling as I saw Stone's name.

Stone: Where are you? Aren't you coming over today?

Penn: You miss me, baby?

Stone: The second you walked out that door last night.

Stone's romantic side was a little overwhelming, but not in a bad way. It was like he had to make up for all the missed time between us, and I wasn't going to complain.

Penn: I'll get one of the guys to bring me now.

Stone: You have half an hour.

I rolled my eyes and relayed the order to Knox, who let out a scoff. "I'm meeting up with Maddox, so I can't take you."

I turned to Drake who winced. "I was going to see Jett while Knox was busy."

"Cruz?" I whined, an amused laugh leaving him as he stood, motioning to Will.

"You want to come for a drive? I'll dump Penn with Stone, and we can go for a beer or something?" he offered, Will giving him a small smile.

"Yeah, that sounds good."

"Took you long enough," Stone growled as I walked into his room, not surprised with his attitude. He really wasn't coping with being chained to this bed. I couldn't even give him a sneaky blow job because it made his muscles flex, and hurt him too much.

I sat on the edge of the bed, leaning over to kiss him. "I'm happy to see you, too. How are you feeling?"

"Ready to commit murder," he snarked, but he

motioned for me to lean down for another kiss, his voice softer as he added, "I'm happy to see you, sorry. Where's the guys?"

"Knox is with Maddox, Drake is with Jett, and Cruz dropped me off so he could have a beer with Will. Sandra left him last night and moved out, and then the shit with Jai happened earlier today, too, so—"

"What shit with Jai?" he demanded, and I could've killed Cruz for not letting me know Stone didn't know. I assumed they'd filled him in.

"Oh, um. Knox handed him over to the Psychos for Archer to pulverize. Jai was the one working with Owen," I said sheepishly, expecting him to strangle me. I was wrong, though, as he took my hand and gave it a squeeze.

"He's been at the compound this whole time, right? Has he bothered you? You should've told us earlier, what if he'd hurt you?"

"I hadn't seen him until today. He freaked out about me ratting him out, but he didn't hurt me, though," I said quickly when he growled.

"I need to get the fuck back to the compound so I can keep you safe. I can't do shit from here," he bit out, making me chuckle.

"The fuck will you do at the compound? Throw pillows at them from your bedroom?"

"I could lock you in the bedroom with me," he grumbled, threading his fingers through mine, his voice softening. "Lopez is pulling back from Lavaro's business deals. He feels like shit because he does a lot of good, but I think this worried him a little bit. What if he'd been targeted by Owen, and Raven or the guys got hurt? He'd never forgive himself."

"I'm grateful that he saved me, but I'd never forgive myself either if something happened to him or his friends."

"He's hoping to find a legal job and pay taxes like a real

grown-up. I think he'll get bored fast, though," Stone grinned. "Speaking of jobs, have you spoken to Harley?"

"Yeah, he wants me to rest for a few more weeks, but then I can have a couple of shifts a week to see how I do. He said he won't give me too many days on, though, so it doesn't interfere with Thieves stuff while I'm training," I said proudly, more than excited to be a regular person with a normal job.

"Have you been practicing your driving? Shooting? Navigation?" he asked rapidly. "You know you won't get better if you don't? Are the guys—"

"Slow down, Cruz has been helping me with computer stuff, Knox has had me in the target room most of the week, mainly to keep me occupied, I'm sure, and all three of them have sat with me in the car while I practice at some point despite the fact I'm technically still meant to be resting. They quiz me on street names every time we come to see you, too," I said dryly, getting a satisfied nod.

"Good. I'm a little surprised Will didn't leave with Sandra. They've been together forever."

"Sandra wanted him to choose between her and the Thieves. He won't ever turn his back on you guys," I said gently, surprise flickering across his face.

"He said that?"

"Yeah. The Night Thieves are his family, and he wasn't about to leave. Sandra's blaming me for Leah's death still, but he doesn't. He's a good guy, I'm glad you're not losing him."

His eyes narrowed. "Don't get any ideas. If he touches you, I'll put a bullet in him and throw him to the crows."

"Jesus, he's a nice guy, not a collectable item," I smirked, but that didn't relax him in the slightest.

"Same shit. You have enough guys, no more."

"Trust me, I don't want more. You guys are a fucking handful," I scoffed, glaring at him as he poked me in the ribs with his finger. "Don't move or you'll hurt yourself!"

"You're lucky I can't move or you'd be bent over this fucking bed getting an attitude adjustment," he warned, no anger in his tone. The nurse chose that time to walk in, eyeballing me like I was the unluckiest woman in the entire world. I couldn't blame her, he really had been an asshole all week to the staff, they probably thought he beat me up in his spare time with the anger constantly rolling off him.

"When can I leave?" Stone bit out for the millionth time, an exasperated sigh leaving her.

"Trust me, Mr. Barrett, when you're allowed to be discharged, we won't delay sharing the news with you. It's at least another week at the bare minimum."

"Seriously?" he snapped, earning a glare in return as she finished checking his chart.

"I know, I'm mad about it, too." She stomped off, and I laughed loudly as Stone fumed.

"You're such a baby! Stop whining and enjoy the rest."

"Enjoy the rest? How the fuck can I enjoy it when I can't keep my eyes on you?" he gritted out, hissing as he got too uptight and injured his stitches. I scowled, laying down beside him and kissing his shoulder.

"You're grumpy, take a nap."

"Make me."

"That's childish," I snorted, snuggling into him a little more until his body relaxed and his hand took mine again. "I'll nap with you."

"You'll be here when I wake up?" he asked as if he didn't trust me, knowing full well that I never left without letting him know. He was just too high on pain meds to remember sometimes.

"Yeah, get some sleep. I told Cruz to give us a few hours," I promised, not surprised in the slightest when he started softly snoring a few moments later. I never would've thought that I had any control over this asshole, but as long as I was by his side, he seemed to listen to what I said as if my word was law. I was completely okay with that. Even though he pretended to hate every damn second of it in front of the guys to avoid being teased.

They had no room for judgment, they all did as they were told, too, because they secretly loved being bossed around. Especially in the bedroom.

Well, other than Knox, but I didn't mind. Who knew the thieves who broke into my damn house could manage to steal my damn heart? I sure as fuck hadn't seen it coming.

I closed my eyes, Stone's breathing putting me to sleep as if it were a lullaby, and I dreamed of a princess locked in her tall tower, and the villains who came to save her.

That was how all fairytales ended, right?

Epilogue

Penn

Two Months Later

"You're sure no one's home?" I whisper-yelled when something moved upstairs in the Kingslake mansion we were currently breaking into, and Cruz peered down at his tablet to find the culprit, his balaclava hiding his face.

"Ugh, they have a cat. I fucking hate cats."

"Apart from the terrifying cat, is it safe to go up?" I deadpanned, making him huff at my teasing.

"Yeah, you're good, baby. Have you ever had a cat? They're furry fucking demons from Hell."

I crept up the stairs with my flashlight, cringing when one of the floorboards creaked loudly. Something thudded two seconds before the tinkering of a bell sounded, the cat in question appearing from the bedroom to stare at us.

"Hey, kitty," I whispered, the asshole hissing at me before taking off down the stairs into the dark. I could hear Drake roaring with laughter through the earpiece I was wearing as he watched us from the compound, and Cruz held his arms out like *I fucking told you.*

Once safely in the bedroom away from Satan's sidekick, I grabbed the closet door with a gloved hand and pulled it open, searching carefully for the necklace we'd been hired to find. I knew it was here because I'd seen the man's wife wearing it at an event two weeks ago.

Cruz wandered across the hall to another bedroom, the two of us silently going through the entire house until we found it.

"Bingo," I grinned as I opened a small box I found tucked inside the bedside table, the diamond necklace shining in the light of the flashlight. It was beautiful, but I really didn't understand why people collected this kind of stuff.

I'd prefer a big, cheesy pizza. That much was obvious from the weight I'd put on. I looked good, my body having a decent figure for the first time in a long time, and the guys couldn't get enough of it. I liked myself more like this, too.

"Got it?" Cruz asked as he walked into the room behind me, his eyes meeting mine with pride. "Good job, baby."

"Hey, guys? Dickbag and his lady are leaving the restaurant. Time to bounce," Drake said into the earpiece, and Cruz motioned for me to lead the way back down the stairs. The first week or two of being allowed to go on jobs had sucked. The guys were paranoid and wouldn't let me do anything other than watch, but now they were getting me to lead a lot. Stone was impressed with how fast I picked things up, and he finally took notice of my eye for detail with expensive pieces of art and collectables. He actually asked my opinion on a lot of things now, which made me realize just how much he'd pulled me into the organization.

We made sure we left the house exactly as we'd found it, Cruz flipping the angry cat off on the way out, then we switched off our flashlights and made our way down the street in the dark. Thankfully, we hadn't parked too far away.

I climbed behind the wheel, pulling my balaclava and earpiece off before handing the necklace over to Cruz as he removed his gear, too, grinning as I started the car. I'd gotten my license two weeks ago, and the guys humored my enthusiasm to drive at every opportunity.

I didn't mean to brag, but I'd only hit one parked car so far.

I drove along a side street, my window rolled down to let the cool breeze in, and Cruz slid his hand onto my thigh. "I think we should start teaching you how to disable alarms next. What do you think?"

"How do I learn that without getting us arrested?" I asked seriously, frowning at the thought. "I won't get it right the first few times, and—"

"I'd guide you so you can't fuck it up. You're good at following instructions." He smirked in the dark, reminding me of the games we'd played last night. Cruz and Knox had gotten bored while Stone and Drake were delivering an art piece to a client, and I let them have their wicked way with me.

Both of them had bossed me around the bedroom for an hour, Stone walking in to find me on my knees between Knox's legs, my hands bound behind my back as Knox filled my throat with his cum.

I slept like a rock thanks to Stone getting jealous and going caveman on me.

I'd say it was a work in progress about teaching him to share, but it really wasn't, and I couldn't complain. The sex was mind-blowing since they liked to compete with each other.

"Need to pull over?" Cruz offered in a teasing tone, snapping me out of it as I glanced at him.

"Huh?"

"You moaned. What were you thinking about?" he asked, his hand trailing higher up my thigh. When I didn't reply, he growled. "Pull over."

"We'll be home in ten minutes," I huffed, but I slowed the car and pulled over to the side of the road, putting the emergency brake on. "We can't just—" My words were cut off as he unclipped his seat belt and kissed me, his hand instantly sliding into my leggings and finding my soaking entrance. My hips jerked as he teased my clit, a curse leaving me. "Fuck, Cruz."

"What the hell were you thinking about? You're dripping," he groaned, pushing his fingers even deeper and making me almost lift off the damn seat. "Tell me."

"Last night with you and Knox," I panted, squeezing my eyes shut as my climax drew closer. "How you guys bossed me around, and then how Stone railed me when he got back because he was mad about it."

"You like making him jealous," he murmured against my neck, biting the skin gently, and I nodded, breathing hard and trying to hold onto the damn door as the tingling grew stronger.

"I'm going to come, fuck, I need—"

"I've got you," he promised, curling his fingers inside me as he sucked on my neck, and I moaned loudly as I came, my hand still trying to grip the door while my other fisted his shirt. "So pretty when you come for me."

My body was like jelly as he pulled away, heat flashing in his eyes in the moonlight as he lifted his wet fingers to his mouth and sucked.

"You don't play fair," I said as I huffed out a tired laugh and reached for his pants, but he swatted me away.

"Thieves don't play fair," he chuckled, sitting back in his seat. "We can continue this later. Let's get home before Stone has a fucking aneurysm."

"I need a second," I whined, and he simply threw me a satisfied look without saying anything.

Once we arrived at the compound almost twenty minutes later, we walked straight into the office where Stone looked ready to explode.

"Here you go, boss," Cruz smirked as he dropped the necklace into Stone's hand before getting comfortable in a chair. "Sorry we're late. There was so much traffic. Where's Drake?"

"You're not fucking sorry. Drake dragged Knox off to the bedroom, thanks to your little phone call. Stop calling us when you're fucking around," Stone snapped, the necklace forgotten about as he put it on the desk and stalked towards me. "You're in my bed tonight, Princess. You can thank Cruz for calling us while he got you off. *Again*."

Cruz had a habit of doing that, rubbing it in their faces at every opportunity. Well, Drake enjoyed listening in, but Knox and Stone turned into cavemen over it. Thankfully, Drake was handling Knox's blue balls.

"No way. I have to get up for work in four hours to help Harley open. I'm too tired for your bullshit tonight," I groaned, but he grabbed my wrist and started yanking me from the room, speaking over his shoulder.

"I want a full report in the morning, Cruz!"

"Yes, Sir," Cruz chirped, giving me a wink.

I ended up only getting two hours of sleep, waking up to Stone pushing inside me again as if I needed a reminder that I was his.

I was definitely going to be walking funny at work all day.

Knox

"She doesn't like it when we annoy her at work," Drake

grumbled, but I knew he was excited to see her, too. It was rare she got a full day of work without one of us hanging around, not that she could blame us. The last time we'd left her alone, she'd been taken and almost killed by a psychopath.

"She's full of shit. She smiles more when we're lingering in the booths," I said flatly, shoving the door open at Harley's and heading for our usual booth. Harley shook his head and tried to hide his smile when he saw us, not bothering to come over since he knew we were here for Penn.

Cruz and Stone were having a meeting with a bunch of the Thieves. We'd split the organization into multiple sections, using people's strengths better. Stone was still the boss of everyone, and he loved to remind us of that, but I was in charge of the protection jobs now, Cruz handled most of the tech, and Drake had started handling more of the stakeouts. With Penn having a good eye for legitimate art and jewelry, Stone had been letting her train some of the others to ensure they knew what was real and what was fake, which made our jobs a lot easier. Training newbies was hard and time consuming, but now we didn't have to worry about it.

Penn had dealt with an uncomfortable handover a month ago thanks to someone who recognized her as Louis' problem child, and Stone had decided we should go back to being faceless for our own safety, bringing in a team of Thieves who could handle the exchanges but didn't go on thieving jobs. Everyone had a part to play, and it ran like clockwork now that we had some kind of order amongst us.

I just wished that Penn didn't want to work in the damn bar so she was safely in the compound.

"You do know Harley and Alex are part of the Psychos, right? I think they're well-trained in how to spot a threat," Penn deadpanned as she walked over to us, but she happily dropped a kiss on both our lips with a small smile. She looked tired, thanks to Stone keeping her awake. "You want the usual?"

"Burgers and fries," Drake piped up, bouncing in his seat as if I hadn't fucked him through the damn mattress for hours last night and not let him sleep either. "I'm starving."

"You want that for breakfast?"

I raised an eyebrow at her. "Says the girl who ate an entire cold pizza for breakfast yesterday."

"What can I say? You guys gave me an appetite," she winked, heading towards the kitchen to give Alex the order. I dropped an arm around Drake, tugging him closer.

"Beckett's racing tonight if you want to go and watch? I think Logan's racing her."

"Yeah, he is. Lopez called earlier to see if Penn wanted to go."

I scowled, still pissed at that fucker for sneaking Penn out of the compound last week and putting her in Ander's passenger seat, letting her go for a lap on the track at full speed. It was hard to be mad at her about going against our wishes because I'd seen the video that Beckett had filmed, and as much as she'd taken it to piss off Stone, Penn had been so fucking happy in that moment.

Ander said it was a one-time-only thing, and he just wanted to give her the one thing he'd promised before going underground. From what he'd been saying, we wouldn't be seeing him for a while. I had no idea what was going on with him, but I got it. Sometimes I just had to shut the world out and get out of my own head, too. Not so much these days, though, thanks to Penn.

I loved her, but I loved Drake more because of her, too. She'd made me realize what I wanted in life, and that I should take what I wanted without apology. Being in public with Drake didn't bother me anymore, and I found myself being relaxed in general. If someone didn't like my relationship, they could go and fuck themselves.

Who knew a Kingslake princess could tame an asshole like me? She'd turned me into a fucking kitten.

Drake

We spent most of the afternoon at Harley's watching Penn work, but when Stone dropped Cruz off, Knox figured we could bail. The one thing I loved about Penn coming into our lives and shaking shit up between me and Knox, was that he was more open in the bedroom, and ten times more insatiable if that were possible.

"Do you think Stone will be pissed if we call dibs for Penn tonight?" Knox chuckled in my ear as he wrapped his naked body around mine from behind after railing the hell out of me.

"She needs some sleep," I reminded him, earning a groan.

"I'll let her nap a little in between rounds."

"Am I not enough for you? Surely your dick is starting to struggle to stay up," I teased, tilting my head to the side as his lips trailed across my neck and along my shoulder. Knox's romantic side didn't come out all the time, but he was doing it more and more when he realized how stupidly horny it made me. That man had been turning me into a damn pretzel for months thanks to some of the sweet shit he'd been doing, and I was soaking it up just as much as he was.

I was insanely relaxed thanks to the post orgasmic bliss I was in, but I was vaguely aware of Penn slipping into the room and quietly closing the door. She padded over to the bed, sliding under the covers to sandwich me between her and Knox.

"How was work?" Knox's voice rumbled in my ear, a soft

chuckle leaving her as she closed her eyes and snuggled into me, her hand snaking around my waist.

"You know exactly how work was since you were there for most of the shift."

"Where's Cruz?" I asked with a yawn, knowing she was close to falling asleep herself.

"Ethan called to check in just as we got home, so he's talking to him." That made me happy. Cruz and Ethan weren't close anymore, but I knew it was important to Cruz to stay in contact. They'd been through a lot together as kids, and I knew Cruz worried that Ethan's obsession with flirting with death was going to land him in the ground sooner rather than later.

I'd seen videos of him and his friends, and the guy was a fucking idiot on a motorcycle.

"Would you like to nap while he's busy?" I asked as I nuzzled into her neck, placing kisses across her skin as she let out a content sigh.

"That sounds amazing. Five minutes won't hurt, right? You'll wake me up?" she asked as she draped a leg over my hip.

"Of course." There was no chance in hell that we'd wake her up. She was exhausted.

Knox lifted his arm, resting his hand on her hip as she drifted off, and it didn't take long for his breathing to even out as he fell asleep, too. I tried to stay awake to savor being between them like this, but I doubted I lasted more than five minutes before sleep dragged me under, too.

Cruz

Ethan was a fucking idiot. I'd spent hours on the damn phone with him, trying to convince him that his bike was a deathtrap, but he really didn't give a shit about his safety.

"You worry too much. You do know you break into houses for a living, right? You like a rush, too," he deadpanned as his motorcycle started in the background, making me huff.

"Yeah, but mine's the thrill of taking shit that doesn't belong to me, yours is mooning the Grim Reaper and asking him to fuck you in the ass, romance optional."

"Damn, your girl made you kinky," he chuckled, his voice dropping. "You'll have to bring her out here so I can meet her sometime. If she's important to you, she must be one hell of a girl."

"You could say that again," I smiled, glancing at the time with a cringe. We were supposed to meet Beckett at the track twenty minutes ago. "Hey, I need to go. It's track night. Ride safely, okay?"

"Not a fucking chance, bro," he laughed, and I rolled my eyes as he revved the hell out of his bike before cutting the call. Mom would hate that fucking thing so much if she was still here to see it.

I found Penn stumbling around the bathroom, frantically washing her face. "We're late!"

I leaned against the wall, hearing the water running and knowing Drake or Knox was in here, possibly both. I was glad they were a lot more secure in their relationship now, and it showed when they did things on their own, then other times they'd spend time alone with Penn. They never made each other compete for attention, managing to balance it well between the three of them.

"Slow down. You obviously needed to rest," I scolded, knowing from the crease mark on her cheek that she'd been sleeping. "I don't even know where Stone is."

"He's in the kitchen with Will. I was just in there," Knox called out from the shower stall, and I rolled my eyes when Drake cursed on a groan. They were worse than Logan, I swore to God. They didn't get off of each other.

Penn slowed a little, and I stepped in behind her and grabbed the brush from the sink, starting to brush the knots out of her hair. "Want it in a braid?" I asked, knowing she liked it when I pampered her. I loved nothing more than fucking her, but I didn't mind spending time with her like this. Just like Drake, Penn's love language was affection, and I tried hard to take note of little things that would matter to her.

Brushing her hair didn't seem like much, but I could tell it meant a lot to her by the way she eyed me in the mirror when she didn't think I was paying attention. I held her entire world in the palm of my hand with this goddamn brush.

Knox and Drake finally finished whatever the fuck they were doing, both of them stepping out of the stall fully dressed, and once Penn's hair was braided and she'd put some mascara on, we headed towards the kitchen in search of Stone.

He looked pissed as he spoke to Will about some newbie who'd fucked up and gotten arrested, meaning we had to cover shit up and bail them out, but we always let them sit in a cell overnight to try and teach them a lesson.

They'd gone against orders, so this was what happened.

Stone had no idea how much of a hold Penn had over him, he didn't see it from our perspective, but the second she walked over to him to wrap her arms around his waist, the anger vanished from his features as well as his voice, his arm absently banding around her in return.

"I'll call and let them know we'll get him out in the morning. They can scare him a little so he doesn't pull this shit again," Stone grumbled, and Will smothered a smile when he noticed Stone's change in attitude, too.

"Want me to handle it? You guys are already late," he offered, and as much as Stone wasn't good at handing things over to people, he was slowly accepting Will as someone he could trust to lead more. Will had good people skills, he had a backbone, but was polite about it, meaning handling cops was something he was good at.

"Fine. Make sure you tell them to give him some grief over it, though, and not to let him know he's getting out tomorrow," he ordered, turning to us. "Why are you all standing around? Get in the fucking car, we're late."

"Yes, boss," I chuckled, walking out with the guys and chuckling under my breath as I heard Penn scold him for being a dick. Like the pushover for her that he was, the asshole grunted an apology and followed us outside with her tucked securely by his side.

Stone

"Shh, Princess," I warned as she screamed behind my hand while I fucked her from behind against the cold, brick wall. Her pussy gripped my dick tightly as I thrusted three more times before spilling inside her, giving her a second to remember where we were before removing my hand from her mouth. She slumped against the wall, the sound of car engines and drunken laughter surrounding us in the dark. Fucking her behind the bathroom out in the open was stupid, but I hadn't seen her all day, and I wasn't going to make it until we got home.

I pulled out of her, straightening her panties and jeans before putting my dick away, not giving a fuck if someone copped an eyeful of that. They shouldn't have been sneaking around behind the bathroom if that was the case. We were completely out of view, but anyone close by would've heard us.

"I need to clean up," she panted, shaking her head when I scowled. "I'm not sitting in your fucking cum tonight, Stone. At home I can handle that, but not here. It feels gross."

"You're no fun," I grumbled, but I gave her a kiss to let her know I was teasing.

We stepped out of the shadows to find Cruz leaning back against the wall with his arms crossed, his eyes scanning our surroundings for trouble. Penn's stalker might have been dead, but that didn't mean something else wouldn't go wrong.

"Thanks," I muttered as I walked up to him, Penn giving him a kiss on the cheek on her way into the bathroom, and he gave me a dirty look.

"You need to keep a lookout, man. I know she's fucking irresistible, but—"

"You're the one who keeps fucking her on the side of the road with no one to keep an eye out, so don't scold me, asshole," I snorted, both of us standing by the door to wait for Penn.

"You guys are usually watching us on the trackers and cameras. Out here, you've got nothing," he pointed out.

Penn emerged after a minute and we walked back towards the track, and Zavier took one look at her before looking at me flatly. "Really? Here?"

"Sorry, your fake sister's hot, man," I said sarcastically, and he flipped me the bird. Penn snapped at us not to fight before stomping away like the brat that she was, but I didn't chase after her. She was heading straight for Beckett and Jett, so I knew they'd keep her safe.

"How the fuck did we end up with a Kingslake princess?" Cruz mumbled under his breath, and I gave him an amused look.

"Because you stole her right out of her bedroom, idiot."

"You're welcome, by the way," he grinned, nudging my shoulder with his as we watched Maddox race Reid. "Admit it, you liked her when I first brought her home, and that's why you pretended you didn't like her. You hate feelings."

"Stop while you're ahead, asshole."

"You two would've hate-fucked so hard," he continued as if I hadn't spoken. "I bet your hate-fuck would've given Knox's a run for it's money. You've got a temper, you know?"

"I'm aware. You're going to witness it soon if you don't shut the fuck up," I replied dryly, my eyes sliding to Penn to check that she was still there. She was watching the race, too, but she sensed my gaze and turned her head, those goddamn butterflies taking flight in my stomach again as she gave me a smile, blowing me a kiss.

I didn't even think before I put my hand up to catch it before blowing one back, and Cruz patted my shoulder with a laugh. "You're so fucking mushy, I love it."

From the way Beckett was smirking at me, too, she was thinking the exact same thing.

"Eat shit. Go play on the track or something," I growled, leaving him laughing behind me as I walked away. Knox seemed amused as I approached, so that dickbag probably witnessed it, too, but he didn't say anything as I leaned on the fence beside him and Drake.

"Maddox said they're heading to Devil's Dungeon after this for some drinks. You want to go?" he asked, Drake giving me a pleading look.

"I want to dance with Penn. Please? I'll be good!"

"Doubtful," I scoffed, but I knew Penn would want to go, so there was no point in arguing. "But fine. Only because I guarantee Beckett's already told Penn about it, and then I'll look like an ass if I say no."

"Aw, look at all that personal growth," Knox joked, laughing as I smacked my fist into his shoulder, turning back to the race just in time to see Maddox speed across the finish line ahead of Reid by a second.

"Ugh, she's so fucking hot," Drake groaned, and I went to smack him up the back of the head for whoever he was checking out, but when I turned, I found him staring at Penn as she walked in our direction, her hand in Cruz's as Jett talked their ears off.

I couldn't help but watch her, knowing I'd jump in front of a hundred bullets if it meant keeping her safe, and for the first time in my entire life, I knew exactly what my future held.

I was going to marry that girl one day alongside my brothers like it was always supposed to be.

Penelope Whitlock wasn't a Kingslake princess, I knew that now.

She was a brat, our future wife, and a fucking Night Thief.

A damn good one at that.

The End.

PREORDER!

Stardust: Home of the Gifted (Standalone)

Stardust: Home of the Gifted (2023)

Also by R.E. Bond

Paranormal

Dreary Shadows series (Completed)

Dreary Shadows Part One

Dreary Shadows Part Two

Dreary Shadows Part Three

Dreary Shadows Part Four

Blood Discipline (Standalone novella)

Co-written with C.A. Rene

Blood Discipline

Urban Fantasy

Stardust: Home the of Gifted (Standalone)

Stardust: Home of the Gifted

Contemporary

Watch Me Burn series (Completed)

WARNING

This series MUST be read in order despite the characters changing. It follows one storyline. These are dark romance books with violence and multiple trigger warnings depending on the book.

Book 1: Pretty Lies

Book 2: Twisted Fate

Book 3: Beautiful Deceit

Book 4: Ignite Me

Book 5: Perfectly Jaded

Book 6: Don't Fear the Reaper

Book 7: Wrath of Rage

Book 8: Sinners Reign

From the Ashes series (Standalone)

(Watch Me Burn next generation)

Book 1: King of Carnage

Book 2: Pretty Little Psycho

Book 3: Prince of Pain

Book 4: Pray for Sin

Book 5: Beg for Ruin

The Night Thieves (Completed)

This reverse harem duet contains spice, violence, and dark content. Although these characters are part of the Watch Me Burn/From the Ashes universe, you do not need to read anything prior to this.

Book 1: No Honor Among Thieves

Book 2: As Thick As Thieves

Reaped series (Completed)

Co-written with C.A. Rene

WARNING

This reverse harem series is full of violence, gore scenes, and a lot of dark spice, with MM included.

Book 0.5: The Reaper Incarnate

Book 1: Hunting the Reaper

Book 2: Claiming the Reaper

Stalk Me!

Stalk the crap out of me you little freaks, I love it!

Facebook:

https://www.facebook.com/indieauthorrebond/

Facebook Readers Group:

https://www.facebook.com/groups/prettypsychos

Instagram:

https://www.instagram.com/author.re.bond/

Goodreads:

https://www.goodreads.com/rebond

Newsletter/website:

https://www.rebondbooks.com/

Tik Tok:

https://vm.tiktok.com/ZSJRKKhr4/

Amazon:

https://www.amazon.com/R-E-Bond/e/B08DV2C21Y/ref=dp_byline_cont_pop_ebooks_1

BookBub:

https://www.bookbub.com/profile/r-e-bond?list=about

Acknowledgments

I think Penn's onto something there. Sounds like a fairytale to me!

This duet has been in my mind since Zavier dragged them out of hiding in King of Carnage, and I just KNEW the Thieves would be a passion project of mine. You have no idea how much they took over my mind, and they're part of the reason I've had the worst writer's block. Nothing else would come into focus, only them.

Selfish pricks.

I think Cruz will always be one of my number one book boyfriends. His bad boy side always flows so well with his good boy side, and I just love him to pieces! I think Penn has a very happy future being with him and the other Thieves. She was always supposed to be a queen.

Now they've had their story told, who's next? Ryder Donovan is chomping at the bit to be let out of his cage, and Tempest Hendricks is more than happy to unlock it. Hopefully they do as they're told, because Zane Evans and Harlow Leary are getting impatient with me.

If you have time, please leave a review for me! I really appreciate it!

I hope to see you soon for my next release, Stardust: Home of the Gifted. You think Penn had it bad? Get ready to meet Salem and her five powerful men!

Love you bunches!

Rachael Xx

About the Author

R.E. Bond is a dark romance author from Tasmania, Australia. She is obsessed with reverse harem books, especially if they have m/m! She collects paperbacks as a hobby, has read or written every day since she started high school, and constantly needs music in her daily life. She loves camping and rodeos in the summer, and not getting out of bed in the winter. Coffee and books are life, and curse words are just sentence enhancers.

Printed in Great Britain
by Amazon

32571080R00247